] *Preposterous*

ALSO BY JENNIFER MASON

The Oddball Gypsy Raconteur

Valedictorian

Sebastopol

Tors Lake

Partitions of Unity

Preposterous

] AN ELIZABETH CROMWELL MYSTERY [

Jennifer Mason

EXPONENTIAL PRESS, SANTA BARBARA, 2022

This is a work of fiction. Characters, places, and events are the product of the author's imagination or are used fictitiously. Any resemblance to real people, companies, institutions, organizations, or incidents is entirely coincidental.

] [

Published by Exponential Press
Post Office Box 3643
Santa Barbara, CA 93130

ISBN 978-0-9980221-3-0 (hardcover)
ISBN 978-0-9980221-4-7 (paperback)
ISBN 978-0-9980221-5-4 (e-book)

Book design: Studio E Books, Santa Barbara

Cover illustration by Sharif Tarabay

for Eric

$$K(s,x) = \frac{1}{2} \int_0^\infty u^{s-1} exp[-\frac{x}{2}(u + \frac{1}{u})]du$$

] *Preposterous*

] *Chapter Zero*

I'D BEEN WAITING for Mrs. Sand to receive me. She was inside dressing. I was at the bottom of a few cracked steps in an old stone wall, not quite thinking and not quite free of thoughts that some ancient commentary might suit the *je ne sais quoi* occasion…that in the middle of the night a wife phones her husband's dominatrix to come out to the house so she can get her take on his suicide note. It wasn't altogether unreasonable. I'd been seeing him professionally since before they were married. He told her I was his therapist.

The suicide note read as vintage Sand:

The partnership of Desmond and Sand, Attorneys at Law, has been dissolved. It is my opinion that (1) Mac-Donald Desmond will never be found and that (2) the assets that might be recovered with Mrs. Sand will not cover obligations. Reinvention is not quite art.

A car was waiting. We were going to Phillipsville. That's where we'd find her husband, hopefully (hopefully?) alive. It was around three hours north of the City, an easy drive up 101 at that hour. We would be there before morning, but I wasn't convinced the trip was indicated. In response to my first question, Mrs. Sand hadn't notified the police because, owing to her way of seeing it, the note was a private matter. There were other things to see that didn't need to be argued at this hour. I went home.

All in all, given the hour, I was more right than wrong. Sand killed himself, but he went the other way.

From the itinerary the secretary, Gail Conrad, found on his desk, the reliable habits of Michael Sand led her to place a call to the Santa Barbara police department right after she entered the office that morning. She said they would find Mr. Sand at the base of the Overlook Bridge. He would be a suicide. His wallet and phone were on his desk. As a matter of predictive fact, she stated that he would have locked the office around midnight and stopped in Paso Robles for gas and an Alpha Energizer, a chocolate-peanut item he had with coffee. The car would be in the La Cumbre Plaza lot near the entrance to the Starbucks. He would have arrived when they opened, and might be remembered for a tribute to the "staff of life." It would be his final remark, or close. It would be his last coffee. He would have dumped the key to his car with his loose change in the tip jar, at which point he would be broke. The bridge is less than a two-mile walk. The empty cup would be in his jacket pocket.

] *Chapter 1*

THE SAN FRANCISCO Financial Crimes Unit operated out of third-floor offices in the Hall of Justice on Bryant Street. The search to evaluate and dispose of materials that turned up in the files of Desmond and Sand was farmed out on channels well established. Michael Sand jumped off a bridge in Santa Barbara. That was six months ago. MacDonald Desmond couldn't be found. Efforts on behalf of clients concerned with the restoration of capital went to Coates and Sinott, who worked off a list of claims against Desmond and Sand that would be settled through arbitration. Clients for whom a service had been performed, or for whom services were pending, were to be notified they should get new representation. On that list was Hannah Kier.

Sarah Feldman was one of a pair of researchers brought onto the payroll of Coates and Sinott for several months of the summer to convey to interested parties the nature of their new circumstances: the firm of Desmond and Sand was defunct. A preliminary letter from Coates and Sinott personalized my relationship to the situation in order to gain a few details in a follow-up call.

In the slot in the front cover of the Kier Trust was my full signature and address, just as they appear in the trust:

Elizabeth Jane Cromwell
The English Department
3724 Stafford Street
San Francisco, California 94109

The number and zip code were wrong, but not by much, not enough to get a letter returned undeliverable, but perhaps enough to invalidate the trust if I'd been the trustee and somebody wanted to pick a fight. I might have been the trustee. It had been a long time since I'd seen Hannah Kier—a long time since anybody had seen her.

Feldman left a message connecting her call to the letter. She'd be pleased to fill in the contents of the letter. No need to go through all that. The letter was open in front of me. They were looking for Ms. Kier and her daughter, Edith Barlow. A guy named Clement was mentioned. He owed the estate a significant sum. They were hoping I could help them out. And one more thing. Ms. Conrad, the secretary at Desmond and Sand, couldn't recall meeting a Countess Alexandrowicz, whose name didn't appear in the trust but was referenced in a note from MacDonald Desmond to Hannah Kier, as if Hannah and this countess were related.

I called Feldman back.

"Kier and the Countess are one and the same," I said. "'The Countess' was the title that fit her elite services. That's the way 'The English Department' works for me. I'm a junior high school dropout. If Hannah used it with Desmond, it means he was a favorite. Lady Amber-Wood was the title on her web page. It advertised her availability to the general public as a professional dominant."

"Thank you very much for the information, Ms. Cromwell." It took her a second. "It's entered." My finger was poised to disconnect the call.

"Anything else?" I asked.

"Well, yes and no. Is this a good time?"

Harrington, my librarian, had appeared in the doorway to the office. A column of books, held together two-handed, waist to chin, was keeping its balance. While libraries all over are going digital, books arrive at the door to my alley by the trunkful. He wasn't moving his mouth, but I could make out a gripe. We needed to throw books out. He was bulging in pink panties, trying to provoke a whipping. There's always that.

I pushed a palm at him. I needed a minute. His cock throbbed. We'd been with each other eleven years. Everything could wait.

I returned to Feldman. I had a minute. "What's it about?"

"The Kier Trust refers to an erotic charity. Hannah Kier ran the thing. It was her wish that the charity continue under the direction of Faith Nichols. At the end of the summer, I'll need a job. I spoke to Faith Nichols. She's not in a position to think seriously about taking it on. She said, talk to you. I just thought you might need an assistant."

Faith Nichols was a name from long ago. I put a fingernail to my scalp and drilled. Assist me? "You've confused me, Ms. Feldman."

"If you were thinking of getting the charity on its feet, I should tell you something about myself. I'm out here in a closet in a house with three grad students at Berkeley throwing nine of every ten cents into *l'essentiale della vita*. Coming across your name, I did the George Washington Plunkitt two-step. You're someone I'd like to meet."

"Do I know him?" I asked.

"He mastered machine politics in New York. 'I kissa you ass,' and so on. You want to hear about Tammany Hall? Or not? Whatever. I talk too much. I can shut up right away if you can use me."

"You know what I do, Ms. Feldman. If you're interested in fetish role-play, check around. The Den of Desires in Emeryville is always hiring. I work alone."

"I have been checking around. That's my job at Coates and Sinott till the end of August."

"Why stop at my name?"

"I didn't. I'm leaving my name all over. The reference to an erotic charity in Ms. Kier's folder caught my eye. Checks were signed by Faith Nichols. I was curious what an erotic charity is. It could be a job. How would I know?"

"I haven't seen Faith in years," I said.

"You have a private library. You went to a Portuguese monastery to steal the design. Ms. Nichols says it's the largest on the peninsula. I mean, she still harbors an immense awe. A bit rubbed off on me."

We left things where my librarian could arrange a tour. It wasn't a job, but she would be here. We might meet if the timing was right.

————

I TWISTED a paperclip unnaturally. In a second it was useless.

A sarcastic sputter, deep in his throat, doubled for a laugh. "I can only hope I'm out of a job." His shifty eyelids were easy to understand. He was giving me stink-eye. The argument that we were going to have about my book addiction could wait its turn.

I asked, "What do you think of her…"

"Plight? Go home to mother. Or move to Austin."

I pulled a desk drawer open, the lower right, where I kept a few things handy just for him. I could have sent him upstairs and tied him down, but I was in a hurry. I dropped a pair of heels on the floor in front of my bare feet. In heels I stretched to a well-appointed six feet and, say, an imaginatively added quarter inch. I was looking down. He wasn't likely to lip off. I latched a finger in his panties and pulled. He came to a stop in the center of the office. I skipped some ritual here, skipping all that "don't drop the books or you'll wish…," and so on. Today would be a quickie.

I revolved an index finger. He rotated slowly, stopping when the finger stopped. I studied the available space, a frivolous delay, an imperious privilege exercised, a random ingredient of the game. After all our encounters, this was by now a near complete waste of time. But it came to me on this occasion, thoughtfully, that a bit of mischief was not to be skipped.

"A tolerable opening for a full swing, Harrington. You are the treasured voice of my superego. No need to remind you of the zest I treasure for whipping my superego. Would you care at this moment to add or subtract from your verdict regarding my addiction?"

"What addiction would you be speaking of? I know only of your perfections, Mistress."

"Well said, Harrington. We shall proceed, then."

My hair had grown the past year to fall over my shoulders, like Lauren Bacall in that publicity shot of blonde satin drapes on a pillow. I cuddled my cheek on the top of his head from behind and dangled leather gloves in front of his face. My hair was an attracting barrier. His lips pushed close to my ear, but I made it impossible to break through. I put a hot breath on his neck, which he received as erotic love, the tripwire of longings that factored through submission. Now he was mine, though the *mine* of the moment was the self of his juicier interests.

The tight morning schedule spared him my insufferable masterpiece. More of that later. The gloved hand roaming here and there was enough. I was now granted access.

The cane was too long for my desk drawer, even diagonally. It stood in a wicker basket. The two tips could be bent together. It had to be long and thin, descended from uncommon stock, to get that spec. The important thing was to get the note. It's the *whip-crack* of a cane. The ones that had it achieved a separation…this cane is *this* cane. It wouldn't strike all at once, but would roll onto a surface, the sonic climax being unpronounceable, usually rendered thicker and coarser as a *swish-crack*. An ear for a thing like that was what happened when a passion fastened to classical forms. Harrington returned in reverie to an *ur*-illusion of Lady Winchester's Mayfair salon. That placed his encounters a hundred years ago, so it was automatically a discipline classic.

I could say we finished each other's sentences. I would mean we were more than close. I made sure he was never sure what he could get away with. I was unerring on that score. He owned a tech outfit in Santa Clara, with a branch in Thousand Oaks. He could afford a mistress every day of the week, but sticking with me was, so far, the best of all possible worlds.

I backed against a wall, looking solemnly into his eyes. "You're sure?" I said.

It was still a go, no-go. He would get two chances. The hard-on couldn't be trusted. He'd called it quits before, while higher than a kite, but the will for triumph had been missing. I was warming up the cane, a half-circle flex, a round-house chop. At the moment it was just sound, but the past never disappears. That's where he was now. The risk wasn't frivolous.

I smiled warmly. "It's time."

"I'm ready, Mistress."

"House rules, Harrington. Same as ever, but every miscreant will take a disputant's joy in claiming ignorance. Am I right? Don't answer. Toes on the mark, legs straight. You're not a choo-choo in heat. Don't act the part. Position!" He was hyper-alert, already bent forward.

10:52:16

"A weak knee…an alignment issue…not serious, but not to be ignored. Repeat the stroke. Two additional. Position."

10:52:27

"Request for pause, ma'am."

"This early? Request out of order. A penalty will be assessed at the end, if we ever get there. Position!"

10:52:38

[A squeak]

"What should I learn from this sound? Don't answer. Where was I? The lapse in posture. Position!"

10:52:48

"Decorum! Position!"

10:52:55

"Position!"

10:52:58

"Please, may we…"

"Request out of correct sequence. Position!"

10:53:07

[Gasping subsides] "Please, ma'am."

"I've been too kind. We'll have these panties lowered for the make-up. Position."

10:53:18

10:53:19

10:53:20

He was swiveling his hips. It wasn't clear what cause he was helping. My hand smoothed heat around his bottom. "Do you need release?"

He was in no mind for reason. When he could turn that corner, I heard, "Three days." He was technically still in limbo. I checked my watch.

"Put the books on the desk," I said.

I tucked his panties under his balls. The gloves and shoes went back in the drawer. I applied a palm full of lotion. I held tight. He did the in and out.

"Every age has its artist," he said. "The technology improves."

"You are attempting a compliment, Harrington. In your favor, you're out of danger. You're not required to explain the indecipherable. However, while we're waiting, where do we stand on important matters?"

"I finished recording the four grocery sacks of books that we tucked away under the kitchen sink," he said. "On top of the books are the cards I just made out. If you would let me know your decision, that would be that."

"Would you please put one in front of me," I said.

Geomorphology from Space: A Global Overview of Regional Landforms, edited by Daniel G. Gunther.

GB

400.42

R4

G46

1986

"How did we get this?"

"Came in a sack. The sacks were in the alley. Anonymous. We talked at Christmas of the overwhelming burden on the shelves. There would be no happy ending."

"What do you suggest?"

"Perhaps the same as the next card."

A Manual of Dissembling: Alibis, Excuses, and Eccentric Defenses, by Henrietta Huggins Easter.

RC 119.5

E 4

"I wanted to have a look at this," I said. "Much to study on, Harrington."

"As you wish, Mistress."

"How are you doing?"

"Closer to the back porch than the foyer."

————

A LETTER had been sitting in limbo at the edge of the desk under the Scotch tape dispenser. The return address was blank, but it was postmarked from the City. No name. Not unusual in a private matter with the English Department. I opened it on the way to the kitchen.

> Dear Mistress Elizabeth,
> I'm Celia Taylor, yes, that one, Board of Supervisors,
> 5th District. I'm thirty-eight, good health, lately foot-
> loose, respectfully asking for your services. I notice
> your contact information has been deleted. I copied it
> down when I was in very strong need of submission,
> but not clear a caning was the experience that satisfied
> the craving. It's a constant hunger now. Please leave a
> message.
> Your admirer,
> Celia

She left a 531 number. Eastern Nebraska.

I left an answer. "Regarding your request for services, I'm not taking new clients. I prefer not to make referrals. I assume you know the City. Good luck."

———

A WORD came to me, "Derriere." Hannah had taught a bullwhip class with Faith Nichols at a talent business, Bare Derriere. An Oakland-based dominant, Faith had shared a house in Oakland with Hannah. Faith was the best evidence that Hannah and a permanent disappearing act to God-knows-where didn't add up.

I texted Faith: "I just learned I'm Hannah Kier's trustee. Why me and not you?"

In the kitchen I mechanically pressed the button that brought the electric water kettle to 212. Two bells and it was time to pour. An Amazon gadget could detect a cup at 123 degrees, my ideal sipping temperature. After that bell rang, I sipped tea in the library.

The phone rang. Faith said, "Did you ask?"

"Hannah's lawyer jumped off a bridge. Otherwise. The bunch that called me is looking for her on behalf of the citizens of California."

A silence ended with, "What are you gonna do?"

"It's California's problem. I don't have to be the trustee. I'll beg off with a gap in memory."

"An untruth to an officer of the state, you could go to prison," she said.

"It'll be a phone call. You have to lie to them in person. Incidentally, I got the news from Sarah Feldman, a young woman making a lot of phone calls that don't interest her. Somehow she dredged up Hannah's charity. She said you told her to call me."

"I assumed *you* told her to call *me*. The charity? What did I ever care?"

"She says she needs a job after Labor Day. Any other idea why Sarah would care?"

"I think I said you were the gray eminence behind Hannah's mission to save the starving artists. There was that Spanish film guy, won the blue ribbon. You were Hannah's artistic conscience. How did that come out?"

"We only had to see the first few scenes. A talented kid, Spanish title, no dialogue, the love of a widow and a stable boy all alone on a mountaintop. Blew Hannah away. The check went to his sister's place. A rare talent, but a long time gone. What's left?"

"What's left of the charity? That's easy," she said. "The Kier Erotic Trust was eighteen hundred dollars lounging peacefully in an endowment fund when Hannah stopped showing up for breakfast. The rest of it's in some boxes in the hall closet here. Who's interested?"

"Somebody gets bank statements," I said.

"Stuff still comes here to the house—Neville's problem, not mine. He owns the house. He was in love with her, if I'm an expert on it. I've held his hand through many a bottle of I'll-never-love-again."

"You still see him?"

"He's a client. We meet at his place, usually. We've been to Europe a few times, the governess arrangement, I explain the whips going through airport security.

"Sand is dead," she said after a pause. She was processing an earlier statement. I heard a thud, like a book tossed on a desk. Then a chair swiveling.

"I'd invite you over," she said, "but I have to get in touch with someone first. How about later tonight?"

"You care to let me know what about?"

"There's a house on Highway One, up near Albion. Hannah owned it, she and Sand. It's not under their names. Some group in Belgium holds the paper. I rent it out. I collect rent and pay taxes. Hannah had a daughter. She ought to get it."

"She does a séance?" I said. "And contacts some group in Belgium?"

"You're not listening. To repeat, if she collects rent and pays taxes, it's hers. I want out of this."

"Out of what?"

We started talking in parallel, Faith mostly to herself. "It was supposed to be an abortion. Sand took care of it. This Edith Barlow that Sarah Feldman was asking about, she must be the girl. I wasn't going to get into it with Hannah about why she gave up her kid."

"Was Sand the father?" I asked.

"Hannah had some strange priorities about charity. Sand set the baby up in Santa Barbara. The foster mother didn't know who the birth mother was."

I said, "With Sand dead…"

"The girl collects rent and pays taxes. I told you. The house belongs to her. Just fuck it. Hannah needed a trustee in a hurry. I slipped out the back door. I guess Hannah filled in your name."

The tea temperature was getting to where it went down in gulps. I rolled a few objections around at the end of my fingers, putting curlicues in the dust on the table. The sequence of swirls looked like I'd signed an agreement.

I asked, "What happens if you don't do anything?"

"What's happening right now? The girl survived. She's an heiress. That's what I was saying, Elizabeth, we have things to talk about. There's a bank account…eighteen hundred bucks… the current endowment of the Kier Erotic Trust. Neville stopped donating when Hannah disappeared. I'll bring that…and…what? I had Hannah's good things put in the attic. There's a Swedish bed and china, some special linens from Munich, abnormal psychology books. I kept all that. And she was in that Ayn Rand society. There are those books. She settled on…it's hard to say what she settled on. She was too beautiful for any one thing. Neville had a dungeon built in her honor. He tore out a sunroom at his estate, had a dungeon put in. One of the eight wonders of the Bay you must see before you die."

"Is this the love thing you were talking about?"

"You want my advice? Do what you want. Look, the beach house is available. We'll meet there. I'll call the renters. They're in Oregon, the Shakespeare Festival. Tomorrow is Saturday. Stay overnight."

I heard the metallic scrape of a sliding door of a filing cabinet, then the systematic shuffle of sheaves of paper.

"I'll send you a map," she said. "You'll see a row of bricks on the side of the road just before the gate. There's a key to the gate in a little box under the first brick."

I rolled a pencil in a ray of sunshine on the desk. Sort of a Ouija board. What to do? Books in ones and twos were on the floor waiting for homes in the stacks. Harrington was gone.

———

I GOT through to Sarah Feldman at the Coates and Sinott number. "You want a job?"

"Depends," she said. "Just kidding."

"What survives of the charity material is in two boxes with Faith Nichols, so I understand. Nobody's been interested for years. I just spoke to her. I'll be meeting her tomorrow. If you get a chance today, if you would, please pick them up at her place. We could meet in Berkeley. Pick a number. It's your fee."

"Then what?"

"In the boxes should be records of expenses, including amounts paid out in grants. Some winners got fifteen thousand dollars, plus a year's support. Faith says there's still eighteen hundred dollars in an account she hasn't bothered to pilfer. I can meet you after work next week. I'll plan on a late night. I'd like to understand why you want to get mixed up with people like us."

"You don't want me. I'm Jewish. There's some *schtick* here. I want to be where people don't think I belong."

"I can give you some Kansas *schtick* my grandmother gave me. If someone throws a baby at you, don't catch it."

"I'm better off picking an art project and applying for a grant," she said. "It's crossed my mind."

We hung up. I got my fingers on another paperclip and got going destroying it one-handed. I played around with a box of straightened-out chunks of wire. When half a minute had gone, I still hadn't the slightest idea for all these years why I never asked what happened to Hannah Kier.

] *Chapter 2*

I CHECKED ROAD CONDITIONS coming off the mountain pass at the coast where the Navarro River enters the Pacific, turned north on Shoreline Hwy for ten minutes to a left turn onto asphalt paving gone chunky for fifty feet. The other side of a gate was unassuming, unpeopled isolation spread out on a grass shelf that hit a beach a quarter-mile downslope. I pulled past the gate and re-hooked the end loops of a chain to a brass lock, and arranged the joined place under a rubber flap. The air was dry and hot at the gate. I released the brake into a roll on a dirt road that was smooth sailing around a zigzag at low speed. The straight line to the ocean wasn't that steep, but the straight line had washed out, and the once-temporary replacement carried on to where a wooden arch mounted an incline onto a fitted stone landing. Three covered parking spaces butted into the wall of a patio a foot higher. On the upper elevation was a house.

The house was out of sight of its neighbors. They were all shake siding offering a life of living off the various views of the ways the sea can catch you up soaking in your inclination for the mystery of existence. I was here for some of that, too, if it worked out. I might stay a few days.

The driver's side window of Faith's silver sedan (FAITH 1) was open. A painting of a sailing ship tucked into a harbor-like crevice on a jagged coast leaned against a front tire. A sack of groceries had been unloaded from the trunk and set on the ground at a rear fender. The trunk was open.

The screen door in front was unlocked. Faith wasn't within a shout. I stashed an overnight bag in the guest room, changed into sun wear, and dumped a survival package of teabags and organic biscuits on the breakfast table. I went back to close the trunk, retrieved the groceries, washed an apple, and put some cheese out to think about in a minute. I pushed the sack deep on the kitchen counter.

I had yelled a hello. I yelled a name. Faith was somewhere, but not somewhere that made any sense that pulled the minute together. Binoculars were on the windowsill. I found a spot on the patio that gave a wide line of sight above trees that sea gales had forced level to the horizon. I didn't expect to see Faith along the near run of rocks, but where else? I blinked hard at spaces snagged in outcroppings.

I went down the back steps to a path through a row of trees that defined a porous property boundary from the sea to the highway. Recent footprints were suddenly visible in the ground on the other side of the trees. One person had taken the beaten path to the closest point of an inlet. There was a last step. The next after that had disappeared in the foam that seeped up from underneath pebbles, which were far from sand, but wet, and held under my weight.

A frontier of rock and water was the shoreline, and that defied an identifying highlight except to distinguish rock formations very locally. Otherwise it was miles of one bunch of rocks after another. Anybody could get into a nook and be lost to a visual search from the shore. No footprints were in the dry area in either direction. Nothing on any horizon except the word that fit what I didn't see: inexplicable. Faith was nowhere.

I lowered the binoculars to hang by the neck strap. To the right a flash of yellow appeared from behind a rock. Practically in hearing of a shout was a woman in a yellow dress. It wasn't Faith. She was too small and had the quick motions of a teenager.

Her dress was coming up over her head. She folded it on a bag and slipped her feet into shoes and took her naked self around the curve of the inlet to where a promontory could be reached without a silly risk. She toed her shoes off at a parapet and pushed off behind arms aligned over her head in a steeple. A shaft of ivory hardly splashed. All around her was a soft tangle of purplish waves.

Her brown head turned to the open sea, threading a clear return channel to the rocks. She hauled herself up and moved on a careful foot to her shoes, and there raised an arm at me as if in some kind of "Look, Ma, how'd you like that piece of splendor?"

I had climbed a rock. I started my descent timed to meet her arrival. She returned to her clothes and grabbed a white hat from her bag. The brim was huge, putting her shoulders in shade. The hat had seen white skin safely through clear summer skies. She was nice. She had always been that. We met in a carrying murmur of tiny lappings of waves.

"So we meet on the neutral ground of a strip club," she said. "Take your things off. We'll take a dip."

"That was some dive you took," I said.

"You swim?" she asked.

"I remember holding the side of a neighbor's pool and kicking my legs. I think I was learning that mingling with the sea plants is not for me. They have the characteristics of a casual contented life. Why disturb them?"

"So that's that. What do we have in common? You don't have a ring. I assume you're not married. I'm not married. Is there love in our future?"

"You dive right in. I'm Elizabeth."

"Najda. I'm assuming you live somewhere else."

"I don't look like I would snuggle up with the seaweed?"

"Just musing. You're too good-natured, too elegant, too curious-looking to live here. You're meeting someone who selects good-looking companionship. A him would be on time, so it's a she, and she's not here yet. You're femme and independent.

You're not in the prime-of-youth set, so she wants someone who knows her way around—if this is a paying gig, that is. I could develop the mistress fantasy. I could go on, anyway. You're not goods off the shelf for just anyone."

She tossed her hat on her bag. Runoff had collected twists in a boyish haircut—one of those chop cuts that were here and there on the streets these days—disaster scenarios, a quick do during a plane crash. She was twenty years old, or would be soon. She worked short rubs down thighs to ankles. In me it would have diagnosed early onset circulation problems. In her it fit a display of vigor.

"It itches," she said. She dabbed the itches around her shoulders and neck and circled her hips and tucked a hand in her butt. She pumped her arms to get up a head of steam into a standing warm-up, then gave her scalp a Dutch rub. She wrapped her arms around the back of her head in a showy tits-lift style. Could I be setting this off? She took her encounters with tall blonde women as she found them.

She grabbed the sleeve of a faded blue sweatshirt and dragged the rest from a bag. She got inside, perhaps aware it was inside-out. Her head popped out on a breath. A twist in her neck put a devil-may-care caprice in her profile. That spun the fantasy that I was watching a mermaid looking out to sea. She stepped into a skirt that left half her bottom available to tease my wanton desires. An arc of curved lettering on the bag was the University of This or That. It had a T.

She inspected the terrain up to the house pretty hard, as though she might make an offer to drop in and join me. Her eyes carried a few thoughts that shared a doubt. She backed away a few steps, the way caution will do against an impulse. She turned, but she wasn't finished with me.

"I think I made a mistake," she said, speaking past me, but with a definite conviction. "If we meet again, I might like a second chance on you. I'll feel bad if I don't get you right."

Her face fell into a verdict: "If we're not falling in love, I won't eat till tomorrow." She walked off. She turned at the rock she had appeared out from behind of. I waved at one of the characters you find along the sea around here.

In the past I'd driven as far up as Fort Bragg. Every acre was a house of wood-shingle siding, but each had been added to in its own fashion. They showed off something special, as unique as a numbered address. The house just north, where the sea nymph was going, had a star where some houses had a weather vane. It might have been hers.

I stuck a look inside the house again, and went out and took a slow walk around Faith's car. It hadn't changed. That left the possibility that Faith had gone on a long swim, except it didn't fit the groceries in the sack. You couldn't reconcile that with the footprints or anything else. A weekend's worth of luggage was in the backseat. I dialed her. No connection.

Thin white clouds had little curls at their tips. A smell of chaparral had caught in the air for a hundred miles. The sky had stopped moving. From the top step of the back porch I had another look at the enveloping arms of the closest rock formation.

I had three goes at getting a lounge backrest inclined to my preference in vacation posture. I set up tea fixings as I took it at home, a green apple in slices at my right hand. I opened a book against doubled knees. I controlled pages one-handed, alternating apple and a napkin, chewing and swallowing on the thought I ought to get up and do something, but merely shifting positions, looking at the same views with more concern.

After noon passed I looked at a page and it came to me halfway down the page that I hadn't been reading. I'd been fussing with how long was too long. I put the book away and sat on the edge of the lounge chair and studied a pool of wet wood around the outdoor shower. The shower head had been dripping constantly. It explained a pool of water in a four-foot radius. A hearty shower? Not likely before a swim. Just a leaky shower.

I tried to phone Faith once more, same result, and ran over

some names. An Oakland cop who used to drop by the English Department was on his day off in Napa with the wife and daughter. They were in a schlock shop. It was his daughter's birthday. He was outside in the shade, and it was hot, and he was feeling good about being a good husband and father. What did I want? I was fine. I didn't actually need advice. I needed to hear myself think out loud. He had some time to listen. I gave him what was there to describe, from when I arrived till now, no theories. After I'd said there was no sign of a struggle, no blood, no dented fenders, and so on, he asked who lived at the house and where were they.

"The owner has a rental arrangement with two women. They went to Ashland for the Shakespeare Festival. We're here today and tomorrow."

"You call them?" he asked.

"Don't know their names. Why?"

"They might know something. Any other cars there?"

"Mine," I said.

"Eventually you may have to think about tracks to the house that look recent. You can eliminate that line…hopefully. What about the groceries? Is there a receipt in the sack?"

"I would think so," I said. "If so, it's a market close by in Albion. That's another thing. She left the groceries outside."

"What were you planning today?"

"Make pancakes and watch movies."

"The marriage experience. But she wouldn't take off and leave you?"

"She was here to meet me."

He said he'd call back. His wife had come out to see if something was too expensive inside.

He called back. His wife had told him to tell me to keep a level head. Check if my friend left a message on the refrigerator. There was nothing to do but stay or go. Start the vacation on my own. Put the perishables away.

"Thanks," I said.

"Let me call somebody in Ukiah," he said. "The sheriff's station there covers Mendocino County. They can get Highway Patrol with you in a few minutes."

"I saw a cop ticketing a car on the road near here," I said.

"Hang on a few minutes."

I watched the phone till his number appeared. He said to expect some company. We hadn't talked about suicide. If Faith was in the water, the sooner they got a search going the less territory they'd have to cover.

A Highway Patrol cruiser was already at the gate as I cleared the last rise on foot. I unlocked the gate. The cop asked if I was Elizabeth Cromwell. I explained about the footprints in the sand. I knew where he should look, but he wanted to do it his way.

I sat on the sofa where he asked me to sit. From then on he was out of sight for the most part. I caught the noise of back-and-forth from the cruiser radio. That and a lot of quiet filled in a quarter-hour. Then it was just like a movie. Two young officers in plain clothes arrived from Fort Bragg, a man and woman with self-assured faces. They really looked over the premises, as if this could be a murder case—their first, from the let-no-suspicious piece of data go unrecorded. It was all evidence. They went on an out-of-hearing walk-around with the Highway Patrol cop. They came back and took standing positions to my left and right, immediately setting up an interrogational atmosphere.

I went through events with a sketchy backstory of why I was there and how this would have been a first meeting with Faith in at least seven years. I left a lot out. Faith was the manager of the property and collected the rent. That ended that line of inquiry and left Hannah out of it, a name that could set off God-knows-what, if combined with my name in her trust.

"You were planning on staying the night, you said. Is that your bag in the bedroom?" the woman asked.

"Yes."

"Faith didn't bring luggage?"

"I saw travel bags in the car," I said. "I didn't open them."

"Could she have changed her mind?"

They ask questions like this. They like to weigh responses. I had an arm over the back of the sofa, a knee on a cushion. I was in it for the long haul, whatever time they needed out of me to get the lay on my state of mind.

"Odd that she would go to the grocery store and then swim out to sea and die, don't you think?" I said.

"What do you think?"

"I can't think of anything else. For that matter, why open the house and leave groceries outside with the trunk open? The milk was still cold. It scarcely gave her time to get the front door open before I arrived. And why lock the gate? I had to open it."

"You called her?"

"I couldn't reach her."

"She owns the silver Kia?" the woman asked.

"The plates would suggest it is. It was the only car when I arrived."

"She ever indicate she might take her life?"

I opened an eye wide and put a little finger at the outer edge of my right eye. I flicked a speck of something off a finger. "I haven't seen her for years."

I softened some. I let go of my knee, and let the hand hold air. I didn't know the shortcuts to explaining Faith. Starting at the top, at her age, like me, she would have a health concern, but how would I know? I couldn't agree with suicide based on a recent conversation. There were no footprints returning from the shore. There was the woman on the beach, she would have mentioned Faith but didn't.

"The name you gave us is not the name of the owner of the car," the woman said.

"It's the name I know her by, Faith Nichols. She's a professional dominant, keeps an address in Oakland under that name. Any other name I don't know. We were in a private chat group. We knew of each other through professional concerns."

"What are those?"

"We basically exchanged observations about clients, what's going on to watch out for."

"Anything recent she might be concerned with?"

"I don't know. A subpoena to one of our group prefigured problems that outweighed advantages. Some years ago I stopped using the chat. I did think she had more concerns than I had."

"Like what?"

"She'd been assaulted. We're all cautious. I'd say extremely. She stood out. I recall she said it wasn't going to happen again."

"She carried a firearm?"

"Might have, but I understood it was more a decision that if someone crossed a line, no warning, she'd deliver a disabling blow, walk away whistling. It wouldn't be a crotch kick. She'd thought that over. They're looking for that. She'd push a couple fingers into an eye socket till they wouldn't go any farther."

The detectives hooked looks.

"It's why I'd write off the woman on the beach," I said. "She'd have had to overpower Faith. She could have had a gun in her bag, but then she's got to drag her down to the beach, and all the rest. I didn't see signs of a struggle, here or anywhere."

I'd been counting off leans and feints to the out-of-doors. The woman stared at a gold-framed photo of the Flying Boat passing over the Golden Gate Bridge, when it was still under construction. She might have been looking for a question. I abruptly stopped a nervous patting of a cushion.

"I'd like to leave," I said.

"We'd like to do a thorough search," the woman said.

"Do I have to stay?"

They let that question sit. "We'll need to talk to the clerk at the market, and neighbors. And the woman you saw on the beach. You wouldn't know where she lives?"

"She called herself Najda. That's all I know."

"Nay-da?"

I spelled how I thought it would be written, with the "j," then the "d." I stood up. They didn't say I had to sit back down.

I put my suitcase at the front door. I put my contact information and the number I used to reach Faith at on an envelope. I gave it to the woman. I'd made it obvious I'd had experience with cops. They get their way one way or another, and it's better all around to let them say when they're done. There was a pause. The woman was exploratory about my leaving. Did I have something to do? I had nothing to do. I wanted to be alone.

I had a hand moving to the door handle when she asked, "You know someone named Toots? A nickname maybe?"

That took a minute. It should have been instantly one way or the other, but I had to stop. It took longer than I expected because there had been times when someone had said, "Hi, Toots," to me. She didn't mean that, but it took a second to catch up to what she meant.

"The painting next to the car," she said. "Did Ms. Nichols own it?"

"Never seen it before."

"You have a look at it?"

"In passing, why?"

"You brought the grocery sack inside, but you left the painting."

"It could wait. It's valuable?"

"Eighteen one-hundred dollar bills are in an envelope taped to the back. 'To Toots,' the note says. You expecting money?"

While I thought about it, she took a few steps forward and held up a photograph of the lower right corner of the painting. I was supposed to notice $K(s, x)$. I gestured it meant nothing to me.

She had looked it up. "It has something to do with a camera on Google."

When you're talking to law enforcement, eighteen hundred dollars to Toots is the kind of thing you're expected to be on top of, like what you were thinking when you were born. The painting was a gift, maybe. The amount taped to the painting was equal to what Faith would have been carrying had she cleared out the Kier Erotic Trust. Another thing I kept to myself.

"She wouldn't call me Toots," I said.

"She was bringing it to someone. Possibly the renters?"

"Possibly."

She looked out the window. "The lights on her car are on. You turned them on?"

"I noticed the keys were in the ignition," I said. "I can turn the lights off."

"We'd appreciate if you don't touch anything."

"Oh." I reached a key from my back pocket and gave it to the woman. "This goes to the gate. They keep it under a brick. That's where I found it. The renters will want to get in when they get home."

"A search team is on its way," the woman said. "They're sending a diver. You might be asked to make a statement at Fort Bragg."

She looked at me as if there was anything else I wanted to say.

I took a picture of the painting and went. Suicide was what was left on the drive to the City. Everything's crazy. You can think about a woman's disappearance five pleasant ways, but not the way I was reading it. It was half past three o'clock on a July afternoon when I pulled onto the grade leaving the secrets of the sea to themselves. And a thought that something terrible had been made to look like nothing. The thought of a drowned head in the ocean, never seen again, struggled on a miserable slope upwards. Against hope.

] *Chapter 3*

A DETECTIVE I WAS lucky to pal around with returned my call. We'd meet at a sidewalk table up a side street from a six-way intersection with Market. I'd left some questions with her.

We were on beers, waiting to be served. She'd reversed a chair, so we were sitting side-by-side but pointing in opposite directions, her way of doing it. That was Ren, short for Rene, which I flipped in and out of interchangeably and unpredictably. She knew what it meant in my unconscious. We got along pretty good in there. She'd stuck her legs out, ankles crossed, an arm in a wandering resting position on the table. It gave her flexibility. She could rest her chin in different arrangements of fingers, a language of simple signals. A vertical forefinger and a twitching middle finger was a posture for debating how much insider police stuff I should know.

"Sarah Feldman checks out, as far as a routine check," she said. "Skipped second grade. English lit from Barnard at twenty. Did a year at Columbia. Quit. Quit Buffalo. A habit of quitting advanced training. Caught on for a summer with Coates and Sinott. Still there. No idea why she would mention a Clement. Couldn't find a Clement mixed up with an Edith Barlow. But a Clement vanished at the same time Hannah Kier vanished. I hope you're not in that, Elizabeth."

"I know a Damien Clement," I said. "What's the other one done?"

She slid a hand in a jacket pocket. The phone stayed put.

"Clement was a big tipper in a bar on Columbus," she said. "It got later and later. Eventually he was pushing a dime at the bartender in place of a twenty dollar bill. He was helped to a car that was called to dump him at his hotel. Clement didn't make it. *Someone* made it. The someone had been paid to leave a Do Not Disturb sign on his door. He ordered room service for a week. Left the luggage and walked off. Never seen again."

"The Clement in the news?" I said. "Getting lost while rich."

"An abduction scenario arranged with some group connected to Hannah Kier. It was supposed to last a few weeks. Nobody has found him. Getting lost for life is harder to do than you'd think. Clement gone for seven years is legally up. The Clement Corporation has moved to get him declared dead. He's not helping. No body."

Ren did her squinting profile. "The health question might answer everything eventually. He suddenly needed medical care he didn't get? Hannah wasn't going to deliver a dead body and swear it wasn't her fault."

"What's Clement to Coates and Sinott?"

"A who-gives-a-shit still hangs over the proceedings. Similarities to a Patrick Byron Westphal, esquire, a case that stuck out back then. He signed a contract with a vacation group. The American branch is headquartered in San Jose. They had an arrangement with Hannah in our little town. Westphal would fly to San Francisco. The agreement of the party of the second part was that within a week of walking out of the air terminal he'd be grabbed. Once under the control of his kidnappers, he was contractually 'the Captive.' Before becoming the captive he was expected to tell everyone who might care about his whereabouts that he was going on a lengthy vacation. But several times an alert went out. Someone in the know forgot they knew, or wanted to know what they didn't know. He was looked for. Quite a lot of money went into a search.

"When Westphal was a kidnap worry, his details alerted the Clement bunch. They joined forces. Then Westphal reappeared. He'd been under the purview of Mistress Aurora, and her story was his story: a match made in heaven. He got his money's worth, she got the money. He'd been in the custody of the Street Girls, some of San Francisco's roughest. The experiences are intense. Pictures of them and Westphal advertise whips that say they aren't kidding. It's all there in the brochure. The joys of men. When the Super Bowl isn't enough.

"Westphal hobbled out of captivity on crutches. He's back in the bosom of his wealthy lifestyle. Clement started the same way but didn't make it. He links to money and boredom. That's all."

"I wish them much happiness," I said. "No point talking to me. Anyone knows I don't do that kidnapping thing."

"My people don't accept personal testimonials. Some piece of good dirt always turns up hounding blondes."

"Are you interested in Clement?" I asked.

"If I need to save you."

"What was Sand's problem?"

She cut me off with a finger doing a windshield wipe. "After a point, no questions asked…no problems land on my desk. A suicide? A mental dead end? Who can say?"

Mineral water and tacos arrived with a straw basket of purple chips. We clinked like she wanted to bring up something. She was changing jobs, off to L.A. It was time for a reveal, but she was silent.

I rubbed her thigh, hello. "Tell me about her…your new girl in L.A., the career on stage and screen, the home in Hollywood."

"That Elizabeth intuition," she marveled. "Where do I get some?"

"You're in love," I said.

"There's a trial period. I might fail."

"You've failed at all the right places. You've never put a foot wrong. She's prettier than me? I could be vulnerable. When are you leaving?"

"They give me a Greatest Law Enforcement Person in the World award next month. Then we get drunk. I promise not to come back."

The tease…the purple garment of glory.

"Thanks for meeting me," I said.

She put a hand in a jacket pocket. "In case you might be wondering why I bothered to do all that investigating for you at the drop of a hat?"

She waved a letter. No return address. No postmark. No perfume. I had a look at both sides. "It was never mailed. Hand delivered. Caught my curiosity."

"A payoff? You want your cut."

"Your city supervisor. She's trying to make friends. She can't reach the friendly you. She asked here and there and got to me… the better way to reach you."

"I'm not taking new clients."

"One of the gaps in your understanding of how the hierarchy takes care of little fish like us."

"My hierarchies are me and a man hugging my boots."

"You're on a ladder, honey. She's not at the top, but she's reaching a hand…down. Take it. Open the letter. See what she wants to give you."

"She wants a caning."

"She's your flipping supervisor. Put the letter next to your heart. Open your heart in the privacy of the English Department. Give her a call. Don't forget to mention me. You know… my needs. How hard is it to express a little thoughtfulness for an ex-lover?"

"I'm retiring. Did I mention that?"

"You're forty-two. You lose your high fast one?"

"Grim-visaged war has smoothed his wrinkled front."

"Jane Krentz. Lord, the people you read. You can't come to

grips with retirement. My mother gave me a French name…I never told you this, did I?"

"Once or twice. She spelled it wrong. Okay. I get the life lesson."

"You've done canes. It's all over. Fine. Explore new horizons. Specialize in paddles. Whole new world out there, Elizabeth."

"You get to make love to starlets. I want something meaning-ful. I want to give back."

Ren picked at a purple chip, then stared at a car pulling away from the curb with a tongue motion cleaning her teeth. "Don't start that. I never told you I loved you. The tears would give me away."

We pushed off from the table. She spread a napkin and dumped nuts in the middle, a little knapsack went in a shirt pock-et. We slow-motioned the end of an occasion, pushing chairs just right to the table, and looked around for how much of ourselves would wait here for us.

"Do I get a movie ending?" I asked.

We'd come out of the curves beyond the Golden Gate Park, but there was still the long sweep onto the bridge and the rise and fall onto the stone platform on the headlands and the twisting grade into the cutoff to an overlook of dreams. Cars were spread out in a personal bias for how they wanted to express admiration. A solitary woman was wrapping herself in her arms. Beyond was what we would all lose one way or another, by design or celestial misadventure.

She unhooked her seatbelt. We watched the lights till the last ferry was lumbering toward Larkspur. It was a twinkly night, but we were on the other side of those nights. She re-hooked her seatbelt. We left.

At the English Department she double-parked. She left the engine on.

"Desmond and Sand was never on the level," she said. "They got away with shit I'd stay away from. That means you, too. The evidence the guys are pulling out of their office is better than the rumors. It's a crime scene, fairly dormant for most of a year while the legends of buried treasure circulate.

"On a piece of disputed paper you're Hannah Keir's trustee, but I don't see that you need to be concerned. I couldn't even find a bicycle in Kier's name to bother an heir about, and I couldn't find evidence that an Edith Barlow is an heir. Not by blood."

I unlocked three locks to my gate and pushed it open and let it close on its own. She drove off. Just above where her car had been was a second-floor window across the street. In the window were shadows settled into bedtime drinks. It was the last time with Rene, less haunted than the first time, when I'd been anticipating the coming developmental stages in my thirties. She was twenty when she first officially arrived at the English Department. The ten-year difference simply meant I didn't know I had to have my guard up. She showed up with a fresh haircut and the confidence of that peculiar appeal of bad girl manners she added to splash grooming.

I'd become aware of her in the news, big in sports accomplishment at City College, which is how we got on to what it meant to be offside in soccer. It was her last semester. She was flunking out. Then I didn't hear from her. Then she was back. She'd returned from overseas intact, an accomplishment that passed between us at our next meeting unspoken, but in awareness, from my side, that these women who'd risked life, the simplest commodity we have to offer, were a befuddled cornerstone of the coming society.

CANING visitors to the tune of hundreds of dollars per hour is the guaranteed income I count on. It's mostly cash, and that's mostly hundreds, which I band in groups of ten, ten groups to an envelope, superfluously notated with $10,000, and off to the bank by secret courier—another story. I'd sealed two envelopes, and counted off an odd lot left over.

I'd put in a system that transcribes calls onto a monitor that

can be attended visually. On the screen was a message from
Sarah: I could call her if I felt like it.

I dialed. She picked up. I said, "I called to say I've been
thinking about you. Incidentally, did you get the boxes?"

"Someone had picked them up already."

"Faith promised them to you."

"Faith said she was busy as she was shutting the door. The
fastest job I ever lost."

"I hear spooky music," I said.

"We're wrapped up in a Charlie Chan film. I know who the
murderer is. 'Guilty conscience always first to speak up.'"

"Speaking of conscience, how do I pay you?"

"Don't. I want you to owe me."

"Think of compassion fatigue, the eternal suppurating wound
of my profession. Can we meet tonight? Two seconds? There and
gone. You won't miss a clue."

"Raise your hand if you talked to more idiots than I did today.
I don't look well enough for IHOP. How about my porch?"

The house was a short walk west of the campus, green with
green trim, green and maroon shrubs, an apron of dried grass
along the sidewalk. The porch was behind an evergreen, visible
halfway up the driveway. Sarah had come out of the porch light
barefoot in a black bikini. There had been a sweltering heat up
and down California, triple digits everywhere except in San Francisco. Berkeley had topped Sacramento today by one degree, and
it would do that for two more days.

Our hellos hung in air that at half past nine was inching lower
in the eighties. Across the street a Civil War ballad was coming
out of a nook in the dark. A baritone was lamenting years creep-
ing by...*the snow is on the grass again...the frost gleams where
the flowers once were.* We didn't hug. We hadn't anything to say
that improved on the guitar. There was always the twinge of our
current situation, that in the next year it would be worse, and in
this year nobody was counting their blessings.

She offered me the plastic bucket seat on the porch. She bent a leg on the top step, stuck her back to a porch post, stretched a leg to the bottom step, and put weight on an arm. The effect was to make her look like a discarded sex doll and to make her look taller than she was. Her hair was a reddish shade of orange pinned up off her neck. We were a fine porch display in a comic lampoon of the privileged class in a golden era that was slipping from our grasp.

I watched her dark eyes. They were the first temptations for the fellows who get a two-way going on the nice things in a girl. She looked me over. What I was blessed with to look over didn't come up.

"You want something?" she said.

"Water with fizz, if you have it."

She looked back from the door. "Green bottle, or blue bottle?"

She came back with ice in plastic drinking glasses and one green and one blue bottle with the classic Coca-Cola contour. I unscrewed the green and poured with care. "Don't want to lose any of this."

She held her glass two-handed, close to her mouth. Three more days and we'd be down fifteen degrees. I pulled three fingers across my forehead that had gone from damp to wet.

"Anything turn up in Emeryville?" I asked.

"Didn't go."

She went inside. She came back with an oscillating fan attached to an extension cord that went under the screen door. Every so many seconds I got a blast that felt like I'd come down with a fever.

"The movie come out the way you thought?" I asked.

"We had a pool. We each put in a dollar. Two of them totally forgot they'd seen it before."

I held out an envelope. She took it in one hand and dropped it on her other palm. "Heavy."

"I'm surprised you followed up with the boxes," I said.

"As far as it went. I'd never heard of an erotic charity. I had a look at what qualified for an award. I write sexy romance. I fancy I'd be a finalist."

She fanned her neck with the envelope I'd given her. It moved air on a Star of David silver necklace.

"I went in person to Atherton to turn in a job application," she said.

"The Drum Erotic Charity?" I said. "They're still listing jobs?"

"The Charity is inside the Drum Foundation. They're giving away money. Why not inquire? I called. One of the call options is to press the five button if you want money. Or read the web page, which describes the procedure for holding out a tin cup."

"You skipped the procedure?"

"People like me get a job if we just happen to know someone who needs someone right now and we're the only one in the room with them. That's how it worked at Coates and Sinott. And that's a summer job in San Francisco, and that was impossible, except there was a girl living in Berkeley who was the older sister of a girl I'm friends with.

"The Foundation asks that an applicant send a formal request in writing, which is reviewed, which may land you in a queue to wait your turn for a second review. If you're pitching a film, don't apply. Yes, to answer your question, I skipped the procedure."

"You dropped off your sexual fantasy in person?" I said.

"They wouldn't accept my application at the gate."

"You write?" I said.

"Flash fiction, not on paper. A sandwich worth of fantasy looking at a male at lunch. I lose interest in lovers, even when I'm telling them what to say. I can't imagine coming up with a novel-length prototype."

She put her chin on a bed of knuckles. It concentrated a stare. "I can imagine the mechanics of whipping men, but…what kept you going?"

"You mean, get a Ph.D. and be the best I can be?"

"I don't mean to be rude. I can't imagine you."

"You mean, where did it all start…the true and real provenance of a snobby dominatrix?"

She raised her eyebrows at the quick surge of belligerence.

"It was when I decided I would get an education, no matter what. Let them pick over the bones of a dumb blonde, but they can't say I didn't see into the heart of their adulterated penitence."

"A religious experience?"

"When I was fourteen I told a man I was nineteen. He could believe it or not. He could go to jail or not. His business. He offered to buy me a leather outfit. Dressing up that afternoon sealed me in a bubble. I saw the horror of walking away from opportunity just because I didn't understand it."

She raised her bottle. "Another green?"

We refilled our glasses and settled into a moment's reconsideration. I knew why the testy mood had surged. I didn't want to bring myself up again. I decided I'd drink up and go.

"Spoke to a woman today," she said. "Her son owned Quantum State Greeting Cards. He died. She's getting advice she doesn't trust. I gave her a slogan: Yesterday is the new tomorrow. Never know what prompts a job offer. That one missed."

"I know who runs the charity," I said. "Neville Drum. He was in love with Hannah Kier. Faith Nichols was his second choice. How serious are you? I might be able to get you past the gate in Atherton."

"And do what?"

"I'll check what's available. When are you leaving Coates and Sinott?"

"The Friday before Labor Day, as of now. They pay me for the week after. I might be kept on. I'm at the brink of an abyss. But. Things keep coming up."

A car was four minutes away. We took a minute getting to the end of the drive.

"Faith tossed out a bunch of stuff," she said. "There were

boxes all over the grass by her walk. My name was on a piece of paper taped to one I was supposed to take. Robert Butterworth was in that one."

I shook my head.

"I looked up the name. A Robert Lowell Butterworth disappeared a long time ago."

I didn't ask why she was interested.

] *Chapter 4*

MESSAGES WERE CIRCULATING in a private network that a woman calling herself Edith Barlow was asking about the Countess. I was flagged because she had a question about the English Department. What did literature have to do with any-thing? Had I written anything literary? Was I published? There was nothing published under my name online. Did I use a *nom de plume*? And did I have integrity? Like what kind of integrity? Any kind. Any kind anybody could think of.

WHEN the letter arrived, the Tres Pinos postmark was interesting enough to open the letter right away. Edith was in Santa Barbara. No way of knowing how I'd entered the story of her life, or why the letter was in an envelope mailed from another return address in Tres Pinos.

> To the Trustee of my Nothing Estate,
> I'm told I'm an heir to nothing. I should understand I
> can thank "Mom." The forecast for this next two weeks
> in Santa Barbara can't be right. It's for paradise. I ought
> to hang around for some clarification, but I have to go
> to Seattle. I'm taking the train. On my way up the coast
> I'd like to meet you. You knew her. Lucky you. Nothing
> personal. I need advice. I'll text.
> Edith.

———

THE trip was down to its last two hours when the message arrived that she'd be coming in on Amtrak to Jack London Square. She called from San Jose to see if a hello was still possible. The day before a person had been killed sitting on the tracks. The odds were high that the schedule wouldn't encounter a hold-up two days running.

Traveling twelve hours by rail makes me think of making ends meet on a budget. She was in an eye-catching leather outfit, the kind that connects professional appointments in my line of work at both ends of a transcontinental flight. Certainly what she was living in maintained a snazzy travel elegance. So the train makes her financial status difficult to nail down. Her figure and height would make it possible to get into resemblances to her mother's elegance—my two cents on appearance.

It hadn't happened before that I'd laid eyes on someone who so impeccably put me in mind of searching for who they reminded me of, not as Edith did when she took the first steps onto the station platform. She'd extended the handle of her luggage cart and gotten the rack loaded, and I was smacked upside the head, weaving through the halls and byways of the flood of reincarnation of the way my body had structured its motions arriving in San Francisco. That was a long while back, when I was seventeen, and watched people carefully and must have emitted some comical tourist manner of knowing my way around. The experience would return when she was on her way again.

"Very nice of you to meet me," she said. "I could have taken a plane. There's nothing so stupidly afflicted as a peripatetic hooker terrified of airplanes."

I had no concern with showing a clichéd exuberance. A tentative second or two of looking her over and I hugged her a fraction longer than a meet-and-greet, almost a goodbye. I wouldn't have been surprised showing a bewildered tear, but her eyes showed a cool head.

"How much time do you have?" she asked.

"I'm here until you board. This your first trip to Oakland?"

"I took this line to Portland on my way to college. I got off here for an hour, not knowing my mother was near."

"You want to see where your mother lived?"

"What's there?"

It was the right question. I stopped trying to give us a common world to share, if that's what I thought I was trying to accomplish. There was a Vietnamese place on Grand. At this hour we could be in a booth in fifteen minutes. Then again, if she was hungry, she could bring it up. She did.

She put a toe to her bag. "I carry what I eat."

"How do I stop being a burden?" I said

"You're looking for a metaphor?"

"You can call toast and jelly whatever you want."

She took her time on that one. Eventually she said, "I've plenty of mood for the two of us. Let's drive."

A car for hire was parked where a street dead-ended at the platform. As we headed his way, he got out. The trunk and rear doors were open when we reached the street.

"Just go up Broadway to Grand," I told him. "I'll tell you from there."

Two blocks passed. We were out of Old Town. I spoke up. "What do you want to see?"

"Just talk. I'll listen."

There was a beginning. I started there. "Your mother taught classes in a multiuse building on Eighteenth Street in the Castro district. There was a coffee shop across the street. I used to walk a lot then. That's where I turned around. We knew of each other. She joined me one day. She thought we had something to talk about. A man had given her his library, some two thousand volumes. I happened to meet her at the precise moment the light bulb came on."

"You can't say no to a free book, I hear."

"My librarian throws out duplicates behind my back, and confesses for a dose of behavior modification. At around five thousand volumes I went to a monastery in Portugal. I restructured the English Department around the design. It became my ultimate ego trip. I'm at fifteen thousand four hundred and some. Books are bearing down on me, a reason for retiring."

"I'm told you look like her."

"From two blocks away maybe. It's a compliment, so I don't sulk. What happened to her is a mystery to all of us."

The driver said, "This is Grand."

"Turn right," I said. "Go down to the theater and get on Lakeshore south. We'll go to the numbered streets and turn left. I'll know it when I see it."

I asked her, "How did you hear about the English Department?"

"Asking questions. You're who I should talk to. I was told… I'm sure you know…you're a snob."

"It's just an act."

"I'm trying to get good at it. What I'm carrying is all that's left of Santa Barbara. What I'm wearing is rented, so to speak. A woman lent me some money to look snooty. I'm on my way to Seattle for an appointment. We're a team for clients who can afford two-women scenarios."

"Your letter went through Tres Pinos. I'm curious."

"You read *Farewell My Lovely*?" she said.

"It's on the shelves. I tried."

"Doesn't matter. The Snap Judgment Press, they're in Tres Pinos. They published my senior thesis on Raymond Chandler. The only father I had."

We passed the Grand Lake Theater. "I called your mother once when she was going in to see *Dr. No*. She's a Sean Connery fan."

Edith cupped her hand against the slant of the sun. The magnificence of the marquee passed.

I spoke to the driver. "We want to get to Seventeenth. You can't get in from Lakeshore. Go down to the next street, and go four blocks. We'll cut over."

"What's the address?"

"I don't know. It was a little white house between apartment buildings."

Seventeenth had grown a new generation, but it was the same hordes of apartment kids riding their bikes defiantly stupidly in and out between parked cars. The driveway was empty. The blinds in the front windows were closed.

"Your mother lived here a long time ago," I said.

"She sold it?"

"It belonged to someone else," I said.

"She was his kept woman?"

"He definitely wouldn't say that. She interacted with him."

"I'd like to get out," she said. "We have time."

I let the driver go. We parked ourselves on the top step like visiting cousins arriving early waiting for the aunt to get home for lunch and let us in. Edith went around back and came around front from the other side. She lowered herself onto a travel bag on the top step and bent forward on her knees, her shoulder bag between us. She spoke into remote events that could be kept distanced.

"Unknown to me, my mother visited Santa Barbara to watch me. When I graduated, she was there. So I heard tell. Now she's gone…which is who she always was. Is there more? It's hard to know. A man said, talk to you."

I drew my knees under my elbows, confidential-like. "She might not be dead. She is missing."

"A la Amelia Earhart?" The sarcasm made a conversation on the subject possible.

"Less missing than that. The generic missing. They have that in common. When I found out I was your mother's trustee I called the woman who lived here. Now she's missing. No point ringing the bell, but you never know. Apparently, your mother had to vanish in a hurry. On the way out the door she signed my name to the trust that names you an heir."

"You're all I've got, then?"

A silence could let the force of pain take root. I caught on to something she'd said. Something to say.

"Your father and Raymond Chandler?"

"That was misleading. I shouldn't make that direct a connection. I've had a fascination with Chandler from way back. I found out he came to Santa Barbara to track the steps of a relative. Some tourist advice: You walk up the sidewalk from the ocean today as if you were in the photo from 1927 when the Biltmore was built. Enter to the left and ask at the desk where Raymond Chandler slept. The concierge of the day refers you to a book at the library that contains claims about Chandler that aren't found anywhere else."

"Literary untruths?" I said.

"Civic exuberance. You know Santa Barbara?"

"I've had offers to meet me at the airport and drop me off. I've some kind of allergy to the place."

"Well…I found a big rock where my body fits a nook. The rock was in a breakwater of boulders dumped on the beach to keep the railroad tracks safe in storms. That's what I was going to say about trains. A long story. They were my companions. I had meals out of sacks on that rock, listening to the *clickity-clack*. It's a one-block community below Santa Barbara with a milkshake bar. I'd wrap up in a plastic poncho and have a milkshake in a storm. That is *security*."

She reached in her travel bag. She unscrewed the top of a thermos, poured coffee, and held up an orange soda. I took it. She showed me how to get the top off.

"You're missing something," she said finally. "On the lawn above the Pacific is still the view of what Chandler saw, an ocean that mixed alcoholic anguish in the seer's imagination and released rays of something strangely honest, a contemporary instruction manual of how the tough guy of any era can get through the mean streets with a soul of sorts. At least while you're reading in bed.

"A throw of the dice. He came up with a first-person narrator paid a penny a word, spoken by a detective whose L.A. had stored up a classic street speech ready to be mined, and a people it could live among. For a while it didn't look like a career. The logic of people who murdered people was so ordinary anybody could make it believable. It was so ordinary it wasn't what books on L.A. were about until a blackout drunk thought it was honest enough to preserve. It wasn't Shakespeare, but it made you wonder before you decided it wasn't. The city he described saved in prose the best of his life."

I took a plug of orange soda. Try anything once.

"It starts a curiosity about the Snap Judgment Press," I said. "How'd you find them?"

"Sofia Velazquez is the managing editor. She knew my advisor. Sofia published her article on Wallace, the *Infinite Jest* guy. What I just said to you is, essentially, the first paragraph of my thesis. Presto, ergo, Sofia published my thesis."

"You mentioned a woman you're meeting in Seattle," I said.

"You're perceptive. Sofia was the leader of a BDSM-themed music group. They brought members of the audience onto the stage, stripped them, tied them to a whipping post and made music. Hyped the gate like all outdoors until God touched Sofia on the shoulder. She heard him say that he wanted her to publish poetry. She was the writer of the group…the poet. It was a snap decision, jousting with the wind."

"You went to Reed?"

A frown appeared to draw her upper lip between her teeth. She made me the subject. "You left school in the eighth grade."

"I've been catching up…not by degrees."

"*Touché.*"

"Touchy. It's almost thirty years later, and my brick-and-mortar experience was an elementary school. You're never supposed to wake up a sleepwalker."

"Or a streetwalker. She'd awakened to poetry, but publishing poetry needs a benefactor, a lot of them. Sofia went back to dominance to support the crew."

"Chandler articles didn't help?"

"The article introduced us. She knew I was in Santa Barbara. She invited me to dominate a guy with her, a big shot on Padaro Lane, a surgeon. His wife was giving him a surprise for his birthday. Sophia bought me an outfit. I turned out to be a hit. We took a drive down the coast for three days…explore how we felt about joining up, you know, as in, the team. We stopped off to see a madam in Malibu…this fills out to a great limerick…Sofia's a heck of a poet…ends in hullaballoo. No appointments necessary. You drop in and fall in with any old talk. She rarely rose from a sofa-chair. Four landlines among the channel-changers. She kept a bunch of housekeeper fellows handy to order around. One of her toys was Webster. He was a finalist in the four hundred meter hurdles at the U.S. Olympic trials in Sacramento. After college he trained with some Hungarian coach at UCLA for a few years. Women in European cars met him after workouts. He lived even then like he was coming into a professional career servicing women. A specimen, a real sperm donor."

"You bought him?"

"We feel safer with him on the road. I can see a steady arrangement. Sofia calls the shots. He's her guy, however she wants him. I guess she's entertaining eventualities. Webster can handle a room full of women. I'm the gasbag in the trio. Webster buys me a book when he prefers I leave him alone. He got me a secondhand copy of *The Wound and the Bow*—Edmund Wilson. These fellows analyze novels like it's a big deal. Anyway, to keep me out of his hair, he told me the story of Philoctetes. I would be his Helen. He ordered *The Big Book of Greek Legends* for me. He didn't feel at liberty to discuss his life until I'd finished it."

Her watch was a tiny thing wrapped twice on a thin wrist. "It's time."

She went in the backyard for a second look. I hung out with her luggage. At the station I took a liking to her choice of color, an open satin blouse, pale green, a crucifix with stones of different colors at four points.

"A showy piece of redemption," she said.

"You need something to tide you over?"

"I was hoping you'd ask," she said. "Cash is appreciated."

I did the no-look casual hand-in-the-bag move. There were hundreds and fifties in an envelope. I squished it up tight in a roll and slid my arm backhanded to my waist, and made the transfer to the hand at the unbuttoned gap in her jacket. We stepped away from each other looking elsewhere.

"I've been meaning to mention something," I said. I took a second to convey that I was proceeding cautiously. "There's a house on the ocean. The woman who lived here was collecting the rent. Before that, your mother was collecting the rent. She might own it. There's probably ten things not legal about the title. If you want to collect the rent, it's yours. In the attic are some of the things your mother couldn't take with her."

"Sofia and Webster are in Seattle," she said. They're my family. "We'll be in L.A. this coming Friday. Tres Pinos is the fixed point in the trips we traverse in California. That's my home. That answer your question?"

She looked up. Looking at the sky cut me off. The public address announcement generated a hug. I walked her to the little footstool that divides the step into two easy halves. She stepped back to let boarders bunching behind go around.

"I'll see you. Thanks for meeting me. Webster thought I lied easily for no advantage. People will notice they can trust me."

She stepped into the crowd at the top of the steps, emerged at the back of the queue on the second level, and arranged a shoulder against a window. The uniformed conductors snatched their stepstools and got inside. When the doors shut a signal came from the back of the train. I waited in the empty space where we had been together. It was all over: she'd stopped a minute in Oakland to tell me something. The question stayed with me on the walk to the street, wondering if she'd said it.

————

THREE weeks later another letter arrived from Tres Pinos.

Dearest Mistress Elizabeth,
I'm sorry for the unconscionable delay. I compose letters when my feet are higher than my head. When I
remember there is something to do, the energy of creation drains off, and the working part of my brain is not
there. This metaphorically excuse-ridden cop-out/alibi
is at most ninety percent wrong. We have been busy,
but I do think of you often while upright.

First, you probably think I've forgotten the loan
you gave me when I really needed it. The day is here. I
can pay you back and throw in a supper in a three-star
hash house in North Beach. The others I owe are opening envelopes of pure cash without the tedium of my
company.

I'm well physically, mentally panicky. It's one of the
reasons I think of you. You are a natural at stockpiling
casual erotic maneuvers that command attention. How
do I learn from you? I can tolerate the dominance
scene within limits. A hundred lashes, and the guy yesterday made a racket like what I would think it feels
like. It's not easy to think I know what's going on in a
guy's head when they don't twitch a muscle. Where are
the limits? To quote Frost, it's like tennis without a net.
Did I say: God, save the money? What's the English
Department all about? We may think alike.

Changing to the sunny side of the street, my table
manners have picked up a shine. I've lost three pounds
and kept it at arm's length, a safe distance for now. We
stayed with the guy on Padaro Lane. He watched over
me growing up. Never had a hint he was there until I
met Sofia. He knew my mother is all he'll say. He was
the one who told me to ask you. I take support from
the bucolic countryside around here.

Life with Sofia means daily compliments I can believe in. She runs a tight ship. An hour is fifty-nine minutes and sixty seconds. I'm the assistant, so that's easy. Strut the allure. The outfits, the scenes, it's the client's call. We love what they love. Don't fall in love. No fantasies beyond protocols. Don't frame the first dollar you earn.

If the itch creeps up on you, I'd love a note. I need letters. I've no biological family–school–society connections to escape to for tea and tennis.

Your devoted admirer, Edith."

I sent a letter to Tres Pinos that day.

Hi, Edith,
It's good to hear from you. When you get a chance, let me know when you'll be in North Beach. Sounds like interesting things are going on in your life.

So you're in the business. Working with a partner is good. I'd guess your "supervisor" screens out the tough nuts. Let her earn her cut. Caution is a talent. Act against your suspicious nature rarely. You'll be a legend some one of these days, or you won't. But don't worry about good fortune, good looks. The gods take the day off now and then. Every generation sees some carelessness in fate.

I don't recommend faking beyond the regular social faking. You know, nice weather, nice day, miles of smiles, when you feel like a rag doll. If you're putting one foot after another purely for the money, then the only advice I have is to just have enough to finance another venture in a career that interests you.

I've been asked what I needed to have in a bank to close the shop and disappear. I never saw it that way. The unusual things that suddenly perplexed me were rarely things I didn't at one time already anticipate. I'm retiring soon, next year perhaps, before I've forgotten what to do next.

By the way, there's the queer stuff. A client I'd been seeing for years mentioned on the way out the door that he'd calculated square roots of primes to fifty places during every session we'd ever had. What agency did I provide?

Best, Elizabeth.

] Chapter 5

DENNIS MEISTERS RETIRED on a physical disability pension from the Missouri Highway Patrol. I agreed to see him just to say yes to a cop I'd never heard of. He was the last link at the end of the favor tree. When it gets to me it's a favor devoid of substance. Nobody cares, or the call to me would have invoked the greater good of the SFPD, and a gold star would be there in the folder for Judgment Day. Not this time, or so the occasion registered.

I wasn't given anything else about Meisters. The circular staircase to the entrance of the English Department would have gotten me into what "disabled" meant. I couldn't see a reason for bringing it up. I knew a place where the sidewalk tables are easy access.

I came up Ginger Road as the owner of Eggs Before Chicken was hauling chairs out of overnight storage to the tables. A delivery truck was double-parked. A block away I could hear the racket of a handcart bouncing down a ramp. A man in an apron had the right-of-way through the side entrance. He was stocking the freezer. It was the first few minutes of a Wednesday morning. The first arrivals were citizens like me who make their own hours. We didn't beat the traffic; we didn't join it. We took our mornings slow.

A big man was letting himself out of a car door opposite

the café. He dodged a few cars in either direction, jaywalking. He propped a briefcase on a chair at an empty table and made a quick turn facing my way. He kept a hand on the back of the chair. From a half-block off it could be I was seeing the fellow I was meeting.

The greeting had a good feel. I'm tall. Within an arm's length hello I was not quite dainty. I was bumptious enough from the lift of feeling of average height to offer a hand to shake. That's not ordinary. The term "disabled" persevered in my mental accounting against his ruggedness. He looked pretty good.

He'd had breakfast. He didn't take coffee. I ordered bottled water and an amaretto biscuit. He had the same. We reclined into looking-each-other-over postures. We were up two tables from the side entrance. A woman with a baby carriage was at the other side of the door, far away, by the stop sign. We could talk without being overheard. I took that to be his concern, that he had something to discuss in private. He displayed those methodical facial preparations that usually signal an impulse to reveal something, but each crescendo subsided in a solemn hand squeezing his briefcase, as if this didn't have to be interesting, but he was trying. I stuck a biscuit on a plate and poured half a glass.

I introduced three topics. He could take his pick.

"The man who gave me your name mentioned a disability," I said. "You were Highway Patrol. And you're from Missouri. And you know what I do. So it's curious that you didn't call me. If you wanted my services you wouldn't ask San Francisco police personnel to pass on your name. I'm surprised they did. However, to clear that up, are you meeting with me in relation to my business?"

"I'm a crank. They forgot that?" The remark came with a curl at the corner of his mouth. The face was handsome once. Smashing good looks young had offered him joys without effort. Quite a few setbacks had taken over, or one long trouble. The smile had turned to stone. We fit. Better than that even. I wouldn't have to look at my watch under the table.

He took a bite, studied the biscuit some, and nodded. The second bite came from the other end.

"What happened?" I asked.

"Looking the wrong way when the gun fired."

"If you excuse my saying, you look okay."

"I can walk a fair distance on a flat surface, if it's hard, without pain. How far depends how much I've been on my feet the day before. Going upslope from here, I wouldn't want to go farther than my car."

"You have to be somewhere soon?"

"Never have to be anywhere soon. Showed my wife your web page. I get questioned even if I'm early for lunch."

"Congratulations on a successful marriage."

His hand wandered off to flip open the flap on his briefcase. The hand went inside. He was prepared for what he was sorting. He pulled out a magnifying glass, a heavy-duty job, a pound or two. He took out some large pieces of paper, unfolded one of them, and ran his finger hard along the crease. He lifted the large open sheet by its far sides and set it where I could pull it my way by the bottom edge. He put the magnifying glass within reach.

I jumped my chair closer and mulled over a couple thousand people in the stands of a sporting event.

"What do I magnify?" I asked.

He reached an index finger to a red circle on the photo. "Just a second." Another sheet needed a crease massaged. He put this photo on top of the first. It was the stuff inside the red circle. The enlargement cut the scene to a small gathering and another red circle. A third sheet did this all over again.

"This is the enlarged image of the red circle in the red circle. Take a look at the three people in the middle."

"What do I see?" I muttered.

"Appreciate if you tell me."

"They're excited," I said. "The man in front of them had his hat knocked off. They did it?"

"You might look closer."

I used the glass. A swarm of bees had collected around their faces.

"Bees?" I said. That couldn't be right. "Do I get a hint?"

"It would prejudice an honest reaction."

"Where is this place? I know I wasn't there."

"It wouldn't help to know. I could tell you. It's up to you. The photograph was taken eleven years ago during the top of the eighth inning in a loser-go-home, single game elimination to determine the wild card entry in the National League playoffs."

"What did these people do? Are they criminals?"

"You're warm."

I magnified the faces. I studied the swarm. The dots weren't quite bees. Still. That was the key. It must have been. A minute later I had assembled the elements of a drug deal gone wrong. A rival gang had put some bees on them. I kept my humor to myself.

"I could use a few more biscuits," I asked. "This will take a minute."

He brought back nine biscuits. "All they had in the big glass jar."

"I need another hint." I suggested.

"It won't help," he said, "but okay. The score was tied. There were two outs. Jackson was on first, Esteves on second, the go-ahead run for St. Louis. Esteves was fast. It was a factor in the calculations. The Moose was batting, a left-hander. He'd worked the count to three and one against the starter, Hermann. Larkin, the Dodger manager, called for a spot reliever, Albrecht, to get a strikeout or an infield out. Keep the ball down. Larkin walked off the mound. Albrecht had his orders: the Moose hits, kill yourself or the team will, and they'll make it hurt. Dana was on deck. He'd doubled three times in three at-bats, the only hits off Herman. If he hit another double, the Dodgers would be down two and maybe going into the ninth inning down three. Albrecht fired a ninety-eight-mile-per-hour dart into the lower inside corner of the zone. The Moose swung. He put it in the air for the next year, plenty of time for the third baseman, Ponce, to park himself under the little speck in the sky. Ponce waved off assistance. Somewhere up there the sky went wrong. Ponce lost sight of the speck. In a cloud? Some say in the shadow of Satan's malevolence. Ponce jumped aside and waved Rodriguez to continue in from left field and finish up. Rodriguez, coming in fast, had gone into his leap to gain altitude. That would get his glove over the rail. He would ignore the geometry of the stadium structure. Whatever happened, he would crash into the iron bars around the dugout. He might end his career. He might end his life. He was paid eight million a year to take this risk."

I flipped back to the first photo. "That's Rodriguez," I noted. "A quality hint."

Meisters put a thumbs up: Atta girl.

"A marvel of grace, what the professional athlete provides in the modern era—in this instance, Rodriguez. His right foot, the one closer to the earth, was three feet off the ground, and he was still rising when he reached the edge of the stands in the third base foul area. He had overshot slightly. His arched body stretched a gloved hand backward to the place that would have created a candidate for the ten best catches in the archives of the game. His neck was twisted, but not enough to see the ball settle into the soft sweet enclosure of the pouch. That would just be the skill of the athlete. What Rodriguez might have seen too, as he swept along in the sweeping arc, was the beer cup above his glove, which accounted for the non-thud of the ball in the glove. No thud. No catch. No out. It didn't happen."

That was it. I caught on. It wasn't bees. It was a thousand drops of beer.

"Rodriguez bounced off the rail, twisting twice into a falling collision with several players of the Los Angeles Dodgers. I watched the replay a dozen times. His teammates caught his fall. They saved his life. Behind him a fountain of foam was spreading into the lower seats.

"Albrecht came out. A reliever, Jerome Tully, took over on the Moose at 3–2, the Moose homered on his first pitch, and nobody remembers the ninth inning. St. Louis went to Atlanta the next day, and no one remembers that outcome either.

"The analysis was fair odds the ball would have landed in Rodriguez's glove and stayed put, but that went into the archives of speculation."

I had it. "This beer guy ruined it for the Dodgers," I said. "You're looking for him. You want to thank him. This is personal. It was his cup that caught Moose's pop-up."

"There was an official Scott Warner free beer and pizza day in St. Louis."

"You're from Missouri," I said, looking up and very pleased catching on. "Scott Warner was the beer man?"

"Scott Warner was celebrated for a week, a poor idiot, a goat for life. Uncounted millions of death threats. Sold his home in Toluca Lake, and nobody knows where he went for the purposes of a follow-up threat. But he and his beer cup are indelible lessons forever in the annals of God's will be done. I had that picture on my wall at home until we moved out here to live with my sister in South San Francisco. When my sister moved downstairs we got the big room. The room my wife and I shared became my study. That's when I unpacked the greatest picture ever taken. That's when I saw it."

There were three oversize glossies on top of my plate. The wide-angle, which caught Rodriguez tilting on his way over into the L.A. dugout head first, was cropped around the splash of beer. The enlargement was cropped around a trio of fans two rows above Warner. I was looking at that blowup.

Images of war and sports provide these instants of minor moment that of some spark of fate in themselves generate a linked past and future that becomes the truest treasures of glory in the claim: "I was there." Moments without flaws, the records in later evenings of a St Crispin's Day of unashamed death or triumph for "we few, we happy few, we band of brothers."

Men concentrate their lives on these moments. But I didn't see it. I couldn't get the shakes over this in two lifetimes.

I had everything I needed. I put a finger on Scott Warner. "Is Warner my last hint?"

I put the magnifying glass silently on the table. I kept looking. While I did, I took my fingers to where they could fit the fingers of the other hand in my lap. I leaned back. I didn't know what to say. I liked Meisters. I wanted to tell him about something I liked.

Meisters sealed the magnifying glass in an inner compartment of his briefcase. A marvelous thing designed for one job. It would never do a job again. Its time was up. Meisters's line of sight could have been stuck on a dried-out crumb on my plate.

"I could look again," I said, as in, "It won't help."

He gave up on me.

"September thirty, two thousand ten, Dodger Stadium. Didn't unpack this photograph till two thousand and seventeen. It's when I saw Clement. I'd only been looking at him for seven years. No reason to see him in a blind spot. The science says I'm wrong."

Clement. A name I'd heard twice now.

"I understand you knew Hannah Kier?" he ventured. "That's her next to Clement, in the middle. The gal on the other side is unknown."

"I was supposed to identify Hannah?"

"It was worth a try."

"You mentioned science," I said. "What science?"

"The lab says it's not Clement."

"You know it's him, though."

"They say ninety-nine point ninety-four percent sure it's not. I'm sure I'm right for what's left over. I say that's Clement."

His face and neck were brown, a dark V at his neck. I put a finger against my glass and slid it thataway an inch. I looked at the check.

He put a bill on the check. I was aware of being with him and enjoying it. I wasn't in a hurry. I could have said that, but it would have been coy, forcing him to agree to small talk. He deserved better. He was looking for Clement. Consulting me was where the lines converged at the end of the road.

"If I'd identified Hannah," I said, "it would boost your identification, slightly, or maybe more, but what then? It's had me wondering."

"I could tell my wife I'm not crazy."

"You want my help to fool her? Before we get to that, I have a bone to pick with you. You people established the slippery slope to secession. I've never forgiven Missouri."

A twinkle happened in his eyes when he saw that I'm a Kansas girl, blond, green eyes, all the curves.

"Bleeding Kansas? One so easily forgets the Pottawatomie massacre."

"Lawrenceville," I recalled, "incited honorable God-fearing abolitionists."

The bite of the remark stoked a bite of cookie. He kept the rest in his fingers, arm elevated, where the part to be devoured could be manipulated for study.

"Am I getting an insight into your profession?" he asked.

"I carry grudges. Quantrill's raid was unnecessary. Uncalled for, actually. You rebels had no right."

"You should have stayed in school. Let me catch you up. We weren't a secessionist state."

"In your hearts, though."

He finished the cookie in smiles and nibbles. It went down pleasantly, or something was satisfying his heart. "I had a look at your web page. Tall, blonde, a stalk of fresh corn. You don't see that kind of attraction where I grew up. Not you're kind."

"It's how you know you're not in Missouri?"

"All too aware of San Francisco," he said to his next cookie. Behind the chef's counter the contents of a row of inverted ketchup bottles were being refurbished. The server asked what's what with the check. I decided I wanted my water. I held on to the glass. We could use a little more time.

"I'm picky with words," I said. "Part nature, part business. We've consulted. You keep rubbing your briefcase. What are we not discussing?"

"Stacey Piersall, if it's anybody. She vanished into thin air when I was fourteen. Getting over it is what my wife is helping me with."

"You loved her?" I was just guessing what his wife wanted him to forget all about.

"My sister has a split-level in South San Francisco. Lived alone. We'd visited her with the kids. The kids are on their own now. My wife and sister talked it over. It wouldn't be a final separation. I could come out when I was ready. See if it worked. It's been three years."

"You're settled in?"

"In a way," he said. He straightened his shoulders, as in a suggestion he was keeping me. He gave a strong impression he was wasting my time, and I was damn good- hearted when it came to listening to cripples.

He'd been twisting a plate, an inch one way, an inch back. His hand slowed suddenly to a stillness. "You're name came up during the time I was looking for Hannah. If you don't mind my saying, the way you're talked about, you know, how you ran away from home, helps me think that Stacey is alive."

"Stacey didn't make the news out here."

He sighed a puff. "She wouldn't. One of a million. All there is to tell."

"There's more, though." I pointed a biscuit at the sky. "I'd like to hear."

"Tell me to shut up," he frowned. The frown waited. I waited.

"All right. She left her house at a quarter past seven to meet Bonnie Knowles on the way to school. For some reason she went through the park to talk to Charlotte Lebaron. Charlotte's older brother spoke with her at the back door. Charlotte had left with her mother just before Stacey arrived. Edward Prince was cutting the grass at the park. He was the last person to say he saw

Stacey Piersall. He saw her go through the park. There's a gap in the trees by the swings. Through that gap he was sure he saw her get in a brown sedan. This must have been after Stacey spoke with Charlotte's brother. There's no reason why she was where he could see her. Officially he was the last to see her.

"I did some investigating solo, mostly piecing things I'd heard people had said with everything I knew about Kirksville. Made up my mind along the way. Became a cop. Threw in with Highway Patrol. I liked the job. Didn't think of myself as a detective, but what happened to Stacey was the cop I really was. Never stopped thinking about her.

"At every stop I looked speeders over like they were child murderers. I figured some must have been. At dinner I'd tell my wife of a peculiar stop that day. I was on to something. I liked murder too much. Too much for her. I had to shut up. Keep it to myself."

"What did Stacey Piersall have to do with Clement?" I asked.

"Nothing. He was a name in my head. Wasn't my case. What do I care about Clement? Always thought Clement ran into what he hadn't expected. Not a man you feel for. He had money. So he was in the papers. He wanted to be kidnapped. Some sort of game you people play out here. I don't have a feel for that. After my injuries had healed, as much as they would, the Highway Patrol had set me up shuffling paper. Chained to paperwork, all I could think about was Stacey. Wife had enough of me and Stacey."

"What do you do now?" I asked.

"Send in a report every once in a while to the Clement bunch. Get a check in the mailbox. Surprised I got the job. A storage unit in Missouri is full of boxes of lists—a lot of data related to Stacey and similar cases. All of it points at guesses. They all dried up. Haven't been near the unit for three years. I'm on the cure. Then I hear about you. How you ran away from home at thirteen. I think of Stacey. I think of what I'm not doing."

He patted the briefcase at the fat hunk of the bulge: "Clement. Don't have any forceful convictions. Wife and I get out nights, weekends. We call it a normal life."

"You were shot?" I asked. Who, what, and so on?

"Looking the wrong way at the scumbag in the car. Didn't occur to me to think about the piece of garbage he was waiting for in the liquor store. One bullet hit both legs." He got off that. "I understand you lost a friend up there at Navarro Point?"

"Someone I hadn't seen for seven or eight years," I said.

"She hasn't been found, I hear."

"They won't tell me anything."

"Ummh. Asking the crew on the case won't get you any-where."

"There were no signs of a crime," I said. "She just wasn't where she agreed to be."

"The team interviewed you how many times?"

"Twice."

"What did they ask the second time?"

"Same questions," I said. "Different order. A bit nastier."

"They're putting resources on this."

Meisters studied me, not quite eye to eye, a compliment that showed a foot wide. "You're highly thought of," he said. "That's verbatim according to one source. One source is good enough."

"I work with Child Protective Services. If I hear of a crime, or seriously suspect one, I report it. I ignore car theft. Then again, never had a client who admitted to stealing a car. The confessions I hear are imaginary sins against nature. Their fibs become part of the act."

———

A WOMAN was gathering leftovers in boxes. The man at her table headed to the restroom. We followed. Then met at the cashier's counter. Meisters followed me through a channel between tables to the door, and we passed into the open air, where a realization hit me that my worries didn't have to be set in the stone I was setting them in. This was a new feeling.

"Faith Nichols," I said. "If you hear anything, I'd appreciate knowing. I don't know where Hannah went. No inkling. Something might come to me. We might want to get together again."

His head shook, like I shouldn't get confused. "I don't care about Clement. I didn't relocate to San Francisco to find Clement. Couldn't care one way or the other. Better all around if I don't. I collect tips, hints, insinuations, inklings, imputations, that baloney. I stay away from clues. I keep getting checks."

"What if I come across Hannah?"

"Tell her to get lost again. I need the job."

It was going on half past ten. Meisters turned onto San Bruno Avenue. I rolled a window down and searched for cars approaching in the rear view mirror. I put on "A String of Pearls," and headed for the freeway.

Chapter 6

TRES PINOS WAS another half-hour farther south off of 101 below Gilroy, the garlic capital of America, at which I've never experienced a temptation to stop at or cut off to. I'd put in a slow breakfast pushing against arguments I'd waste a day going down there.

Edith had had a plan for us to meet there, but that was a month ago, and nothing since.

I rolled down the window onto a line of sight over a morning spread across the flat golden California of schoolbook history, say of a hundred and fifty years ago. A purplish ridge of hills a way off ran along with me. It had a Spanish name, I'm sure.

Tres Pinos had two lettered streets, C and F. F Street had the quaintness of Lompoc from a W.C. Fields movie. No curbs or sidewalks, no public areas off the road that stayed solid when it rained. The age of white picket fences fronting single stories, perhaps from the 30s, perhaps from earlier, before the benefits of cement, was a look into a kid's memory of an old-time matinee. I parked where F didn't quite end, but where the paving stopped.

A dirt road was the continuation left turn between the last two houses on the one side of the street. The second to the last house was 473, and the last was 475. I wanted 475½. The road went along a wooden fence, past a bungalow, to agricultural sheds that stuck out beyond a vacant lot. Over there a man was unhooking a trailer. He watched me cross the road. Out of sight I climbed two steps to the porch to knock on the door of the house with the number 475.

I knocked three clear knocks and stepped back from the screen and listened, then another three knocks and another nothing to step back from. I took a look in the front window in passing, and stuck my head past the edge of the porch, sighting the man across a family garden. He'd kept an eye out, waiting for logical developments. When I waved a hand he broke off shining irrigation pipe and headed for the corner of the yard, the place to meet and face the expected question. I was lost.

He hadn't been young for a time, but he'd kept the power of his youth, adequate to the jobs around here, which on evidence took a good day's worth of endurance. He'd jerked a trailer hitch off the back of a truck and lifted it onto a barrel barehanded. Regarding me, he spared a break in the day, folding an orange cloth against itself twice, neat edges, putting some thinking into the third fold, no hello, no name, no welcome. He knew what to do with me. He delivered it straight, eye to eye.

"I can't say anything," he said. "I gave my word."

This is always fun. Some guy thinks he knows why I'm somewhere, and I know he can't possibly know that, and the thought creeps up on me that he's working too hard on an orange rag not to believe he knows something that I'm here to ask about, but that I would have no interest in knowing except that I'd have to know that bit in order to get to what I do want to know. Of course it's always just possible that what he's keeping quiet about is helpful to know. I get too mixed up about this stuff.

I had one shot at this. No smart-ass.

"I'm sorry to trouble you, sir," I said. I waited, but that didn't subtly pry loose anything. My best feature formed a snug bulge in my right hip pocket. I'd turned it his way. It didn't buy me any additional information.

I went back to a car soaking in an Indian summer. I got in and left the door open and a foot on the ground. A dented sedan was planted diagonally up to the back of the garden of 475. Not everybody was somewhere else. I made up my mind, to hell with it. I pulled forward into the dirt and made a left turn, beginning the maneuver out of there.

As my eyes came off the rear-view mirror, the guy I'd spoken to was coming up the path with a hand waving, but pretty neutral about it, making his intentions look dubious, or lazy. He'd left his rag on a stake. He tapped a finger on the window. I shut the engine and rolled the window halfway.

"Hang on a second," he said. I waited. I had an honor code governing behavior with men who might be trying to help me. Get out of the car. Meet him on my feet, polite, nod, reach a hand if the occasion arose. His phone was on speaker. A woman's voice suggested that he ask me if I was Willow.

"Elizabeth Cromwell," I answered, and rolled all the rest out directly to the phone: "I send letters to a Ms. Sofia Velazquez at 475½ F Street. She forwards them to Edith Barlow. Any way I might reach Ms. Barlow, or Ms. Velazquez?"

"Just a second," she said. The man collected his rag on the return walk. Time passed…thankfully in dry heat. I dropped dull glances into the vacant side of a hill beyond a garage. No evidence what I was waiting for. I refreshed circulation in my hands. A weird warp in sky color from sparkles flashing in blue. It was hot.

A woman put a step into the road from the back of the garden, a stutter stop looking past the man passing her, who might not have liked her. He didn't slow. She didn't speak to him. She was in black string fringe, the stuff you put on a rigid handle and whip a penis with. The black resolved into components, black lipstick, straight black hair, black tattoo on her neck consisting of the name Medea superimposed on a severed head. The black eyes weren't God-given, but they weren't fake. The black appreciation that life's fucked.

She put her face to the rear window, then walked around the car to check out the flowerpot in the back seat. From there she could peek at me.

"You're giving her a flowerpot?"

"I picked it up on the way here. Edith isn't here by any chance?"

"You send letters to Sofia? That's the agreement? You want Sofia to tell you where she forwards the flowers? Wouldn't Edith tell you if she wanted you to know? Here's what I suggest. Go home and write a letter. Go through the drill. Ask Edith if you can bother Sofia to give you her address."

"Idle curiosity," I said. "What does Sofia do around here?"

"She's a dominatrix."

"In Tres Pinos?"

"What did I say? She's a dominatrix everywhere. She and Edith met in Santa Barbara. A wife wanted two women for her husband's birthday whipping."

"She wanted to speed it up?"

"Or double it."

She squinted. "Elizabeth Cromwell," she said. "Edith heard it was your real name."

"The name was on the suitcase when I left home. I kept both."

"Where'd you go when you stopped leaving home?"

"A ride slowed at the corner of Hollywood and Vine. I got out. Why?"

"Domme interviews sell. You mind?"

"What I would tell you is common knowledge. Incidentally, sell what?"

"We started a poetry zine in Oakland: Snap Judgment Press. Look around at the economic conditions. This is where we had to move. Tell us about yourself, the great moments in dominance and submission. You can use a pseudonym. You'll sell."

"You were expecting Willow?"

"She owns a baby store in Oakland. She sends verse. We prefer verse that sells magazines. Our age group is in decline, has been from birth. We want to survive."

"She doesn't understand she's not publishable?"

"She? All of them. They wander around, all over the fields. They get lost on the other side of the hill. They ask the chickens for directions to four seventy-five and a half. Looking for the way out of a petting zoo."

I pointed down the dirt road. "The guy with the orange rag, he went out of his way to be of help to me."

"Lucky you." She had no interest in topping that. Something unscrewed a change of expression. Imagination could make a sick smile out of it.

"What are those flowers in the pot?" she sneered.

"I was hoping to get it to Edith," I said. "Cymbidiums. It's a kind of orchid, the diamond of the cut flower orchids. You can keep them outdoors in the warm months, but out of direct sun."

She was squinting less sarcastically. "We could run a piece on it. You could lead off with it on the interview."

"I'm a nobody," I said.

"That's who we do. We're your launching pad. We used to be a music group. The Bee Hive? No? Five years pumping erotic sound. *The Dead Salmon*? Never heard it? No? We were a big name when we moved to Oakland, linked up with bigger name groups on tours. Three albums, going on a fourth. Sofia used fetish props, fetish décor. The creeps were stimulated to seek abuse. Sofia met them in private. We put that dynamic in the act. It fed on itself, grew the following."

She waved her hand to follow. I brought my cymbidiums. I must be out of my mind.

———

THE home of the Snap Judgment Press had inherited the loading dock at the back of an agricultural equipment barn. The floor was six or so feet off the mud on the occasions it rained, and about the same off yellow dust.

At the landing was a screen door that kept itself ajar. I pulled it to the shut sound behind me, but it recovered its own comfortable angle. Inside on the right were mail sorting slots above shelving functioning as stuff storage: STUFF ON ITS WAY IN,

STUFF ON ITS WAY OUT, STUFF IN LIMBO. A guitar hung on pegs stuck in the side of a desk. The door that was supposed to keep the weather out was backed open a hundred and eighty degrees to a wall. It had been repaired. A painted plywood sheet patched a square in the center. A bulletin board of sorts was a place to store or recover a thumbtack. The weather strips around the door frame were shot. The whole enclosed business was three paces of width along a dozen paces to an open doorway at the other end. I would have called it a corridor if it were empty. Along the wall were two skinny double bunk beds and a cot. Thorn pointed to names. At the far end was Edwina. Next this way was Ariel, then Olive.

Olive said, "She's Thorn. First and last name."

The two work areas closest to me were vacant. A wavering hum in the air had no visible source. It had a life, like life on a train route.

I was introduced. "This is Elizabeth Cromwell. She's the owner of the English Department in San Francisco. She stopped by to give Edith some flowers. I haven't told her Sofia is missing. We all agree the explanations for their disappearances go together."

Thorn held her hand out at three faces: Have a look. The opportunity to study the debilitating effects of poverty. Three sad postures. Their concerns were way ahead of mine. I was a two-second attention-grabber, an instant in the schedule.

"In case you have some suggestions," she said, "we know we could call the police. An investigation would bring them here. You have no idea how much there is to conceal that can't be concealed."

Olive spoke to a window: "She's dead. She would have called."

Ariel threw a bottle out the window. "She deserves justice."

Thorn swiveled sideways to indicate I had the floor. I gave it back.

Ariel said to Thorn about me, "She's not here to tell us what to do."

Thorn brought everybody into her thinking. She spoke to me. "The man who owns this place gave us a week. You met him. We get this place for free. Sofia takes care of his sick needs. They have an agreement. Or, as of today, they *had* an agreement. I've tried to work out a revised agreement. He doesn't want it. "

"She plays, Zara, Queen of the Black Tower," Ariel said.

"We hear him scream in the barn," Olive said. "We hear Sofia laugh. Cruel romantic whip encounters, the teen romance he missed."

The thought came, and the thought left. Then it came back. "You want me to talk to What's-his-name? I fill in temporarily for Sofia?" I waited for the silence to die down.

Olive had five rings on her left hand, worry beads fingered in sequence with her other hand.

"The spare change ran out," Thorn said. "Our printing staff has expenses. Sofia paid them directly. We've thought of solutions. We could stop answering their calls, but they would stop calling. Our drivers have expenses delivering. We can't renew our business license. To repeat, we wouldn't do well under investigation."

Her hand didn't collapse, but could have lost its desire for expression. The hand was planted on a box of staples.

"You've hung on for a month," I said. The implications were obvious.

"We've read the dominatrix instructional books on Amazon," Olive said. "We got the perspective. He won't accept anyone else. He's spaced out on this life-mate connection with Sofia. They had a ceremony. They filmed it. His facial tic scares me. The Erich von Stroheim of Tres Pinos."

Ariel stabbed the peanut butter. "You were at the house? The steps in back go to the basement. On the other side of the washing machine is the ladies room. We're his home entertainment system. We pull our pants down. We show him. Edwina dry fucks us. We're filmed. We've hung on, so far."

"We thought we'd be an exclusive poetry outlet," Edwina said. "Ha! Look what that got us… English majors. A design error in the human race. A word processor, the gloom of night—the aphrodisiac of *writing*. It's all we get for visitors: poets who, thankfully, can't find the address."

Ariel shut her eyes. "This is leading where? Edith sends us things about this guy, Raymond Chandler. He was a real person once. The five of us vote. Has to be unanimous usually. If Sofia throws a doubt at a leak in the roof, we give in. The Chandler stuff sold on campuses. They crib it for assignments. We have an expanding skimpy reputation on the edge of starvation. We're highbrow, literary annotated anal punctuated shit."

"If Sofia doesn't come back, how long do you have till Michael Moore appears at the door with the sheriff?" I asked.

Ariel had her finger on her pulse. "We're in a Michael Moore documentary? My mother will see me. That's a dead dick."

"What happened to your band?" I asked, just getting the possibility of a reappraisal out and about on a career that worked.

"A problem with our drummer," Thorn said. "You can't just get a new drummer. We were a myth organism in people's minds. Sofia composed lyrics. Take the music out and what do you have? Idiot poets. We couldn't afford Oakland. Moved twice. She got us this loft."

"No air conditioner?"

A discussion followed. The committee on committees of the Snap Judgment Press had a meeting with a unanimous decision, as rare as a road not taken. Thorn had an idea. She didn't prefer to pitch her strong point on an empty stomach. I should be tied to a chair where I would hear her out with an open mind. The Snap Judgment Press would cover gas and mileage. They ordered me to go to the store on the through street. Pick up bread, jelly, and peanut butter and a red? And come back.

I got in my car and took my cymbidiums into town. On the way the opportunity to talk to myself presented itself and I took it. A big decision. Did I ever want to remember I stopped in Tres Pinos? What did I have against Tres Pinos? Not exactly nothing. But I hadn't decided by the time I'd entered the strip. The historical Tres Pinos is too short to make a big decision like that, so I availed myself of the memory of Tres Pinos in a restaurant for the convenience of the facilities, and while I was there I had a BLT and a carrot juice, and thought about the message Thorn had just left on my office number, which didn't have to be attended to till Monday. But I could divide the view of the truck stop with a call. Why not? I called her. I'd be back in a jiffy.

The sun had moved in an advantageous direction while I wasn't there on F Street. I could get some of the car in the shade and figured the shade would keep working in my favor.

Edwina took the groceries at the door. He was a gender in yellow curls, the Swinburnian target of sadistic men. He consumed air and water, or so the ingredients that kept his slight design in balance suggested. It would break under the years and the drugs, telling of its beauty with a sigh ages hence, as all of us beauty mongers sigh.

Olive Gottschalk was a hard-thinking intellectually coordinated face supporting some granny spectacles. She was going on to a well-proportioned thirty in a two-piece bikini. She had a scribble going at papers in her lap that coordinated with a stack among stacks on a U-shaped desk arrangement. Stuck in a chair in a deep backward lean, she signaled a foot in a white cotton sock on the desk to wiggle a welcome back. She had her own private window that rotated on a horizontal axis. It was propped open by a shaped branch. A battery-powered fan sucked air in. I think that was the hum. It replaced hot air here and put it there. On a shelf under the window was a yellow/blue slice of bread, maybe French toast, dried out on a greasy skillet. A half-loaf of bread reclined with a fluffy bear on a refrigerator about the size of a car battery.

Ariel could shop all her life at a mom-and-pop grocery and not be remembered. She was the youngest, a twenty-somewhere, most reticent to engage me in chat by the meaning I took from a flat stare that never left a flat line at my belt.

I should have walked away within the chime of the Old Town

clock. I laced my fingers, leaned an ear on a wall, and did my best trouble-layered-in-trouble, tortured, out- of-solutions gaze—and could not fool myself I could help this bunch.

"I have a favor to ask," I said. "I have a client. He wrote his take on Gatsby. It's different from the run-of-the-mill article in the *New Yorker* on this and that anniversary of Fitzgerald's birth, death, or a new movie release. You know, put out the piece that doesn't rework the previous piece that appeared merely to kiss-ass advertise the latest Gatsby nonsense. I would like to see this client get a fair shake. Can he get space with you folks? I know a little about writing. Who knows? Someone might pay a couple dollars for it. I have other clients. They write decently, but they're under the impression they're no good because they don't do psychotic serial murder mysteries, or cozy murders on the speeding Zephyr. They would just like to see their life's work in a library other than mine."

"We're already in the quote-unquote valley of the shadow of very bad choices," Thorn said. "You're suggesting we try a sub-cultural dive into, say, F. Scott Fitzgerald, starting from scratch? I see. We're within a hair of our only advantage: be the disaster?"

Ariel raised her hand. "Elizabeth might be right. What was once known and forgotten: that old bitch, hard times. Try that out. We can write poems that tell everyone it's come back, the new old America. The piece just might sound trendy."

Olive spoke. "Absolutely. Live the dream. The owner says we can dig a ditch in back and lay drainage pipe. We walked it off, eighty-four paces, five feet deep, wide enough to squeeze through—say two and a half feet wide. We have a bucket. Four shovelful's doesn't make a dent in the earth, but it fills the bucket." Olive looked at me. "Now make a suggestion."

"How long will the owner accept sweat equity in place of erotic joy?" I wondered.

"He wants a fence on the other side of the trees. A good one, post holes every six feet. He gave us a post-hole digger. Shit. We're artists."

"Is anyone going to the Bay Area?" I asked.

Edwina raised her hand, "Oakland, why?"

"We do an interview on the way. You publish it or you don't. I send articles to you for consideration. When we get to Oakland, we go to my bank. What did Sofia send you guys?"

"Twenty-five hundred stretches the entire operation over a month," Olive said.

"Everybody trust Edwina here with a company dollar?" I asked.

Ariel stopped spreading peanut butter. She pointed a knife at me. The sudden effect on the room was complete, as if she'd struck a gong. The looks she received granted her permission for something or other, the right to take aim, the willful indulgence of a smile with power to deliver a verdict. It was up to her. She licked the end of the knife, studied its taste, or whatever, for something out of reach, as Macbeth questioned the dagger in his mind's eye. The moment passed. The knife went back to its job, now with a way of knowing how to say something, a something that was in reach, but not in words. I was just told I was a big talker.

Chapter 7

EDWINA HAD CHANGED to jeans, his slave design—rips, frayed threads, rape apertures. His ornaments were packed in a velvet pouch, a distinguishing color at the crotch. Pastel ribbons dangled from a waist thong. A hairband held curls off his neck.

The bank in Gilroy would be quicker than the bank in Emeryville. The envelope I brought back to the car squished cash, a sacred commodity, as water in a desert. It found a home between his legs. We were on our way.

Time for the dominatrix interview. My "Okay, you get three questions," hit it off. The air moved in my personal space, so I noticed. He moved two fingers to not quite brush off an invisible substance a fraction of an inch from my right wrist. A thank you?

EDWINA: "Is your mind open?" He rolled a few pages over the top of a notepad. This was old-fashioned crack journalism.

ME: "This is the non-reveal reveal. I'm twenty-nine years old. You can figure when I was born. Put that in bold type."

EDWINA: "Okay. How about your stupidest mistake?

ME: "I was seventeen. Just four months in San Francisco. I had a reputation of international proportions. It snagged a newsworthy figure from Toronto. I was the hottest thing of the year, but not in possession of my senses. He asked for seven hundred and fifty lashes. I couldn't figure out how long that would take. There was also the question what he would look like. I told him I didn't have an odometer. I got blowback on that. You can't believe what can be made out of 'odometer' to taint a reputation."

EDWINA: "Obviously you recovered. We'll title the interview 'Tales of the Maladroit.'"

ME: "When you set yourself on a pedestal, your mistakes aren't youthful indiscretions to be forgotten. I cried some. I thought of getting my junior high school diploma. Move on. Get a honey bear. Fortunately I didn't make the front page of the *Chronicle*. And there was a warm pool of self-sympathy to wallow in. As usual people don't notice the end of the world when it happens to you. The demand for discipline went on. An understanding client gave me his porn library. He said that I probably hadn't read *Psychopathia Sexualis*. He didn't think I could be surprised again. I could respond rationally when asked to nail a penis to a board."

EDWINA: "Did you?"

ME: "Passed up all requests."

EDWINA: "How about stapled?"

ME: "Have you been?"

EDWINA: "I ask the questions. You don't look like an English teacher."

ME: "It's all make-believe."

EDWINA: "What characters do you play in sessions?"

ME: "A surprisingly high ratio of English teachers to everything else. Governesses of various descriptions are popular requests. An enormous number of walks of life I turn down."

EDWINA: "Such as?"

ME: "Military types. Also, I won't do any role if I have to wear a hat."

EDWINA: "How about terrorists?"

ME: "The turn-off factor is too large. That's another thing. I get calls to help someone embark on a new regimen, like they're off cigarettes, or booze—addictions culturally frowned on. Their doctor won't cane them for lapses. They really need me."

EDWINA: "You say no?"

ME: "I want no part of a death wish. Masochism in its most destructive forms comes on little cat feet."

EDWINA: "Masochism inhabits a large terrifying terrain."

ME: "You're telling me?"

EDWINA: "Okay. Explain pain as fun."

ME: "Pain as fun? I would just use a bunch of words that go around in a circle."

EDWINA: "A circular evasion? I'll take it."

ME: "A test of strength. They're brave. They pass. They feel good. Call it triumph."

EDWINA: "Fair enough. Any others?"

ME: "I know the triggers of sexual excitement in a few circumstances. I know the particular sequences of commands, motions, stops and starts. When the design is good, I can feel the real. They know they're in knowledgeable hands. Sometimes the release occurs before we get there."

EDWINA: "Just the thought of pain? That's a trigger?"

ME: "I'm not sure this is a circle."

EDWINA: "You were past circles. You're on triggers."

ME: "The triggers are located on this pathway we've worked out. Once they've been through this pathway, if enough flashes go off, the accumulated experience to that point releases the climax. Some swoon, go lightheaded, faint."

EDWINA: "Pain isn't what you're providing?"

ME: "Not exclusively. Often, not primarily."

EDWINA: "You receive offers of a hand in marriage?"

ME: "And offers to let me pay them."

EDWINA: "That's almost communism."

ME: "Plenty of crazy out there."

EDWINA: "No sexual contact permitted in your sessions?"

ME: "Read my web page. Most questions are resolved that way."

EDWINA: "What's your weak suit?"

ME: "All my career I've been accumulating an emotional turn against modernism. Sex arousal along bookish lines is getting used up in millions of conversations over drinks, but here I am in renewal and therefore hoping I might repeat, without fear of boring anybody, that I entertain a private appreciation of a notion of development in writing styles being none other than minor confections hypertextually attached to what went up when they planted the trees."

EDWINA: "You want to say that again?"

ME: "My weak suit. I truck in long hyperventilating phrases without substance. A propos. S.M. porn is like any bad writing. It sells, like a lot of bad writing sells. People like what they like. My verbal stamp is a type of garish phraseology, not in type unlike the designer dialogue in soft porn. Scorsese may be an artist, but what his characters show of life doesn't interest me. Reversing this, I'm sure Scorsese doesn't give two beans for my language. 'Who does she think she is?'"

EDWINA: "Aren't you talking about art when you talk about what sells?"

ME: "The art is earning a living in my case. And I'd leave art out of it."

EDWINA: "Have you been caned?"

ME: "Yes."

EDWINA: "Nothing more to say about that?"

ME: "Every dominant should submit themselves."

EDWINA: "It gives an insight?"

ME: "I've always had a responsible streak. I wondered why anyone would pay me for it."

EDWINA: "Who did the honors?"

ME: "The couple who used to have a leather store near the Noe Recreation Center. I'd purchased a few items from them. Canings were free for repeat customers. I asked him for a caning. He said there was no such thing. I knew what he meant. I told him just do it. I'd see what I could take. His wife was away. She had to be present when a woman pulled her pants down during business hours. A husband-and-wife thing. I showed up for four sets of six. It's how I decided I don't go more than twenty-four with a client. It's my limit. I'm called a sadist if I won't deliver twenty-five."

EDWINA: "You don't mind rejection. Sofia didn't argue with the market. They could call her Sally Thrashbottom for all she cared. It's the good word. Can't get enough of those. Moving on. S.M. is a huge collection of activities. You're very narrowly compartmentalized within the field."

ME: "Extremely."

EDWINA: "Saying no all the time, how do you pay the bills?"

ME: "The bill collectors are clients?"

EDWINA: "Let's change the subject. Do you read dominatrix books?"

ME: "Name one you'd read."

EDWINA: "Well, what's your favorite movie?"

ME: "*Five Fingers*, with James Mason. I love upperclass English snobbery, as practiced by anyone, including me. I feel self-confidence welling up in me."

EDWINA: "What's the English thing about?"

ME: "I could give you a reason. Some clients would see to it that I'd regret it."

EDWINA: "I'm interested."

ME: "Stay that way. You'll have a worthwhile life."

EDWINA: "Let's wrap up. I'm going to say a word or two. You say what comes to you, okay. Here's mine: *After apple picking time*."

ME: "A client's pure thoughts about a wife, children, neighbors, about me, will harbor some pretty disgusting subsidiary thoughts that, as far as he believes, are not his own. But they have this annoying capacity for popping into his head. This happens at the most awkward moments...like when he is feeling good about himself. After whipping him for quite a few sessions, we get bored and more and more begin talking about what makes the world go around. In time he notices I'm rather nonjudgmental about the things that bother him. It's quite surprising that I seem like a decent person. I'm not shocked at these disgusting thoughts in his head. I encourage him to explore. Use me this way. I like to feel useful."

EDWINA: "Admiration."

ME: "Leering."

EDWINA: "Strict behavior modification."

ME: "A club in Amsterdam. A copycat I'm dropping you off at."

EDWINA: "What won't you do?"

ME: "I'll keep you guessing."

He pointed. I cut through the parking lot of an abandoned motel, breaking diagonally to the side of a gray three-story wood-frame that was going to be bulldozed, from the looks of the block across the street. I cut the engine in an alleyway off 9th.

"I was coming here to beg," he said. "The owner is one of our distributors. She's closed her heart."

"What if you can slap an envelope on her palm and call it macaroni?" I said.

———

IT HAD to happen. Just getting it stuck in my mind that I'd be home in twenty minutes dialed the law of averages and the drive home is how the City treats an honest taxpayer flipping her coin. The reminder. Times have changed. Regular disasters are the daydream-poppers. You wake fast, you grab your survival reactions in one hell of a hurry. Dropping into the City off the Bay Bridge, the scream was turning into focus.

Taillights were pumping. I was one of the first going into the tie-up. Analyzing very fast. It was a congestion reaction to the huge puff rising off the 8th Street off-ramp, fiery flares shooting into a black cloud. Explosions. Physical shocks hit my car as they were heard. A gas tanker had gone into inferno. The sky was disappearing on the right of the freeway. A fresh blotch, spreading, enclosing, attacking. Escape was open on the left.

The left two lanes were clear space. They provided an opening for the lucky few not yet past the 5th Street exit. A few of us were getting off. In the right lanes, and in all lanes beyond the exit, doors were opening. People were running back my way. No stopping at the stop. I'll get to 5th Street. Got there. Progress suggested okay to keep going. Don't press luck at 8th. Not the first to get that thought. Decision. Get clever: Back to 7th, thinking my way ahead. Cross Market up above Church, below Castro. This will need luck. Skip King. Barry to Alameda. Stupid. Ends at Bryant. Jammed up on 16th. What's that about? Northbound stuff getting off? Sneak around to Alameda continuation. Not bad. Left on Harrison to 15th. Truck stopped ahead. Right on Folsom. Hit 14th, bad, wrong way, a quick U, right on 15th. Just traffic lights to Castro. Home in forty-three minutes. God, made it. Either that, or tonight I sleep with the fishes.

] *Chapter 8*

NEIGHBORS I KNEW only from street level encounters were on the roof when I got home. We watched smoke wiping out the known world. It filled a common awareness that it was the thing that would get us. For four days it kept me inside. The stink that would only dissipate in time and in the coming rains went on, perhaps in imagination, for months.

It was fourteen days later when restrictions were lifted. One lane had opened, letting traffic cross Market both ways between Van Ness and 8th. For several blocks in the housing area to the west of the freeway, the scar of the fire was a weird double S shape. It had entered structures, consumed the interiors, and leapt spaces, entering structures on the other side. Then it stopped. The connective tissue of the destruction was the new temporary landscape, a picture expressive of nonchalance in the mood of a beast. The fire had danced along streets, one side blackened, the other side left for consumption on another occasion. On the final work of the beast, plans would be submitted, and new rules correcting flaws in code would come into being to make us safer.

We had been lucky. It had been a damp, still afternoon. The fire had run out of gas in two directions within a block of where the truck had gone off the freeway. The papers showed that the other side of the freeway had remained untouched. I remembered an image over there from that night. I wanted to see it again. I called a car and told the driver to cross the intersection at 14th and pull to the curb. Across Folsom a decorated sheet metal frame bounded the corner of a car repair business. Three panels of fading street art divided its collective image into ten-foot sections. A middle section stood out between comic book characters. The day of the fire I had been making a U-turn when my lights had stopped on the piece illuminated in crimson flashes.

Fence art. Enough black strokes were placed to identify ships in a harbor. Fewer strokes, and it became the abstraction of black strokes. I got out to look at it. Something uncanny was going on around here. I think I must have been showing an awareness that I was seeing more than other people could see. I was having an effect on the tent-dweller across the street. He'd looked up from a slumber. He had a deep tan and a briefcase. This was his home. He yelled to me.

"Can't get in this side. Can't go around the corner. One way. Go around the block." He swung his arm through a circle. "Come down Fourteenth. Turn left. Gate's open. Electrons and protons combine on chromatic diffusion dust."

I crossed the street at the corner, going with the green light at a good clip, no conferring with the science guy, deliberately keeping a faraway focus. Inside the gate I took the step to the door of the office, and closed it behind me. Coffee and a plastic seating arrangement along two walls. Certificates behind an empty desk. In a minute a man came from a side door. Standing at the desk, he waited for me to sit.

"I'm interested in the painting on your fence facing Folsom," I said, pointing at Folsom. "Some ships in the aftermath of a storm in a harbor. It's the one in the middle. You wouldn't know who did it?"

He had a crucifix on a chain. Jesus in agony loomed large on a powerful chest. He was, or had been, a weightlifter, gone bald, and kept a peaceful interactive seriousness. He took a second, nodding. He knew what I was talking about.

"Mickey Mouse was there when I bought the shop. I was never hot for it. The artist noticed I'm a Christian. She gave me some Bible choices. I could have gone with a garden with a tree in the middle."

"The Garden of Eden?"

"Could have been. Woman had a fig leaf. Could have been Eve. Long hair covered the front. I took the ships in the harbor, gave her fifty dollars."

"You didn't get her name?" I asked.

"We left a lot unsaid."

"Haven't seen her since?"

"Not her, but I saw the garden, somewhere on Valencia, or near."

"Clarion Alley?"

"The gang that runs wall art up there might go for it. I had a condo off Valencia. I came that way once in a while. Saw the garden. She had a strange signature that started with a capital J. It was on the painting up there, too. If that helps.

———

THE driver dropped me in front of the City Art Co-op on Valencia. The reception desk in the center of the room was vacant. An alert man at a counter in back noticed me, and kept on noticing, as if he knew me or planned on it. I was the store customer, anticipated all the way from the door to the counter. I showed him a photo of the painting abandoned against the wheel of Faith's car. He asked if he could hold my phone. He put his elbows on the counter and leaned his face to where he could breathe on the screen.

He traced the tip of a pen on her $K(s, x)$, as if fingering a meaning from the structure of the symbols. He picked out a name.

"Joanie Bessel," he said. "That's her signature. She had an imaginary twin sister, Kylie. This *Kay-ess-ex* I'm looking at is a

Bessel function. They come in different flavors. Just quoting, or trying to."

"*J* is another flavor?"

"She used the *K* when she was on her own, before she met Ward Flowers, then switched to the *J* when she worked with him. There's the *Jay-ess-ex* design embedded in the logo. If you hunt, it's in everything Ward did in San Francisco.

"When did they work together?" I asked.

"Fifteen years ago? Let me think. I can do better—ten years ago."

He logged onto a desk computer. He motioned me to stay put. He had caught the sound of a church bell in the mist, and stared at the place where the memory sees what it needs, and said, *"Showdown!"* He turned the screen to me, enlarging a full-page image entitled *Showdown*.

I stuffed my phone in a back pocket and took a look, as I was here now and gone in a minute.

A thirty-ish man, black hair slicked in a twenties style, continental playboy, bow tie, legs crossed, cigarette at rest in two fingers in a hand at rest, was killing time in a chair. A woman in a side room was adjusting the upper end of a second elbow length glove. Her face was close to a mirror. She was inspecting her lips.

"Joanie Bessel," he said. "His Mona Lisa. Good image."

The woman was dressed: heels, stockings, corset. Her hair was rolled tight, exposed ears, bare neck, the boudoir dominant. A gown and she could have been going to the opera—if she hadn't been sharing the scene with a coiled whip on the dressing table.

Showdown. As for renditions of mature female dominance, the artist wouldn't be copied. It wouldn't be impossible, but who would take time to pull all these details out of himself? You're looking at craftsmanship that spreads appreciation into the nooks and corners of a room and then pulls your gaze beyond doors into another room. Two acts of a drama, soon performed together were waiting in a cheap lodging.

"That room is where they lived, just down here over the Art Market, the next block."

"She's not bad," I said.

"The arresting image, if you're wired on the type. She wired Ward Flowers."

"She's wired," I agreed.

He opened a drawer. An advertising brochure made an argument for a high step into classy erotica. Above the fold was a once-in-a-lifetime run of 100 of the original. The blurb said the original sold for $700. Price tag for one of a hundred, lifetime copy today: $1200. What the collector would release it for these days accents the mystery of investing.

His fingers did some wiggling to the spoken word, "strict," as he typed, scanning rapidly the contents of several pages. He drew his finger under Strycte. It appeared as a brand name of a mail-order art outlet.

"You look at how the women are dressed, and you think it could be a line of undergarments, like Spanx. You see the schematic cane/chair logo, and you know you're not shopping undergarments. That Strycte logo turns on the spigot among the disciples." He scrolled to *Doubledare.*

Two women were bantering, tall, slim, French rolls, hands on hips, made up to put a blouse on and go somewhere, but more likely they had arrived and relaxed into bras and slips. Three Champagne glasses were in a row on a table by a window that looked out on a dozen rows of windows in another high-rise. The man sleeping on the sofa would happen. No hurry.

"It's eventually sex with a sleeping man," I said, "if they want to bother."

"They're bothering with four figures in the galleries."

He highlighted a column of small dollar amounts running across to titles of copies obtainable via mail: *Initiation Ceremony, Pay for Play, Job Interview, Misgivings.*

"*Highball* made Flowers. He was too big for Valencia after that. But he never did anything new. His inspiration fit right onto

Joanie's medium of isolation, two people in orbit around a center of gravity. That was the strange thing, Ward's eroticism obeyed a crazy law: the force got weaker the closer two bodies came together. You see how Flowers puts Joanie in the next room. She's getting ready, but it never happens.

"Joanie gave him that—it was all Joanie—an eroticism at absolute rest. She could have annotated his stuff and made it immortal, but her brain put her too far out ahead of him. She would have said things that elevated his work by undercutting it with his buyers. There are alternative theories about those two. To my sense of romanticism, they were your classical lovers, doomed to separation, hooked together hard the farther away they are from each other."

"I'm looking for her," I said. "Where do I find her?"

"I could have told you ten years ago. I couldn't even have guessed nine years ago. She painted on walls when Flowers left. The wall paintings had a few fans. Drop in on the galleries over in Oakland and Berkeley. I'm trying to think who you could talk to. If it comes to me I can leave you a message."

"I'd appreciate it. I can leave my name."

"I know your name." He brushed his hair. "We don't swing on the same chandelier," he said.

"Another exercise I can suggest at the moment?"

"In the service of clarity and brevity, I wish you could."

"Call me if a couple hours at the English Department works. In case you call, you're…?"

"Stewart. Not likely. A woman came in one day looking for a Whistler. We're married now. Art for art's sake."

I stepped outside and looked up and down Valencia and decided on down, intending to hit the next art emporium when a "Hey!" caught up to me from behind. Stewart was waving. He took a step in my direction. I did the rest. I met him inside the door. His phone was at his ear. He motioned me to stick around. The call had to do with me.

"Hi. It is indeed…pretty good, yourself…been busier…say,

I have a question, you know those placards you had in the basement? You sold them. Don't worry about it. No, figure of speech. You remember who bought them? That's what I'm getting to. There's someone here asking. Elizabeth Cromwell. Absolutely, it's her, right next to me. Yeah, English Department, the blonde. That's the one, a spank and a smile. Absolutely, goes more than that. I don't want to go there either. Yes, if you remember, give me a call. You, too."

He hung up. He let a siren go past. It reminded him. "A heck of a fire last week… sirens all over the City. I thought there was a riot. Who knows? Then we saw the smoke. Anyway, a lady on Twenty-third, just around the corner, was being evicted. That was in two thousand ten, or twelve, near Easter. Stirred up an uproar.

"Two cops were shot," I said.

"They turned the whole neighborhood upside down, shook us inside out. The FBI arrested a guy who lived up here on Twenty-third Street on the other side of Valencia. Picked him up in Bellingham. The shots came from his window."

"They made two arrests," I said. "Didn't stick. They never found the killer?"

"Still unsolved. Must have been someone in the neighborhood. People came in from all over. There were thousands in the march. That's what I called you back for. It was Joanie and Flowers who made up the placards they used in the demonstration. They roomed upstairs in the top floor of the Art Market, which is in the next block down. A couple years ago the Art Market changed ownership. They're Global Graffiti now, same location. When the previous owner was cleaning out the basement, she found these placards that had been stored there. She called Flowers. She said Flowers didn't want the placards. They were money, but he didn't care. He mentioned Joanie. He didn't know where she was at that time. The owner couldn't locate her, so she put out the word she wanted to sell everything in the basement.

"I thought about it," he said. "Placards, I don't sell. Somebody got it all, including the fliers. She doesn't have the name of the buyer at hand, but she recalls the buyer said she knew Joanie. She'll call if she remembers."

A woman had been making her way around the wall. She was in wool/linen trousers, a velvet jacket, auburn hair to her shoulders, delicately pulled apart to look windblown, a clean part in the middle, white designer sneakers, around twenty-five, looked like she knew what she was looking at. Could be a better business bet than me. Stewart appeared at her side. She remarked that she'd ask if she needed help. I'd formed a sense of how gratitude should be handled in my generation.

"I notice Flowers sells a coffee-table book," I said. What if you order it, and I pay the freight here? There's also a 2022 calendar. How about one of those." A couple hundreds thanked him.

"Kylie and Joanie?" I asked just to ask. "There might have been a screw loose there?"

"Couldn't say. Why do you want to reach her, if I might ask?"

"I came across one of her efforts, the one I showed you. I'm surprised I saw it where I saw it. The desolation certainly fit the view of the ocean."

"I was going to say her take on desolation never caught on, not to make a living off of, not to say many do on anything. She wasn't marketable for shops on Valencia. Her street work expressed the hollow inner domain. She had to put it on garage doors. You could steal a garage door. Make less on the art than what you'd make running off with the metal."

———

WARD Flowers was under his own name in my card catalogues, cross-referenced in a category my librarian designates: "Simmering Heat (Straight, Art)." Books scattered around the stacks cover several times over what's in the coffee-table item I ordered. Kylie Bessel didn't exist.

I'd been drifting about in the library when I got a text referencing Stewart. Did I want to know anything about Joanie

Bessel? Am I the right person? I could call if I was. I called. When a voice came on the line I said, "Hi, Phyllis, I'm the right person."

She was unpleasant and brief. "You're looking for Joanie Bessel. Why?"

"I like her work."

"That's what I heard," she said. "I find that hard to understand. You realize a policewoman was killed. She died where she dropped. Simply doing her job. Her son grew up without a mother. Her partner was killed, too. For what? So some poor picked-upon helium head can live in San Francisco for free. Give me a break."

"You recall where Joanie went?"

"Check the massage parlors. The placards she and Flowers did for the march, they left them, like please clean up after me. We sold as is. Who would want the stuff in their basement? Apparently you. Forget it."

"Who took them?" I asked.

"One of the organizers wanted them. Helen? Whoever. She was getting a divorce, though, if that helps. She claimed she knew Joanie."

"Any idea how eighteen hundred dollars might be taped to the back of one of Joanie's paintings?" I asked. "Was it worth that much?"

"God knows what they were thinking."

I was putting her through hell. All these thoughts of socialism avalanching through her afternoon. I'd been dithering, poking both ends of a pen against a blotter, pushing the shaft through my fingers. Ward Flowers kept coming into my head, and I'd push him out.

"I heard Joanie split up with Ward Flowers?"

"They cleared out. That's all I needed. Made my day."

"Was he famous by then?"

"Famous? You're not entitled to live anywhere for free," she reminded me.

This was a big subject, best left to throwaway occasions over drinks. I left it at that.

————

I'D SEEN Flowers's work, missed the fuss then, and would again today. I wasn't of the opinion that where femdom porn slid out of its know-it-when-you-see-it hardcore domain, there was art. His work radiated some long-term project in that outer territory of intense hard work. I'm okay if you call *Showdown* your preference in art.

Chapter 9

S TOPPING OFF AT A CITY with an airport to meet a red-headed Scottish lady. Two hours getting mixed up in her English."

It was that kind of message from Rene. It didn't mean what it said, if read as it was said, or mean the opposite of what it said, or anything like that. It had originated in a quirky routine I do of a Scottish Mae West, the unmarried Auntie Elizabeth persona I'd greeted her with one night in a ladies' dive. At that instant she "knew all about me." She never stopped laughing.

The "city with an airport" was a deep, between-the-lines reminder to call my damn supervisor, like, you know, like she had taken the trouble to stick a letter from her in my damn hand. No two ways to read that.

My brain was stuck in a poor humor that called my supervisor's number in the Nebraska area code. It was going on ten minutes after six o'clock when the Nebraska line opened.

I heard, "I'm surprised you answered."

"What are you doing tonight?" I said.

Another pause. "We're meeting?"

"It's what you requested in your letter," I said.

"I'd given up hope."

"A detective passed on your letter. Credit where credit's due.

You mentioned a caning. I'm available tonight. Let's say in two hours."

Now she ran into her troubles. "Ummh…tonight…tonight… I'm still here. We'd be meeting at the English Department?"

"It's what I was thinking."

"I have an appointment tonight…after dinner. How about the English Department at seven? Tomorrow morning?"

"Seven? What kind of scenario are you looking for at seven in the morning?"

"A caning from you."

"It's an after afternoon thing. Marquis of Queensbury rules."

"It would be a first for both of us," she said.

"I have to get back to work," I said. "It's tonight…here…or find someone in the next office. This is San Francisco, for God's sakes. You can get off in a hotel lobby."

"Eight," she said, indifferently. "That's out of the question."

"Nine, then," I said.

"All right, nine. I'll be there…and I thank you."

"Wait!" I said. "You have something to write on?"

"I have your address."

"You need instructions. There's a reason. Call me when you get to 3274 Stafford at nine. You'll be facing a ten-foot setback between two buildings. In a metal barrier is a gate that opens when you press three numbers known only to you. There are five buttons with Roman numerals. Push 2–5–3, as if you were a Latin scholar. That is your sequence. Do not change the sequence. When you do things as you've been instructed the gate opens outward all by itself. Step through the gate and pull the gate shut behind you. Listen for the click. No fear of a stranger attack. You've been on camera for your safety. Step forward onto a circular staircase. Go two full turns. You don't have to count. You come out in a narrow passageway that goes about twelve good strides to a door on the left. Not the door on the right. Another three strides forward you come to a dangerous drop to an alley. I've put up a guardrail in case you wish to check out an alley that doesn't deserve the honor, but statistically, if you do, you are one of the fourteen in fifteen who do. When you ring the bell to the door on the left, the door will open. I don't shake hands. I don't hug strangers. I am friendly.

"If you wouldn't mind, please repeat the instructions I've given you."

"Let's see. Ten o'clock sharp; 352 Stafford; sequence: 4754; fall over the guardrail; land on my head; come back around; door on the right. How am I doing?"

"Six strokes of the cane in order to help you forget the knot on the head."

"Thank you, Mistress. I look forward to your kind attention to my shortcomings."

I called Mr. Liu. He looks out a second-story window across the street when I tell him I'm expecting a client. If the client decides to leave, I get a call—or if he pulls a gun out of a back pocket and sticks it in his ankle holster, I get a call. Anything I should know about—like a heart attack, indications of distress, vomiting, wobbling—I get a call. I have an assistant who lives in a flat on the next floor above me. He watches over the proceedings when I'm coming to an understanding of what I can expect of a new client. He's in charge of the monitors. They cover our activities. He keeps an eye out.

Celia hung out at the corner for five minutes. She timed a slow walk to the Roman numerals, arriving by the atomic clock on my wall sort of on time.

Arrivals can go a number of ways. Evenings are generally anticlimactic to the long drag through the day, the drink and traffic, the internal resistance to getting up to speed on the fly. Visitors are at their best in evenings, good behavior-wise, relatively speaking. They're tired. I'm not as perky either. I always expect the unexpected. I never damn know.

She pulled her coat collar *noir* style, sniffed the air, one drag evidently enough. I was ready for whatever response I could muster to whatever she might throw at me when she came to the door. She wasn't in a little girl's spanky skirt. Black leather pants, tight, a satin shirt, long sleeves, high-heel boots, hair collected in a bun, decorated with a fleur-de-lis and crossed toothpick swords.

"You want to prowl the City with me?" she said. "If not, may I come in?"

She'd unbuttoned a leather jacket. It hung open hinting it could keep on opening. We bumped shoulders on her way over to a publicity image of Alida Valli. The sultry, the sexy, the severe, are on the wall to produce revelations. Alida supplies my first look into clients, meaning, invariably, they never heard of Baroness Alida Maria Laura Altenburger von Markenstein-Frauenburg, Valli's biographical title.

She took her time with Irene Papas, as she appeared in *The Trojan Women*. She daydreamed through a procession of images, and said "The jury of my peers?"

"They could deliver a good lecture on sin," I said.

"But the sin of what?"

She swiveled a hip with a sliding two-step that provided her coat with leather-under-stress sounds.

"What sort of atmosphere are you looking for?" I asked.

"A man who analyzes juries told me he couldn't figure out his mother. Life's a puzzle."

"You're looking for a strict mother?" I said.

"Not a mother!" The reaction was a laugh, a huff, and a puff, but converted quickly to instructions. "You and I are lovers. I've had a fling with a girl. I repent sincerely betraying you. You accept my sincerity after a good caning. I'm into betrayal this year."

"What does *good* mean?" I asked.

"Good and hard without the literary stuff." She had a glance around the reception area. "I don't see a cane."

"There must be one somewhere. They get misplaced. First things first. You want a red ass. I have a color chart upstairs. You'll tell me how red is good."

"Not just good. It comes with a scolding. I kneel at your leg and seek forgiveness. We'd take our time on the scene, let it develop naturally." She set up our central theme: "You own my sex life; you sentence me to a term of chastity, but I always rebel; it's what you punish me for."

"I see," I said, "I ignore the symptom, treat the resistance."

"God! I thought I didn't have to hear that stuff till Thursday. But yes, you demand a full confession."

"I beat a confession out of you."

"I'm a liar. You're very one-way on that score."

"These admissions," I wondered, "pretty lurid stuff? They shock me?"

"You're a woman of the world. Nothing shocks you. Think of me as Anna in *The Third Man*. I'm walking out of the cemetery, a rebellious pinhead. Alida Valli did it better, but you're Joseph Cotton, and you want me to be a better person. The lie is the sin."

She managed people, kicked them around, and didn't use up much time doing it. She looked past me, found a thought and let me have it.

"I don't bond over literature. I read alone on airplanes and forget what I read."

"I'm not a proselytizer," I said. "What do you read?"

"Two girl vampires meet in a bar."

"Let me guess, they terrorize a boys' dorm."

She took her eyes off my chest, and checked her chopsticks. "What happens now?"

"As this is your first visit, I'm taking the opportunity to get to know you. Anything I should understand?"

"Hard."

I pushed a door open. "Follow me." She followed into the domain of more than fifteen thousand catalogued items. I'd removed the ceiling, imitating the dimensions, but hardly the grandeur, of a Portuguese library, in order to provide for stacks that went to the heavens. A staircase in the corner spiraled to a U-shaped walkway along the edge of where the ceiling used to be. Another three thousand volumes on those walls were broken by three doorways.

"You've read my web page?"

"Sort of."

"You remember the three rooms upstairs. You have a preference?"

"I'd like it down here."

We stayed downstairs. I put the soft lights on, and closed the library door. I took her to a small clearing at the head of the stacks. I leaned my bottom on the black leather surface of a table. To my right was a low dais. The leading edge pooched out in a semicircle, as it was in Portugal. On either side was a cabinet. Those were the two card catalogues. A large mirror between them was built into the wall above a cabinet. The top of the cabinet was decorated with Scotch tape and yellow pads, the stuff my librarian insists he needs at his right hand.

She looked at a stack of uncatalogued titles on the floor, then a gaze up to the ceiling, around and down, past me, and back to me. I saw the question.

"Second drawer down," I said. They had to be somewhere.

"As long as you know," she said. "I'd like to see you in the mirror," she said.

A vaulting horse was pushed under the table I was sitting on. I rolled it in front of the mirror and pulled the lever that took it off its feet.

She was still, all motions on hold. She used a reliable sigh of disapproval. "Not on that."

"You wanted to see me in the mirror," I said.

"I don't want to touch that."

I wheeled the furniture back under the table. Here we go… part of the game. My move. I put a hand on the side of the table, a toe forward at a line on the floor. "Toes here. Hands here. Face the table."

She pointed at the opposite mirror. "That one's too far away."

The contretemps had its moment. I scoured her face, arms akimbo, and converted it into English. "Understand something.

If you say you're done with our meeting, we're done. You go your way. No hard feelings. I'll walk you to the door and wish you a pleasant night, and I'll have a pleasant night. If I say we're done, same thing."

I saw something coming. I stopped her. "You're about to say something. You can keep the smirk, but if you say anything before I give you permission…we're done. To acknowledge these instructions, take off your jacket."

I shuffled canes in the middle drawer, called up some sound effects cutting the air, picked one and took the old walk-around-the-table governess promenade.

I ran the cane along a line for her toes. She fell forward hands on the table. I unbuttoned her pants, worked the waist to her knees, lifted the panties to tuck in the blouse.

"Stick your bottom out." The butt came out a tad. I tapped the curviest section to keep it coming till…"Good enough." Her hair was up. Twisting her neck, she could see the whole me and could see it coming…a blur, as always. It's all over in a jiffy.

She twisted to a knee with a sound like a corkscrew going into wood. Putting her weight on an arm let her replace the knee with an arm and a thigh. She rubbed her knee, which brought her breathing under control, one of those struggles at the root of these in-between intervals that make me a witness to courage. She decided to recover determination somewhere else. Bouncing along, foot and knee, was how I saw the first few steps. Then up on her feet, bent over, her right thigh held tight in a two-handed grip, she jerked away toward a card catalogue, kicking at the skirt, at her shoes, doing what it took to protect balance. She was staying for another…if I'm a judge. She was not bored.

So we began.

Most of my clients would be all too aware of what I'd just witnessed. What's the fuss? It wasn't a real whack, but I'd learned to monitor reactions from the flicker of a tongue, the involuntary quiver of a thigh, and the varying assertions of silence.

"You can speak," I said.

"Up yours."

"I'll take that as a compliment. Here's the bad news. On the lowest scale of one to ten, that was a four."

"What?"

"It wasn't hard."

"Liar."

"I'll take that as a compliment, too. But I don't lie in a sacred temple. When I say something here, I'm infallible."

"*[Unintelligible]*…Pope shit."

"Have it your way," I said. "If you want it hard, we go to eight…at least."

"Whore."

Ah-ha. Got me there.

"You ain't seen prime time, sweetie, not yet."

"Don't call me names."

"Just beat you?"

"Shut…up."

"You'll miss the best part of the service I provide."

"I'm paying for this. Shut up."

She got a right toe under the pants. She'd yanked them off one-handed. She shook them out, threw them at an arm of the chair, missed, and didn't try twice.

Her hindquarters showed a streak, physiologically normal, comported with what she got, hardly a knock-out blow, but it's been said, it's all relative.

"You have a clean stripe. Have your friends sign it. If you're staying, put the heels back on. Keeps the stroke level, and—"

"Can't you shut up?"

A dignified breathing caught up. I tapped the floor at the toe-line. Taps got the legs aligned. Perfect. A big breath, then a resting state.

"There's eight, and there's eight," I said. "Call them hard if you like. I'm here for you. It's your nervous system."

"Could you please just do the eight?"

She got it. Down she went…not passing through any of the

luminous territory that fits with masochistic pleasure. Her forefinger pressed circles into the floor in some hard despair of not knowing how to ask for what she wanted. This was not it. It was a shipwreck…the triumph of hate.

She was determined to get it hard. Okay.

At the sixth stroke, on the come, her legs were quivering. She could take one more eight, and not the one after that.

She was on her elbows and knees when I put the cane in the drawer.

When the drawer was closed, she asked, "That's it?"

"Six. It's old-fashioned, the Victorian tradition. And here we are, the time where I say, 'good show'…if you want to join the numberless predecessors in the classical closure. Technically, you didn't get all the trimmings. I should have offered you the cane for a kiss. A blindfold reveals much of the unknown of yourself."

"Will you see me again?"

"Give me a call," I said. "When was your first experience?"

"I have to fill out a form?"

I gestured thataway: "Through the door at the other end of the stacks there's a bathroom. Have a look up close. You have my number. It won't be a regular schedule."

She came back as she had come in. Small talk at both ends of a session is welcome. I interpret banter to mean I'd remained a nice person in the real-world aspect of caning.

She said, "My neighbor's an Italian from Philly, my age. We talk coming and going. A faithful Catholic, member of the NRA, follows Rush Limbaugh, he tells me Obama went to a Marxist school. I ask, really, which one? He knows I know, but he likes to put shade on Harvard. Through him I get all the lowdown on how the Republicans will squeak out the next election."

Her life illustrates what can happen when a bright mind locks onto politics.

I waited at the door until the gate clanged shut at the top of the stairs. I waited some more. Then I went out and stood at the edge of the drop to the alley until the call arrived to say she'd gotten in a car at the corner. Mr. Liu had the license number.

Her first time, my concern was protecting her from herself. How this thing would develop with us should show itself next visit. Looking into a dark corner, I saw Pompeii, an image of a woman getting whipped over another woman's lap. I would see her again. Should start a file.

I sat at my desk. I smoothed a hand across a fresh new page of a notebook:

CELIA TAYLOR, S.F. BOARD OF SUPERVISORS
Initial request for caning: Polite letter. Emphasized political position. (Wash each other's hands some-day? How does that work?) Follow-up request comes through Rene. Not a commonly known fact! Six, no extras, no fetish, no whining, no begging. Not a Softie. Mild strokes, big reaction. Once underway, no deliber-ate attempt to manipulate. Surprised when I stopped at 6. Took what the doctor prescribed. I am confused. Unclear what she wanted. Not caning, but what? Knew Alida Valli! The mysterious twists of the mind of the perfect childhood.

Chapter 10

THE REQUEST, FROM A Ms. Crackenthorpe of the Davidovich Turlow Law Group, on behalf of a Stan Davidovich, arriving during hours reserved for client contact, was what it was. Stan made an appointment at the English Department through a secretary. During a confused few minutes she kept saying he wanted to meet me to discuss a proposal, and could I call Mr. Davidovich back directly. And I kept asking for a few details, like call him about what. She wasn't at liberty to get into specifics. And I didn't care.

It transpired in the melee that Stan headed the team that kept the legal affairs of Neville Drum in order. Neville Drum was Stan's boss. It revealed everything but explained nothing. But Crackenthorpe had accomplished her assignment. I called Stan.

"Glad you called," he said. "How's your day going?"

"Maybe we should keep this call short," I said. "Just say you want to give me money. Is that correct?"

"Yes," he said.

"Let's meet, then. Where do we shake hands?"

"I'll be at the English Department at two this afternoon?"

"I will be here."

"Nice talking with you."

"Looking forward to our meeting."

At two o'clock sharp, Mr. Davidovich had skipped lunch, thank you, down to business. Challenging circumstances lay ahead. We commenced with a selection from a row of five jars of coffee beans. I keep four old oak chairs at the kitchen table. Stan's briefcase had a chair of its own.

"Where did you get these cups?" he marveled. He marveled through a full rotation. "The design gets you."

Stan had unbuttoned his jacket, charcoal gray. He shifted an off-maroon tie askew. He hooked a corner of an Austrian-manufactured napkin, Legends of the Forest, in his collar, covering his chest. Appreciation took him a long way off.

I crossed my legs. I waited for the statement manufactured in the appreciation. He turned his cup a half-inch for a look from another angle. He'd done this twice already. He explained, "I'm involuntarily pushed to think about why they've an artistic appeal."

"I know a man," I said. "How he said he found the set, I won't claim absolute recall, but Switzerland is close. He'd been caught in an avalanche, carried to the safety of a secret cave by a dog with a brandy barrel to keep him company. A lost tribe of potters let him take one server set on condition he keep their location secret. Say 'bingo' when you're ready to tell me what I have to do for Mr. Drum in exchange for what I want."

"If you like, call me Stan."

My eyes narrowed.

"In a word," he said, "Mr. Drum called me at bedtime. Never mind. I work for Mr. Drum. I dressed and went over to see what he wanted. We met in his living quarters. This has happened before. He ordered sandwiches from the kitchen. He showed me your name. He asked if I'd heard of you. I hadn't. He filled me in on the things he thought I should know about you."

"To wit?"

"Mr. Drum hopes that you, Elizabeth Cromwell, will take his place as chair of the Drum Foundation."

"You argued. To no avail?"

"You were not my first choice. I ran you through the wringer to get my objections on some solid ground. The more I studied your dossier, the more I saw the sand running out from beneath my feet."

"He's having a breakdown?"

Stan pulverized a grain of sugar. His face relayed the diagnosis.

"He's my boss, Ms. Cromwell."

"How about this? I'm not qualified."

"It's your argument to put to him. You can say no thanks, but I will say that worries me. At midnight I was thinking of getting him in to a doctor. Four hours later, I was leaning both ways on where the changes in the will were taking things, whether you'd stepped in or not."

"You can't want me to step in?" I said. "If he's dying, just say so. He expects to die soon?"

"Don't know what he expects. His father died at eighty-one. His mother died when he was two. He's fifty-four. He's past the average. A Mistress Anne periodically attends to his needs at his dungeon. I can't say the activities are especially health-inducing. He's a hypochondriac, however, which effectively means he can move his fears to wherever he likes, while removing them from whatever he doesn't care to think about."

"The plot thickens?" I said. "Just quoting."

"He didn't mention your name in connection with the dungeon. Which reminds me to ask, how did the two of you meet?"

"How valuable is your time?" I asked. I headed for the counter. A coffee cake was on the counter. I cut the string off the box and unfolded the sides. The aroma did its thing. Stan made yummy sounds. My pastry shop asks for a phrase. What would I like on my cake? I put THE FLESH IS WEAK on the table with accessories. The occasion called for the plates with the signatures that appear in the lower corner of the last page of the Constitution. The signatures were blue swirls on a porcelain background. I moved the knife perpendicular to the long dimension. His choice. The cut slice lifted delicately onto New Jersey. I took mine on Delaware.

"I think I said call me Stan. May I call you Elizabeth?" We clinked cups. We washed the first bites down and came back to what I was trying to talk about.

"I once asked Mr. Drum to do some carpentry for me," I said. "He agreed in return for a bullwhipping."

"A hell of an exchange of services for carpentry? Care to tell me about that?"

"Then as now I employ help from within the BDSM community. I'd had a carpenter in mind. I'd seen Mr. Drum at Hannah's bullwhip class. He'd volunteered as the target for the final exam. He'd put up all the scaffolding. Somehow my mind takes things like this and converts them to facts, like he's my handyman. That wasn't going to be the first time I'd gummed myself up creating a Neville Drum fact on junk evidence."

"Might I dip my cake in coffee?"

"And please ask for seconds, Stan. Live a little. Or I could say, you only live once."

"The Foundation was an erotic trust with a friend he knew a long time ago. He hasn't given up holding on to her memory, I'm afraid."

"Hannah Kier?"

"She left him. The trust is what's left of her."

"Faith Nichols was seeing Mr. Drum after Hannah left," I said.

"Faith and the trust? After Hannah they were names. Mistress Anne has been filling in for a while in the dungeon. The dungeon is downstairs. You're upstairs. You'd have living quarters on the estate. Kitchen privileges. Access to a private gate."

"Am I stepping on any toes?"

"Mr. Drum doesn't want a lawyer with a minor in some old masters. My toes are well shod."

"I might want to use the grant to support a poetry zine. Does anybody argue with Mr. Drum?"

"Bring that up with him. What worries me is what he'll do if you turn him down."

"If you were to worry out loud?"

"How about we both see the bright side. Mr. Drum suggested two hundred fifty thousand per year with a one-year trial period."

My breath caught on a gulp. Stan turned his face away. He'd brought that number on a gold hook, dangled the line, and reeled me in. He was taking me over to the scales. The prize catch. It certainly looked like a bright day. The least I could do was share in the joy.

"I couldn't possibly say no, Stan."

He looked at his briefcase confidently, witness to women's great game of performative reluctance, the initial volleys before he hauls out the contract, clicks the pen, and the contract is signed.

Stan was too decent to pin me to a yes or a no. He found a neutral smile, clinking his plate, catching frosting in the prongs of his fork. He took his plate to the sink. "It's how I was raised. Don't drop crumbs. Take small bites. Ask if you can lick your thumb. Leave a good impression."

"We're not dating, Stan."

"I read your dos and don'ts," he said.

"That's if I cane you. You seem silent on a simple question."

"Just one?"

"Start with that one. What kind of troubles do I contend with when I tell Mr. Drum he can't have what he wants for a quarter of a million?"

"What he wants? He likes your brand of what you do."

"Hannah put up with his brand. They're both pythons. I won't let him wrap himself around my finger."

"Hannah used the trust to support her friends. He knew it. The price he paid to keep her. You mentioned a poetry zine. Here's your opportunity. You're only the second person to my knowledge to have this opportunity."

"I work outside the literary canon," I said.

"The what?"

"The one percent of the one percent. I'm a snob. Hannah specialized in masochists. She was a sadistic beauty, perfectly designed for billionaires who never had the time to grow up.

"I met Mr. Drum here. I can only say that on that one occasion he seemed nice about it when I refused to agree to what he wanted. It has me wondering. After all this time he wants a woman in his organizational chart who once said no to him."

"It seems an awful long time to nurture a revenge fantasy," he said.

"Is Hannah Kier in the will?"

He opened his hands. "Can't get into that. Sorry. You can ask him." He folded his hands. "Hannah once told me that she lived a fortunate life, Neville-wise. I might venture the opinion: you're his type. You could always quit. And by the way, you should know that some in the firm are having a tough time getting their minds together about you. If you sign on, they won't wish to accept the existing contract as the document of record."

"Who's the boss?" I asked.

"A few of them have Mr. Drum's ear. You can march in like a lion and screw up. Anybody can."

"I don't get it. Are you trying to excite my fighting spirit?"

"If you say no, you don't get to see how the top one percent of the one percent plays the game."

Stan buttoned his jacket. It was all the time he needed. "I'll meet Mr. Drum after dinner tonight. This will go bing, bang. When do I announce your visit at the estate?

He had a laugh he shared through the whites of his confident brown eyes. They got a little bit whiter and brighter at the door. He looked at me with a question on his face. We stood there waiting for a hand to grab the doorknob.

"What is it, Stan?"

"This chair of the Foundation. I never would have thought of a subconscious revenge fantasy. You really know people."

"That's not what you're thinking," I said.

The door closed. I had taken a few steps, then a timid knock.

I opened the door. "Hi, Stan."

"I mean no disrespect."

"Please say it, Stan."

"I'm not sure I heard a yes."

"I'll be thinking about it. If you find someone else, no hard feelings."

He started to turn, but stopped to offer a smile that might want to stay with me a while.

Chapter 11

A S A COURTESY, Stan sent some calligraphy of the lay of the Drum land, along with a page of history from when the first shovel scoop left a dent in the ground in 1922, and a note on procedure. When you visit the Drum estate during business hours, you take your turn inching forward to the visitors' mansion. Most arrivals aren't there to see Drum. I was, and Stan saved me an hour, cutting out all but the last step. Have the driver let me out where the traffic slowed, walk the rest of the way on the curved path on the estate side of the street. He'd inked in a bypass. That eliminated the front gate, the most direct of three shortcuts onto the grounds.

At one corner of the gate was a building that ran behind a brick wall along the property line of the street I was on. The building had been a mini-mansion acquired by Drum as a location later to be incorporated into a security center for the primary estate. Before reaching the gate, a walk perpendicular to the curb connected shortly to a pedestrian gate. A tall man in a yellow T-shirt was standing at the pedestrian gate where Stan had put an X with a circle around it. It's where Stan said I was to meet Lane Shepherd.

Lane waved me past the gate to where a bluish light blinked on from a covering dome of oak. A diffuse beam wandered over the area till it settled on me, and then wandered over a lot of inches of me, perhaps recording vital measurements to be compared against future visits.

"Lane Shepherd," he said. "Nice to meet you, Ms. Cromwell. This way, please."

He pulled the gate shut and pushed buttons on a panel.

"You'll get a passcode. Memorize the code. In case you have a mental moment and can't get out of it, get a grip on a bar and make a racket. Wait a decent interval. Someone will come out and act over-the-top polite, but he wishes you weren't born. But you're in. You can park your car right here. You'll get a permit. If you accidentally bring the wrong car, a green car comes from up that way and circles around the center island. A woman in a traffic variety police uniform will get out and pull her belt up and act polite as peaches. And so on. Any questions?"

"I'd like to say hello to Mr. Drum," I said.

"He may not know you're here."

"I'm on time. Anything the matter?"

His eyes explained: plenty. "Last night I had three calls to come over here. I said no to the first two."

"How long do you entertain me?" I said.

The short incoming walk connected to a walk that joined the corners of the building. We returned single file in the direction I'd come. He stopped just past the corner of the security center, coming into a dense arbor, an immaculately sculpted arrangement, a place to describe someday.

"It wasn't put to me that way," he said finally.

"You work for Stan, but you get to say no to two out of three requests?"

"Good observation…if you understand what you just said."

"Okay. You don't work for Stan. Why the yes?"

"I'm the extremely temporary representative of the chair of the Erotic Art Foundation welcoming you to the Drum nuthouse. Twice I asked myself why I would do that. The third time was to say goodbye to Neville, if the occasion should arise."

I was in jeans, sort of tight and pre-faded into a spring sunset blue, as I've seen transient hues from Twin Peaks. Lane motioned I could walk ahead. Get a look at me. When we passed the corner of the building, the light intensified. My mind was whistling "Dixie." It was a clue. Clear this up, or leave.

I imitated the immovable object, hands on hips. "First question, did Mr. Drum change his mind about me?"

"Mr. Drum is having an episode. The intervals are getting shorter."

"At the moment?"

"Stan says we're in an interval. Stan very much hopes you can wait."

I had a look at a late afternoon. A high wind was jumping the sun's rays around, penetrating the forest cover. I was wearing sunglasses, experiencing a constant flicker. The effect was to stop the thing in me that argues with forces beyond my control, like watching a soothing explanation from far away that I couldn't hear and didn't have to understand. I planted fingers in front pockets, a gesture that planted my feet where they were. This little space had patched a warmth onto my thighs. I could hang around a while for the feel of contributing to the common blah-blah.

"Second question," I said. "I'd like to start with your T-shirt." I stared some, utterly frozen out of the meaning of S&*T(b)2@q. "What does that mean?"

"It doesn't mean what it did yesterday. It's the code that was. If it's on a T-shirt, it's so old. When I turned forty this year, I decided it's not me. So I wear it. I'm complex."

Lane was smarter than anyone else. Tall, dark, not classically Hollywood handsome, but nice looking in middle age, a lot more appeal if he lost the kid stuff. I find them fun at the English Department before they grow out of exuberance. They've got some life in them, and some appreciation of give and take, taking pleasure in dancing around simple questions. Puzzle boys with the attributes of fresh cuddly material, asking for attention.

I took some steps. He took some steps catching up. We took a quick circle of the grounds.

"You and Mr. Drum met where?" I asked.

"Yorktown Heights. The IBM research center. I had a summer job my senior year. They asked me to show him around. I'd heard about him, the wonder kid in California. He had this thing when he was a teenager, the wherewithal to make choices that in retrospect read in interviews as nothing so much as a career collecting free money. He patented inventions, and sold the patents, all except an operating system incorporated in a gadget manufactured by Raspberry, Incorporated, a local bunch you don't hear much of, as the item goes directly into more sophisticated systems as one component of no commercial value by itself—the essential story of Mr. Drum. He's another billionaire backing a fruit company in the great passing show."

"You worked with him?"

"I was in grad school at MIT. He flew me out here. We hit it big—bang, bang—five ideas, right out of the box. I got a thesis, and money. He bought me out. I then had options. I could quit work. Put my feet up, but I love algorithms. So I kept a position half time with Pairwise Prime."

"You left all this, though."

"Not exactly. A woman captured his interest. Mine, too. She used Neville. I liked how she did it. I wanted some. Then she disappeared. I'm interested in what happened to her. Just say I knew her well, say very well, a lot better than Neville did."

"What brings you back? Memories?"

"Stan asked."

On the tour Lane threw remarks in the direction of things that stood out physically. A racehorse was buried in a corner in 1927. The statue was a landmark photographed regularly. It was outside an iron gate that had rusted tight. Iron bars filled in for a brick wall on this side. A dog had lived nineteen years. The dates of his life were on a stone nearby. We could get a look later.

He went inside to find out what was what with Stan. He left

me off where a door to the mansion was open to a reception room set up for an occasion. A buffet arrangement on two tables looked worth a walk around. We'd passed a bent figure showing some curiosity at an object that didn't belong on the ground. He was attending to what a toe might design in a sand walkway. He had a tired look, moving his toe.

Bottles of water looked as colorful as domestic olive oil, the light factored through many shades of foliage. While I was thinking about water, I heard "German wedding cookies" from him in connection with cookies.

He ground out his butt in a stone receptacle. "Awful habit. If you care to join me, I'm finished for now."

We stood facing a bowl that contained a bowl holding another bowl. At the top was a stone ball over which water flowed through lion's teeth to pools that overflowed their bowls down three levels to an intake valve that connected underground somewhere to a gadget that hauled it back up. The cycle conspired to keep up a pleasant trickle.

He was in a dark business suit, a striped dress shirt, dark tie. He had a hand in a pocket, where change jingled. He massaged the part in his peppered hair with a middle finger, as if stimulating growth or thoughts of something to introduce.

"Been waiting long?" I asked.

"I'm asking for money," he said. "I was scheduled yesterday and the day before. It's been three hours this morning. Four hours this afternoon. As long as it takes." He caught me up to the purpose of money. "Protect the Future. It's our group. We're running a candidate for city council in San Jose. Mr. Drum is on our side. Some of his people aren't."

"I have conversations with politicians," I said. "It takes money to run a copy machine. What's your platform?"

"Get rid of the internal combustion engine in two years— nationwide. Then all petroleum-operated machines. Spread it out over a year—eliminate interurban traffic in one-month steps as alternative transportation networks are put in place. Flexibility is the essential. Anything that gets it done for you—walking, bicycles, underground, pedicabs. We show people it works. Then it spreads. Catches on nationally. That's the first step."

"Anything else if you're asked two questions?"

"Busses are on the chopping block, and planes. Cut airline travel ninety percent in a year. No strategy. Just do it. We've a documentary prepared. The calculated effects, estimating conservatively, are extraordinary."

"You have an office, a place somebody can drop in?" I said.

"The candidate has an office in her house. Name is Edgar, Sylvia Edgar. She's in the directory. Her sister seals envelopes, stamps them, gets them over to the post office. Doubles as the campaign manager. We could use a volunteer."

We were watching water flow gently when a woman joined us to say that the gentleman should follow her.

I went around the fountain to the fish pond. I hadn't much of the circuit covered when a voice came from the house, "Over here."

Lane reached fingers to a back pocket. He pointed a gadget at a door that caused a click. A light went on inside. The door opened outward on a push inward.

I went inside. It's where we pros put substance to the nonsense. The store's open for business.

The lighting was a subdued red-and-yellow combination at eye level, enough so you wouldn't bump your head. Coming in from outside, at the other end of the room, facing in the long direction, around ten paces, was an elevated throne, the same dark wood as the platform it sat on and the board floor. A flat plank ceiling covered rough-hewn beams with brass plates that secured two chandeliers. A wall-winch operating a chain was driven by hand. The object was to raise and lower a ring from the ceiling. The ultimate object was to attach wrists to the ring, and raise and lower the wrists. Two tables were tucked in black leather with brass rings. A third table was in the middle of the room.

I covered ten paces over two carpets. I took a reclining stretch on the throne. The raised platform was curtained on either side. There would be devices for this and that activity hidden behind them. To my right was a vertical rigging of red rope—the spider web—placed opposite from where they see it all happen in a gold-edged mirror. Around the mirror was shelving for ready-to-grab bondage straps, a two-foot shelf for books, leather-bound classics—Swinburne, Rousseau, von Sacher-Masoch, plus a selection of whatever you want to call the moderns, being the coordinating window dressing that filled out two shelves.

Lane hung back, then swung behind the center table and put a hip on it, a moody Dane posture. "Behold! The house that Hannah built."

An oil painting of the S.M. brothel in *Ulysses* was behind a row of books. I pulled out a book bound in red leather, and went back to the throne and read a line and closed it.

"You couldn't resist her."

"Didn't want to resist. See something?" He lifted the leg of his pants, underlined a scar on the calf with a fingernail. "She was ambidextrous, whipped from all sides. One time she lost her balance. The point of her boot caught my leg. She said I'd carry that forever."

I set *Flowers of Evil* on the arm of the throne, the highest level of poetry in any room.

"What's your favorite?" I asked.

"I wrote it, *Mistress from Planet X.*"

My posture was better if I shifted to a hip that let a heel casually escape a shoe. The shoe dangled on a set of toes. I used the strict voice that stroked the right instinctual apparatus in business hours. The effect carried over the space between us. Not negligible. A surge brought his hand into motion. He smoothed a thigh that couldn't be smoother.

"You knew Hannah?" he asked.

"There's knew, and there's knew, as you knew her. Let's skip the rest, Lane. What am I here for?"

"This was our world. I'd like to show you another someday."

"Hannah was part of it?"

"I drove her around."

"This is the world you're showing me now, and if I take the job, I'll be around, and from time to time we can get together… in a worldly way. That it?"

"I've an interest in this."

I looked around at what he called "this," as familiar to me as my address. Six feet of floor plan on one side of the dungeon was occupied by two parallel sets of three vertical drawers. These supported glass cases. I'd spotted the storage arrangement of the longer whips looped on pegs. Canes were the artistic decorations in umbrella stands. Function was evident in the artistic set-up.

"When Hannah hooked you up in here, how did Mr. Drum react?"

"I was the one who kept her here. Anyway, I imagined I did. Anyway, she stayed. We spent most of our time on the road driving. That's what she wanted me for. She told me I wasn't fun to whip. She called it puppy love. Neville was her dog. She shopped her precious beauty for favors, for power. But she walked off, and didn't come back."

"You wouldn't have the hots for Mr. Drum?" I asked.

"Not that kind. It was sad watching him."

I got off my high horse and went to the case. I knew what was in the drawers in some order or other. I untied a binding rawhide thong of a long whip in the cabinet, and got back up on high and held the whip over the arm of the throne and let go. The loops fell open under gravity so easily that the leather dropped into an unkinked shape at the ready, no massaging needed to get an operating flexibility.

"That's one fine weave," I said. "Mr. Drum liked this. What do you know, Lane, you're not telling me?"

"Next week's winning Lotto numbers."

"I was here to meet Mr. Drum," I said. "He's not here."

Lane's eye was dull with information. "He's here—here." His finger points up.

"But not here—here—here, as you are, Lane. When you see him, please convey my something-or-others. Don't unzip your pants, Lane. I'm passing up the fun of using this whip. I'm going around to the front entrance. If Mr. Drum is not there, I'm calling a car."

Chapter 12

A HARD SAND PATH took a wide curve around the mansion as the river of *Finnegans Wake,* bringing me back by way of its commodious vicus of recirculation to the front drive. The security system had picked me up when I came out of the dungeon. I took three brick steps directly into the gaze of a man waiting for me with his hand on a harp-shaped handle on the front door. Stepping onto the landing, I passed a nod and a wink entering the grand foyer. I winked back. A logbook was lying open on a glass desk. An empty chair was pushed snug to the desk.

The man I'd met earlier at the fountain was occupying a state of waiting in a high-back chair at the wall. His hands were measuring his life out flipping the lid of a cigarette lighter open and shut.

"How'd it go?" I asked.

"I thought he said a hundred and ten million. That's what I told the woman upstairs. She called Mr. Davidovich. I was thinking Mr. Drum meant a hundred and ten thousand. That's still worth talking about. How'd it go with you?"

"I didn't meet him," I said.

"You have to put in your time."

Lane called. The front door opened as he was saying he'd be

right in to get me. Lane had changed his appearance. I should feel honored. He'd changed his T-shirt from the last time we shared admiration.

On his chest: WE CAUGHT THE WHITE WHALE.

"Don't you feel stupid?" I said.

"Not if you notice."

A windbreaker was clamped in his fist. He walked fast. I kept up with him to the fork in the path. We went clockwise around the security center.

A black limousine was at the curb by the south gate. A Mercedes ornament decorated the hood of the car behind it. Mr. Drum was in green satin pajamas and slippers. A man with a medical bag was paired off with a nurse in uniform. Stan was keeping Drum in his peripheral vision. A chauffeur was ready at the rear door of the limousine.

A step beyond the wall, Lane and I were part of the gathering, and not part. What was about to happen would happen with or without us.

Drum clapped his hands, summoning attention. He addressed us individually as "you," in a not-open-for-discussion: "You, get lost; you, take a long drive on a short pier; you, leave me alone for a year." Who was who was clear and interested nobody.

Drum got to Stan. "I'm fine. Don't worry your little pin-head. I'm going for a drive. I would like to borrow your car so I can talk to Elizabeth, who is here to talk to me. I want to show her something. On the way we have important matters to discuss. Alone. Thank you. Everyone else, the drinks are on your nickel. Find another bar."

Drum slid along the passenger seat of the Mercedes. The medical team did a good job of serious looks of concern. Lane broke off from my side, shifted a few shuffles and counted birds in the trees. The chauffeur deferred to Stan. Stan nodded, yes, shut the door. Stan produced car keys from an inside jacket pocket. He spoke to me.

"You're driving, thank God. Please say you will." His eyes sparkled with begs.

"Has he threatened anyone? How much danger is he to me?"

Stan couldn't manufacture a guarantee, but he was upbeat. "At worst he'll call me vile names. But not you. He's in phase two. He's come down—much better—vectoring to depressed. Might go to sleep. No promise there. The doorlock is on your side. The doctor got some pills ground up in his tacos."

"I have a life, Stan. I don't need this one."

"This isn't about you.

"What? The continuity of civilization?"

"It's about Hannah. He's been psychoanalyzed. It's all about Hannah. He wants to go where he last saw Hannah. Every year I take him. Please drive him there and back. If you're a Christian, you'll get in heaven for this *mitzvah*. He just needs someone to listen."

"Does he have a gun?"

"You frisk him."

Suddenly he remembered why I was here.

"He'll bring up the trust. He wants you. If you ever had a sacred moment to get my undying gratitude, this is it. He promised a man one hundred and ten million in precious stones in the last half-hour. It all went wrong at seventeen minutes after nine this morning. StyleTech was off two hundred points. No better at eleven twenty-one. Dropped another two hundred. He took it personally for a few hours, long enough to leave a personal message with his broker. He was coming over with a dominatrix. He meant you, I think."

He thought a second about money. "I'll take care that you're made totally whole."

The keys fell into my palm.

"Oh, by the way," Stan said, "he called Mistress Anne. She'll meet you. You won't be alone."

My weakest hunch was that Anne had written Drum off. Stan knew it. He was pulling tricks out of a bag. "You're a lifesaver." That baloney.

The motor switched on. There was a faint murmur of a smooth flowing brook. A tire snapped a twig. We were off.

"You want to go to a pajama party?" Drum asked.

"If they keep their pajamas on," I said.

"They think I'm every which way tonight. Every time I'm crazy I make fifty million."

"At a pajama party?"

"Push that there button, a tray comes out," he said, "self explanatory from there, coffee, cups, Irish additives. I want to bore you for an hour."

———

YOU leave Atherton in a westerly direction across an intersection. It's not a street crossing a street, the usual kind of intersection, but you notice a change, as a shift in a travel documentary from Technicolor to black and white. A sudden physically new sign of wealth marks homes with little lawns, brief hedges, and a fruit tree or two stuck on rectangles measured in modest fractions of acres. We were a block over the line when Drum asked me to stop. He nodded at a house. We were going this way to the freeway so he could say a few words.

"The brown one," he said. "A yellow house is what it was."

He got out and headed straight onto the lawn, apparently just to be under the canopy of a giant oak. He reached a leaf, got the feel of it, left it on the tree, got in the car and said to go.

"I knocked on the door here once. The woman who answered asked why I didn't ring the bell. Was I raised in a barn? I told her I was raised here."

He opened the glove compartment. He pulled out a pair of sunglasses and waved them down a side street. "Down there, once, long ago, and a long time ago it was, we collected golf balls at the university course. Sold them a quarter a dozen."

He spoke in the direction of a single-story wood-frame house. A skinny garage was squeezed by four sycamore trees.

"Donald Roach had these comic book subscriptions. They sent a new comic each month in the mail. I got to read them before he wrapped them in plastic and stacked them in racks. One day, I turned a page of a Blackhawk comic. On the other side, on the top, was this woman in high-heel boots. She had a long black whip curled out on the snow. She was standing against a snowdrift above the arctic circle in a skimpy bikini.

"I was at a loss for words, but when I grew up and saw the word *paroxysm*, I realized that's what I'd had experienced when I was nine.

"I could've snapped my fingers, and a million dollars would've fallen out of a tree, and I wouldn't have cared. I've been snapping money out of the ambient sky because I found out I could do it, not out of a hunger for money. A beautiful woman with a whip is the only hunger I ever had.

"I sound psychotic," he said. "The staff is instructed to keep sharp objects out of my suite."

We entered 280 north from Sand Hill Road. We'd beat the late-afternoon clog at the Bay Bridge, but I was leery the bridge hadn't run through its bad luck. The gadget that mapped areas of congestion suggested 92. Did that. Then a slowdown showed ahead on 880, currently a ten-minute delay, but I knew the Bay, you get between exits and it's a thirty-minute delay and rising. I swung over to 185 and stuck with it for the continuation on International Boulevard for a long, straight blandness getting somewhere sort of fast without losing cool.

Drum was mid-fifties. The body had kept a memory of virility in his weight room, a physique, ranked for age, in a respectable percentile, not the top. He was snagging a few extra Twinkies per visit to his in-house deli. I would never agree to meet him anywhere except in company on business. Hence, there I was driving him alone to Oakland.

I asked for the address of our destination. Seventeenth Street. No surprise. Been there. I punched that in and thought some on what the trip to Atherton added up to. Less than an hour ago I was thinking I might take the job. Now I was deciding how I could slow down and push him out the door.

"There's some indication that a hundred and ten million in precious stones and art is buried where I'm going," he said.

"You're not sure?"

"The strangest things pop up at a pajama party."

A right off International dropped into a district below Lake Merritt, mostly apartments. Isolated homes waited their turns for the wrecking ball. I stopped in a drive. A sedan was ahead of us at the top of the grade. A tall brunette was sitting on the front step with a man. I recognized Anne. I'd been here with Edith.

––––––––

I DIDN'T say hello to Anne. No handshakes, no hugs. She was not happy. The front door was open. She'd been in and out. We went in and saw the back door. It was open. The house had started into its historical treasury period a generation ago. I'd never seen black and white hexagonal stones in a kitchen floor. You could turn from the sink to the stove without taking a step. The back porch was a narrow step that looked out onto wild grass and shrubs and clusters of bamboo stumps and a tree that went up three or four stories. A tree house had gone up with it. Decayed ropes over a main bough were beyond reach. A sitting board was dangling on a tough thread. At the right corner of the yard was a woodshed.

The side entrance to the shed might have had a door recently. A door was slanted against a flowering bush. All around were scattered piles of items that belonged in a shed. The front wall of the shed had been pushed out. It was flat on the ground.

Drum draped his pajama top over the handle of a lawn mower, the kind you had to push. It was pitted metal, less pitted where spots of red paint had hung on.

The rest of us were three figures loosely packed in an audience standing at the open side of the shed. A sledgehammer was propped against Drum's leg. A finger pressing down on the top of the handle took some of the burden off standing while thinking. He moved to the center of the shed, kicking dirt around in exploratory sweeps of a slipper. His right hand was bleeding above the fingers. A gash on his forearm was a red stripe. He'd cut himself on a nail.

"Let's go get it, troops. Get your cut. Diamonds or rubies?"

Three shovels stood at the end of a row of vertically stacked yard tools. Above was shelving. The man with Anne put his jacket on a stepladder. The paper wrapping of several packages of light bulbs had disintegrated. The man screwed a bulb into a socket where two wood beams crossed. Drum got the switch. The light didn't work. Drum dropped a hand straight down from the bulb to the point of his slipper. He crossed the spot with two lines in the dust. He took a shovel and dragged the dust with the flat side of the blade until a large board was cleared. He pried up an edge with the shovel, and lifted it. Underneath was the clean imprint of a wooden door in the dust.

He jabbed the point of the shovel into the dirt. He wiped his mouth with the back of his hand, opening a cut. Blood streaked his mouth.

The man with Anne had moved the ladder to the wall. When Drum pointed, "dig here," the man loosened his tie. He was young; he was ready. He left his shirt on and the buttons buttoned.

The first shovelful came out of the ground easy, and it kept coming easy. A pile of dirt accumulated thud after thud outside the shed. He went at the center till the sides caved in on it. Then he widened the hole and increased the depth uniformly for three feet. As it got deeper, he had to keep excavating wider. Going down took longer. I thought about calling a car. But it's one of those things that come once in a lifetime. Why not scoop up some emeralds? Then call a car.

The guy in the hole was digging steadily, like he didn't care to have a thought if this was work in the right location. His chest was at ground level when the sound of the shovel was different. It was a dull clang, metal on metal. Drum came close to an edge. He looked into the hole. I hung back. Anne had gone off for a talk with herself. The clang and chatter of discovery brought her back. She was semi-mesmerized.

"There's something here, Mr. Drum. Looks like a sheet of metal."

Drum put a knee on the ground and leaned over the edge of the hole. It was a large corrugated surface. Most of it was stuck under ground that hadn't been scraped off.

Drum pointed. "Clear out the edge down there. See if you can pry it up."

The man dragged the point of the shovel along the long direction of the metal. The top of a metal section cleared a bit.

"Dig that one side out. Can you get the shovel under the top and pry it up?"

The man in the hole couldn't do it. He couldn't bend it from the end pulling with both hands. He grabbed a corner. A groan didn't help.

Drum pointed to a pick. "Get the point under the edge. Pry it up and bend it back." It didn't work. He changed his mind.

"Just go with what you're doing," he directed. In a few minutes a triangle was exposed. The pick worked.

Anne summed it up: "Oh, tap-dancing Jesus."

They weren't precious stones wrapped in a covering. Not yet anyway. I'd seen buried treasure in movies. This wasn't that. It was a Halloween foot without a shoe. Bones protruded from a few windings of canvas.

I had a hand over my nose and mouth when Anne passed the corner of the house calling for Kenneth. She was headed for the street. Drum was a step outside the shed with a hand on his head. He waved me over to join him. When he said nothing, it occurred to me that we'd left a guy in a hole holding the bag.

I put two hands on a thick brown rope and introduced myself to Kenneth. Kenneth got a high hold on the rope and walked a step up a slope. It was clear that I was going into the hole faster than he was coming out. He tried it differently. He lifted a leg onto the floor of the shed beyond a knee while I pulled the rope in the direction he was coming out. He rolled over and came to his feet, brushing his shoulders, moving dust out into a smelly atmosphere. He coughed continuously. I hit his back. The coughing went on.

I asked twice, "How you doing?" Kenneth took it as he heard it. If he got his tie on straight he was fine.

I held him in place. "You're sure?"

"I'm fine. What should I be?"

"You should ask for a raise."

He shrugged a "can't complain," and asked me, "I have a date tonight. How long do you think we'll be here?"

I reached a hand from my pocket to the pocket in his jacket. It was plenty for a date. "Don't tell Anne," I said. "She'll want ninety percent."

Anne was in her car. She told Kenneth to get in. I leaned in the driver's side and spoke past Anne.

"When the police arrive, they'll ask who dug the hole, because they'll be slightly upset at what was done to an area that might end up being a crime scene. They'll find you. They'll interrupt your date. You'll be asked to recall what you saw, shovelful by shovelful. Don't say anything more than personal identification— you know, name and address. You'll believe you're obligated to answer. They'll ask you questions you won't believe they're asking. If you stole a watermelon when you were fourteen, you could do time for it. You're in the Drum Corporation employ. Your troubles will be covered."

I shifted emphasis.

"Might your date meet you here? I have a modest reputation for honesty. If I can say a few words on your behalf, don't hesitate."

"I only did what I was told," Kenneth said in all candor.

I faced him, hoping for verisimilitude or something. "A lot of Nazis dangled on the end of a rope arguing exactly that point."

I turned to Anne, addressing her, as to whom it may concern.

"Don't anybody leave. The police might not inform you of your right to remain silent when they get going. They'll start up buddy-buddy. You'll get sour looks. They smile if you're following their lead down the garden path. They can be rude, accusing you of watching too many cop shows. I don't think you'll run into that stuff here, but the less they smile the quicker you're out of here. So it's in your interest to remember one answer to all requests. You ready?"

I took the podium: "I respectfully request that you direct your question to Mr. Stan Davidovich." I spelled the name.

"I'll call him. He'll be here as soon as he can. He'll bring free legal help."

I spoke to Kenneth. "And one more thing, do not say you have a date. You're here until they say you can go. I'll bring this up with them right away. Even then, patience and respect for the rule of law is all we have."

"I caught all that," Anne said. "I know somebody in Sacramento."

"That works, too." I pointed a finger at my temple and pulled the middle finger.

Anne said to Kenneth, "Don't listen to her."

"You know better, Anne," I said. "Besides, Mr. Drum's car is blocking your car, and I have the keys."

She got out. "We'll push it into the street then."

"It's locked."

"Fuck you. I have nothing to do with this." She looked at me with a cold fury. "You don't have to tell them we were here."

"Who dug the hole, Anne?" I looked around for Drum. "Incidentally, who's in the hole?"

"Why were we here?" Kenneth ventured. "They'll ask. Won't they?"

"Good point. Remember. Stan has the answers. He's on his way."

A patrol car stopped behind the Mercedes. Two uniformed officers got out. They looked at me. I was the only one on their feet on the premises. The curious had come out of a row of rentals to see what the police were doing. One cop looked through the window of Drum's car. I gave him the keys and one sentence. I made the call. The other cop asked about the two people in Anne's car.

"That's Anne, and that's Kenneth. The body is up there in the shed."

"The detectives will be here in a minute. Who are you?"

"Elizabeth Cromwell. I've called a lawyer. He works for Mr. Drum. He's on his way. He'll answer all your questions. I prefer to speak with him when he arrives. I can sit on the porch until then."

It wasn't fifteen minutes till the area of the shed had gone through an initial inspection, and a detective had come around looking for me. I was up with Detective Heffelfinger. She asked my name and address. It seemed that checked against what she had learned from Officer Hogarth.

"We see the bones of a foot." They had powerful flashlights. "How did you know there was a body there?"

"A lawyer will be here shortly," I said. "I will be speaking with him."

She gestured past her shoulder to Anne and Kenneth. "They said they came here at the request of Neville Drum. They said Mr. Drum arrived with you in his car. The car is registered to Stanley Davidovich. The house is in Mr. Drum's name. Is this what you remember?"

"I respectfully request that all questions be addressed to Mr. Davidovich."

"Is he your lawyer?"

"I'm going to ask him."

"I'd like to ask you if you'd wait down here."

I joined Kenneth and Anne at the street. We exchanged non-glances. They were cooperative. Doing all they could, except they had no idea where Neville Drum was. The detective tried one last time.

"Ms. Cromwell, we're looking for Mr. Drum. Could you help us out? We can't find him."

"He should be in the house," I said.

"We looked. Where in the house?"

"Just great," Anne said. "Just fucking great. He skips out,

leaving us with a skeleton." She walked as far as a stretch of yellow tape. It blocked the sidewalk. A cop was there to see passersby didn't slip underneath. She appealed for reason. "If we don't know anything about anything, why do we have to stay here?"

"You don't," the detective said. "We're all going down to the station."

"*Au contraire*," Anne said. She could as well have said, "Peel me a grape, copper."

We all went downtown.

Chapter 13

OUT OF OUR DEPTHS, we were suspects in a possible homicide. Everybody provided eyewitness testimony to more than they should have. Its brighter qualities were contradiction and confusion. Mr. Drum had stated that Hannah was in the grave in the shed. That's what Kenneth was sure he remembered as he was climbing out of the hole. No question. Anne had seen Mr. Drum stretch out on the grass, flat on his back. It wasn't her responsibility to keep tabs on him. Whenever she put "fuck" in a statement it underlined the true ordeal of a completely innocent victim. Mr. Drum was wealthy. I'm not given to the self-effacing life. I wanted some wealth. That's why I was with him. Kenneth was attracted to what a pile of gems looked like. Nobody had been warned about a body. Stan disentangled threads in a complex weave, shaping the subsequent context: Mr. Drum was hardly a font of accurate information, no matter what anyone remembered. His remark upgraded all our evidence.

A witness in an apartment several doors from the crime scene had seen a man running. He had a gun, but he didn't have a shirt. He might have been barefoot. He ran down the street toward the lake. Nobody was found to say where he went from there. The cops had a hole in the ground. It was up in the air who they'd pull out of it.

I went home early on Stan's lawyering skills, taking for granted that Hannah had been found. For several days the event was in the news as an unidentified body in a backyard in Oakland. The newspapers were a rolling release of statements, today's no more true than those earlier, but rearranged, as old news becomes new news in that line of publishing.

Neville Drum was missing. They looked in all the places a billionaire might wait out personal difficulties. They were working off of the wrong list of difficulties. Drum came out of the woods and wandered along a scenic stretch in Big Sur. A couple strolling the cliffs didn't like the look of him. He was half-naked and smelled like he might be capable of anything. They took off. On the drive down the hill he wasn't where they'd last seen him. The next day they read about a body found in the rocks below the cliffs. They could put the time of death to within three minutes. The Drum estate entered more than one protracted legal proceeding.

Niles Clement had been missing for eight years, three months, and nine days when his remains were identified. They'd been removed from the backyard where Hannah Kier had lived eight years and three months ago, in which case Hannah was not merely missing. She was the prime person of interest, alive or dead. I was still thinking I was not her trustee. I was whatever I wanted me to be. Drum's fate was a full stop. Having passed through a historically significant moment, I was out clean, no unbearable memories.

———

I'D CLEARED the breakfast dishes and set the table anew with free time to wonder what to do with the coming years of free time. Into the meadows came thoughts of the little things, the leftovers that go on the bottom shelf of the refrigerator.

I'd been halfway into the chair of an erotic charity. I'd composed a note to Stan that he should forget about the other half. Only that note hadn't gone out. There was as yet that situation over the coming year in Tres Pinos—four artists and twenty-five hundred a month. For weeks the thought had gnawed at me that sending a dozen charity checks, one per month, would not induce the right effect in their minds. It would surely dampen their sense of their talents. Inevitably, they'd be in the same position in a year as now. It might be better if they could experience a foundation acting in the belief that their work was worth a grant. In this regard it might help if they thought through a plan of action with a representative of the foundation, someone who could steer them to drop the vanity stuff and get a bit more hard-nosed on what sells. Poetry that comes out of Berkeley had its practical effect: I texted Stan, let's meet, see if we can work something out. I might take the job. Famous last text messages.

———

IN THIS period of decompression, Dennis Meisters had called to ask if I'd listen to a message on his machine. Take a deep breath and assemble my reactions in a clear, constructive evaluation. Well, okay, I called. A woman's voice introduced Detective Meisters and provided instructions for reaching him, and have a nice day. I had to say, it boosted his professional appeal. You shouldn't just call a detective and reach him.

"My blessings to your marriage. Call her Effie, and treat her good. I'll bet she's got you a phone that takes movies. As a professional dominant in good standing in this great City by the Bay, I confer on you the title: gumshoe."

Another thing, something I hadn't realized: I was his first liberal. The meeting had had an unpredictable effect on him. His wife had seen it right away. He'd come home from our breakfast and taken off on a tangent. A tree stump in the middle of the sister's backyard was a big sore thumb, just looking at it out the dining room window—the kind of job a big man could take care of on a weekend, but not a hint anybody makes in the presence of a cripple. And he was wrestling with the burden of thinking of a second job, a security job, breaking an eyeball on surveillance monitors. And the stump sat there. But right after he came home from our meeting, he'd got the tools together, frontier style, no chainsaw, broke out a pair of sweats and work boots, and went at it. The surprising thing was how much he had to think. You had to think your way through a job like that. This comes first, this next, and so on, or you can bang away at a little root and hardly get nowhere. Anyway, he sent me these pictures of a hole in the ground. Next to it were piles of little white chips, bigger chips, all the way to chunks, and bigger chunks, and then this *piece de resistance*, the size of a car engine.

His call brought to mind the small matter that the Clement investigation had been a steady dollar. I assumed the work had dried up, a development which began bouncing around in my thinking with a name, Edith Barlow. I could give him some business. Her disappearance fit with his expertise in the field. I could bring that up with him, a professional matter. So when he relayed the message that his wife wanted me to know he'd talked about the biscuits at our breakfast, I said I'd like us to meet again.

It took half a minute to make that work. We set it in concrete, same place as before. Whoever got there first waited for the other. I looked forward to it.

Meisters was still big and he was still quiet when he had something to say to me. But the quiet had changed. It had an earned quality, like he'd lucked into more than a winning streak. He was sitting like a winner, leaning back to take in the size of his stack. He had the posture of a man who knew how to play. He owned the table. The stack would take care of itself. An arm snagged a water glass and two helpings of almond biscuits in free fingers. He kept a supply in his lap. I was snooty enough to think I was a part of the metamorphosis. It was a healthy relationship.

"About Hannah Kier and Niles Clement," I said, "you were right all along,"

"I guessed right all along. About the photo at the ballpark, the third person at the game is still bothering me. I don't think it matters anymore. I haven't tried to make it bother Clement, Incorporated."

A name didn't come to me, not out of the circle of people I could tie to Hannah, business or pleasure.

"How about another problem?" I said. "Two people have disappeared, Edith Barlow and Sofia Velazquez. I care about Edith. Some people I met in Tres Pinos care about Sofia."

"Tres Pinos?"

"A little stop on a road below Gilroy," I said.

He licked a finger, dried it on a napkin and folded the napkin twice. "I can tell you. The police down there have taken statements, put out the pictures, run checks on their phones, whatever can be done with the time they have available and their level of concern. What do you imagine I can do?"

"They can't go to the police," I said. A slump in the conversation didn't look like it would end. I added irrelevancies. Soften him up.

"They used to be a music group based in Oakland. Sofia composed lyrics. The atmosphere around the music was bondage and discipline, hardcore. Sofia worked customers on stage and on the side. She had a reputation for working men over hard, which, with the music, gave them a niche notoriety for a time. When they lost their drummer, the group decided to stay together doing this post-imaginative poetry sheet in Oakland. Two moves later, they're in Tres Pinos.

"Post-imaginative," he said. "What's that?"

"I don't know. I pretend to have a philological mastery of post-this, post-that, and use it in sessions. Doesn't have to mean anything. It's the nonsense after the previous nonsense."

"Money in nonsense? Who would have guessed?"

"They run a catch-all poetry-newspaper-discussion sheet. They don't know what to put in it. Poetry was the dream. A lot of snap judgments what to include, and so, *voila*, the Snap Judgment Press."

"Who's they?"

"Olive, Ariel, Thorn, Edwina. They're at four seventy-five and a half F Street. A hundred bucks if you can find it."

Meisters got online and said, "Aha, Tres Pinos. They say no murders, no rapes. Not enough citizens for hard feelings. Nice friendly people, whoever they are. They don't have a department. Nearest law enforcement is another town I never heard of."

He had enough of collecting crumbs in his lap. He stood, brushed off, and moved his chair to where a forearm rested on the table. I braced for a hard truth or two.

"The Snap Judgment Press was advised to launch an investigation by contacting a blonde lion tamer? How'd they get you?"

"Edith Barlow is Hannah Kier's daughter. I'm the trustee of Hannah's estate."

"You say Edith and Sofia disappeared. Drugs make people disappear. The gangs have their own rules. You want some advice?"

"It's too late. Edith Barlow and Sofia Velazquez haven't checked in at the office for two months. It seems to me that it just might be good that Sam Spade stops in at Tres Pinos. You know, it will look like someone is trying to help. They're scared, even if they say there's no reason to be. And there's something else."

"Something I have a chance to solve?"

"Faith Nichols. Possibly the third person at the ball game you're looking for. She lived in the house where Clement was found. She disappeared, also some two months ago. We were supposed to meet each other."

"And long about now, I'm supposed to square the circle."

"You're not getting off that easy," I said. "Hannah Kier lived in the house at the time Clement was killed, or was that in the papers? And…"

"And my fee comes in around now. We're at one hundred grand."

"This is for your memoirs: Hannah knows who killed Clement…because Neville Drum knew."

"He was the jumper?"

"I was there two days before it happened, watching the faces of the people Drum owned. He'd assembled them in a crazy farewell, kissing them all goodbye. He'd earlier sent his legal beagle to the English Department to grab my attention with a literary offer—and a ton of money. The cover story was that I would run an artistic trust. His lawyer still operates on that request, but I'm sure Drum wanted me there when Clement was unearthed. Why? I looked like Hannah? No idea."

"Elizabeth, look, if we're getting to be my first official case, and I hope we will be getting there, I need an assignment I can understand. You remind me of a high school English teacher… in a roundabout upside-down memory."

"An interesting position to catch a boy's interest."

"I shouldn't have said it. Please. Erase that. You were saying."

"I'm sure Drum paid a large sum to find Hannah. That's when the scent was warm. Now? I'm not asking. I have a vague hunch who the second woman in your photograph was. She may know where Hannah is. I believe she's alive, because only one or two people know where she is. It's not a theory. I don't have a theory—except the police can't do this. In time I'll try to run it down."

"I was about to say," he said, "you're paying for this breakfast. And I'm ordering another pot of coffee."

The server had been by twice and from there on had left us alone doing the take-our-time boy-girl routine. It could go through lunch. The server wasn't the same one we'd had last time. Meisters went inside to speak to the guy in charge of coffeepots. He must have been nice to him. A pot came out right after he sat down. I told the server how much we appreciated all this, putting emphasis on what was folded under a salt shaker. We were good to keep yapping.

"There's something you don't know," I said. "The day I showed up at the house where I was supposed to meet Faith, there was an oil painting propped against the front tire. On the lower right corner was a *Kay-ess-ex.*"

I put a *K(s, x)* on a napkin.

Meisters moved the napkin sideways an inch to make something happen. Then he moved it back. Then he turned the napkin over and back in a flipping motion that didn't turn up anything.

"It's the nitty-gritty of detective work," he said. "I'll take a clue, if you can spare one."

I put a *J(s,x)* above the *K(s, x)*.

"An *L(s, x)* comes next?" he asked.

"You're looking at the signatures used by Joanie and Kylie Bessel. One person."

"What does Bessel have to do with Barlow?"

"I care for Barlow. I want to know what happened to her. I'm interested in what Bessel knows about that."

"A look here, a look there, and if nothing turns up?"

"Then you tried. What would you like? Half now, half after nothing turns up?"

He was now having coffee in a perplexed thinking man's stare at the sky and the trees. "She's not where a few questions can find her?"

"There are other ways, I hope."

"Not on those napkins," he said. "How'd you get to Bessel?"

"A fire forced me off 101. I made a U-turn on Folsom. I saw a ship in a harbor for a second. It was on a metal panel. A fellow named Stewart owns an art shop on Valencia. He recognized the *Jay-ess-ex*. An artist, Ward Flowers, used the signature. It's the signature on the images he did in San Francisco. He's famous, so Joanie Bessel gets her name mentioned when he's mentioned."

He pulled a napkin next to his phone and entered something. Then something else. Then, "Hmm," slowly. "They don't know this." He entered something, spelling silently, adding a definitive, "Yeah, Bessel functions. That's how I tell a detective I know you made Bessel. Clever. You get points off this. Not many. I can't call it a lead."

I did a minute of polite thinking. I went for a few more

points. "I have an ulterior motive. You have contacts with the department I can use."

He gave me a direct look that was meant for someone else, someone who wouldn't like being looked at like that.

"I'd be interested to find out what they know about Faith Nichols. Her name's not in the papers, so there's no body yet… not one that's been identified. Are they even bothering?"

He ignored Faith Nichols and said, "Ward Flowers," and scrolled around and said, *"Fan Mail."* He put the phone where I could give *Fan Mail* a glance. Another Ward Flowers creation.

"Stewart knows this Ward Flowers?" he asked.

"Flowers and Bessel lived down the street from him. Ten years back. Ward struck it rich. His business has been in Georgia since then. He's a rarity…an artist millionaire. Joanie Bessel lent her image to him many times." I tapped *Fan Mail.* "That's her."

He studied his screen. "They look married."

"Another thing, probably nothing, but about three years ago someone collected these Ward Flowers placards that had been stored in the basement of an art co-op. Flowers and Bessel had done them for a protest march. After the march, they were dumped and forgotten. When the co-op was sold, the owner sold the placards to someone who knew Bessel. She knew who bought them."

"How do these placards fit in?"

"I think Hannah knew Joanie. Hannah had the painting, perhaps a piece of art submitted in a contest. Hannah must have liked it, but not enough to take it with her when she vanished. It was at the house that Faith and Hannah shared. Faith brought that and eighteen hundred dollars to a meeting with me. Then she disappeared."

"I should find Faith. That's Faith, Edith, Joanie, and Sofia. Sounds like a third-string infield. I still don't see where Bessel gets you."

"I don't either."

"It saves you a couple thousand if I don't bother."

The smile restored itself. A gentle nod relaxed his eyes. It was a kind of thanks. He opened his wallet and removed a plastic package. He rolled it open and fished out a green tooth flosser. He turned his seat sideways so the side of his face was in shade.

"That's all I know about Bessel," I said. "I have several of Flowers's books in my library. I bought a catalogue. I can give you the catalogue when it arrives."

"You bring a problem, you bring a solution."

"Good to know. I won't owe you anything?"

"Tres Pinos. It's a couple thousand in gas money before I turn the meter on." He shook his head. "I'll go. If my wife comes along, no charge."

We walked to his car. I got in the front seat and asked him how much to get us even. "I pay in advance," I said. He wouldn't talk to me. I rolled off ten bills, folded them in half. I stuck them in a napkin in a loose change compartment.

Meisters put a paw on the napkin. Whatever he was thinking, he shook it off. "I had an English teacher in the tenth grade," he said. "She had a thing: Who's buried in Shakespeare's crypt? She said she was afraid to find out. She was a looker. We knew she was from Kansas.

"Anyway, she loved to stray from the syllabus. We knew when it didn't have anything to do with anything we had to know. We liked things that wouldn't be on a test. We had to memorize lines: 'Now is the winter of our discontent.' Had to remember that. The War of the Roses. That ended, as far as anyone was aware, when Edward IV was coroneted in Westminster Abbey. That was the twenty-eighth of June, fourteen sixty-one. Jugglers, musicians, dancers, the joint is hopping, the happiest day of their lives. Then the king gets up and leads them all out into a beautiful summer day—all but one man, a malignant cripple, curtailed of fair proportion, rudely stamped, cheated of feature by dissembling nature. He hangs back, plots to be king."

He was telling me I was wasting money. I was entertaining. He'd found his crazy lady. He looked at the keys in his hand. "The plot doesn't thicken around here, Elizabeth. I keep it simple. If Edith and Sofia are playing Parcheesi at the same resort, I can give you a rate cut."

"Another thing I have to look into in Santa Barbara," I said. "Why did Edith Barlow follow in her mother's footsteps?" I got out and went behind the car and wiggled my fingers *adieu*.

He tossed his hand. "Tinkers to Evers to Chance," he said. "That there was an infield."

Chapter 14

I SCANNED NAMES for Hungarians in the track-and-field subsection of the UCLA athletic department. Alma maters and dates of graduation were next to e-mail addresses of the coaching staff. The data pointed to one conclusion: the coach I was looking for, if he existed, was no longer on the payroll. Or had never been. Regardless, that wouldn't solve a problem. I wasn't looking for a Hungarian. I'd be asking after a particular someone he had coached—a guy who might have graduated from UCLA, who might have answered to Webster, who would have been picked up by older women in expensive cars after practice. It's the type of offbeat question that could spring a name to mind, if you catch a break. I took down the department number of track and field in case something changed. As things stood, all I had was a Webster with the odd collection of features that fit the criteria of employment pleasing to a pair of traveling dommes looking for protective companionship.

There were eight finalists in the four hundred meter hurdle trials for the 2004 USA Olympics, but no Websters. Had I expected any? These fellows were good—they had top rankings. Their names and brief athletic histories popped up in online searches. They had backgrounds in other states. I could rule out the three who had made the team, the data point I would expect Edith to have included, but I put them as questionable. That left five names. There had been a late-minute scratch.

I pulled up the event on YouTube to get a look at the finalists lining up in lanes. A mild stroke of luck. Four were black. Of the four with white appearance, one had finished second, had been disqualified—in itself not a reason to include a question mark. That left three and an extra possibility with a mental check mark. The finish of the race was a running shot from the side. Follow-up images of men recovering the ability to walk upright carrying disappointment covered other angles for a few seconds, none of which threw out a strong hint of gigolo material. I could think of where to get other pictures, but I wasn't there yet. The losers wandered around picking up their clothes.

I got a toasted bagel sliced and buttered in blueberry preserves. Waiting for water to heat provided a minute that included a note to myself that an American wouldn't call an American with a Hungarian name a Hungarian. I set up breakfast in the study and looked up Hungarian track coaches in California. There were two hits, both deceased, no indication of a UCLA connection in their résumés, and no hurdles. Okay. Not every Hungarian hurdles coach gets a mention under that description. I chewed thoughtfully with a foot on the desk. Two minutes later it hadn't produced an aha where to look anybody up.

On a walk, it occurred that there was a deceased madam in Malibu to put under scrutiny—and put on a back burner. I could track down somebody who knew somebody in L.A., get a name and address, an associate or two. The thought of the effort never had its charms. I put it off.

At the English Department I had three candidates on a lined pad. Kenneth Wilson was a Wisconsin grad, David Mertens from Arizona, Hamilton Van Eyck from Duke. Flip a coin where to start. Flip another coin. Suppose I do get somebody at Duke. I say hello. I'm looking for Hamilton. I give my name. Does it matter who I say I am? I'd like to know where he is. Yeah, sure, he only left Duke fourteen years ago.

The next day the call I was intending to make to Duke hadn't changed from the call I was going to make yesterday. No improvements had come to me overnight. I reached the secretary of the athletic office. The track coach was away from his desk. How far away was that? He was in Pennsylvania. She would leave a message in his box. I got the number of the head coach at Arizona. Leave a message.

The coach at Wisconsin knew the name Kenneth Wilson. He was the assistant coach until year before last. He had been a hurdler. He also recalled the name Van Eyck, another hurdler. Hold the line. When he came back he had a Michigan number. Try Kenneth Wilson.

Wilson had been with the Santa Monica Stumblers, a group of guys training together in the L.A. area preparing for 2008. Van Eyck was a 400-meter runner who'd switched to the hurdles. He wasn't fast enough for the open 400. He switched to hurdles and did better than expected in 2004. More hurdle experience would give him a shot at the team in 2008. Any Hungarian coaches? No. There was a Honig. Honig was a Hungarian runner training over here. He wasn't a coach. He made the Hungarian team, but he's been in Hungary since the Beijing games. Who might know where Van Eyck was? Wilson sure didn't.

The second time I looked at the clock it was time for lunch. I stood in the doorway not particularly interested. I was thinking I ought to skip a lunch. I wanted something to chew on and work it off walking. I went out. I made a selection from a row of health bars at a liquor store when the phone buzzed. It was Wilson. He had a name. Nora Kolenick had been in a club out there on the coast. She would have made the Olympic team in the 800. She was at a high school meet. A discus skidded into a parking lot. Hit her leg. She couldn't start over. She was currently head woman's coach at San Diego State. She might remember Van Eyck. She was social. Got around to parties.

I left a message with Nora Kolenick. I was looking for Hamilton Van Eyck. It got an answer a few minutes later. She wanted to know if I was the Cromwell of the English Department. I said I was. Then we lost contact. I said hello twice.

"You called about Hamilton? What's he done?"

"He's not where I can ask him a few questions," I said. "I'd like to know where that is."

"I haven't the slightest interest where he is."

That was all I wanted to know unless she knew where he was and simply wasn't slightly interested. I held on.

"He's one of your customers?" she asked.

"Never met him," I said.

"Why do you want to?"

"You don't know where I could find him? Is that correct?"

"Correct."

I was listening and looking at the change I was sticking in a pocket. "I think the cashier just charged me a dollar extra." I said this out loud to myself, like a random "damn it."

"Is this a sense of humor? Sorry I can't join you." The line went dead.

It was the next day, and Kolenick's call was still odd in the same way. I had to say hello twice again, with the silent gap and all.

"Who are you?" she asked.

"Everything you heard yesterday is still true."

"I'm looking at an ad in Erotica San Francisco," she said. "You state you're not a submissive. I assume your customers don't do things to you?"

"I'm not submissive. I can be agreeable. What do you want to know about me?"

"I don't want to talk about this over the phone. We have a race at Stanford a week from Saturday. I'm arriving by air that Friday morning. We can meet at the airport."

"When do you come in?" I asked.

"Eleven thirty, American. There's a bar near the gates."

"Friday afternoon is a problem," I said. "When do you return?"

"I'm bringing some people back with me. Look. There's an earlier flight. Arrives at nine ten. Can you make that?"

She would call if there was a hitch.

I leaned back. The lean puts a gaze upwards to Louise Brooks, full body, head to toe, the perspective looking down onto a leg crossed, a sheathed thigh poised in a publicity shot in the corner of a sofa. Brooks had the natural vamp look of the twenties, when European decadence had it all over American booze. American decadence didn't exist—if you edit slavery out of our history.

————

I GOT a table on the left as you enter the bar from the concourse. There was nobody passing, but I could hear a herd. In a minute the corridor filled with a crowd, first the fleet of foot, then back a ways the riders on conveyances. From a slower pack, people entered in ones and two. Three men with thin attaché cases had settled in before me. They had built up an exuberance, breaking the silence in quick bursts of laughter at whatever made them happy at an early hour. The one with his back to me was pushing a straw up and down, making ice tinkle. It gave him the idea to get another napkin from the bar. On his return he took a look. I took a look. Neither look got a thing going.

A few crowds later, a woman wheeled a bag to my table and said she'd like to move to another table. I took my water to an area of empty tables beyond the bar. She slipped her arms out of a backpack and looped the straps over the chair between us. She was in a designer sweat suit, running shoes in black and red. I was looking at a black D penetrating a red S over San Diego State.

"I'm not having anything," she said. She pulled a zipper across the front of her bag, pulled a snapshot-sized photo from a manila envelope, and identified the man in the arms-over-the-shoulders pose with a woman, obviously not her. She held the upper corner.

"That's Van Dyke," she said. "This was taken at Zuma Beach not too long before the Beijing Olympics." She turned the photo over. January 2008, was on the back. A strip of tape covered names, presumably. She put the photo where it came from.

"My leg was in a cast when I took it. I left for Indiana a few days later. I haven't seen him since. I'm here to find out why you're dragging me into this. I don't appreciate the position you're putting me in."

I put in a moment on a theory that helped me make sense of her asking me to explain what drags her places. If I was going to comment on anything, I was going to thank her.

"I appreciate your taking the time to meet me," I said. "Thanks for letting me see the picture."

"Anything else?"

"A woman I know vanished. She mentioned traveling with a finalist in the U.S. Olympic trials in the four hundred hurdles. That and Sacramento was all I had to go on. Why I didn't go to the police? That would hold us up a while. I'm happy to get into it, but to repeat, I appreciate your time."

She didn't get up. If she didn't get up, she wanted to get into something. Time passed. She didn't say what it was. More time passed. I added another two cents:

"You might know more than anyone else," I said. "That's why I'm here."

I moved my water to the side to clear a lane. I was guessing there was a run at five o'clock in her mornings. There was a Thai design on a pendant, little blue stones on drop earrings, no wedding ring, but two rings, one on each little finger. Her face made itself available to listen. What did I have to say?

"He was traveling with two women," I said. "One I know, the other I haven't met. The three of them seemed to have taken off to parts unknown. The woman I haven't met has friends who very much depend on her. They haven't heard from her for months. It leaves a strong assumption she's in trouble. They come from a world that doesn't trust cops. They didn't report the disappearance. They wouldn't expect help if they did. I know a retired cop. He asked about drugs. First thing in his eyes, I see the lights go off."

She used an intense gaze. "Keep going."

"The two women I'm talking about are, like me, dominants. They travel jobs here to there. They found this guy, took him into employment as protection. He fit their needs. He wasn't expensive, quietly entertaining, didn't need tender loving care. He called himself Webster. Kept his penis out of sight unless it was spoken to. The woman I know mentioned in a letter that he was in the finals of the four hundred meter Olympic trials. That's how I got to Van Eyck. A coach at Michigan was in a track club with Van Eyck. He remembered you."

I showed my hands. "That's what I know."

"Did he mention Philoctetes?"

"Yes. It didn't sound like a defect in personality. He was consoling a girl. She'd lost her family."

"You said you didn't meet him. I did. It's a mask of compassion. He's utterly immune to giving a shit about anybody, but you don't start to suspect until you're involved and you're convinced you're out of your mind. You think the two of you have to have a talk. You have to iron things out. He helps—oh so helpful. He takes all the blame. A man mans up. I kept falling for that."

"You're recovered?"

"I had a look at myself."

"That threw you?"

"I tried anything in high school. I was the hotshot. I finally decided I set a bad example for myself."

Her eyes closed. When they opened, the dregs-in-memory had passed. Her hand did the rest, moving nothing you could see, but I could feel the few feet between us had cleared a little.

"Hamilton know you're looking for him?" she asked.

"I left my name with some track coaches."

"That could do it. Not likely. How about me?"

"A Kenneth Wilson connected you and Hamilton. He was in your track club."

"I know him," she said. "All right. This is from more than twelve years ago. We went to clubs, one in particular, Black Lash, it's a place off Sunset, up in the hills, where I was whipped and people took pictures. If it's still there, you could ask…but it's all new people, I'd think. If someone could help, they could put you in touch with people who know more than track coaches. Another thing that might help: There was a picture in a magazine. Hamilton was collared on a leash at some BDSM jamboree in L.A. I was in Indiana then. You could run that down. The woman was a big shot. Another thing: Hamilton used to talk with a guy in San Francisco. He went up to see him a few times. The Side Door, or the Sliding Door. There's a restaurant in Redondo Beach by that name. It's the one in San Francisco. They met there. You could ask there."

"Seems like a long shot."

"For what it's worth, asking me isn't helping you. Think about it. If your friends are safe, they're where they want to be. If they're not, I don't understand your problem. Tell the police. It's easy for me to say, I know that. But Hamilton wouldn't hurt anyone. Except I couldn't trust him. To his credit he didn't say I should."

I had a sip of water. I looked at the glass to see what would go with it—if we were getting into something. "You want to order?" I asked.

She shook her head. "I've never told anybody about Hamilton. When I got your call, it was a flood."

I said, "Incidentally, for the record, I'm Elizabeth." We didn't bother to shake hands, but I got the first look that acknowledged I might be related to a human.

"Nora," she said finally. "I still don't know how that happens."

"What? The escape? Or the capture?"

"It ended," she said. "When we were together he'd borrowed some money to make the rent." She drew her knuckles together. She stuck her chin on them, like that was another story.

"He brought this old guy to our apartment. He's going to watch Hamilton and me. He tells me what the old guy is paying me for. I refused. Hamilton apologized to him—to him! They walked to his car. He drove off. The amazing thing is how thoroughly decent Hamilton was about the mix-up between us. Sorry it didn't work out."

"You stayed," I said.

"I was incredibly free of self-reflection. I had a knack for never being bored enough to wonder why I loved Hamilton. I could have been an actor. I was, actually. We made porn movies. We liked to watch ourselves. Another genius move I made.

"That being said," she started, "I wasn't a prostitute."

I filled in the thought. "Hamilton had you wrong."

"It was an honest mistake, I told myself, given what we were regularly doing. It's still a guilty feeling. I must have been telling him at sex clubs that he wasn't enough for me."

"I was a prostitute before I was fourteen."

We breathed in and out on Great Confessions of the Damned.

"I'm going to ask you the sixty-four-dollar question," I said.

"He never paid me back."

"The other question," I said. "Could he kill anyone?"

I waited. Some serious time went into the answer.

"I didn't think that," she said slowly. "I heard about some girls he was shopping around as slaves. He was shopping himself around as a slave. He did things as idiotic for him as it was for them. I don't think he'd kill anyone…but you put an apple on someone's head and fire an arrow at it, it could happen. He lived on a high wire."

"He lived at the pleasure of a lady in Malibu," I said. "She farmed him out. He made ends meet servicing women. No evidence he was out to make a fortune. More to the point, why would two women vanish while he's looking after them?"

"A woman who was in some of his movies blew her top when she found out he'd sold them. He did that. He did the 'I'll never do that again' shit with a straight face. He always needed money. The movie went to a private collector, so nobody would ever see it. That was nice of him."

"What happened to your movies?"

"Good question." She took a few seconds. "Once a year I

wonder what happened to him. He got calls from all over. He was at his best when he just stood there. Beautiful body, a sculpture. There were some beautiful women at clubs we went to. When I saw you, you reminded me."

She checked the time, and sat up. She looked into my eyes in a line to the bar behind as if checking a clock. "There's a meeting at two. I'm meeting people for a run. Nice to meet you… Elizabeth."

I could see she was thinking about advice she could lay on me, tough love for Webster. But. Life goes on. She arose ready to go, and not with me. She was out of sight in the time it took to dab my mouth and crumple a napkin. I looked up the Side Door. The closest to anything you'd call an establishment in the Bay area was in Sacramento. But it could have been anywhere ten-twelve years ago.

Chapter 15

I MUTED THE TELEVISION and reached a hand out to fish around in a pile of clothes to find the phone. The call was Nora, which didn't have to interrupt a Gérard Depardieu film. I caught the message absently, having to suspend disbelief twice that a country bumpkin could violate the inner sanctum of a Parisian dominatrix—all he had to do is pry open a window. And start up a conversation.

"I'm at the emergency room. One of my runners is getting tests. She called me after a snack this afternoon. It got worse. Could be nerves. This has happened before, but she was screaming, so I'm hanging around until I get the results. You never know. While I'm doing nothing, I have a question for you. Hamilton? I'd like to know if he's alive, but I don't want my name involved. Leave me out of it."

I returned the call. "You're out right now," I said. "You want to leave it that way?"

"I can see myself in fifty years. I'll still be thinking about him. We went out on walks. I'd look at anybody. They'd be looking at him. He wasn't a jerk about it. He wasn't full of himself. He didn't have to be."

"Can I pry a bit?" I asked.

"I don't pry open."

"Another thing, then. I don't remember a Side Door in San Francisco. Could it be Sacramento?"

"Then he would have taken a flight to Sacramento…you know. They advertised a mural on a wall—the Side Door."

"It was a painting?" I said.

"He couldn't bring the wall back with him," she explained. "Think."

"How did Hamilton know this guy he met there?"

"They grew up together in Georgia. The friend's father's was in the Air Force. There was a base in Marietta."

I booted up, and typed in "The Side Door," as before. This time I added, "wall art." There was a hit: Ward Flowers. I opened the page.

A woman, relaxing her back in a doorway, could be offering a conventional negotiation of this much for that thing. Or it could be a hot night, and the man is just passing, or he's broke tonight. Nobody's in a hurry. It's not that business is slow. There's no business. Flowers has breathed a bit of life into your imagination. A man and woman are meeting at a side door. The man is in a hat from the 40s. Chiseled bold features, he's his own hero. The woman is taking the air in high heels, no flashy fetish, a line of cigarette smoke foregrounds an untouchable essence—a freeze-frame is extracted of the best moments of their nights.

"You have a laptop available?" I asked.

"I'm online."

I gave her a name.

"Flowers," she said, "That's why I thought he was gay—the name. That was the friend…Flowers…yeah…have a look at *The Final Handshake*."

I brought up an image. It was another door in another alley. The man was a replica of an advertising executive in a television series. The woman in the doorway was of another interest. She was in heels and a necklace supporting a word, PRINCESS. Her hat was a Dick Tracy caricature. Her underwear was in a jeweled hand at her side. The line of smoke from the cigarette in her fingers crossed her hard-on and, up some, passed a perfect pair of tits. Her face was an exquisite face. Their cocks were showing off.

"Hamilton showed me this picture. We laughed at it. He wasn't gay. It was a joke." The memory amplified light moments from the past, memories of pleasures that had been stifled in her silence. A gusher opened.

The masculine jaw on Hamilton was a decent image of the photo she showed of Hamilton at the airport.

"You free?" she asked.

"To meet? Where?"

"Palo Alto. I have to stay close."

"Give me a minute. I'll call you back." I dialed Stan. He interrupted the second ring.

"I'll take the job," I said.

"I have no words, Elizabeth."

"I can come down there now. Should I wait till I finish banging my head on the wall, say in the morning?"

"The British danced the minuet in Philadelphia while Washington's army starved at Valley Forge. The British decided Washington could wait till the morning. I'll have the forms ready. Lane is upstairs going through the archives. If you're here in the hour, you'll get the signing bonus."

I called Nora. "I'm on my way in your direction. Another matter altogether. You can join me."

"Can you pick me up?"

"What about your runner?"

"She's sleeping. They have my number. How should I dress?"

"It's a big topic," I said. "What were you thinking of?"

"Going over your lap."

When she came out of the lobby she was showing it off in heels and tights that gleamed like a fresh coat of black lacquer… bare tummy to a runner's halter that was less a brassiere than a hiker's pack for hauling tits around. The lipstick and nail polish were a seriously coordinated red. With eyeliner and tight bun it wasn't an ensemble I'd spanked before.

"You look fast," I said.

"Waddle in all-comers meets. I'm closer to thirty-four than thirty-three. Where is the nice woman taking me?"

"Might I say you are perfect material for a dungeon."

"And I thought you were too nice for my tastes."

Most clients get around to telling me I'm too nice. Clients are a lot like articles in a magazine. They make a point and shoot it down, or use it to beef up another point, like a big word in a limited vocabulary. She used "nice" in contiguous sentences. That seemed like a dangling topic on the fringes of something she might not want me to let her get away with.

We were the only car for the last several blocks arriving in Atherton. Nora had been sizing up what we'd passed so far. It was dark, so these places didn't look as close as they did in the daytime. You weren't in a development, to start with, and solitude added a pricey ambiance depending on the imagination you'd invested. The grounds of the Drum estate weren't visible from our approach. The first block was just a wall holding up vines and shrubbery.

Stan was waving a flashlight, tracing a red dot on the street, crawling it from one curb to the other, emphasizing a line. The driver assumed this was where the front wheels should go. Stan and Lane could as well have been the hourly help out to unlock a side entrance. Lane was on the sidewalk. He opened the passenger door. Out popped Nora. I didn't get to see his reaction. It wasn't gone in the time required of me to disengage from Stan's welcome. Once we had grabbed hands he made sure all ten digits had a deal.

Lane was poking his finger at the corner of an eye. This disguised what the other corner was up to. Nora was assembling impressions. I transmitted a frown at her. Two women, a Rubicon to cross. She frowned harder, a frown that segued from leave to stay. Lane passed the test. She was willing to get looked at a while. I let the driver go.

I did introductions, first names, no titles, no explanations why Nora was here. Stan pointed at the gate. Nora had the lead.

The security building had been a neighboring mansion once, so getting around it to the other side was already an impressive introduction to the grounds. Turning the corner were moonscapes spread out underneath light cones from hidden bulbs in trees, a smearing of light and dark regions all over, a directionless design, though the steps to the main entrance could be tracked by sight from the spot on the sidewalk where we were.

Stan took the right fork to the majestic fountain in the garden. We stopped where he stopped, in a triangular unit plus Nora, the electromagnetic center. Now that six eyes were on her, some chit-chat was Stan's duty. He was having trouble. Could be hard not to put a foot awkwardly, given our business. I jumped in.

"How high is this fountain, Stan? Did you tell me it was named for a dominatrix?"

"It's what I miss about Mt. Kisko," Lane said, "café society."

Nora studied…Lane? Could be.

"Lane, do you have that clicker handy that opens the dungeon?"

"Mistress Anne…you just missed her. You know, I'll bet she walked off with it."

"How is she?" I asked. "Haven't seen her since we dug up Clement."

"How is she? Remind me. I got the whipping. A hundred lashes."

Stan saw the next hour going up in smoke. "We have two dining salons upstairs," he offered, "one inside, one outside. You name it, our chef can whip it up."

"The chef fills in for Anne," Lane said. "Shit, that was brilliant! How about an ice cream sundae out here?"

Stan had a clincher. "There are five interior staircases to the second floor, three on the outside. We might wish to have a walk-round, Elizabeth. Builds an appetite."

Lane did his impression of a man whose mind is not into staircases. He left.

The fountain was convenient. I lowered myself on a stone ledge, leaned sideways on an arm and crossed my legs.

"Stan, I'm not giving you my word," I said. "You have my word. One year. If I'm expected to sign something, my lawyer will talk to your lawyer. If you expect erotic art is stuff you can leave on the coffee table, you overrate my taste. I'll keep within the parameters of my budget. And, I hope, you may come to admire the results."

Stan bent over symbols on a sundial, stuck a finger in the water and scrubbed a symbol.

Nora coughed. She tilted her head in the direction I should look. Lane was holding a door open. As good as a wave, "over here." I accompanied Nora to her escort. Stan put a phone to his ear and ordered a drink.

Lane had turned the glow on in the chamber of submission, a low-intensity pale orange of artificial log fireplaces. Nora showed an interest conventionally, museum-wise, not squinty-eyed, but checking casually *vis-à-vis* what's that used for. Passing reading material, she put a finger on a blood-red cover, traced the title, but her hand wilted on a second thought. She leaned in at a mirror.

"You whip Stan?"

"Stan answers to the courts," I said. "Makes the trains run on time. Keeps people happy. Haven't detected an interest in all this."

"You and him?" She meant the guy next to me.

"Your costume has his attention," I said.

"I could tie him up. Get his undivided attention."

Black has a knack for catching a curve. Her buttocks were lit in a sexy dark versus a very sexy dark-intriguing, as a half-moon that makes you think of the shape that's there, but missing. Her back to me, she tapped the glass triangles in the cabinet doors, window-shopping, her reflected gaze taking a decisive turn. The power of selecting might have been the experience she wanted to remember, what the psychology write-ups say you feel in a place of worship, connecting with the divine.

She'd made up her mind. She put a hand on Lane's shoulder. "I have some time," she said. "How about you?"

"All night," he said.

"You take orders," she said. "We aren't intending to waste each other's evening, are we? Lane, is it?"

Lane smiled quickly. The smile didn't hang around. The quick yes of experience. The less said the better. Put Nora on firm footing. Gave confidence that a scream didn't mean a scream that would take the fun out of anything.

Nora unbuttoned his shirt. She gripped his chin and swiveled his neck to the side. His shirt dropped to the floor as she put her lips to his ear. Sweet nothings…a question I didn't hear.

"Sounds good," he said.

"I don't know if I like that," she said. "You don't know what sounds good to me."

She searched over her head. High up in the darkened places of the mind were wrist straps. She followed a chain across the ceiling and down. She inserted an index finger through a brass ring and wound a wheel, while looking down and left, then making a complete turn searching high and low. Red nylon cord was compacted in loops in the cabinet. Next to that was the best money could buy in a blue whip. She'd put it all together, whip, rope, wrists, Lane. It's a comfort realizing somebody else cared about this way of reaching the soul.

"Can he take it?" she asked me.

"Every whippee I've ever known boasts the unremarkable statistic that they can take more when tied up than when not," I said. "His potential is unproven."

She passed up the blue whip, settled for the conventional, a rich variable brown. A smoothing stroke worked its way to the business end. She stretched the fall tight between two fingers. "Satisfactory. It'll do."

"I think I'll take off," I said.

"His pants are coming off. You'll miss the part where I size him up."

"Be sure to ooh and ah," I said. "Make it loud. I'll hear you. I have a job to see about."

"This your new office?" she asked.

"I might drop in here now and then. I'll be upstairs. Paperwork. But I digress."

"Stan's the owner?"

"The owner passed. The will insists on the preservation of a charitable trust. They need an artistic maven. I'm it. Lane might be my assistant, if it works out. He'll be a help showing me the ropes."

————

WHEN I got back to the fountain, it was hard to say where Stan was in his drinking. He'd pushed a cushioned chair to the fountain. He was slouched with an unlaced shoe braced on the side of the chair, a leg straight, a foot propped on a cushion on an identical chair reversed in front of him. An arm lay on a table. A hand covered a glass. A finger was stirring the contents of the glass.

Casablanca? The greatest film of all time? He looked to be at the end of thinking through a position on that.

My hands grabbed the back of a chair. "Any questions?" I didn't give him the second to think about it. "I have a few. You were working upstairs with Lane. That's where I'll be working?"

"Going through some archives," he said.

"Archives? A record of all applications, granted or not?"

"Plenty of filing cabinets. We were at the point of throwing everything out. You hadn't called with an answer. Archives are a record of the life Mr. Drum cared about, and nobody else. You're in charge now. Your archives."

"You want I should throw everything out?" I asked.

Stan jumped to a worry. "Is there a problem?"

"I don't know," I said. "Let me see if this helps. I got around to the document you sent me. If Hannah shows up within a year of Mr. Drum's death, she gets all this, plus whatever else I haven't been made aware of. I'm supposedly her trustee. Her heir is a woman who claims she's a biological daughter. I know her as Edith Barlow. She says she wants nothing. I told her there was, essentially, nothing, at the same time that I thought there was nothing. If she were here now, who knows? If I decide I'm the trustee, I owe her a call. But she's missing. People can stay seriously missing for a year on a lark. They'd never know they're not at the meetings they should be attending. It's enough to make me wonder who knows more than they're saying out loud."

Stan was working out how far along I'd gotten to the punch line—that I'd talked myself into quitting. I was sure he knew plenty, but it was all disconnected dots in Drum's past. If he could say something to unravel what was bugging me, he'd have it out there about now…smooth me down. I wasn't helping. I could't help. My dots were all over a blank brain, splintered.

"Hannah had it all," Stan said. "Mr. Drum asked for her hand. She had the brains to say no. They had this pillow talk when he was tied up. She had a say in decisions. Then she vanished…like there is a God."

"And I get rid of the last Post-it and paperclip Mr. Drum touched." I raised my hand. "Where does a working girl get a chocolate sundae around here?"

Stan held a dungeon key up to his chest, found what he wanted, and put it in a pocket. A door opened and shut behind a man in a service jacket who passed through the room open to the outside and onto the walk. He said, "Yes, sir," to Stan. I was introduced to Jack.

I took the three steps to shake hello. "I'll be working nights. Not tonight, but in the future I'd like us to work out a one-calorie ice cream sundae."

I was a card. Stan looked at his sock.

A silver goblet, not larger than a punch bowl, arrived on a silver platter. Stan thanked Jack for a glass that threw off dark green and maroon rays. Jack saw no reason to keep my drink's identity to himself.

"Only five-star Zombie on the peninsula." Message to me: Jack massaged his heart. "Wish you a bright view of the sun tomorrow."

Jack turned. He looked at me sideways. "Comes in at eight hundred and thirty-two calories. Leave the cherry and don't lick the inside, you're sneaking under eight hundred, Ms. Cromwell. Enjoy."

For a minute I withdrew into myself. Oh, my sweet bippy, this was ice cream in here. This was chocolate from a Swiss vault. Be deathly afraid to ask for seconds. I made good headway for that minute.

Stan left me alone. He waited till I looked up at the stars. "You want to see your rooms? You'll be living here. Up to you."

A door opened and shut. The enchanted couple returned. Nora wanted to take her whip home. Not kidding? She was getting it in shape to be rehung, loop by loop, but not how it was done. Lane helped her get the science of it. What are new friends for? Hold it here and here, *et cetera*. It seemed I was hearing an in-joke.

Stan was standing. He'd put one shoe on and tied it.

Nora did the goodbye gesture on Lane's arm. She loved seeing us, would love to see us again, but it was late. She followed that up with formalities with the boss.

"Nice to meet you, Stan." Nora nodded at me. "Time to say *adieu*."

"One for the road?" Stan said.

"I've a ten-mile run at five-thirty, tomorrow? Today? Is it midnight?"

Stan called a car. "Side gate. Two minutes."

I went with Nora.

Stan said, "Just for today, Elizabeth. How many seconds in the current year? Answer: three-one-five-three-six-zero-zero-zero. In case the gate shuts accidentally. You get the permanent code when you meet Ms. Crackenthorpe. You'll get the lecture about you can't write it down."

We made it to the curb in silence. Nora asked the driver to

wait. We had some girl talk. "I'm out of line." She pointed her thumb away from her shoulder at where we were. "You sleep with him?"

I smiled in a way that made many possibilities possible.

"Yeah. Sometimes all we have is self-control. I'd like to see you again. What happens now? You go to the cops about Hamilton?"

"I can take it in easy bites. I start with a cop who appreciates a woman dressed for mom-and-pop places. He's a retired Missouri Highway Patrol officer. I've been having breakfasts with him. He can advise me. He can pass on the information you gave me… you know, buddy-buddy, to get inside. I have no idea what a look at Flowers will turn up. He's in Georgia."

"We all lost our baby teeth, but why bring it up with the Highway Patrol?"

"If the bite of a small child solves a murder, you do. I have a question. What does Hamilton get working for professional women…above and beyond?"

"He gets to walk around in his underpants."

"Help me translate that."

"He'll figure out what he needs to do to get women to feel they can't live without him."

"You went to Indiana. Your way to get him and you far apart?"

"I remember thinking I might have to support him the rest of my life to keep him. I remember thinking he was worth it. When I got to Bloomington I didn't make enough to fly back and forth to L.A."

Nora gave the old dump a last appreciation and got in the car. "In case you want to know, you've got a decision with Lane. He wants it from you."

I went back to my goblet thinking what a quarter-million dollars looked like in a suitcase. I was disguising my intake with fewer sips, but larger. There was then one sip that was a bit woozy, but I could see okay, and then I couldn't. There was a word for that.

I was trying to remember the word. By the time the word

showed up, I'd cleared another half-inch of goblet (okay, an inch or two or whatever), down to a cherry stem I'd planted as a referent, this far and no farther, a thing I'd picked up from an Irish movie. I mean, I'd need the discipline. I was explaining the beautiful night in the manner of holding my spoon above my head, as if studying the heavens in curved reflections, that precursor to an even more embarrassing thing, the main event, whatever was coming up. I couldn't hold my ice cream. Lane had his feet up, watching me, the big easy, who's perfect.

I put my goblet on the ground out of the way of where anyone might kick it over.

"There's more where that came from," Lane said. "Another day, say?"

He was not resonating. I was not a hundred percent to resonate with. I stared far off, and stood up to see farther. Lane put his arm around my waist. The guy had his talents. He got me off the premises to the street, and then brought up the question, would I like an emergency bag from the kitchen, which would be a jiffy to go get.

"Why…oh why," I said. "A bit more walking…no talking. No arm, thanks." A hundred steps along, we slowed. "Why do I do this?"

Next bit of doing something new, I was in a car. Houses went by. We passed the house he owned, the house that we could have walked to under brighter skies. I was in Misery City…well enough to understand I'm an idiot.

Chapter 16

A SHARP CLICK AT SUNRISE started the sound of water gurgling. In the clutch of stupor, my nervous system sent out a hand to strangle it. At least bend it to my will. No can do. First thought: A new day had dawned. The morning was afoot. I lifted my head from a pillow on a chaise lounge in a backyard in suburban foliage. I was next to a swimming pool. The pool's filter system was up and running, competing with a roar in the sky.

I sat up, coming to terms with me and a man in chaste sleeping arrangements between a house and a high stone wall. I wondered at what I'd never had to wonder: What do I do with a man in the other chaise lounge in a morning more or less in certain respects, in this place, like any other morning, except…I was here. They walked, they talked, but were they human as the sun came up?

"Avoir les yeux plus gros que l'estomac," he said, then intimating it was his fault: "I should have warned you about the ice cream. Hundred and eighty proof. Jack will store the unused portion. Waste not, you know."

He grabbed a pair of shorts from the ground and slipped them on under the covers. He'd slept in a T-shirt: MIT.

A single-file brick path meandered around the swimming pool to the back of a hedge. Most of the yard was garden. A low wooden gate was built into a stone wall higher than me. Lane operated a click from a box on a post. The gate opened. He went first, planted himself, and held his arm out, keeping me close to the wall for a count of three. I should collect my thoughts and watch my step. He took the first steps. We were on a strip of grass struggling for life in a shade of brown. A gazebo looked down on a mile of Highway 280. A few strides beyond the gazebo was a short jump to a strip of bare ground. Beyond that edge was a long, steep slide, eroded between cement drainage channels.

To the left, the stone wall kept going. "Down there is another gate to another house I own. It's the house across the street from this one. We can see it if you want. That house doesn't have a pool. How do you feel?"

"Getting better," I said.

"I don't have a bathing suit for you."

"Not that much better." There were spy cameras high on poles. "You put in a lot of security."

"I'm the only two houses on the street, so I'm isolated. The two houses on the streets next to mine, on the outer sides, you have to go all the way down to the Alameda and back."

"Didn't we pass a house last night?"

"Menlo—my city abode. I don't come here during the week, when the gardener's on the premises. Nobody's inside. I'm going to catch a shower."

He left me alone to handle a high-tech coffeemaker. He was a drinker—twenty-ounce mugs. No matter, the milk had crossed the bar. Ah! The non-dairy creamer had not. Back in business. I had a look at the bookshelves. Paper markers were stuck in the unfinished paperbacks that tempted another try, old second-hand buys, some hardcovers without jackets. *Extraterrestrial Whorehouses* were awarded one to three stars on stopovers. They say there are no new perversions the Romans didn't know. They hadn't met the gals beyond Alpha Centauri. The author had some fun with five of everything. The opening sentence got Lane going to a bookmark on page 33:

"Axial Torpedo was programmed for a short life of eight mega eons, a perfect cube, on which he figured conservatively he'd get a suck and a fuck in every galaxy in the sixth Stupenagel angle out to one hundred light years, give or take."

The epigraph was Mozart:

"I pay no attention whatever to anybody's praise or blame. I simply follow my own feelings."

Lane sat on a couch opposite me two-handing a mug. Nothing gained for either of us launching a discussion on the title. I could look into his eyes longer continuously than he could look into mine. I had a question.

"I'm trying to tackle the matter of why you keep three houses."

"Hannah and I took drives. She saw a house for sale. It was her idea we come up here and buy it. We were half a power couple. She was in jodhpurs, slapping a boot with a whip. She said the owner was afraid. The owner thought the hillside would slide onto the freeway. It will, carefully considered, but life's a gamble."

"That's one house." Not that that made any sense. "What about the other one?"

"He had the house across the street…took a little off the aggregate price. I was new money. Had a lot of it. I took them both."

"So…?" I didn't know where the question would go. He understood.

"Don't be timid. Grab it. It's the one true rule of the economy on the Bay."

"You bought the houses for her to watch traffic on 280 from two places?"

"Lucky I don't have to explain," he said.

"What if I ask?"

"Like what?"

"Did Mr. Drum know? He must have. So…?"

"He wasn't special to her, if that's what you mean. Okay. He might have been the wealthiest. She had a deck of cards, a man on each one. Pulled one out when a moment needed a bump.

He bought her a house in Oakland, another gent bought her a horse ranch in Phillipsville—and some other places. I know, I took her there."

"It's a long drive," I said.

"If she wanted me for the night, we'd go there. I didn't merely drive her here and there. She did things for me that suggested love on her side. And then she disappeared. Not a peep. I'm still working on forgiveness."

"She's alive…you're saying…other than you loved her."

"I told Stan she's alive…if she had anything to say about it… not sure that was the case. She didn't kill anyone. It's beyond ridiculous."

"Subsequent events caused you some doubts, though?"

"She came up here terrified one night, sputtering about some gang. She spent an hour peeping out the window, went out and hid out up around the corner of the hedge to watch the street, just waiting for a sound. When she didn't hear anything, she interpreted the silence: the death star was coming after her."

"It was about that time Clement disappeared?"

"She'd always been in control. Like she could make the wind change direction. Clement's disappearance made her afraid. That house, where Clement was found, the first time I went there she told me to wait outside a second, which meant she'd be back when she was back. I had a look inside from the front window. She was talking to a girl at the kitchen table. A naked boy was standing next to the girl. He was thirteen—if he was even a teenager."

"These were her kids?"

"She said they weren't. She ran an art school, where she kept runaways amenable to a resurrection program of arts and crafts. The older girl was in charge. I think there were other girls…older ones, mentors. I recognized the girl inside the Oakland house. She had a bed of her own at the Phillipsville house, but vacated when we were there."

"Why were they in Oakland?"

"Hannah had them visit. They did things for her. I didn't ask."

"Mr. Drum went to Phillipsville?"

"Phillipsville was for me and Hannah, and hiking. One of the four pillars of the good life. Teenagers won't hike, or they bring their phones and dawdle. They rest when they need to talk to their well-rested friends. They're no fun. She kept the workable projects, the kids that found a purpose, up somewhere in the hills. I detest hiking. I kept that quiet like I loved the outdoors beyond words."

"If they're no fun…what do I want to say?"

"They were artists. The girl was a tutor. Look, Hannah taught nude bullwhipping to housewives and grocery clerks. Ten bucks a lesson. She did all kinds of things. People paint naked people. See for yourself. Go to Florence."

I leaned my elbows on my knees, aware of an empty highway during a quiet spell, then a roar, dozens jammed up in a convoy. The whole brain was analyzing traffic to get past this nude painting in Florence.

"That house where we dug up Clement," I said. "Clement must have been killed at the house. Hannah operated some abduction scheme. She couldn't operate a business of that sort on her own. People worked for her. If you peeked in windows, you must have seen more than nude painting?"

"I didn't know about Clement till a month ago. No reason to know anything. Then Mr. Drum's dead, and Stan calls and says there's a new will. Then there's you and this crazy apparition. Hannah's come back."

"I don't look like Hannah."

"Not at this distance. But you share the vital similarities."

"Stan called you," I said, shifting, a steady voice, modulating insinuation, "to liaise with me?"

"Hannah was now in the will. Stan thought Mr. Drum knew she was alive. Raised deliberations at Raspberry, Incorporated. It was a viable contingency, anyhow. Stan's always had my end in focus with Hannah. At long last, when she 'disappeared,' he asked what we were up to. Its time had come—the question, after all that driving her around. Who's been watching me? Nobody. Well, who does he ask? Stan offered me an exploratory lunch. Until the plate was in front of me, He was sizing me up. Ever notice? Anyway, another thing about him—anyway, another story. The question: Do I know she's alive?

"Then it didn't matter. Mr. Drum was dead. He was nuts, the predominant view while he was alive. Opportunity knocked. The corporation insists they will contest the will. It's the war cry at Raspberry."

"Is she alive?" I asked.

"The hell with her is what I recall going to sleep on when I didn't hear from her for three years."

"Your interest in Hannah and me, roughly comparable? Do I have to go deeper?"

"I was more impressionable then."

"She was your first?"

"Every sick way, yes, but technically, no. What I experienced was a first. I hadn't had my cock hooked up to an electric current. At the time it was love. I was at a loss what she got out of me other than bright people like to be amused. She entered Stanford at seventeen, left after three classes, then Santa Rosa J.C. and a monastery for eight weeks, then Honduras and points south. I was unique in her world, like Mr. Drum. We did things she wouldn't invest the time to really understand, but she collected data, like the CIA collects every photo taken on an iPhone. It amused her that her private shots were all stored in Utah. According to me."

"Stan and Hannah?" I said.

"Stan never seemed to be more than a guy who can get for Mr. Drum anything he yelled for. 'Get Elizabeth!' Mr. Drum's words at midnight. Stan got you."

"I had a reason to speak with Mr. Drum," I said. "It was a long shot that just might keep a bunch calling themselves the Snap Judgment Press on their feet. Call them artists. There had to be a lot of others like them. In the background were big plans. If I got the Tres Pinos bunch past their vague outlines as artists in desperation, I'm sure I could find another deserving dozen that fit the mold, and ten times that number in another mold—if I had the opportunity."

"The Drum Foundation fits the mold," he said.

"Mr. Drum brought you to California," I said. "I hear that right?"

"I'd been making my own fetish magazines since high school. I was in a worldwide network, everybody doing their own take on bizarro stuff in every language. You know—the hobby. Mr. Drum saw something I did on corsets with neat cut-outs, and we started corresponding. I'd been at IBM at the research center in Yorktown Heights. I knew the problems they were working on. I knew the research—a bit of it. I knew what they needed, and I told Neville, and, snap your fingers, he had that lock opened. I'd just help him write it up. Our patents are classified.

"As for settling in California, I had other interests. A friend I hung out with in New York took a job out here with Pairwise Prime. She's a mathematician. They were hiring math people. She gave me encouragement. I didn't need it. I followed her. We were open-ended. She dated around. She'd modeled for my magazine."

"Anything still going on?"

"She's my second choice. I like you. I have to do a good deed today. You're welcome to come along. I could use a strong back."

Chapter 17

A LIMO-LIKE CAR WAS in the drive. Lane was wearing a long-sleeved light blue shirt with dark blue buttons. I was being courted. Goodbye, MIT. I slid onto the front seat. He shut the door. It didn't seem as if it had closed. I pushed on it.

"It never sounds like it closes," he said. "Better still, it's the kind of car that doesn't pay parking fines. I called Stan. He had it dropped off."

"D 5. Easy-to-remember license plate. A meaning?"

"It says, no traffic citations."

"A good deed, you said?"

"My words. Not sure exactly. You ever been to the Alameda? My friend has seven boxes of illustrated Bibles in his garage. He promised to get them to the owner. He can't do it. It's a marriage snarl."

"I see the general outlines of a good deed," I said. "You sure you know the whole story?"

"His wife wants them off the property."

"How far off?"

"Didn't come up."

The Alameda house faced a large playground. An addition over a narrow, single-car garage had a small window that looked down on five bicycles, all little, leaning against the garage door, one of them upside down in a red wagon. A larger window was next to a narrow entryway. The two windows presented an aesthetic balance. It was a cute house.

Rachel Cohen met us at the door. She was eight years old, the oldest. Her mother was at the beach with her three sisters and baby brother. Her father was indisposed. Did we want something to drink while we waited for her father?

Lane was a mathematician, like her father. Lane was a fixture at the house on Sundays, research day. Rachel was currently examining the digits of π. Anyone could see the number represented by the sixteenth letter of the Greek alphabet was not twenty-two sevenths. She wrote that up for class. What it was at its core remained a three-thousand- year-old mystery. It was she who, for personal reasons, convinced her dad to purchase a Bible, the Bible that came with her mom's parable about how you're not your brother's keeper. A man had come by the week before selling Bibles in three categories, classic, deluxe, and premium. He was with his grandson, who showed her the two-page illustration of Daniel in a den of lions at peace with the world. Her father's name, being Daniel, was what prompted the boy to appeal directly to her, but later her father said he simply wanted to help the man. The coincidence of names had nothing to do with anything. He had forked over $199.00 plus tax and incidentals for a premium edition. And the ball was rolling—actually two balls. The purchase got her mom into it. The issue was, as always, money. In every other respect her parents loved each other.

The second issue developed later. The man had gone to his car to get a pristine copy of the Bible. When he came back he asked her father if he wouldn't mind looking at his car. The engine was smoking. It had been smoking for several weeks, but when they'd entered the Alameda that morning it was harder to breathe. The car was a 1937 One Twenty Packard pickup. The hood came up in two parts. Daniel yelled at the man to turn off the engine within a second of ignition. The gasket at the top of the cylinder was leaking gas. Gas was trickling down the side of the engine. That it hadn't caught fire was not a lucky break you wanted to push any longer. The temperature was high enough to evaporate the gas and sludge as oily smoke. A fortuitous warning signal. Daniel advised the man to face what had to be faced. Tow the car and go from there. There was a safe way to do everything, but the man didn't have the money.

Daniel had asked the man to wait a moment. He had to go home. When he came back the news was it was not possible to drive the man to Bayo Vista. His wife needed her car the rest of the day. The man assured Daniel he and his grandson and the Packard would make it home fine. The Lord is our shepherd and all. Daniel had one other suggestion. If the engine caught fire on the drive back, get out of the car fast. Wherever it happened. Don't try to get the Bibles out. Just get out. There are other trucks. Solution: leave the Bibles with him.

This had been the state of play for a week, the subtext being that Daniel had begun to worry that the situation had gotten too deep under his skin. The man's life predicament had a hold on him. I began to wonder if an enormous parable had been engineered for my benefit, but when Daniel opened the door to the garage, there were the seven sealed boxes and a half-full box. It just seemed Lane and I were exactly where we were needed. On the drive to Bayo Vista I thought about what a life would be like with a daughter like Rachel. What could I give her?

———

Good deed done, Lane posed the question: "When we cross the bridge, where do we go?"

We were on our way in the direction of Phillipsville, hinting of obscure, salacious purpose, while the destination was still an hour away in the conversation.

It was four and a half hours to the exit off 101 onto the Avenue of the Giants. That ran us along the South Fork Eel River, the largest tributary of the Eel River, the last leg to Phillipsville. I'd never driven to Eureka, so half the scenery on the drive I'd never seen, and it does change, so it was new and worth it, and I had Lane to thank for someone willing to drive. It's what he had done for Hannah.

Lane had something to show me. We were in luck. It was a week-end. I probed a few times, but the experiment wasn't worth anything unless it just happened, like a discovery under non-laboratory conditions.

Just past the Reindeer Inn was the right turn I was supposed to look for. I'd see it after the first houses, cars, propane tanks, a birdhouse, a plastic pool. I saw it. A paved lane curved to a cleared field, a row of trailers, a restaurant/inn, and four structures that looked the same, two with names that catered to tourists. A car and a Winnebago with Colorado plates were pulled up to Bud and Mary's Mobile Luncheonette. Open nine to three weekends. Closed all day Mondays through Fridays inclusive. A mother and father were at a picnic table with a brood of three.

We had driven with the windows down for ten minutes. The cold air was gone.

"Are they air-conditioned over there?" I asked. My thumb meant one of those places we'd passed.

"I wanted to take you to a place on the river. We can bring a snack."

"This is important?"

"Incredibly."

A large board at the front of the stand had been swung from vertical to a level position waist high. This served as the counter to the luncheonette. The wagon was painted a many-layered deep green. A large, blunt script was hand-painted within parallel white lines, typed-looking, by someone with the knack. There wasn't much choice. Every item was a specialty of the house.

The woman waiting for my decision said to the cook, "You won't guess who's here: 'Onion Slices on White, Lettuce, Tomato, Light Mustard.'" The phrase was expressed as you'd address someone, a substitute name based on a culinary oddity.

I looked for Lane. I had to turn completely around. In half a second I saw he'd swallowed the whole canary.

Bud was wiping his hands on a rag. The occasion called for amazement. "You're pulling my shorts."

"Look behind her," Mary said. "'Two of Everything.' Where you been hiding?"

Lane stepped forward. "Spending money." He must have signaled. I got it. I was Hannah in the flesh.

"We thought you two would get married. Thought you'd settle over on the other side to road. Business sure took a dip when you left. Most of them kids is gone. No goodbye. We had a hunch…but button it up, back to work. Grab an oar, Bud. Feed these folks."

Lane lied the lie. "We woke up this morning and said, you know, let's see Bud and Mary. Here we are. You two haven't put on a day."

"Tell my knees. Have to sit these past years. Can't move fast. Don't have to. Thank the sawbones."

"You've changed your hair," Mary said to me. "Looks pretty. What do you think, Bud?"

"Always looked pretty. You still have that dog? Alphonse, wasn't it? Havanese. I remember that day you cut his hair. I said, 'Where's Alphonse?' Whole new dog till I put the burger on the end of a fork. You can take the hair off the dog, but those big brown eyes. Gave hisself away."

"No more Alphonse," I said.

"Bud, these people are hungry. Can't eat words. Staying overnight?"

"Maybe. We were thinking of taking some of the old trails," Lane said. "The house across on Crooked Rock, thought we might have a look."

"You notice anything different?" Mary looked sideways. "They cleared all the land back a hundred yards. Goin' on two years ago. We had firetrucks down from Crystal City. Hardly a wind the day it started. Could have been a big blaze."

"Woulda been all she wrote," Bud said.

"We don't have to be told twice. Get it done. The wind from over there can be terrible fierce. Well, you know. A lot of folks thought twice. Can't steal fire insurance."

"Can always go sit in the river," Bud said.

"Old buzzards like us drown before they care to notice."

"Hannah has a nose for smoke," Lane said. "Always asking, do you smell that? Smell what, I had to say honestly. I know what she meant."

"Somebody should have the fear of God in 'em." Mary winked. "If we don't, look out."

Lane handed Mary a fifty. He waved a "no change" at her and took the sack. She looked at me. "We always wondered about you two and all those artists. A couple of counterfeiters, we imagined, but the bills always got a clean bill a health at the bank.

"Anyone ever ask for us?" Lane asked.

She paused a second. "Sharon stopped by. She hadn't seen you. Asked if we had. She was with a boy. Didn't know him." She turned. "When was that, Bud?"

"We were in Redway, the off-season at the Copper Kettle. Before the election. She was wearing that Black Lives Matter sweatshirt."

"Yes, she was." It went quiet. Thinking of the sensitivity of liberals. Mary let it go. "We didn't talk much. Our business practice. I tell Bud that you sit out here your whole life you'll meet every one of the friends you've ever known. Very nice seein' you again."

We got in the car and got the air conditioner going. Lane continued in the direction we'd been going, stopping at the intersection with the Redwood Highway. He let go of the steering wheel, tapping it with his fingertips. The wheel told him to take the highway south to a right that went toward the river on a paved road. Another right ended in a few car lengths at a gate. A U-turn in back-and-forths brought us into the shade of a thicket.

"You want the window down?" he asked.

"I hadn't thought about it."

"We can eat at the river if you want."

"You're going to eat that onion sandwich, Lane, hike or no hike. If it helps, roll the window down."

"'Two of Everything,' you'll recall they said. That was me: two burgers, two fries, two pickles, two ketchups. I always took one set home for after. The second set is for you…in case."

I opened the sack, figured what was what. The onion thing was at the bottom. "Hannah ate those things?"

"Weird creature."

"You wanted the vanilla shake." I set the milkshakes in the cup holders and tapped his. I rolled the top of the sack closed. "I'm donating my pickle, and all but one fry. You were giving me options." I had a bite.

"That Zombie you had last night," he said, "I was meaning to say, you handled that pretty good. Up to a point."

"I've got a Zombie you can kiss." I handed him his burger, thin, even distribution of ketchup. I had another bite of mine, small bites so I could talk. "We forgot napkins, unless I'm sitting on them. Got 'em."

He put his tongue on a fry. "I'd kiss it." He swallowed hard. What he kissed went with it, if it was supposed to be lapidary.

"I didn't see it till you were on the edge of sleep last night. I was thinking. The CIA would know who killed Clement. I'll go one more: Hannah is in the CIA. What better way to be in Mr. Drum's nightmares? The CIA has stuff going on in these hills. Notice all those gated roads? You can't get to them. Their cover is that they're marijuana growers. They shoot intruders on sight. That's why we can't find her."

"What are we talking about, Lane?"

"It's the first step of the scientific method: This bullshit is interesting. The second step is: I know what I'm talking about. Then you wise up to the third step: This is bullshit."

"What's the bullshit?"

"Hannah is up there in the hills…somewhere. Something that went on up there was important to her. I asked her to show me around. She shut up about it. It was for my own good. She said shut up about that, too."

"The CIA?" I asked.

"She never used initials on them. It was a bunch that didn't want to get looked at, that's for sure."

"I'd think just about anything that happens around here goes past Bud and Mary."

"You have to ask the right question."

"You didn't ask the right question."

"If it had been right, it wouldn't have gotten me anywhere. Bud and Mary are in the CIA."

"Hannah is alive?" I asked.

"You tell me."

———

As WE started back we got onto the meaning of Phillipsville, as it was in the days before yesterday. Hannah had lived in the corner house around the trees from where we'd parked. Rejoining 101 he picked up the rest.

"Someone stayed at the house off and on, someone far more important to Hannah than I was. He kept closets full of clothes. Most were women's clothes. In her wardrobe were men's outfits. They hung around as a couple of women on holiday. They may or may not have fooled Bud and Mary."

In some way the story magnified the misidentification of Hannah and me at the luncheonette. Why it bothered me didn't register.

"I was thinking of taking you on a walk. There was another house for Hannah's art students on the other side of the highway, fairly far up the hill. Hannah's idea was to get the students out of the city. One trail went close to that house. I'd seen people moving around the grounds from higher up. So we could have dropped in. I didn't ask. It's how she wanted it."

"Mr. Drum bought the houses for Hannah?"

"Hannah carried rich men in her purse. The house back there that we saw was just for her and for whoever was the company she was keeping. One time when we came here there was an older girl on the porch when we arrived—the art tutor, the one I'd seen in the house in Oakland. She had a cake waiting on the table for Hannah's birthday. The cake was huge, intricately lay-ered on a network of tunnels and rooms. Tiny figures in the rooms were edible, but I couldn't look at a body part let alone eat one. I picked them out on a fork. You could see their faces. Like they were thankful. I thought dried coconut was the strengthener that held it together. It was preposterous anyone would go to all that trouble with a cake."

A minute later he said, "The cake-maker, I was carried away with how much Hannah meant to her."

He stopped at the English Department to let me out. I'd been telling myself at forty I had two years to get the next stage of life up and running. All I did was use them up like the oth-ers, making a living, more sharply attuned to life moving on, but casually expecting that the unexpected would produce a someone who checked the boxes. Lane wasn't the one.

] *Chapter 18*

B ASICALLY, IF YOU WERE to turn in a missing person report for someone in Tres Pinos, you'd fill out the forms in Hollister, the larger town north of Tres Pinos. Hollister was Meisters's first stop going south. He was looking for Edith Barlow, missing from 475½ F Street, Tres Pinos. She wasn't on file. Neither was Sofia Velazquez. And that would have been that for a breed of cop who encountered witness statements whose stories don't fit and happen to be extraneous to the job at hand.

The missing person that year in Tres Pinos was Trent Tubman, and Meisters was in Hollister at the moment and gone in a minute. He asked if he could have a look at witness statements.

Trent Tubman's car had pulled out of his garage on the night of November 4 during a commercial break of NCIS, The next-door neighbor had heard that sequence of sounds a thousand times, although he hadn't actually seen Mr. Tubman this time. Another neighbor had seen Tubman in a car turning left onto the highway in the direction of Hollister. She'd been at the minimart. She was timing her return home to have her snack ready for NCIS. Mr. Tubman wasn't driving. The driver could have been a woman. She didn't recall a car that stood out for particulars. A sedan, four doors, a shade of gray came to mind.

Tubman had two foremen who managed the personnel employed to work his farming operations. One of the two always started before daybreak in the kitchen with Tubman, coordinating the day, checking that they were on schedule and adding instructions for what to do if they were behind. Tubman didn't come to the back door on the morning of November 5. He wasn't there at noon, and he didn't return calls. The same for the next day, the sixth.

That day the foremen noticed two things. Tubman's car was gone, and the grounds hadn't been watered. This was concerning. Tubman had a device that would operate the system of lawn sprinklers from anywhere in the world. Why he hadn't used it caused them to contact the police. Trent Tubman had been away from home for several weeks when he came to the attention of Dennis Meisters, who noted, merely to himself, that Tubman owned 475½ F Street, the location of Snap Judgment Press. Meisters had been intending to stop in and ask about Sofia Velazquez and Edith Barlow, but an instinct for when not to bother people before he knew what to bother them about decided him to save his questions.

In spite of the pain in his legs, he met with several of Tubman's neighbors and took a walk around the boundary of Tubman's western acreage. That took him up and down two hills and to a conclusion that Tubman was land rich, childless, friendless, not exactly a kidnap target. He left a message with me on the drive home. He'd see me tomorrow. A second message pushed the date back a week, and added a few remarks to help me follow his steps, because he had been sidetracked into something he didn't think he could ask me to pay for.

He asked if I knew a detective Rene Forrest. If a pin dropped, nobody mentioned it.

————

WE HAD the same outdoor table in San Bruno, the same blue skies and warm, gentle breeze, less worth a remark on arriving. We were regulars. We had to train a new server. There were thirteen almond biscuits in the jar. Dennis followed the Golden Rule: leave three.

Right off I knew his legs hurt. His face looked like they'd hurt worse if I'd asked. He'd been to Tres Pinos and found out Trent Tubman was alone in this world. Why that interested him, he couldn't say except that Tubman was another missing person on F Street. About Edith and Sofia? He hadn't stopped in to meet with Sofia's partners at the S.J. Press. So nothing on Barlow. Point being I didn't owe him anything if I wanted my money back.

Clement was dead. The Clement people hadn't notified him he was out of a job. I inquired when that would happen.

"When they stop singing and dancing. Real question is what you said the other day about this *Jay-ess-ex.*"

Not the question on the tip of my tongue.

"Let's put aside how I know things," he said. "I mean it doesn't get up with us and leave the table."

I nodded. Our secret.

"Well," he said thoughtfully, "a body washed up downstream of Caryville, Alabama. This was a year ago. He'd floated some in the Choctawhatchee River. A bullet stayed in him. Didn't make him sink. The dead man was an ex-Army corporal. He'd been in a feud with two brothers, also Army guys, a couple of brain deads they raise in the woods down there. The corporal took on too much for his own good. The woman involved with him got hurt. He had smacked her around some, and her ex was one of the brothers. He figured the corporal deserved a dishonorable death. Afterwards he dropped by to see the woman to say he'd restored her honor, noting that he'd earned a romantic favor. She didn't think so. She went to the police. On her testimony they obtained a warrant and found the gun involved. It was in the ex's closet. This was also the rifle that killed two cops on Twenty-third Street in San Francisco some ten years ago. The ex went inside. He's still there.

"It was a cop murder, and those never go cold. The guy who headed the case retired. Detectives Forrest and Kremer were added to the team. They went on assignment to Georgia to the gun shop where the gun had been brand new twelve years ago. The man who bought it runs an art dealership in Lawrenceville. He's known worldwide, a Mr. Ward Flowers. Detectives Forrest and Kremer interviewed Flowers. How the rifle got to Alabama, Flowers couldn't say. How it got to California he couldn't say. A fantastic deal had fallen in his lap right after he'd bought the gun. He'd put up two Lugers for a LeMat Civil War pistol. The other guy wanted more, and Flowers threw in the rifle. The day of the deal, Flowers had driven to an address where the exchange would happen. While he was waiting in a café, the guns were stolen out of his truck."

"He shot the cops in San Francisco," I said.

He scooped a slice of bacon through sunny-side-up eggs, got his mouth closed, and licked a thumb and finger. He chewed some and got it over to one side of his mouth.

"Is Flowers lying? Sure. I'd electrocute him, but where does the law go? That's a very technical row to hoe. There's enough for me and you. Not enough for a death sentence. Detective Forrest has to establish possession beyond a reasonable doubt at the time of the shooting. All you can say is Flowers owned the gun. He and the gun were in the same city at the time of the shooting."

"A LeMat Civil War pistol," I said. "The alibi is too good. Can't be that many owners locally selling a gun like that. Rene would run that down."

"Flowers said he remembered that the man had grown up in Lawrenceville. He was visiting his mother. He was coming down from South Carolina. Flowers hadn't met him, so he couldn't describe him."

"Must be records you can trace," I said.

"Not how Flowers tells it. Some guy heard Flowers was thinking of selling two Lugers. He tells someone who tells someone. A lot of people call Flowers from South Carolina. Almost all the calls go through the art business. And Flowers lost his Lugers. Never had a chance to sell them."

"The guy in prison," I said. "Talk to him."

"Charlie Abbott," he said. "All Abbott has to do is say he got the gun from Flowers. And provide a few details."

"So Flowers had the gun when he came back from California," I said. "Offer him a deal."

"You let Abbott out of prison early for his testimony, and a lawyer takes the wheels off of that car with a light laugh. Listen to yourself. Abbott is talking his way out of prison on testimony that relies on a business contact with Flowers? A prosecutor is chasing that rainbow? The prosecution is making the case for the defense. Abbott stole the gun. Or he got it from someone who stole it. End of case. Charlie Abbott would have a hard time proving he was born."

"Abbott got the gun somehow," I said.

He shook his tired head. "You have to understand the region down there. Good rifles are the only decent piece of property halfwits own in Georgia, and they lose it on a pair of jacks. That goes for Alabama and every other bayou swamp. Charlie Abbott can't be put in California. He was never here. Flowers owned the gun in San Francisco. Nobody saw Flowers in the vicinity of the shooting, with or without the gun. There are your facts."

"Rene wouldn't give up," I said.

"You can think of something, I'll pass it on."

We ate with the noises of anything that went by, compared todays biscuits to the ones we had last time, took turns on trips to the restrooms, looked in each other's eyes for glimmers, and had a consolation piece of pie. Dusting my place for crumbs, I said:

"There is that painting," I said. "That *Jay-ess-ex* is how Flowers signed himself for a time. That's Joanie Bessel."

"Tell me where that goes?" he said. "Ward Flowers? He lived on Valencia when the killing happened. Moved away in a hurry. Forrest and Kremer have this Joanie Bessel living with Flowers at the time of the shooting. They nailed that much down hard. They're looking for her. Just answer one of these questions: Where was Joanie born? When? Where did she go to school?

How about an address? Name one relative, say a third cousin. Joanie almost never existed. Neither did her twin, Kylie."

"Faith Nichols didn't walk into the ocean," I said. What a gun has to do with her disappearance, I don't see."

"There's a dance step nobody can follow," he said.

He walked me to my car. I rolled the windows down and let the air circulate.

Chapter 19

DURING THE YEARS he was seeing me at the English Department, Michael Sand had been mixing our appointments with visits to the Ladies Academy, a single-owner operated place, like mine, but unavailable in a public directory. Désirée had worked there. Désirée was the contact name of Joyce Ellers, the future Mrs. Sand. The night I received her call and went out to the house, I didn't get around to asking her why she thought her husband would end it all in Phillipsville. Now that I knew more than I knew then, I'd caught up to the question from another direction. But the phone number Mrs. Sand had used that night was no longer in use. The house was vacant. That was the problem this moment: how much effort I'd have to invest if I was going to ask her in person. After her husband died, a guess was that Joyce had retreated to the old plantation, resuming her routine under Felice. Felice was the owner of the Academy.

The Academy was situated on the fringes of the Castro, on a street not ordinarily thought of as within the district. Spaced appointments provided privacy coming and going. Two-hour parking wasn't abundant in the area. Of course, don't arrive early and hang out at the corner and make people wonder. We're all big girls now. Figure it out. The coffee shop on the streetcar line nearby was my first stop for ten minutes. The street was deserted when I got there.

The establishment started at the sidewalk. No sign, no welcome mat, no sounds from inside. An eagle stood guard next to
a surveillance camera in a high corner. It was about all you could
tastefully put over the door with the space you had to work with.
The black paint on the security grate looked fresh. The entrance,
not wide, not deep, was set into the structure. A pair of potted
cactuses on a terracotta landing framed the alcove. Inset astro-
logical designs in a double-door filled a maze of glass panels with
intense reds and blues. The door buzzed and sprang free of the
frame. Felice was inside, invisible to the street.

"Follow me for the tour, young lady. Put your quarter in the
little box at the door."

Felice might have stepped out of the scenes on the wall, tab-
leaux from front to back from Little Women—lakefront gardens,
children playing croquet, girls with books in window nooks, uni-
corns and real species not native to the same continents, lolling
and gamboling on hill and dale. Felice was in a dress with a white
lace collar and blue fringe at the wrists. Gray streaks you could
count were pulled, to the last hair, into a black bun.

A narrow hall passed two closed doors on both sides. It came
to an end at an elevator on one side, a stairway on the other.
A lady-in-waiting emerged from the elevator and gave me the
whole nine yards. A heck of a lot of training went into that curtsy.
Eyes lowered, she awaited instructions. She could have been the
mayor of Dubuque. Could have been anybody from anywhere,
showing off her storybook responsibilities. The final product, having long graduated boot camp, upholding the high standards of
the establishment, could make a lady welcome.

Felice introduced me in the fashion of the Academy.

"This is Mistress Elizabeth, Priscilla. She will be my visitor.
She is my colleague, a dear friend. Your conduct reflects the highest standards befitting the high honor her presence bestows on
us. You will show us to my suite."

Some males start as girls, not as a choice but for an awkwardness of nature. For some the defect is hidden but remains

lifelong as conflict. They work it out variously as they would fit a mind and body to society, and societies work out the manner they will be accepted. It's been a hell of a grind of intolerance and cruelty. Priscilla had broad shoulders and a strong physique, the prime qualities of the standard version of masculinity. She might have been an athlete some two dozen years ago. She might have excelled. She had come to Felice to transform into a particular psychedelic image of femininity.

We took an elevator to the third level and stepped past a goldfish-shaped pool with goldfish moving sinuously, as they do, when undisturbed in softly lit plant life. Double curtain panels in antique gold dressed a street window. They were open a foot or so. A faint light from outside illuminated a customized trim along the lead edges, sort of bluish. The curtains were badly cut, to my taste. The lower edge lay six inches of velvet on variable brown wood flooring. The whole side of the room was a wall of windows that looked out on a full patio with ornamental plants drooping on railing every so many feet apart. Blackout velvet drapes were open to what was left of the afternoon light at this hour. Waterfall valences added a beige to the gold curtains on the window looking out on the backyard.

Felice was a woman with a cheerful smile at ten after three in the afternoon. "I don't drink, but you're not in Rome. What's your pleasure?"

"Water that makes a fizzy sound when you unscrew the cap."

Behind elegant, subdued cabinetry was a refrigerator. Inside were bottles. Priscilla showed off exports: Swiss, French, Canadian.

"Never had a Swiss," I said. "When in Switzerland."

Priscilla stationed herself at the door to the patio. Felice said, "Interest you in the patio? It's cool, but bearable without a fur coat for another half-hour." That ended that. We stayed put.

We were served, a special occasion folded into the afternoon of the Academy. Priscilla was dismissed to somewhere, wherever the elevator took her. The welcoming atmosphere went with her.

Felice lifted her glass. She watched it come to her lips.

"I've reconsidered," she said, as if reading a label on the glass. "I don't think you and Joyce should have your get-together here." Her hand flopped: that's decided. I'd called. I'd asked. Meeting granted. That was before. "I prefer we not complicate our friendship."

She gave me the floor. Her eyes held a warning. A long silence was the line in the sand.

"You're not wondering what drags me here?" I said. "Should I go?"

My use of "here" referred to the tranquility of the Academy more than to the premises. I was dragging dirt into a refuge. She started to fold back the fabric at her wrist, thought about looking at her watch, probably just did, and got a grip on her arm and held on a second and let go.

"How about an interesting subject from a book I recently read, Elizabeth?"

"A thinking person's meeting we're having, then?"

"*The Economics of the New Woman*. Here we are, no degrees, no pedigrees. How do we make money so easily, you and I?"

"Fortuitous circumstances," I said. "It's the new explanation."

"A smart woman watches her p's and q's. That's how we do it. We watch where the wind is blowing and stay out of it." She made a grimace. A smile absorbed it, a cavalier recovery of lightheartedness.

She made a meaningful gesture. I could have a sip or two and take my leave by the fire escape. No loss in decorum there, the fastest route out, if I was looking for speed.

"Nice sparkle in this," I said. I might stay a bit. "How are things with you?"

"Well. At the moment I'm twiddling my thumbs in silence in a circular argument with a client—an argument, I'm afraid— that's going to break out again, when he gets around to it. We're in a cycle. It's my turn to listen, but he hasn't satisfactorily refined a new point."

"What do I need to know?" I asked. A hint that I didn't.

"He wants to redesign a room—his room, he calls it. He'll pay. That's fair. That's his point of view. Fair is fair. We both know it won't happen, but we pretend he can talk me into it based on I'm not fair."

"What would be his point?"

"He's wealthy. Thank God we're not married, my point in the abstract. His point, see a negotiating team, thinking deep there." She held her wrist again to keep her watch handy. "He's run out of interests. I haven't. He gives me money."

We were into "life is out of whack." Two middle-aged women who have decided a sip of water won't fix it.

"You look good, Elizabeth. I won't ask. It's your secret."

"How's she doing?" I asked. Time for my question about Joyce Ellers.

"Suicide. It's a shitty kind of divorce. He gave her a house in Utah—a poison pill. It's way off the books. California doesn't know about it, and I don't know about it. For God sakes, she's a beautician out of Montebello, the flophouse of L.A. Had nothing, had it all, has a room in back. The life cycle.

"Look, you want to talk to her? I'm not telling anybody how to live. She'll be finished soon. How about this? She'll find you. It's not my fault if she decides not to bother. Which way are you going?"

"I'm in the mood for a walk home. I'll stop at the market at the corner on Haight."

———

I BOUGHT a candy bar at the corner on Haight. I tossed the wrapper in a bin at Buchanan, and decided I'd savor the last bite all the way to Laguna. I was going home. It started that way. I got to the hump on Haight and started the downhill. A car heading up Haight turned right at Laguna and stopped at the corner. The driver got out and put his back against a door, waiting. Judging my rate, he waved, preparatory to a motion to catch me at a point of intersection. We would meet, if I wanted it to come out that way. He was my age, professional looking, deferential, and got to the point before I could brush past.

"You don't recognize me." He had all the polish he'd ever need meeting a woman. A handsome frame, the fitted shirt gave the frame a swimmer's body. I could give him a minute.

"Mrs. Sand, I presume?"

"Not bad," he said. "If you still want to talk to me, this is my car."

He opened my door and tucked me in. "I could say lady's choice where we go, but years ago I ran out of cute remarks." He turned the ignition. We didn't go far on Laguna. We headed back in the direction of the Academy and meandered a sweeping circuit to Corona Park. He pulled the car into a tennis court.

"I play here with a college kid. I still kick his watoozi."

We walked to a deserted kiddie area and sat where the moms hang out. "How'd you know?" he asked. "Michael tell you?"

"Michael told me nothing. The night I was supposed to meet you, you spent a long time getting dressed…with me outside. It could mean a couple things."

"You knew Michael. He hinted something about me?"

"Our little talks were often nothing more than humdrum *du jour*. The energy that went into his frustrations was the perpetual subject."

"What about me?"

"A day came when he convinced himself a creature tending him at the Ladies Academy had what he was looking for. One particular lady suddenly got to be all we talked about. He put her into his thoughts of the future with quite a bit of zest. That woman was you… the second Mrs. Sand."

"He kept seeing you," he said.

"I stayed on his appointments schedule as the strict maiden aunt," I said. "It was never clear what relationship he was trying to strike with me after the marriage. I definitely missed the warning signs. He gave me a wing of his library, though, so maybe he did."

"You and Felice? I had no inkling you two had something. She trusts you. That's why I'm here."

"A bunch of us once upon a time used to rotate themed parties for birthdays—a Mayfair brothel, a Bloomsbury knockoff group, a Marie Antoinette barbecue. The years went by. It had us winding up earlier and earlier, but depending on variables, a few girls would hang on later and later. Some years back a friend, Violet, had an appendicitis episode at two in the morning. By pure luck, Felice was the sober operator of a hurry-up hatchback. We got Violet to surgery and hung out in the hospital lounge. We met this father waiting for the arrival of his fifth child, a boy. Not exactly expected from a service station manager twenty-three years old.

"Felice and I spent the rest of the day together. One of the great encounters for both of us. We knew it would never happen again."

"What do I know that you want to know?" he asked.

"Mr. Sand had two houses in Phillipsville, that I've heard of. A woman named Hannah Kier lived in one of them a long time ago, perhaps in both. I'd like to find her. Was he going to see her the night you called me? If he was, she's alive. She might want to know her daughter's alive."

He looked at the ground, then stared in the opposite direction from me, then silent deliberation scraping dirt back and forth between the two points of his shoes.

"Walter Coombs," he said to his shoes. "It doesn't matter now. I didn't know till a year after he died."

Chapter 20

W ALTER COOMBS DIED in this place he built up in the hills. Michael buried him, dug a hole and buried him."

"Walter Coombs," he repeated. Three short syllables, a final playing of Taps. He stopped breathing, putting the sound of the name to rest. Very deliberately he filled his chest. "There's a tree. Michael nailed a headstone to it. You wouldn't hike there…so that's that."

"Who was he?" I asked.

"Never looked him up. Might find the name online. I don't think his birth was recorded. There was no school, no vaccination record. There was a family…a long time ago."

He made very slight motions warming the tips of his fingers.

"One day we were packing and Michael said October tenth, and we stopped packing. We were leaving for Chile. He asked me if I wanted to take a drive. A man he knew had died one year before. October tenth. It was a coin flip. We could take the drive or go to the airport. The crossroads."

"You took the drive," I said.

"Walter Coombs…landed with a B-17 crew on an Oahu golf course during the attack on Pearl Harbor. Twenty-three years old, bouncing around in the Depression since he was fourteen, until he'd lowered a wounded navigator onto a stretcher on a wide swath of green grass. Up until that moment the grass knew more about how the world worked than he did. Hickam Field was in flames. In two weeks, after they got that mess cleared, he continued on to Melbourne, set up shop for the duration of the war as an Army Air Corps medic. How he did that with no schooling, that's Coombs. That's war. After V.J. Day he reconnected in San Francisco with a doctor he'd met at Pearl, becoming a doctor himself."

He raised his finger. "You could find him through his service record. He won some medals. They're listed on the tree. You could find them with his name.

"Anyway, he and this friend stocked their own clinic. They assisted an abortion. Afterwards the woman had a breakdown. She would have had a breakdown if she'd given birth. Coombs said it was like the atom bomb. If we hadn't dropped the bomb, millions would have been killed in the invasion. When he read we would have looked weak to the Soviets, he stopped listening to reasons for anything."

"Am I beginning to understand Phillipsville?"

"You think so? What do you make of the German phrase for the outbreak of war in nineteen fourteen, *Das Kind ist geboren*?"

"I don't speak the language. The child is born?"

"All hell breaks loose."

"His mission? Keep that under control?"

"There was no mission. Coombs lived outside the rules of the world at large. He found in the mountains what he always was—a cave-dweller.

"The land up there wasn't Phillipsville then. When it was, the hill he owned remained in the unincorporated area, separate from when the city was permanently named. He built a collection of housing units that included a women's clinic. He buried each baby with his own hands, a barely articulate coming to grips with what a scheduled death is about. He gave them names, and maintained records. That's where he got the idea, or rather, where he started having ideas, like some Edison in the boonies.

"During the war he'd met soldiers in dissociated states,

semi-professionally and often just bumping into a random drink-er with a problem that pretty obviously had been a psychosis for quite a while. The poor guy had been holding a string of delusions together in a story. In an hour he could be any number of charac-ters with different genders that were fluid, this one this moment, that one the next. Sometimes Coombs would merely see a signal, hardly a second and it was gone, but it had registered. And they'd meet up later, and the gender behind the signal would emerge. In the absence of any tomorrow in wartime, where you'd be ship-ping out to who knows what blasted-out atoll, signals became confessions of strange hungers.

"Unofficially his people all carried multiple identities for those little moments—nominally men or women on their dog tags, but the true path went through a secret life. It was real fun when it got dangerous, when they simply risked everything, and too dangerous when they lost everything. Not everyone was a risk-taker. The Army kicked a lot of people out, 4-Fs."

"They needed multiple identifications," I said.

"After the war Coombs forged papers," he said. "There was a network. They had experts who supplied names and birth data for your standard problems, like providing documents for women who had thought too long about ending a pregnancy and didn't want the kid they had. Coombs realized this need would go on for a long time. It wasn't just the backlog from the war. He decided he would give them all names, the living and the dead. Some of the living grew up with him. To understand that, maybe it would help to know he grew up in a household of eighteen children, four mothers, and a patriarch in Nolo, Utah. It was a solid sys-tem—an educational regime shepherded through the offices of a community of women."

"I'll venture he had four women at the clinic," I said.

"Astute you. One was special…the psycho nurse who had come with Walter in the beginning. She was an inbred disci-plinarian. But Coombs had a rule: never hit a child under any circumstances. And he meant it."

"What if they're six foot ten and coming to kill you?"

"You deserve it. Take your medicine."

"Coombs could abort a child, though."

"He had a special drug for bad nights. Another rule: If a kid wants an ice cream, they get an ice cream. Coombs took this nurse under his wing. He kept a diary of her transformation—fifty years of kindness. She was high-functioning. Worked for California as a midwife."

"Michael vacationed with Hannah," I said. "Did I get that wrong?"

"They were close."

"Is Hannah alive?"

"Two years after Coombs died, I met her at his grave. There was a formula for locating the grave. You pace off steps from two trees, turn and walk, turn and walk, and if you have the number of steps just right each time, you're there."

"Why a secret grave?"

"They all are."

"All what?"

"Babies."

"Babies?"

"The unborn," he said. "A midwife reported live births to the State of California, but they were only names. They weren't born. The plots are along a fence. The fence is missing posts, but you can pace off where they are."

"These names grew up?"

"Went to those who needed a new name. Some of those names had children of their own. They inherited those histories."

"Hannah had a child?"

"She went to Coombs for an abortion."

"Abortions were legal then," I said.

"Hannah wanted the kid. She wanted her to grow up not knowing her or the father. Coombs made those arrangements. A nurse working for him had overdone some S.M. She'd been strapped black and blue…her form of erotic release. She was in ecstasy. She couldn't go back to her boyfriend with an explanation for either state. Coombs worked out an explanation for her absence. A quarantine story was constructed around a medical necessity that explained a month's seclusion with a dangerously communicable virus. Survival was all nip and tuck. Then Hannah's baby arrived. The nurse was in the right place at the right time. Michael had arranged a bungalow for her in Santa Barbara.

"There she was, a nurse with an all-expenses-paid life in Santa Barbara. It didn't look so shabby. The nurse was issued an identity for herself and Hannah's baby."

"Adoptions are routine," I said, "with a long list of regulations. Coombs bypassed that part?"

"Hannah wanted to watch her daughter grow up. Michael got Hannah into contact with this surgeon in Santa Barbara. He was the network down there. Hannah had a place to stay for visits. She took a local identity."

A crisscross of rooftops was a tree-shrouded squarish design falling off past the slope of the park. One second it was its own darkly tinted Technicolor. Then a white cloud dropped over us. Cold as hell, it obliterated everything beyond what you could reach at the end of an arm.

"Let's get in the car," he said. I was already on the move. Inside I rubbed my arms up to my shoulders two-handed. He got the engine going. I put my hands open against the vent.

"That's why nobody was here," he said. "When we play, we calculate what sun we'll get. We know to the minute when it's due to end. It's close to clockwork. If you care for schnapps I know a place. You want to call me Joyce. They'll know we're on very good terms. Nobody will interrupt us."

The Land of Milk and Honey wasn't far. A billowing mist, almost a horizontal rain, covered the mile getting there. Joyce handed his car keys to a hand sticking out of a fur parka. He went ahead through Gothic curtains and pointed at the ceiling. The maître d' put a two-fingered salute to his forehead. He snapped his fingers and made some hand signals that meant we were to be placed in the last booth on the right upstairs. And so it was. The signature on the publicity shot on the wall between us was Marilyn Monroe.

"She was my inspiration," Joyce said. "I used the persona in La-La Land when I was trying to get into the girl's network. Little good it did getting a job. I never made it off the sidewalk in Hollywood. Plenty of make-up artists in line ahead of me."

He ordered a Coast Guard cutter, a rum concoction, and a quartet of cannelés de Bordeaux. I had a hot tea, and promised assistance with the pastry.

"It's possible," I said to promote a thesis, "we're not here by sheer accident. An unseen hand guided you and me to Marilyn."

"How's that?"

"A man showed me a picture not so long ago. An attractive lady is in this picture with Hannah. Three people are at a Dodgers game. A woman is with Hannah and a man named Clement."

"How do you know?"

"Doesn't matter. It was either Michael or you. It had to be Michael, which I'll leave to one side. You claimed Michael's body?"

"I identified him."

"MacDonald Desmond was already dead by then?"

"Shot dead by then—a freak death, shooter unknown. Tipped Michael over. He'd been leaning since Coombs died."

"Who buried Michael?" I said.

"Thorndyke, the surgeon I mentioned in the Santa Barbara area. He and Michael were close. He had a document that granted release of the body to him. Not a surprise to me. I just thought it made sense, whether it did or not. When it was all over, did I care?"

"Michael didn't provide for you?"

"While he was alive. It was a great ride for a no-talent mediocrity. The house was mortgaged as far off as a bank in Cypress. I have no income. I couldn't make payments on a bicycle. There's also the—the hell with it. End of a chapter of life. I walked off into the past."

"Who got Coombs's property?" I asked.

He thought a second. "Not Michael."

"Someone's living up there," I said.

"For sure. From way back, there were always a bunch of kids on it. The first two generations of kids have grown. Hannah brought her reclamation projects up there…an art retreat, modeled on Coombs's education. The older girls teach the young ones. When we went to Coombs's grave, we had to take this hike. In one section we could see people moving around at the compound from the trail. Hannah was terrified. She thought of them as a kind of Manson family."

He took a sip and stopped. "Thorndyke. That's the one. He's the surgeon on Padaro Lane. I met him at the funeral. Michael was buried in Santa Barbara. Thorndyke helped me out. I wasn't in the will."

"Hannah wasn't there?" I said.

"Not with the same appearance of the woman I'd met at Coombs's grave. The repast was at Thorndyke's estate. Hannah's daughter was there. Michael had relied on Thorndyke. The woman who'd taken care of the daughter came to Thorndyke with the problems that come up with raising a kid. Thorndyke passed them on to Michael. Hannah's kid went off the rails a few times. Moved out of her house to a rock on the beach, Michael said."

"She said she went to Reed," I said. "Worse ways to go off the rails."

"Thorndyke was a Reed graduate. The rock the girl lived on was just up the street from his estate. He was the rock.

"Hannah had been watching her daughter from a distance. She had it all worked out till the girl graduated high school. A funny thing happened on the way to the Forum."

"Plans went haywire."

"As they will when a girl realizes the person taking care of her is lying about who she is. At twelve or so she was strong enough for answers. I get the truth, or go fuck yourself."

"I was thirteen when it happened," I said.

"You're a late bloomer. Anyway, the girl and the pseudo-mom lived in modest surroundings, seemingly the beneficiaries of an inexhaustible inheritance. Miraculously, whenever the girl needed a door opened, it happened. The explanation from the pseudo-mom reached the breaking point. Quite a year."

"Thorndyke was the crisis management team?"

"And Michael. Michael showed up when he was needed. He packaged the truth as only his dual gender could. Parallel lives were his specialty. It's what sold him to Coombs—to a lot of citizens of the closet."

"The girl got a parallel truth," I said.

"Whatever he provided, Thorndyke patched them together, the girl and the caretaker."

"Strange."

"I don't know. What is strange is how blind people are to themselves."

"She became a dominant," I said. "I don't believe in that kind of bad seed coincidence. Some truth must have leaked out in some fashion. Someone gave her my name, that I was her mother's trustee."

"Thorndyke would be my first guess."

A plate went to the center of the table. Four mounds were at the corners of the compass, labeled in flowery script…N, S, E, W. Red and blue swirls filled in a background.

Joyce translated: "None, some, excess, wow—the rum scale. We should split the Wow. I'll drive, you hold the wheel." He let me have all of N.

"I get your S…you get the E?" I tilted my plate. Half of N slid off mine, landed on his. All done. I got the whole E.

Joyce raised his glass. "Thank God for the guy who makes these. Only in the Castro—as far as I can testify."

Joyce cut a first bite from S. He tapped it with a fork. I had my hands in my lap. He looked at me as a test of a mental exercise. Why wasn't I eating? What did I want to know?

"Felice says there's blood in your eye," he said. "The fog of metaphor?"

"I don't want to cause you trouble," I said.

"Suppose in the act of protecting my right not to say anything to you, I act suspicious, which makes you suspicious, and then you go to the authorities with your suspicions. Nobody wants to hurt anybody."

"Just tell me."

"You want to hear about the time I was getting fucked and the bed collapsed?"

"Not in any more words."

"Michael had a talent. He could buy you a property, and God wouldn't know how to find who owned it."

"So what?"

"So, he talked a lot with Coombs, and Coombs told him about some unexplained disappearances of prominent individuals, quite a lot of them. Coombs had engineered that stuff. There were some disappearances he didn't take responsibility for. Michael knew about the death of a man first hand from Hannah. It was the work of a group that grew up in Phillipsville. Dropping a body in a hole in the ground was second nature to this bunch. Michael didn't tell. There was no connection to him that the police could know about unless they heard about something that got a very smart domme thinking to ask him questions. Like you."

"Like a Missouri Highway Patrolman," I added. That went past him.

"Felice said to think twice before I spoke with you."

"She's a sufficiently talented business person to bottle up what she knows."

"Michael is dead. Coombs is dead. The dead don't talk, and I go on dressing up the world as Marie Antoinette. What a talent. I'm only queer in the usual sense. I don't kill, cheat, rape."

Chapter 21

SUBSCRIBERS TO THE *Santa Barbara News-Press*, having passed through the largest fire in California history and desperately looking forward to news of rainfall amounts from the weather front that had blown through on a January night, were astonished by a front page, above and below the fold, of utter destruction. Overnight a mountainside of mud had wiped out wide swaths of Montecito all the way to the freeway. No freeway for weeks. There was a picture of two firemen. They had hiked to the summit of a boulder. Stuff that big had rolled from somewhere up Romero Canyon. The mud had removed a mansion from its foundation, leaving it stuck in a trough in a bend. It couldn't make the turn.

Eight months later there was a story in the *L.A. Times* about a daily search for a missing husband and wife. Many were missing. There were twenty-one names for the missing. Most fit households where I would have expected to find Hannah. Hannah might have died under another name. Or not.

Thorndyke would provide the whereabouts of Hannah Kier.

I booked a room in Santa Barbara. Some bridges were still out, but I could get around, sightseeing a community that had struggled through. I expected dried mud all over the place, but not a trace when I arrived. Hard to know what had once been the real world around here.

I took the slow way through Montecito to Summerland. Via Real picks up from Lillie Road in Summerland going south along the mountain side of 101 for about ten miles. Padaro Lane cuts off Via Real, runs under the freeway and turns parallel to the coast for a couple miles, then cuts back under the freeway and rejoins Via Real. Along one side of those two miles a dozen walled estates and upwards of fifty or sixty lesser places were blessed with private access to the Pacific. Thorndyke had a stucco wall on the other side of a strip of desert garden. A metal gate was open. The open drive beyond curved around an orchard. An old lesson I listened to: Think about it. Don't go there.

I followed Padaro to Santa Claus Lane. That was in one of Edith's letters. I crossed train tracks. That was in a letter. I pulled off Santa Claus onto a sand shoulder where an open space to one side of a nursery was clear all the way to the tracks. Across the tracks were large boulders that held the ground away from the sea, just as she'd said. Not far from where I'd come out at the end of the footpath were two boulders that bounded a hammock-shaped valley in between. You could stretch out on it with your feet braced on a lip at the bottom. On the next rock over was a flat section that was as good as a tray. It was a well-chiseled blend of rugged isolation and comfort. This is where she wrote letters and fattened a bit on breakfast snacks.

A hundred yards out a collection of fins slowly rolled above the surface and dove out of sight in a steady rhythm heading south. Dogs chased sandpipers off the beach, only to gather again up the beach. A woman swam out to the family of whatever was migrating. I didn't wait to see what happened in the encounter.

They were finished for the day when I got to Santa Barbara High School. The visitors lot had plenty of places. A deserted police car was parked along the curved drive in front of the school library. They were open for business for another twenty-two minutes, but no students. I asked the skinny, gray ghost behind the counter for the yearbooks for 2011 through 2014, inclusive.

"I'll be closing soon. Come back tomorrow."

I pointed at a bank of shelves. "I see them right there. I can find what I'm looking for in ten minutes. I'll stand here at this desk."

She collected the four volumes, dropped them on the desk stacked, doomed to be who she was, and went back to whatever she was doing. I started in reverse order. I found the face I wanted in 2013. The name was Edith Barlow. She was listed on five pages. I looked at all five faces. It was her. I stacked the books as I'd received them.

"Would you have a city directory from two thousand twelve?"

"The current year is on the table as you leave."

I could tell her she's been very kind. I couldn't think of a way to say it. I hadn't had that hard a life.

I looked in the directory for Barlow. Not there. I went back to my car. I called the reference desk at the public library. The fellow at the desk found an Edith Barlow on the fourteen hundred block of Alta Vista in the 2012 directory. That was just up the hill from the high school.

"Another question, if you have time?" I said.

"What's the question?"

"You have a local author in your catalogue. He wrote, *Raymond Chandler in Santa Barbara, Day by Day*. Xavier Thibideaux. He wasn't in the white pages. He's published a string of mysteries with a Santa Barbara backdrop…*Monday Dorothy Died…Tuesday, Jeanine Eloped*."

"There's a bookstore on Anapamu, just off of State Street, the Book Cave. It's right across the street from the main entrance to the library. You might ask there."

The house at 1482 Alta Vista was partly visible behind a hedge. A man and a husky on his haunches were at the corner. They had the right-of-way. I nodded. He waved me on. They were practicing a human-dog-car maneuver. I swung a loop in the intersection and pulled to the curb past the mailbox of 1474.

A curtain was parted in the front window at 1482. A teen in the window saw me on the walk. A girl's voice emerged from a

circular plate overhead on the porch. They weren't buying anything. I said I wasn't selling anything. Time passed. The music
in a distant room stopped. I heard a door shut, and then steps. A
woman came into view on the driveway at the side of the house,
drying her hands. She smiled with a look of a natural inclination
for human decency.

"How can I help you?" she said.

"I was looking for a Ms. Barlow. This is the last address I
could find for her."

"Who are you?"

She knew something. The truth, the whole truth, and so on
wasn't yet where we were.

"Elizabeth Cromwell," I said. "I know Edith Barlow."

"She's not here."

"I'm not looking for her. I'm looking for her mother. It's possible the woman who took care of Edith knows where she is. I'd
like to ask her."

She thought a minute. "How does she reach you?"

I gave her my number. I skipped a beat, let it sink in, a 415
area code.

————

MY PHONE buzzed at eight o'clock that evening. A woman's
voice was familiar. "You were at my house this afternoon," she
said.

"That was me."

"You wouldn't be the owner of the English Department in
San Francisco?"

"I am."

"She looks like you. What are you doing in Santa Barbara?"

"Hannah Kier is Edith Barlow's mother. She's disappeared.
I'm the trustee of her estate. The woman who took care of Ms.
Barlow might be able to help with what I don't know. She might
have information I can validate."

"Ms. Culler, you mean. She had a stroke."

"How bad is she?" I said.

"We send a rent check to where she lives. It gets cashed. Last year Christmas she was alive."

A man's voice came on the line. "We were wondering something," he said.

"Sure, if I can help," I said.

"We're not sure who owns the house we're in. Ms. Culler is not on the property rolls. Neither is Edith Barlow. The owner lives in Belgium. We got as far as a name. He pays the property taxes. We were thinking we might want to buy the house, but how do we contact him? Our letter never came back."

"You can't ask Ms. Culler?"

"She's lost her memory. The woman she lives with doesn't know either."

"Where will you send the checks when Ms. Culler passes?" I asked.

"We haven't brought up the subject. Ms. Culler hasn't raised the rent since we moved in. We're wondering, though."

"Suppose you stopped sending rent?" I asked.

"We don't want to find out."

"You want to know something?"

"We don't care to make waves."

"Then keep this to yourself. The one person who knew what there is to know is dead. He provided the house to Edith Barlow until she finished high school. It looks like the caretaker arrangement with Ms. Culler was in effect as long as she lived. The woman she lives with now I don't know about. I don't imagine anyone thought it through that far…but again, I don't know."

"The house just sits here?"

"Seems to me you're sitting on a good deal."

"How long are you in the area?" he said.

"A week at the outside."

"Ms. Barlow left some boxes in the shed—school things, books, yearbooks, music albums. We agreed to store the boxes for Ms. Culler. We were only planning on staying a year. It's been over six years. Nobody has asked to see them. You think Ms. Barlow's mother would want them?"

"If I see her, I'll ask."

"You have our number. If you can get us in contact with the owner, we'd appreciate a call."

———

I'D NOTICED her out on the pier, a tall brunette, alone, casually dressed, a wandering planet in front of an outdoor menu at a fish house. An hour later, dressed for domination, she was at a table along the wall of the patio at the hotel, just as alone. She took a glib stab at the two of us, a couple of executive-style independent contractors, killing time before an assignment.

The server leaned his head close to my shoulder. He whispered to my right thigh. "The lady at the other table would like to waste a bit of your time. She promises no politics, no culture, no art, no mention of any literary goings-on in France."

I put two palms up weighing the atmosphere. Then a hand waved her over. The server held a chair for her, tucked her in, inquired if he should be back.

"To quote somebody," she said, "are we a couple of nitwits sitting around wondering what time it is?"

"Been mulling the economic irrelevance of national borders…so…yes."

"I'll have to leave in four minutes," she said. "I'm done at ten. If you feel like doing something after, I'm staying at the Biltmore. You?"

"I'm here. Anyone joining us?"

"I can assure you, just the two of us."

"Can I assume it stays there?" I said.

She slid her palm a sharp half-inch parallel to the table. "Absolutely. You don't need to be anywhere?"

"I'm here. Elizabeth Cromwell. Stop by my room. Two-oh-eight. When?"

"Name is Adriana. See you at ten, say?"

She recovered a stiff posture, put a tissue to her lips, looked at what came off, and pulled her hair evenly over her shoulders. And was on her way. Maybe we were two dames in the same racket. Two curious corks had bounced into each other. When the door closed behind her a chill filled the vacuum. I knew now that Thorndyke and I were just possibly about to be on near speaking terms. Adriana wanted to talk about that. I had his number, the one that records messages. I called him and left a second message. No reason to speak with each other through Adriana.

The oceanfront went a long way to a rise into the mansions in Hope Ranch. I'd passed a deserted lookout coming up to a sharp turn inland. From there the road took me to a shopping center, and I brought a coffee back to the lookout as a soft sheen of pastel was following the sun over the horizon. Then it was points of lights out there, and the low whine of a jet on a glide path from the direction of the ocean.

I went back to my hotel and had a look at the bar menu in my room. I ordered a stiff thing with an attractive picture of Tahiti in the background, and laid a robe on the bed to sip it in. I'd just got my phone hooked to the house charger when two knocks seemed awfully fast for a goblet of ingredients blended with loving care.

On the other side of the peephole was my favorite brunette. The eyes were hazel, but they weren't as curious as they'd been earlier. I stepped to the side and closed the door behind her. My time was her time. She pulled the curtain open an inch and had a look at the courtyard. It didn't take long to stretch her legs, all very on time, and overwhelmingly sexy.

"How'd it go?" I said.

"Before we come to that, I should wash my face. I didn't want to be late."

A look in my eye took her attention. I saw nothing that indicated I ought to let this drag out.

"Before you do, I wonder, where'd Thorndyke find you?"

She caught my meaning. It was not time to wash her face.

"Someone doesn't care to meet you," she said pleasantly.

"Thorndyke?"

She wiped her fingers on the curtain. "You could ask him."

"I asked you."

She turned to the side to give off the full effect of truth, the whole truth, and all that. "I don't know. He doesn't tell me what he's thinking."

"Call him back," I said. "Tell him I'm in the mood for what he's thinking. You could tell him to drop by tomorrow. Tell him to call first, introduce himself."

Her mouth was very still. She had to think about this mission, how she might rephrase her statement so that it would be more persuasive. "You'd be surprised at how much he doesn't want to meet you."

"At this hour of the night…yes, I would be surprised."

I answered a knock at the door. I had the delivery fellow put the tray on the nightstand. I asked him to wait a second.

"Will you have something with me?" I said. She shook her head that she would not.

I paid the man, and asked him if he wouldn't mind leaving the door open. For what I gave him he was willing to take the door off the hinges. I pulled a chair away from a table, and indicated I was looking forward to flopping myself into it alone.

"We're letting a fly in," I said. As she was shutting the door her phone buzzed. It could have been Thorndyke.

———

I HAD the hotel paid and snacks stashed in the car for the drive back to the City. I was sitting in the coffee shop at 8:15. I retrieved a message recorded in traffic. The voice was a woman's in surround sound zipping along on a whoosh that must have been a freeway, or it's on television.

"This is Amber," the voice informed me. "We talked about Edith's things? We didn't hear from you. Have you been able to find her mother?"

I called back. "The man who could answer that wouldn't talk to me. It would be hard to find out for sure any other way that I can think of."

"That's what we thought. We went ahead. My husband put her things out this morning. They're at the end of the drive with the barrels. The trash people come by around nine. You didn't seem interested, but I thought I'd call. The neighbors took the tricycle and the wagon."

I swirled the stuff in my cup. I left it on the table with only the intention to go under the freeway, head around the roundabout, and get on the on-ramp north, and listen to a Ray Charles disc. In the roundabout I got off one exit early, and stopped at the boxes on Alta Vista. I put all three of them in the trunk. Then I got on the on-ramp north, and thought about the money wasted on this stupid trip till Gaviota, and then, coming out of the tunnel, I put on my music.

I pulled into the alley behind the English Department just after 3:00. I dumped the boxes in the basement and put the car in the garage, and checked messages.

I left a message with my librarian.

"There are three heavy boxes in the basement, some textbooks, some personal things belonging to an Edith Barlow. Don't keep paperclips. It's been a long drive. I'm trying to be cute. Let's see what we can throw out. Give me an inventory when you can. Wait. On the serious side, I'd like that assignment finished in an hour. If not…a penalty should be expected, and will be imposed. Sweet dreams."

] *Chapter 22*

IN TWO MINUTES my librarian will be at attention at the head of my writing desk, in a Victorian flat, as it were, at Audley Street, Mayfair, also as it were, one of the three upstairs spaces I provide for the Olde Worlde drama we play at—a caning. Day-to-day polish and refinement in personal behavior is provided in the Throne Room and Monastic Cell, or anywhere the mood out of nowhere will alight. For what we were about to enjoy on this designated occasion, Mayfair was his preferred scene. Here was where I took him in hand.

Not every caning is a caning. One person whacking another for kicks goes way back into illustrations on proto-Indo pottery. What I'm talking about is a school of caning that evolved a highly stylized test of endurance that purges something mad in the mind. As a perfectly tuned art it saw its development finalized a century ago—not nearly as far off as the spelling, Olde Worlde, would indicate. From there on a few of us have been playing it as it lies—an homage to a theater of dehumanization, trapped and powerless, and entertained, by one's own obsessions. Callers to the English Department know the box to check: strict discipline.

———

I WAS seated at the writing desk in a Weddington white blouse with stand collar edged in lace. My hair was up in a Victorian do.

For the pale appearance of a quiet afternoon my cheeks were lightly dusted. The bustle effect of ruffles in a black twill bustle skirt would show itself when I stood. Of course when I stood he'd be undressed, and that's another act. Just for now, before he opened the case on the desk, the leather boot on the crossed leg was a favorite, the whole lash-up tightened in a dozen inches of lacing.

The case on the desk?

I needed an edge. We've been here upwards of many times. That doesn't count numberless quickies, the spur-of-the-moment happenstance, undies down, *whack-whack*, undies up. The high priestess of boredom…he's used that on me. A bit of trolling. I try not to let that stick. As always, the design was on me.

That would be provided by the unrivaled grandeur of Lovesey-Marburg & Sweeney workmanship. They're in London, Edinburgh, and Fort Lauderdale. I'd called the domestic number. A woman by the name of Monica Walker answered the phone in person. The firm charged for the personal touch in pounds sterling. They hadn't converted their stock to Euros. The item I wanted was available at £185, plus £52 for the original carrying case, plus thirty-six dollars next-day delivery, the English Department, San Francisco.

Harrington placed a folder on my desk and stood with his hands at his sides. One eye indulged its thing for the toe of a boot. A well-turned wiggle gets the front of his pants into thoughts that, from who knows where, seem to belong to him. This was the silent period when the governess gains from a projection of inner superiority the mantle of divine right to tease the limits of doing whatever I wanted with him.

I'm the messy type. He holds my contradictions together with order. Keeping my literary collection from sweeping me out to sea is where our affections are joined.

"What's the problem?" I asked.

"We've had this discussion."

"What am I thinking…if you know so much?"

"Eventually we'll come to the place where you're concerned that you bore me."

"You're saying you're bored."

"Anything sound familiar so far?"

This is about how it goes. We fight the honest fight, order versus disorder, but his complaint taps into maternal failure. In that ground is its root, the woman in the mystery of why the world is pain.

"I want to know," he asked, "are you getting rid of me? A yes or no will suffice."

"You need to be taught a few manners." I always remind.

"Ah…down to brass tacks. You love me. I knew it."

"Yeah, well, what's the expression…ye who are of little faith, go sit on them?"

"You wouldn't waste the money. They're tin. Am I right, or…"

"You want to get me angry. That's…"

"Not what this is about, no matter how many times you insist it is. It's not transactional, I'll do this for you if you'll do that for me. We're filling our glasses from the same pitcher."

"I'll take a sip. Your conduct is judged by the natural consequences of your behavior."

"Oh, Betsy! You still retreading that mumbo-jumbo?"

"Do you want to be whipped or not? You don't act like it. Not if you get me angry."

"I'm a little tired of St. Augustine," he said, "that's all."

"A bit snotty, that. I admit that what is taught here at the English Department does appear in the Great Courses. What aren't you tired of? I'm searching."

"What have I been asking for this year…two years…three…if we might pause to touch on a bit of someone else's frustration?"

"Okay. We've run out of shelf space. You don't have to go on. The complaint is registered: one more book will enter the premises, and I will, on the laws of viscous fluids, be oozed out. I'm beginning to acknowledge this as a real possibility. I'm not debating."

"Oh? The material you brought from Santa Barbara is in the visitor's powder room…on top of the other boxes. Something for the visitors to read on the can. You're oozing them out first."

He let go. Mere words don't move me anyway. I would agree to throw one thing out—some law of compensation in my quest for harmony. It's my smoke and mirrors. The books this past year are filed in overflow sections along walls. The walls are closing in.

I stood up and came around the table and stood close. I held my arms out…not a suggestion. He'd get it. I locked his arms within mine. It was the hug he had to endure. He shut his eyes. I kissed his cheek, not once. My lips kissed to his ear, the play within the play, while I got past the button, the zipper, the elastic. Absolute confirmation was on its way. His arrogance could be extravagant. That was pleasing. His punishments were earned.

"Open the case," I said.

He picked up the case at the ends and put his ear to the brass nameplate. "Lovesey-Marburg and Sweeney. Ecstasy already."

"Pick a sin," I said. "While you're deciding, over here on the carpet. Keep your eyes lowered. You are not to look at me. Now is the moment, Harrington. Make yourself available to me. Regarding my pleasure, I want you to strive for the truth. No evasions, no matter how trivial. Can I trust you?"

"No."

"My God, you are a handful. On what does your obedience depend? Don't answer. Do you have names of characters you think about when you daydream?"

"Salome."

"Significance?"

"My music teacher in the fourth grade. A goddess."

"Your tastes are immaculate."

Shopworn aristocratic patter brought the past close.

"Strip," I said, and he stripped. A not infallible body, an attitude with the arrogance of a royalist, too pious for man or woman, having a love affair with itself. At least it's a love of equals.

"Get your socks off."

The whip was vintage dressage, 1951, catalogued as last in the ownership of a Lady Jane. I paid for a true fact. A rare item, a unique pedigree, the classical note as it snapped the air.

I opened the folder and ran a fingernail on a piece of paper, a list. A gliding motion caused me to look up. His interest had grown. The whip swished three quick strokes in air. He was on parade, tip-top.

"Despite the picture you're painting, you will not be experiencing a seduction, Harrington. This will not be an X-rated session. Our next move is the discernment of the extent of culpability. You kept me waiting an hour this morning. What do I do about it? This is not a question. I am talking to myself."

The tip of the whip drew a line. "Hands clasped…behind your back…higher…a good lean…excellent."

"We shall begin at eleven…when the clock chimes the eleventh chime."

At the eleventh chime, I said, "Position."

11:00:11

"You have disappointed. A slight curvature in the legs. The stroke will not count."

"Yes, ma'am."

"Position."

11:00:18

There is an eerie calm of extreme carefulness.

"Position."

11:01

"A long journey ahead. We are on our way. Now. About the list. I see a Chandler bio I don't recognize."

No response. "Would it be impolite to ask you again?"

"No, ma'am."

"You're gasping. You're not well? It seems I must."

"No space…on…Chandler shelf."

"Am I not entitled to full sentences, Harrington? Take your time."

"On top of Hammett…slipshod…I do my best."

"I would not ask for more. Position."

11:03

"Oh my, what did I hear? Heavy breathing…and a high note. I need not remind you. Two extra. Position."

11:03:22

"Position."

11:03:27

"Position."

11:03:31

I read from the list. "What's this pocket diary? It says nineteen forty- two."

"A moment…ma'am…please."

"Say again? The liberties you expect have become quite trying. But…a moment granted. I won't get anything out of you otherwise."

"January twenty-third…the first entry."

"Whose diary?"

"I don't remember."

"I'm going to all this trouble with you for nothing?"

"No, ma'am."

"I am, apparently. Or are you contradicting me, Harrington… a second time?"

"I'm not sure, ma'am."

"What was I recalling of Augustine: 'Men pass by themselves without wondering.' Do you wonder about yourself, Harrington?"

"Yes, ma'am."

"Might you unravel the results of your examination?"

"I wonder that I wonder, ma'am."

"Ah, a Sophist. Have I admitted you to the school?"

"No, ma'am."

"Position."

11:04:41

"A notebook. Whose notebook?"

"A moment, ma'am."

"Not granted, Harrington. Answer the question."

"I didn't notice… Please."

"Request is out of order, but granted, if you make some sense. I won't wait forever."

[The sound of a boot beating off an interval of time]

"Well?"

"I don't remember."

Oh, the little more, and how much it is!

And the little less, and what worlds away!

"Position."

11:06:32

"Position."

11:06:32:03

"Stand up straight."

[Inappropriate remark]

"You're losing control. I suggest for your benefit you recover."

"A moment, ma'am. Double-U. See."

"What's this, Double-U. See?"

"Initials. Please."

"Out of order. Position."

11:07:06

"Position."

11:07:08

"Position."

11:08:10

A struggle. He won't last much longer.

"You're faking."

[Complaint]

"A clear case of oppositionalism, Harrington. Are you contradicting your mistress?"

[Gross remark]

"Profanity Harrington. Automatic penalty. Position."

11:08:22

"I asked you a question."

"I am faking…ma'am."

"You lied, then. The penalties will be assessed presently. For the moment, where were we?"

"Forget, ma'am."

"A further penalty. Must you be this tedious? Apparently, the answer is yes. You express a need. But I remind you: Double-U. See? What am I to see in two U's?"

"The twenty-third letter in the English alphabet."

"What should I *see* in a double?"

"The third letter in the English alphabet."

"Do I seem in a speculative mood, Harrington?"

"The same initials in the diary and the ledger," he said.

"Initials. Finally. A stroke of clarity. Am I a mind-reader?"

"The same printing. The same man."

"A man?"

"I assume."

"I'd like to see this. Before we go downstairs, we need to calculate. Regarding penalties, I need a number. We will not skimp here, Harrington, will we?"

"Two, ma'am."

"We'll make that three to be on the safe side. Your performance has slipped. Might I not add a few additional strokes on general principles?"

"You may, ma'am."

"And what might those principles be?"

"You paint on a large canvas, ma'am. Your vision is limitless."

"A bit snippy, are we? An even six, then, soundly applied… in case I'm failing you."

"I apologize, ma'am."

"A little late, Harrington. You exhaust my kindness. Position."

Time passed.

"Done, Harrington. You deserve a reward. Two more. A character-builder. Over the desk. No safe words. You've been warned."

————

IT WAS a half-hour since Harrington finished placing his backside to a mirror, evaluated my purchase from Lovesey-Marburg & Sweeney, and rendered his verdict: about average. I'd passed. There's always a next time to raise my grade.

Harrington knocked a light knock on the doorframe of my

office. He had a look in his eye that went with the plum G-string. Until he gets off he won't let me relax. I had a question for him, right up his alley, but we wouldn't get to it without first things first.

"I was feeling particularly kind today, Harrington."

"No need for apologies."

"I can call Abigail," I said. Abigail was a sex doll who worked in a three-way arrangement with us. She wound up in all sorts of positions, but she'd lost air, and, hence, convenience. "It takes a long time to set up. How about we take a page from *Ideal Sex Life*?"

"Remind me," he said.

"We haven't used the Goddess for ages."

He put his hands flat on both thighs and rubbed. The motion pulled the pouch this way and that. His cock got going. So the pouch got tighter. This was a feedback loop that has once or twice worked all by itself.

"You know where everything is. I'll be here when you get back."

The goddess is a popular apparatus for men who want to put a spark in their relationships. I helped him put his cock in an opening of an object that had the bulk and bulge of a toaster. The inner material imitated the real thing. It polled superior on average among comps. I wrapped a wire around the base of his cock; another went around the balls. These hooked to a console with dials and buttons.

"Stop moving," I said. "Mistress rules…you follow orders."

"Yes, ma'am."

"How about some sensory deprivation at the other end?" I took a hood from a peg and sawed it down snug over his eyes. He could hear sounds and lick his lips.

"Another thing," I said. "Before I turn the dials and press the buttons, I have something to ask."

"Should we call this a favor?" he asked.

"I forgot how to work this dumb thing."

"Okay, ask."

"You're way ahead of me," I said. "Catching up, I have a problem. I'm trying to find a word in this ledger. I'm sure it's here. If I even knew it was on a particular page, it would take a week to find."

"You want me to scan a page?"

"Not, a page, exactly…all three hundred fifty-five pages." I gave him a shot of juice. "Do I hear a groan?"

"Please…go on."

"I need a name, Hannah, or Hannah Kier. Also, Michael, or Michael Sand. Try that, too. And one more thing. I needed it yesterday."

"I can do words," he said. "Just program symbols as contiguous if the space between them is less than some assigned amount. Might have to experiment. I can do yesterdays. There's a trick with a calendar."

"You're sure? We have an agreement?"

"I'll have some more pleasure if I may. Oh, yeah…"

Harrington was a fluctuating Catholic, lapsed and practicing, obsessed with imagined flaws that combined well in compensation as penitent and perfectionist. He read Augustine in Latin. He learned who he was in Latin. His obedience to me as a librarian was surrender.

He went through a string of motions and a whisper as soft as the trembling of a leaf, then the release. As I removed the hood, he succumbed. A token of appreciation slipped from his grasp. He caught my eye and held it. A powerful influence on each other, we were successful as a couple in what we've chosen to articulate. I patted his bottom, creating again the experience of the first stirrings of love.

Chapter 23

A POCKET DIARY, NOTEBOOK, and ledger, with the initials W.C., were distributed on a table on a low dais in the library between two cabinets that each housed half the English Department's card catalogue.

Walter Coombs had put what he'd witnessed of the Second World War in a book of about nine by eleven inches. January 23, 1942, dated his first and longest impressions of a reconnaissance flight over a jungle on an island he didn't name. The Japanese had been expected in the next few months. Typographically minute, precisely spaced words went straight onto the page during three and a half years of enormously varied conditions on land, sea, and air. The printing duplicated a typewriter.

A notebook covered postwar San Francisco and Phillipsville. Ten years of an unfolding life ended on a lament. A bald spot and receding hairline were recorded at 7:14 in the evening of December 11, 1958. He was forty years old. Four days later his initials went into the upper left corner of an eleven-by-seventeen-inch two-tone green ledger, heavy cardboard, light green paper, dark green spine. Three hundred and fifty-five pages were most of a long life. The final entry in 2012: "I forgot my birthday. I was ninety-four yesterday."

The ledger ended in a meticulous compression of closely

spaced lines. Coombs had evidently started out planning on an entry a day per page, perhaps calculating a jump to a new ledger in a year, but switched to the consideration of the consumption of space with more caution. The new economy put a month's worth on a page. He then switched to pens with extra-fine points, cut the size of his letters in half, and quit leaving margins along edges, like he had done in the war. However long the long haul would be, it would go in one book.

A gooseneck lamp divided a brightly lit elliptical region of fine print from everything else. I was looking for Hannah in the 2000 timeframe, for anything that rang a bell with something I could associate with her. It was like studying the Gutenburg Bible reduced to a postcard.

Harrington took the Walter Coombs stuff home. He thought he could do something with it.

————

It took Harrington four days to get back with me. We met in the evening at his place in Moss Beach. He lived alone in a white house with a bronze statue of an equestrienne inside the front door. He took my coat and hung it in a closet. In the den was a two-by-two square of boxes with a box on top. The stuff prepared for me was in five boxes. The intention had been to drop them off two days ago at the English Department, job over.

He had had the ledger copied, the print enlarged, and two copies of the material of each page isolated in its own jacket, once in the same order as it appears in the ledger, and again in a lexicographic order of his own choosing, but rational. At least he could explain it to me. In the second arrangement a peculiar repetition of certain symbols had caught his attention. At the office, before locking up, he'd taken a minute to check a name against his memory. A stab in the dark had produced a coinci-dence, and he'd stayed another minute to check a second name, with the same result: scribbles he'd made on a notepad were evi-dence of the same coincidence. It was getting to be an attracting repetition. A pattern, it seemed, was crying out to be validated.

That had been two days ago. The cause of the delay was what he wanted to talk about.

Harrington jotted "αω–Niles Clement" on a pad. "This Greek combination—alpha, omega, dash—turns up nineteen times."

I raised my eyes in a casual "so?" He turned pages on the pad to a numbered list of names. I picked up the pad. The first four of nineteen were αω-Niles Clement, αω–Sloan Abbott, αω–Robert Butterworth, αω–Brady Fitzpatrick.

"I'd noticed a Greek letter, psi, here and there," he said. "So Greek had to be factored into the way I was going to alphabetize. I decided I'd put the Greek letters before English. That put any alpha at the top. I went back and sifted for occurrences of alpha. There were nineteen of them—those you are holding in your hand."

He pulled the drapes, brought two glasses to the table, filled his glass, and backed against a doorjamb, a handful of knuckles against his lips. "Anything in a bottle, pour it to your heart's content. You'll need it."

I did as I was told. A Kentucky blend reached a generous two fingers. A chunk of ice made a neat splash. I kicked my shoes off and took the big chair in front of an oil painting of a math equation.

"I'd seen a Niles Clement in the papers," he said. "He'd been gone a long time. Then he'd been found. I looked him up. That clicked."

"Abbott was in an article in the *L.A. Times*. Not big, not small, figured in some early years with Reagan, had enough to operate in country club circles as basically a medium donor and overall second-row guy in group photos. The wife went to the police in nineteen eighty-two. Abbott had missed his return flight from somewhere. There was mention in the article of a young thing on the same flight with Abbott. Reading between the lines, the article was saying they had adjoining seats."

"They missed their flight back?" I said.

Harrington carried a cheese tray in from the kitchen. He cut a triangle of hard cheese, and sat with it on a sofa. "Neither of them came back. The interesting thing is how ordinary it all is. Done and gone."

"Greener pastures?" I said.

"Same with Butterworth. Found himself a young lovely. The lovebirds stayed with an up-and-coming Republican cougar in Vail for a night. The cops got that far. Then the trail went cold. That was in ninety-one, same pattern as hundreds of other aging gents, nothing special. A well-to-do lifestyle meets an adoring virgin. They both disappear. If anyone was a suspect, it was a wife, who picked up the inheritance, invariably a bundle."

"Amelia Earhart in the ledger?"

He laughed with his finger pointing at me. "Funny. Great minds. I checked. No Jimmy Hoffa. That would have been something out of *The Martian Chronicles*. I looked up Fitzpatrick. Why not? That was 1952. Alpha, omega, dash, Brady Fitzpatrick has pride of place. I found him in the archives of the *Orange County Register.* He walked off into another world, recorded ever since as a missing person. That's seventy years he's been gone. Butterworth is sixty-six years according to the ledger. His status is not in the public archives."

"Not been seen?" I said.

"The only body they ever found was the last…this Clement fellow."

I poured another finger of smooth and delicious. He had a hard time with a gulp that I could have heard in another room. He waved his whiskey in circles and had another gulp. "This W.C. was running a homespun Murder, Incorporated."

He went to a second thought: "There's a glorified thumb drive on the box there. The top box is the diary. The thumb is everything. It's yours. What I was getting to, there are several cases of a capital Psi in the diary, a lot more in the notebook. At first I had a hunch what they meant. The occurrences spanned a lot of time for one person. Now I think it is one person. The first Psi died or went away. The second one took over."

"Hannah?"

"Hannah is named explicitly. That's by far and away the case. It's not her."

"The thumb will have Hannah?"

"The thumb will have everything. You want a look in the thumb?"

He booted up. He inserted the drive, drummed his fingers, put in a sequence of instructions, and there it was: a list of all occurrences of Hannah, numbered, with all relevant coordinates. "There she is, nineteen ninety-five…on page three hundred and one."

"I go to that page, and what?"

"Depends. You're looking at list B. You want A…the original text. Here, I'll show you. It's kid stuff."

"It never helps, Harrington."

He put in his kid stuff. He was right, there they were, an entry on page 301.

"The original is blown up. And I've spaced things out. You get fourteen new pages for one old page. Here, scroll to page three, line eleven…there she is. She's had a kid…Edith. There's a dollar sign and a reverse arrow. That's money coming in to W.C. Easy to guess that. He doesn't list amounts. If he did, you're missing the ledger the IRS wants to get their mitts on."

"Here's the next Hannah coordinate, page three-oh-two, line six."

I pulled up "Edith to M.S."

A good guess was Michael Sand, which I knew from Mrs. Sand.

"I was curious about those reverse arrows," he said. "You want to see a lot of arrows?" He did his sequence and said, "Press this button."

He was right, pages and pages of arrows…with coordinates.

"This W.C. was rich. That's a lot of arrows moving dough. It's all going duty free through his wallet. Safe to say it wasn't stored in financial institutions."

"Abortions," I said.

"And adoptions."

"He named them," I said.

"These are dead. That's what the crosses are for." He went back to Edith. "Here's an arrow from M.C. to a woman named Culler.

"Culler took care of Edith growing up," I said. "When Edith moved out, Culler rented the house out and moved to another place. She left some of Edith's stuff behind. The ledger and diary were in boxes with Edith's things."

He stared at the screen. "How did that happen?"

"Follow the arrows," I said. "When W.C. died, Michael Sand took the ledger and diary. Took everything Walter Coombs ever wrote, I'd imagine, and left it off in Santa Barbara with Culler. She would throw everything of Edith's in boxes."

I typed in $J(s, x)$. "Try that."

"Here, you do it. Go to List B. Excellent. Hit these two keys."

"Why?"

"That's the way it talks to you. Now press that button. Bingo. You struck it rich…Joanna Bessel." He put his fingers on the keyboard waiting for the brain to send an instruction. He tapped the table instead. "This is a Bessel function," he said. "What's that about?"

I said quietly, "She is, or was, a street painter, did walls, fences."

"W.C. has some connection to math. This *Jay-es-ex*, maybe? He tagged her. Not many get the math symbol. It's an honor?"

He pressed buttons, with the result "Bernice Farragut and daughter, Joanna Bessel." He hummed a tune from *My Fair Lady*. "There's the birthday: January five, nineteen eighty-eight. Bessel was the father's name. I'll bet you something. You're not liable to find any of this in any bureau of vital statistics. This was all offline. That's his service. A lot of spare change in that profession. Anonymity, step right up, folks, buy some anonymity."

"Walter Coombs," I said. "A law unto himself?"

Understanding spread over his face. He put his head back and put his glass upside down over his mouth. He spit out an ice cube, poured another and tapped the bar. "You drove. You don't need a ride?" He sat on his sofa chair. He cupped his glass two-handed.

"Something I said earlier, or did I?" he said. "You have to go to the cops. Before you get to them, who knows you have this ledger?"

"Nobody. The couple in Santa Barbara could say I took some boxes."

"Wouldn't that mean somebody knew Sand had given the boxes…" He broke off. "What about this Culler you mentioned."

"She had a stroke. She can't remember her name."

"I don't like this character Psi. I don't like it when W.C. uses a math symbol. Somebody gets whacked."

He put his glass on a table and folded his hands. He didn't look at me. He was seeing me where he was looking. "I don't want to lose you, Elizabeth."

"Only me and you, Harrington."

"And it was me who suggested the cops. Numero uno, you don't know who Psi is. Coombs was in the Pacific. You can see a Psi in the diary. Psi is absent for the first years Coombs is in San Francisco. Then he shows up in the Phillipsville years. It's implausible he's one person. A cop at the top would be a nice Psi. Two cops at the top is better protection."

"The big cheese?" I said. "A multiple personality?" I was trying.

"I wouldn't get too giddy."

He carried his glass to another table and sat on the arm of a sofa. He was still talking to the floor. "Coombs stopped organizing disappearances some years before he died—twenty, thirty years, give or take. Somebody added on disappearances and kept him up to speed. I'd hold off on the cops. Psi might kill you for a quarter.

"Considering the worst case…that somebody would kill for

those boxes. I don't think you should take them home. It's not my usual packrat complaint."

He pushed his glass an inch. "I better switch to prune juice, or I'll start suggesting the governor of California is Psi. It fits with the current logic in vogue."

"I should be on my way." I moved a foot. It didn't get the other one to cooperate. He swiped his hand across his face. He slapped the ice cube in a cheek lightly six or seven times. The look he gave me said he didn't want to say the obvious.

"I put some pizza out to defrost," he did say. "Too much for me. Waste not, and so forth."

They weren't big circles, but they were big slices, four pieces on two cuts. I did a slice, then reoriented my chair sideways, stuck out my legs and began the long haul of moving pieces of peperoni around, making neat little decorations.

Harrington had been thinking the whole time. "This first guy, Fitzpatrick, it must have been a grudge. Coombs came up with the disappearing angle. He puts a bullet in him, and he's at the head of the line of characters the cops want to question. A guy disappears? Coombs can spread that event out over a year or more. Plenty of room for an alibi."

"Nineteen grudges?" I said.

He wiped his mouth and folded the napkin carefully. "That is a good question. You'll notice the names go in the ledger before they're announced in the newspaper. He's up to his ears in grudges. Might be a cause, though, and activities in a symmetric organization. As long as they keep themselves unlinked, a little group can spread suspicion all over California. Nothing points in any one direction. They'd have a shared purpose, a philosophy, a crazy philosophy, but the crazy thing is, this went on for a long time. Still might be going on. Coombs got old and died. Who took over?"

"I don't see Hannah devoted to a cause," I said.

"You want some rocky road? I got mint chocolate chip. There's another kind with cookie dough."

I had a scoop of all three. "I love your mind, Harrington."

He held his spoon at me, and wiggled it. "Try this then. Coombs always put Psi in a box by itself. What does your mind add to that?"

"A burning bush. Coombs talks to a burning bush to get his guidance?"

I rinsed my bowl. I washed and dried my hands and called a car.

"The Old Testament version. Psi appears in thirty-seven boxes in the diary. These could have been events, but I'm leaning to a sort of hybrid. In the ledger, the boxes contain a contact of some significance, a private voice only Coombs can hear."

"A ghost, huh?"

I put my coat on. I put the thumb drive in my pocket. "Do I need to know that?"

Chapter 24

IT WAS MY SECOND week on the job. The Drum Foundation was up and running. I'd been getting a feel for the dimensions of the backlog in a second-floor corner area of the mansion. It had always been the Foundation headquarters. A big room, the Foundation was not squeezed for space. That wasn't the problem. There was a backlog, always would be, right up until the day, minute, and second we'd go down for good and throw everything out. We? That was me and Tilly and Gretchen. They had been here with Mr. Drum. Stan coaxed them back with their old salary and their old space, an adjoining suite around a corner from mine. I was the boss, but I had no inclination to stamp a hierarchy on this operation. We were all three interchangeable hourly labor, making acceptance stacks and rejection stacks out of applications. We had put up a new web page the week before; this week the deluge.

Around noon we'd been at it for three hours, and Tilly went down to the fountain and scraped a chair. The noise was like a whistle at quitting time.

I called Dennis. "Could we meet tomorrow?" I intended to share some bother with him regarding Walter Coombs. No telling how much bother.

"Looking forward to seeing you," he said, "if you're in the neighborhood. I'm at the New Beaula Cemetery. That's on the

Ronald Reagan Highway just outside Tickfaw. That's in Louisiana. I passed a red brick diner down the way. They're open."

"Oh," I said. "You want to go first, or me?"

"You have anything interesting?"

"Not really. I was in Santa Barbara. Looks like I've uncovered nineteen murders. Clement was the last of them."

"You been to headquarters with this?"

"I'm up to my ears sorting artists who get a dollar from the Drum Foundation. A lady here set up the system. Of every five applicants, one, and only one, makes the first cut. Same for the next cut. The survival rate plummets until dinner. In the evenings we review the day's decisions. More cuts. It's like the aftermath of a bus crash. We only save one body from each wreck."

The sound of the word he'd used, "Louisiana," caught up. "Am I hearing this Louisiana thing right?" I asked.

"Your hearing's fine. I was thinking about Charlie Abbott wasting his life in a cell in Alabama."

"For killing someone who deserved it," I said. "Must have been raised by his defense team at trial."

"Abbott took a plea. It worked in his favor."

I leaned back and put a foot on the desk. "Compassion. Am I right? You want to find something else working in his favor?"

"We all agree. A piece of dog meat like Abbott doesn't get his hands on a fancy rifle from Ward Flowers. Forrest and Kremer had a chat with the arresting officer. He's the chief down there now. All agreed, Abbott stole the gun, but they couldn't put him near Lawrenceville. Not ever. He didn't steal that gun out of Flowers's truck."

"If I understood you before, they didn't get much out of Abbott back then. What's changed?"

"That gun they found with Abbott," he said, "the one Flowers bought, that wasn't the only gun they found in Abbott's closet. There was a Civil War Remington revolver, a collectors' item. They looked up local burglaries where guns were reported stolen. Nothing stolen matched."

"Aha! That's where you came in. You looked in Louisiana. How'd you think of that?"

"I didn't. Detectives Forrest and Kremer were digging into assaults and murders wherever they could pinpoint where our boy Abbott had been. He'd killed once, and you never know. An art collector in Tickfaw had been killed in a robbery, a fellow by the name of Driggers, by itself nothing of interest, except Abbott had shacked up at an Army buddy's place in Hammond, Louisiana."

"…And that's up the road from Tickfaw," I said. "I'm looking at a map. You're saying what? Rene found something in Tickfaw?"

"Not what she was looking for. Ms. Driggers remembered her husband had some guns in a cabinet in his den. They had been taken in the robbery, but no description of the guns had been preserved. Your friend went down there to show Ms. Driggers some photographs of guns, see what she might recognize."

"And something turned up then or you wouldn't be down there. Or wait a minute, I'm confused."

"I was, too."

"I'm still confused. If something did turn up, you wouldn't need to be there."

"You got that much covered. And rub your lucky charm. Something did turn up. The people who investigated Driggers's murder took pictures of the crime scene, the house, the grounds, the cemetery across the street, the whole neighborhood. And they took pictures of a painting in the cabinet. It was still there. All they could say was the killer had better taste."

"Not much of an identification." I said.

"But interesting. They shipped all the photos to San Francisco. But the Alabama officer I was talking to, he had a copy of the photo of the cabinet. He wasn't sure he would have stolen it, either. The picture was this woman, undressed from the knees up, getting on a horse. Her naked groom was helping her fit a boot into a stirrup. The posture left her overly exposed to the groom. That snapshot went into the police files."

"That's what Driggers had hanging in his cabinet?"

"No. It got talked about, the way the boys will talk, and there was this other thing: the picture was signed. Nobody could make anything out of it."

"I don't believe it," I muttered.

"The chief sent me a photo. There was your *Jay-ess-ex* inscribed in a chair."

I knew Rene. The rest was easy. "And Rene ran that down to Flowers."

"She checked art shops all over. Bingo. She identified the signature. It was unique to Flowers. So she had Driggers with a piece of art that Flowers supplied, but no signature on a bill of sale. Driggers could have picked it up anywhere."

"And no bill of sale on a gun?" I said.

"Detectives Forrest and Kremer had located e-mail and phone calls between Driggers and Flowers. Flowers was charging in the thousands for anything he produced, yet he didn't have a record of the painting of his that Driggers had hung in his den. Perfectly reasonable. Flowers had stopped using that signature when he left San Francisco. Flowers surmised that Driggers got the painting in a cash transaction, not uncommon in those days before the move. The signature referred to one of his models, and she hadn't come with him to Georgia."

"The trail stopped there," I said.

"Driggers is the connection between Flowers and Abbott, no question. But no way Abbott gets an advantage admitting to a theft of a gun where a man was murdered—and it drives you crazy, it's the only testimony a jury would believe. They just can't fit the noose on our boy, Flowers."

I moved a lot of brain cells to help him out. Nothing moved, and nothing was said for a moment's catharsis. Back to square zero.

"You still there?" I asked

"I'm here."

"What for?" I said.

"Had a guess. Called the widow. She'd sold the home. Changed her will some. Moved in with a daughter who lived nearby. They went to the same church. The pace of life didn't change much after the funeral. I got a feeling talking with her on the phone that she's going to remember something—and don't press it in a phone call—get down there and drop in like folks and say hello. We had lunch today."

"She remembered Flowers gave her husband a gun?"

"Mrs. Driggers remembered a natural redhead, six feet, one blue eye, one green eye, with a sense of humor. Don't ask."

"I am asking," I said.

"It's that bingo business. While I'm with Ms. Driggers enjoying some damn fine cornbread waiting for a bingo, it's in the back of my mind what I'd been thinking all along…Flowers is a stupid idiot. Here's a stupid idiot with a multi-million-dollar art business without the brains to put a few weights on a gun and dump it over the side of the Richmond ferry. And then it came to me from the sound of the sheer common sense in Ms. Driggers's voice, and the sauce they lather on these ribs in Louisiana, I was too damn smart. I had an oar. Only I was up the wrong creek. I'm the stupid idiot."

"You're joking about the redhead?" I said.

"Sure, we see it funny, but Mrs. Driggers didn't. Flowers supplied real live models to Driggers. Flowers had a harem. He'd send his best patrons photos to choose from. The photos were under the floorboards in the den. Don't ask."

"I'm asking."

"Mrs. Driggers sold the house. As part of the sale an inspector crawled under the guesthouse. I can go on. You want to ask?"

I didn't see what Dennis was so worked up over. "You discovered you're a stupid idiot?"

"Try this," he said. "Flowers didn't know the gun had been used, not when he packed up and went back to Georgia, not till Detectives Forrest and Kremer hit him between the eyes with it. He did give the gun to Driggers. I'm convinced of that. No other way that gun could get to Abbott. And I'm convinced about Abbott. Flowers didn't know it was *the* gun. People that smart making money are smart in other ways, like surviving, and he was already smart in San Francisco. It adds up to zero he's shooting two cops and keeping the gun, much less giving it to a porn patron. Nothing there."

I was glad I'd hired him. Maybe he'd work on my problems. But then the signature came back to me. "Bessel shot the cops?"

"She was living with Flowers at the time. Let's say she knew the guy in the room where the shots came from. He was out of town. She got a key, got in, took a clean shot, and got out. She put the gun back. She washed and dried her hands."

"They separated around then," I said. "Flowers took his business to Georgia."

"Ten years or so down the road your detective friend showed up at Flowers's door and started going on about this gun used in a shooting in San Francisco, and how the sales records showed he was the purchaser of record, and how, by the way, he had been living down the street from two cop killings—at the very exact time it all went down. Now I'm wondering what your detective saw in his reactions.

"Assuming I'm the stupid idiot, and not Flowers, anybody could see how his face would express itself when San Francisco dumped that ton of bricks on him.

"Say he wasn't guilty. An innocent mind with guilty knowledge could work it all backwards, maintaining the five stages of total cool. When he got to the not-so-blank blank stare, that would be him dealing with a very good guess who took his gun without him knowing, did something bad with it, and put it back.

"Now, all of that thinking happened too fast. There was all that circumstantial evidence up against the only thing he knows: he's innocent. Very suddenly, he looked like the guilty party grabbing for an explanation. What came to his mind was a slightly delayed, but obviously silly explanation that the gun had been stolen out of his truck before he went to San Francisco. Given advance warning, he might have come up with the same thing, but more likely he would have stood his ground on the simpler lie: he had the gun, then he didn't. How it was lost, he can't say. He moved a lot. Things got thrown out."

"I'm with you," I said. "Flowers would know where he stands: prove me a liar, copper."

"It's a hard sell for the defense, that a gun stolen out of his truck gets to San Francisco and back to Alabama. It's more than a totally impossible possibility, though. The gun did just that. Flowers has the gap on his side, the gap that the prosecution has to fill. It's the word of a successful entrepreneur against evidence that leaves out some crucial dots."

We chewed that in silence.

"Bessel," I said. "She was his muse, but I'll bet Bessel and Flowers haven't exchanged a penny postcard since he left San Francisco. She'd see to it. Bye-bye."

"They couldn't indict her."

"Bessel is a name in a ledger I found. Her birth date is there, and data that attached to her when she was born. And maybe data she acquired, if I search. I won't need a magnifying glass. The setup is high tech. Incidentally, when will you be in our town again?"

"I'm swinging through Missouri on my way back. Be back end of the week. We have to get Bessel's data to your detective. I can't bug Flowers to get at Bessel. Not much chance anyway, but I'd need another country if I pulled that stunt. Cops have fragile egos. What will you be doing when I get back?"

"Dropping out in the eighth grade is finally catching up to me. Our freshly minted web page at the Drum Foundation kept intact the old wording, with a section honoring the memory of Neville Drum, but my name heads the new management. The place where I'm supposed to put all my degrees is blank. My qualifications are accessed in a hyperlink of the sex industry.

That's where the powers at Raspberry, Inc. stuck their claws in. Elizabeth Who. I'm signing replies to tenured faculty that begin with the word 'Unfortunately.' They're asking where I learned such big words. The pushback I'm getting from Raspberry came through Stan's assistant, Crackenthorpe. It means the trouble coming is official. I've penciled in a meeting with Stan. We meet in the shadow of the Stanford law school, and I have to hold my own."

Chapter 25

IT WAS THE MONDAY of the next week when the access code to the gate of the Drum estate didn't work, a hint at the *faits accomplis* that Stan had been predicting in our meeting at Stanford. A minor miracle it hadn't happened sooner.

The guard at the main gate put his magazine down and stepped outside the security building.

"I work here," I said. "The private gate I use seems to be stuck. Anything you can do about it?"

He devoted a moment to what we might do for each other on the same side of the gate and wrestled a life-is-tough goodbye out of disappointment. "The estate is closed."

"It was open Friday," I said.

Whatever that meant to him, the "too bad" shrug suggested I understand that things change.

I dialed Gretchen.

"We went for groceries on Saturday," she said. "When we came back, we couldn't get in the gate. Our things are there. We can't reach Stan. He has four messages from us he hasn't answered. Are you inside?"

"I'm out here with a box of applications and no a trash can. You called Crackenthorpe?"

"We're extinct."

I called Lane for his code. He gave me a number.

"It doesn't work," I said. "There's a vine on the wall by the statue of the dog. I'm sure I can climb it."

"The doors are locked," he said. "The key you have won't open them. It's a step they don't overlook. Leave Crackenthorpe a message where you want your possessions delivered. She's waiting for you to catch on."

"You knew about this?"

"After it got as far as hiring you, it looked like Stan was right, the triumvirate at Raspberry would accept a year more of the Foundation as Drum envisioned it. That's what it looked like."

"I have a contract. So do Sheila and Gretchen."

"You'll still get the salary checks. They're saying you can't use the estate. Read the contract. What Stan provided was the way it used to be."

"They can get away with this?"

"Stan has nothing to fight with. Watch out for non-performance, or malfeasance…some damn term that says you're not holding up your end. The checks can dry up. You can stay at my house here in Menlo. I'll leave the back door unlocked."

I hung up, and forgot I'd hung up. I put the phone to an ear and spoke to Lane and caught on to the impression I was getting. I had a free day. I had a chance to lie down. I could do anything but put myself on the other side of the gate.

————

McKenna's has been in San Francisco under that name from before the Big One, the one that's overdue, average-wise, calculated over ten thousand years. They redecorated once years back, settled on a 40s look with a phone booth and without a television, unique for mid-budget eateries that served alcohol. Customers paid for a place to get out of a house and get away from the house. You call a friend and float a proposal that you get together with the Squires. It's still used to suggest a drink at McKenna's. I had a use for it.

I called Celia. I heard her ears go up. She expected to hear we were firming up the nine o'clock hour of the coming Thursday evening at the Drum estate. She heard instead that the dungeon was closed. I dialed the outreach back a bit, but made myself available if she cared to sneak off the job.

It was eleven in the morning at McKenna's. Two men were in a booth sipping alternately from the same straw. I heard one of them say, "That's that dominant." It didn't strike up a conversation.

Celia stopped a second at the bar and pointed to the booth I was in. The guys looked up from their straw but didn't say, "That's that supervisor." A politician off camera at the end of a morning has been on his or her ass soaking in other people's terminal miseries ever since his or her toes got out from under the covers. They look like anybody drinking before lunch. When I took the hand she offered, she leaned back, and her shoulders dropped, but there was a glint in her eye. I was still worth the fuss. A couple of beers arrived with nuts.

"Are we breaking up?" she asked. What she knew of me told her she knew better. A social arrangement with a client wasn't my style, either canceling or setting up our next meeting. It was a politician's fair guess I wanted to be with someone who made things happen. She had put her naked self under my control. She was leaving the field open to a proposition of what she might be asked to do in return. We were going somewhere from there.

"You have a few minutes?" I asked.

"I'll be sitting at another table in front of another beer down the road at noon. You might compress your problem into a thimble."

"I can't even get my hate in a thimble."

"Oh, that," she laughed. "The soothing balm for when you are in bed alone in the dark. You want to think cool, clear strikes of the rapier before lunch."

"I done did cool lunges with the rapier."

"May I still call you Mistress Elizabeth?"

"You're still welcome at the English Department," I said.

"At this instant, yes, but it's more than likely I won't feel sorry for you. I don't want to lose you. It's why I'm here."

"Fake it. All I'm asking."

"There's a private room upstairs with four views of paradise. You might not feel so bad. I wouldn't have to fake as hard. What happened?"

"I was a sexual excitement editor. Artists get me excited, I give them grants from the Drum Foundation. I liked the job. The two women I worked with liked the job. The Drum estate is in the hands of three male trustees who kicked the Drum Foundation off the premises. I went with it. I've had a few hours pissed off, plotting a retaliatory strike."

"You can't simmer down. I can relate."

"I want them to beg me to come back," I said. "I give them the finger."

She grinned. "Sounds like a lot of work for a two-second punch line."

"I was hoping you could come up with a cruelty too cruel for my imagination."

"How about a solution well within your imagination? Please don't be insulted if I speak to you as a commoner. Given any three billionaires, a person with your talents can get a grip on at least one, and one is all you might need. His pleasure is your pleasure every Sunday afternoon, whatever that might be. Everyone wins."

I shook my head. "I would have to beg. Men like women on their knees. I'm not used to the posture."

"They're each worth a billion, say. They're saving mere millions denying you the use of a few rooms. Do I have that much right?"

I scooted over and put my back to a wall. A knee went on the seat. I held on to an ankle.

She was getting annoyed. I expected flags at half-mast commemorating my low place in the capitalist system? And a caring shoulder?

"Men wipe a life off the map for lack of imagination as to what they can do to feel like men. Think of Anna Nicole Smith. If she could do it, come on, you're being silly."

"Not what I'm saying," I said. "They're not wrong. What gives me the right to pass judgment on anyone's work? I'm a joke, an embarrassment. The two women working for me are U.C. grads."

She hadn't touched what she'd poured. She moved her bag an inch closer to the edge of the table.

"Okay. Abstractly." She paused. "In a nutshell, that dirt under your fingernails, you'll never get it out. How long do you need to have a good cry?"

"Two years, and I get my high school equivalency through City College."

"You see the lines coming together, then. When you're sixty you'll have a Berkeley law degree. They admit the random old lady on pluck and vinegar."

"In the meanwhile I marinate in my own bile until I shit myself and reemerge a processed piece of harmony."

"How'd you get the Drum job? I mean, being so devoid of talent."

"Drum wanted me. I looked like someone he liked."

She stood up and twisted her lips into a reserved smile. "There's a play you're invited to on Sunday. Let's meet. In the meanwhile, take the money. All it cost was a slap in the face. Someday I'll show you how to fix that."

Chapter 26

FROM WHERE I LIVE the quickest way to Sausalito is the Golden Gate Bridge. The trip occasionally overlaps hours when a bit of bad luck sticks its nose into it. My ride crawled across the bridge in one of those days, in a near total white-out. Orange headlights concentrated on the mystery of what was beyond twenty feet, silence being the prayer to nature that the rest of the bridge was still there. And then somewhere we were out of the soup, as if a door had been opened, and on the other side it was Technicolor. We climbed a hill and took a curve off 101 down to sea level, reaching a section of oceanfront where you could see who looks at the water along here, if you tilted your head back far enough.

The driver said he had a passenger, Elizabeth Cromwell. A man's voice said he copied. A door in a hill swung open. The car turned into a cavern, climbed a ramp, and stopped. I'd been delivered. Another man took over. He got me out and tucked me into an elevator all alone with an inset aquarium that brought all the fish up with me.

The gentle sound of a bell opened the door to a life-size Venus de Milo gracing a sculpted stand of Japanese trees. I stepped into what exposed, in the 20s, when the house was built, a hundred and eighty degrees of ungraspable magnificence. Eventually it had become the Lamond estate.

Robin, an editor in the art section of the *Chronicle*, had taken the décor in stride. He'd ducked behind the statue of a Spartan getting his sword ready. His columns exercise a general responsibility to his fellow citizens. After the play he'll be off slumped in a corner, discouraging social intercourse. I'm his mistress. I'll pull rank on him, find out where the money verdict is at. I made a head motion that we could bump into each other now. He was in a thumbs-down mood. He knew something.

I spiraled around, landing in his shadow like a tip-seeking journalist. "I'm not disturbing our friendship, am I?"

He shut his eyes. "Thank God it's you. You brought chloroform. My kingdom for a dose."

"I was watching you staring at feet. You're not into high heels, or have you turned that corner?"

"My complete-unto-myself disguise. You and the Lamonds? What am I not aware of?"

"Just slumming on a beautiful Sunday afternoon," I said. "Who are these Lamonds?"

"The Lamonds, Thomas and Jill, a numbered pair in the neighborhood, currently number four on the list who can call the governor and be connected at midnight. They receive their fair share of sunshine. Their home locates the first serious filter for plays and actors. Impressions will commingle in the garden after the performance. Nobody bombs at the Lamonds'. Praise, mere praise, profoundly influenced by a view of the Bay, will sparkle for works that die on the premises."

"Good place to start."

"You missed them. The Lamonds cruised past me through a continuous maneuver welcoming the multitudes. They're very much looking forward to meeting the whole bunch of us in the garden after the play. You will behold and rejoice."

Celia passed, touching my arm intimately above the elbow, gone in the wake of high voices and laughter. I was in, but not like Flynn.

A ten-minute bell dinged. Drink up. Phones off.

A sequence of tapestries were pulled shut across a vast wall of glass. The stage was on risers with an open space of one long stride to ground-level seating. Staircases around both sides of the center audience supplied supplemental seating. I went to the next- to-the-top step and put my back to the wall with an elbow on the floor of the second level of the house. My left foot could slide between butts on a step below that, with the knee bent. The other foot got a spot a step lower. I waited for the cramp.

I was looking at a printed program of *Expecting Bonnie Jingles*: Kitty Herndon, Manx Lindner, Naomi Nystrom, Al Titus, reading clockwise in a circle of faces around Myles George, the playwright.

The first act. A room with a massive four-poster bed in the middle of mirrors. Whatever they're doing on the sheets, we see it from multiple angles. A brothel? A table and four cushy chairs were the rest of the furniture. The chairs stood where you might shove them to sweep under the table. Drinking glasses and playing cards were on the table. Four players have suspended a game for a break?

Two men and two women entered from the wing. The men had been in tuxedos. They'd lost ties and coats. They were about to lose their shirts was the impression. The women were showgirls. They didn't have much to lose, and hadn't lost any of it. They were lucky, or they were better players. It was an ambiguous sort of strip game. Three sat down. The woman who would have had her back to the audience didn't sit. She imitated an asthmatic, making a desperate struggle for air, the cause of the distress unknown. She was next to a full-length painting of a man in dungarees, like the man in Grant Wood's *American Gothic*. The doorbell rang. She opened the door. From the other side of the door came the first line of the play. "There's been an accident. Bonnie is delayed."

"We've been waiting a long time," was the reply.

"I'm the messenger. That's all I am."

The indefinite wait among the card players was intolerable.

Bickering broke out. It ran the scale from the personal torments of a hangnail to the observation that God can damn the utility companies. Vital services were kaput. Hence the candles. The men lifted their glasses, but the liquor was gone. The audience got it: middlebrow society under debilitating stress. A transformative day had arrived? Bonnie had a handle on it. If only she would get here and tell them what to do. The first act ended with the woman sitting at the table sticking a needle in her arm: "Nothing we can do until she's here."

During intermission I wandered onto the lawn and into a women with an adolescent son. I can't hold my own with parent talk. I took a step around them and got pinched in a knot with a man who looked bored. He'd heard the buzz. He knew what to expect. He lived in Bel Air, and I looked like I was in entertainment, and I heard, "Have we met?" He was leaving within a minute. He could drop me…somewhere? No? Another day, then. *Hasta luego.*

I zigged and zagged to Robin and used a smile to pry.

"Okay, Robin, let's have it. It's an order from your mistress."

"Keep this under your hat. He's got *The Iceman Cometh* reconfigured without the charm. Bonnie Jingles? Not a person. It's a drug. Solves all problems. Big clue? The shit she stuck in her arm didn't help her rhetoric. That's the way you'll read it on Wednesday. Around a quarter-hour in I was hearing far too much of a thank you to *Waiting for Lefty*.

"Second act begins with the four players as they were. The woman with her back to the audience will go to the door. She'll say, 'I thought I heard the bell. Did anyone hear a bell?' Nobody bothers to theorize. They'll bitch and moan and take turns with the needle. They might perform a medley on the bed. You know, the Dumbed-Down Chekhov Principle. After an hour torturing the mattress, a sharp bang startles them. They jump up naked, ready with a prepared reaction. 'That's a shot! It's come. It's started.'"

He poked his chest. "The bell. It started. You coming?"

"I'll wait out here."

"The woman on her feet," he said, "she's worth watching. She's trying not to throw up. It works. Concentrate on her. Kitty Herndon. Learn." He tapped a finger on his ear. "The third ear." It was the name of his column.

Within the center ring of the garden the help were positioning utensils around a gigantic cake. I heard Robin say, "See that bulb of frosting on that corner there? Stick a finger in. You're out fast. They'll throw you over the parapet."

I poured myself champagne and wandered over to the cake, amazed at the enormity of the space it took up and startled at an awareness that I was witnessing this preposterous work of art for the second time. A server backed into me. Without turning, she excused herself. I could help myself to champagne and get out of the way. Periodically there was someone schlepping a box from a service elevator in an efficient counterclockwise motion around the table, depositing a labeled container in a prescribed position. Three women took turns removing contents, discharging many small tasks setting up the main table. Every so often the whole side of the table was vacant, and from where I was standing this incredibly lyrical monstrosity existed as one enormous vision.

A woman at the bar had bent over an opened case of champagne. I leaned over the bar and asked who did the cake. I guess I meant to ask which bakery. She pulled herself to a full vertical and nodded to a fellow carrying a box to the service elevator. He was in white—white leather shoes, white pants, white starched tunic: Continental Caterers.

I caught up with him at the elevator. "I'm interested in your cake."

He was shorter than me and busier than me. He looked in the direction of the cake. My tits blocked off his discretionary angle of vision. He looked them over without jeopardizing his employment. The elevator door opened. Two women in white pushed a cart out. Behind them the trail boss saw it was her guy I was talking to. She was getting no work out of the conversation.

She suddenly had three things to say. Discretion was in order. She made a conciliatory nod to me. She had a pocket watch level on her palm. It was chained to her wrist.

Her guy slipped into the elevator. "She wants to know about the cake," he said.

She put her finger on the hold button. She said to him, "We'll be short. There's champagne in the truck. Up here. All of it. Dawn left five cases at the shop on the back step. Get that right away." She twisted his wrist to twist his watch, so he could see it. "Have it up here on ice—forty minutes. We need clean silverware. Get what's in the truck washed at the store and back. Same forty minutes."

Gray-headed, fifties, pale blue blazer, name of Adele, no-limit energy.

"This is a big job," I said. Perfectly sympathetic, utterly irrelevant.

She made a face at her watch. The same face seemed to honor a possibility I just might be future business. "How can I help you?"

"I was admiring the cake. I'm interested in meeting the cake-maker."

"It's not ours," she said. "We picked it up at Hillside Bakery."

"I've seen things near that size, but those fancy decorations… that took an eye for detail."

She put an arm out to get attention from a woman at the table. Her right index finger pointed somewhere over there at A, then B. The woman looking at her from point A went from where she was to where she should be.

"You might call Hillside Bakery," she said to me. "We do special deliveries for them. Our brochure is available in our truck. You going down?"

I went down. The fellow I'd met upstairs was studying a clipboard.

"The woman upstairs," I said, "she said you have a brochure."

He pressed down with his palm, which opened a metal clamp

on the clipboard, slipped a small sheet of paper from underneath, closed the clamp, dropped the clipboard in the door pouch and climbed in the driver's seat. He taped the piece of paper to the steering wheel. "I'll get you a brochure. Be back in forty minutes."

I called Hillside Bakery. A young woman answered and passed me to an older woman, who said the hieroglyphics on the cake were offering three cheers to the author. The woman I was speaking with knew one more thing.

"Have you cut the cake?" she asked.

"Not yet."

"You haven't seen anything, then. Don't take the first piece. Wait. Whacking away into the layers uncovers secret passageways to a tomb. Myles George—you'll see his image when they open the sarcophagus."

"I'm thinking of an occasion coming up," I said. "I'd like to drop by and meet the genius who made it."

"She doesn't work here. We gave her half the premises for a few days. It was a special order for a friend."

"I couldn't get on her schedule?"

"She uses us infrequently. You could talk to her. She's going to be expensive, I don't need to say, as you can see." She asked me to hold on. Then I heard, "My husband says she left some equipment here. She's picking it up when she gets back."

"She say when that would be?"

"She might not have left yet."

"Could I have her name? I'd like to call her. You have a world treasure there. I am flabbergasted."

"Leave your number with us. I'll see that she gets it."

She hung up and that was what there was to know at Hillside Bakery. One heck of a specialist. A labor of love for a friend. "Don't get your hopes up," I said to a bright yellow flower.

———

I WAS let out. I crossed the road and climbed the guardrail and followed the nature trail to the left to where the road divided at Pelican Park. I'd seen the Bay enough. I called a car. It was an unsettling ride back to the English Department. Coombs's ledger was in a hollowed step at the foot of the staircase. On top was a concordance. I looked up "cake." Used twice in the phrase, "that takes the cake," the word didn't occur otherwise. I was looking for a connection with an event or a name.

I dialed Continental Caterers and heard an older woman's voice. She identified herself as Charlotte. She would be pleased to help me.

"I very much hope you can," I said. "I was at the Lamond mansion for the performance this afternoon. I was amazed at the cake your people delivered. It's hard to believe it's the construction of one individual, but that's what I understand. I'd like to meet her. Would you have a number I could call?"

"The invoice comes from the Santa Annalee Retreat. They have a number."

"Would it be possible to stop in at the retreat? I'd like to speak to the artist."

"Oh, for sure. I can give you the business address. It's worth the visit anyway. We used to ride our bicycles on the grounds up there when I was a kid. The homes above the retreat weren't built then. There was the one paved road that went over the hill to the observatory. It's still there. Still the only way to get there. We'd go over to see Darwin Hooke. He owned the observatory. It's been a state park for a time. There's a boat landing and a few places where trails come up from the bay. It's free access to the shore. That's all undeveloped on that side of the hill."

"Who lives at the retreat?"

"Women. They have a spiritual core in their lives. Dress like anybody. Drive cars, so they're not isolated from the world. They stop in here mornings. We have a shop that sells baked goods. We pick them up from Hillside Bakery."

"Why do they have someone who makes huge cakes?"

"Just do. Hasn't always been that way. When I inherited the business, we made everything we sold on premises. Without my parents, I had plenty to do with the catering. Sometime after we set up an arrangement with Hillside, this woman came in and asked if a friend of hers could use our facilities to make a cake. I referred her to Hillside. Let's say, not quite ten year ago. What did you think of the play?"

"Why do you ask?"

"No particular reason. I see the playwright."

"He lives in the neighborhood?"

"I'm in the game. Over on the far corner of the retreat there's a dark and spooky wooded area bounding the parking lot, darker and spookier from the flash of a cigarette at night. They're unloading and waiting. Writers. You'll see writers when it's all in their heads, a silhouette skimming a loose-leaf manuscript over the trunk of car, a pocket flashlight in their teeth, word processors being unpacked, thermos tops unscrewed, coffee poured, sips and slurps, a phrase on a cellphone in between, the rhythmic booting up of technology on which the modern galleons will lumber through waves of imagination. The sound of zippers never stops."

"You can sure turn a phrase."

"Myles George. You saw his play. We meet every other Thursday night at the Tree Whisperer. It's the writer's hangout up there. You'll see it. The far corner. I'm working with Emmett Eastbrook. He's one of our stars. We call him 'Ask,' for Almost Stephen King. He's almost published, has a Manhattan agent. We walk together, when he's preoccupied with a pain in his chest. It doesn't have a source he can explain, not like books can give him. He was a violin prodigy, but stopped at the age of five. Drop in. I can introduce you."

"He's entitled to his privacy," I said.

"He's five-four, almost. We almost had an affair. Awkward sex kinship. Another Ask. God, once in a while I'm almost good. A bit of advice if you meet him, don't bring up Hemingway. He'll call you a derogatory name, a phrase from the French gutter. The bright side: you won't understand what it means."

"I know a little French slang," I said.

"Okay: 'You should be licking the toes of a parasitic centi-pede.' How would you render that in Marseilles?"

"I see what you mean."

"I went to Greece, an Aesop's Fables kick, follow the trail of a great teacher. On the cruise I came up with a pain in my chest."

"Speaking of trails, who uses these grounds up there at the retreat…other than your group?"

"An historical society meets at the upper parking lot. It was more than that at one time. I grew up hearing 'retreat' used as a visual reference. It was at a fork in the road to the hiking area over around China Camp State Park. Other than that the address was a women's sanatorium in my great-grandmother's era, officially the Palisades Rest Home. Otherwise, for my parents, it was the Lazy Ladies Looney Bin—inmates of means and social position."

"They were generally understood as having plenty?" I said.

"Enough to exist as sufferers from merely transcendental concerns. When my father was a kid, the asylum was converted to a military hospital. That was during the war. That was World War Two. The area remained under the control of the Defense Department up through the Korean War, and was sold off to private developers after that. It was quite a while later that it was fixed up as the Santa Annalee Retreat."

"It's great for escape," I said.

"It's still where the wilderness starts. Too many years ago we rode mountain bikes on the foot trails. The developments built up to it from the west. The inmates these days come and go in all kinds of cars, nothing you'd call expensive, but it still must cost plenty living there. The grounds are under constant care."

Goodbye was on the tip of my tongue. I got more than I expected from one phone call. I had a look in the ledger. An unnamed property, designated as the Santa Annalee Retreat, appeared in a 1967 entry, with a mention of a transaction, refer-enced as a sale to a partnership of Walter Coombs and Martin Bebe, for March 1, 1955. Right below came a list of four women's names, presumably occupants. These gals would be old ladies getting Social Security checks. One of them was the name of a lady on her last legs in Santa Barbara.

I looked up Myles George in the ledger. I could bet the farm on finding him. Born in 1981 as Paul Gifford to Angelica Gifford. No dagger indicated he participated in a killing. He was a writer. They get it in other ways.

———

I WAS in the library picking at the crumbs of a breakfast cake, cleaning up the look of an overworked table. I opened the coffee-table edition of Ward Flowers's illustrations and removed the slip of paper I'd used to bookmark *Handshake*—the drawing where Nora had recalled the link to Hamilton. I riffled the remaining pages from there on, pages I hadn't looked at carefully. On the last page was *Bicycle*. A cyclist has dismounted. The back of her tights are missing. Locked out of inspiration, and stalemated by temperament, Flowers had fallen into the fetishist's logic for elaboration. On the previous page was a fantasy Transylvanian castle, lost for a thousand years, reemerging from the clouds in the form of a monster cake. I remembered. This is where I first saw it. I shut the Flowers book and had a moment with what it was that stuck to me, or stuck me to the chair.

Chapter 27

IN THE MORNING I drove myself to Phillipsville. Bud recognized me: "Onion slices on white, lettuce, tomato, light mustard. Where's your fellow?"

"Workaholic. Gets his face in the computer…six hours later, it's been two minutes. Say, I've come across a fantastic cake. Have you ever seen a monster like this?"

I pulled a picture of a cake from an envelope. Bud reached a pair of glasses out of a shirt pocket. He didn't have to lean into it. "Ms. Apple Pie a la Mode." He tossed a word over his shoulder, "Mary. Remember this?"

"Had a sweet tooth a mile wide," Mary said. "She made them cakes. Was by here…a year back. What did she say, Bud?" She stopped herself. A thought rolled slowly over her face. "You had some birthdays in those days."

"Hadn't seen her for a time," Bud said. "Now and then. Had to bring that baby over in a pickup. Have a picture somewhere. All them kids had smarts. Talent to burn."

"Where'd you come by this picture?" Mary asked, drying her suspicious hands on an apron.

"In an art book," I said. The jig was up. "It's a long story. I should start with I'm not Hannah."

"We thought so. Any reason for pulling our leg?"

"Can I blame the man who was with me?"

"If it's true. If not, why bother?"

"Fair enough," I said. "I'm not positive, but I'm almost positive…the man you call 'Two of Everything' was trying to get a conversation going with me on a long drive. If you'd recognized me, which you did, then I'd measured up to his standards for his private joke. Earlier that day, we'd visited a married colleague. He was introducing marriage as a topic we could get into. He wanted to settle down."

I shrugged. I was finished…for a minute.

Bud said, "Gather he'd talked his way outta his marriage."

"All cats are black in the dark," said Mary. "What I told Bud. Bad way to talk to a woman."

I switched subjects. "I appreciate your patience. I wanted to ask another question. Did any of the kids who came over here with Hannah, or by themselves, behave in some way that made you suspicious? You know, like me and Lane made you suspicious, but you could slough it off. No big deal. It wouldn't be a big deal. It would be something you remembered."

"You with the police?" Mary asked.

"No. A friend was murdered. One of them," I pointed, "from up there in the hills killed her."

"That's some accusation," Bud said.

"Some of them murdered a man because they could," I said. "They terrified Hannah."

I opened the playbill, *Expecting Bonnie Jingles*. I pointed out the photo of the author. I put my finger under the face in the center. "He's older now."

Mary looked past Bud's shoulder and stepped back. Bud said, "He didn't eat, not here."

"Like we was servin' poison," Mary said. "He kill someone?"

"He's a writer," I said. "I doubt it. They have other customs."

"Kids loved Hannah. Hannah loved them. You got yourself way off somewhere. They was good kids."

"They played their roles. They fit in. You put anyone through the lives they had, it's the hardest thing separating who needs a bit of counseling from the others, the kids who have given out. They bore into you, in every which way. Hannah was sick. She knew it. She gave her kid away. Watched the girl grow up from a car."

I don't know what Bud and Mary were hearing from me. They were too sharp for my profiles in psychosis. You feed people, you laugh with people, you shrug off quiet people, you ignore impolite people. Their world spun right. I wasn't here to put a wobble in it.

"I have a request," I said. "You have chocolate ice cream. You have wheat rolls. I want a scoop of chocolate on a wheat roll in one of your sundae cups…if I may, please."

"Funny she said that. Isn't that right, Bud?

"She is funny. Won't forget her. Chocolate on wheat in a sundae cup."

Chapter 28

I'D STOPPED FOR A STRETCH on the drive home when I called Celia to acknowledge the disappearing act I'd pulled at the Lamonds'. The call reached her on a trail behind her little shack on the Santa Annalee estate. It started us on the back-and-forth to another get-together.

"You didn't miss anything at the Lamonds'," she said. "All that attention we give them, and two hours of artsy-fartsy antics is the so-called performance we get? You can buy quality furniture, quality just about anything, a quality moon shot; but a decent play that will hold your interest, forget it."

"I've recovered," I said.

"I'm sorry for putting you in a position that left you no option but to flee. I would love to atone."

Sensing the hook had gone in, she gave the line a tug. "In case you haven't noticed, I've been trying to interest you."

"We agreed you want the cane. Is that still it?"

"What else could we possibly be talking about? My wiggles aren't obvious?" Her voice suggested the most boring class anybody ever caught up on their sleep in.

"Your wiggles are vague, I'm saying."

"I'm suggesting we strike a balance within your no-sex rule. I suggest we drop the play-acting. Let's get real. You would be my lit instructor. We'd be meeting off-hours in a secluded château exploring a passage in a text. You'd attach a device. The operating control would be on the desk. When I got something wrong, then you'd…"

"Go to the juice." I got it, the perfect English teacher. Get something real going.

"I have a favorite. It's Japanese. There's an older American one with a different feel. It's not sex. We're within your rules. And we have some fun." Her voice mingled secret hideaways and happiness and laughter. So much for the myth of women's masochism.

"We might be friends one of these days."

"How about an hour or two first on the prepositional diphthong?" I said. These things take time is what I meant.

————

I DROPPED off 101 onto a frontage road that settled into a five-minute uphill that saved the best for last, a long sweeping arc of California sea-level forest that came out at a short run of picket fencing. This stretch ran along the upper boundary of a garden that, so the brochure claimed, perfectly recreated the Quinta das Lágrimas. I pulled off the road onto cleared ground, backstopped by logs, and locked up. A legend of a Galician noblewoman murdered in 1355 was on a plaque at the edge of the garden. The Villa of Tears locates in America the national love story of Portugal. A lush bamboo grove threw a magnificent green arch over two stone columns. A chain supported a redwood plank with fancy script announcing the Santa Annalee Retreat.

Across from the parking lot an isolated road went up to an isolated residence with a designed frontier appearance. Its shingle siding had seen some weather, as it was supposed to look in this area, contrived on the drawing boards of travel agents, the wood aged under sunlamps in the Philippines. It was the right address.

A bikeway went upward on the right to a slight crest. I took a stone walk to a door with a knocker in the middle of a combination of Chinese characters. A yellow porch light was on.

A husky "Come in" welcomed me from behind the door.

The entrance was a narrow alcove that led into a room that had been designed for exactly what a spare elegance should look like. A few items strung together on a theme and not one item more. Two overhead lamps dropped on chains to spherical arrangements of thin iron bars, sort of a Ptolemaic universe, the earth at the center. A cocoa leather three-cushion sofa and chair had a collector's look of salvaged sofas out of the Bohemian Grove of a hundred years back.

When I turned around, I saw what I hadn't noticed coming in: a naked body in a red G-string.

A beverage server in a corner was the place to head for. An oak coffee table was a repository of initials, some fancy, some plain, some this way, some that, prominently carved into the surface and lacquered over for permanence. Dates showed that many of the signatories were dead. Their owners had put them in one or so at a time over many years, as a long signing ceremony from when California had became a state: September 9, 1850.

The mirror above the fireplace made a large woman's head look enormous. The piece had been carved from a single chunk of driftwood. The head was balanced on a platform held up on three narrow iron pillars. An historical map of settlements in the Central Valley was on a wall with a gold rush scene, men sloshing water over silt in pans. The face of the bust allowed me the opportunity to get a compliment on record.

"The Chinese goddess Guon Yin," I said. "You come up here when you're in need of compassion?"

I picked a cane up from the table and tapped the tip to the top of the head. "She's granted mercy to your prayers?"

"So far." She spun a bottle of wine to show off a label. She saluted, "To my panacea."

I held a palm up, no thanks.

"You're a loner," she said clinically. "To what should I have paid tribute, the algae?"

Her fingers had been wandering along the underside of her thong. She'd been giving her crotch a standing ovation. I hadn't laid a serious eye on the G-string. A seriousness had wrinkled my face. I was working on an introduction to a subject that was already solidly set in conviction.

"How did you get possession of this house?" I said. "I thought the units were leased short term."

Her face took on all the nonchalance in the world. She poured a glass on a cork coaster with a blue cloth napkin. "Technically, I'm not part of the retreat. The retreat was carved from a larger unit of property belonging to someone else. I inherited. When it was sold, the land up here didn't generate income. This house is on that larger original unit. It's not complicated until I have to describe the history."

"You own the house?"

She took her time raising her glass to her lips. She nodded in agreement as she swallowed. "You're thinking of buying up here?"

"This was government land during the Second World War."

"Is that a question?" she said.

"You have an appreciation of California history. I guess it is."

"Could you get to your question? You're worried about radioactive soil?"

"Isn't everyone? Who wants to glow in the dark?"

She took two steps to the window with the southern exposure. The light caught a hip sideways, brightest where the softest and roundest section of the curve touched the top of the thigh. She touched her hands, wrist to wrist, bondage style, over her head and turned her head to catch my look, a long, hard turn past her arm with one eye. Enough said.

"Glowing at any time has its appeal," she said. "I would think."

I pressed the ends of the cane down and in. The half-circle of the shaft brought out my best smile.

"You're hard to get to know," she said. She pushed her bottom backwards, a highly simplified invitation. It doesn't take no for an answer.

I tucked the cane under my arm and smoothed the few inches of her bottom where three separated tracks still had a faint dark tint.

"You keep your bruises," I said.

"In the bedroom closet," she said, "you can add some more. It's set up for anything."

"Anything? Must be a big closet."

"If you can't find what you want, I'll be shocked."

"You and me," I whispered. "Don't tell me about the equipment. I want to know why me? If the answer comes out so I can live with it, I'll work you over, whatever you want. I'll try, anyway. But don't tell me you're into getting your ass whacked."

Her nakedness suddenly had that chill of unwanted exposure. Her face saw that she didn't have anything to show off, nothing that caught my interest. She lowered her arm and turned to smack me a roundhouse with some authority.

Tactfully, I backed off, so I wouldn't have to smack her back. I put the cane on the table and poured myself a few inches.

"It's easy to get my vote," I said, "but I don't make friends. If it happens, it just happens. If it would have happened with us, it would have happened by now."

Except for the double exposure, the smile was fine. Underneath, the face was shifting a gear out of a bold little murder into a show of minor stress and annoyance. It was a performance worth the visit, a fury transforming itself into petty exasperation, hiding in a dirty look.

It was the first time with her that I felt like myself. I'd pathologized a stunning range of social conventions. It kept my true self at a safe separation. I could be manipulated, but I could watch anybody figuring that out.

"I've been trying too hard," she said. An awkwardness in the phrasing made it obvious she hadn't landed the right expression. The rage was not responding to the art of cool. It would take another minute to polish up the smile. I gave her a minute.

"I have a guess what you're trying to say," I said, "and I don't like it."

"You want to know what I don't like?"

"Save it for now." I had a sip, and then drained the glass.

"Suppose I gave you the name of a man who died some seven years back. I wonder if you've heard of him, a Walter Coombs?"

Just like that, her face stopped and became an utterly revealing stare. And she became attractive, as a woman hiding a detached past draws attention to some mystery. Her upper lip caught in her teeth. Her eyes might have dried out. For the longest time she couldn't blink.

The pause that conceptualizes. I'd hit a dangerous note.

"I'm going to assume you did know him," I said. "In bed tonight, you were going to suggest, oh so theoretically, that I didn't have to bother with some scumbags down at Raspberry, Incorporated. You could help me get them out of my hair. It's how Walter Coombs would have helped me out. Disappear one or two of them, all three, if necessary, and that little problem is out of my way. I'm back on the Drum estate again. And who can say, with a clear field ahead of me, how many years my contract gets renewed?"

She was sipping and thinking and moving a foot, and not moving, but the thinking was going somewhere.

"I've met a few Walters, but none that would, as you said, 'disappear' three billionaires, who, in point of fact, are substantial contributors to my campaigns."

"There was just the one Walter," I said, "and he's dead. You and somebody else took over his outfit. The somebody else wasn't Michael Sand, but Sand was somebody Walter Coombs relied on. Sand could make a mansion in Sausalito, or a dump in Hicksville, look like it was owned by the man on the moon—a valuable talent, and I'm guessing you used it when it suited the occasion. Things were going well until Sand decided he'd had his fill of whatever had kept him getting up in the morning.

"Coombs was dead, and then Sand was dead, and I was Hannah's trustee, and God knows what the hell I was up to. You're the decider now. And Faith was terrified. A body had been out there in a shed going on eight years, right outside her kitchen window. How many nights did a bag of bones crawl out of the ground dragging his chains into her sleep? When I called her the Friday I heard about the trust, she was in a horror movie and the doors were locked. She couldn't dump the whole miserable racket in my lap fast enough. She hit on the abandoned daughter angle to get me to meet her the next day. A Friday meeting was for some reason inconvenient. She had someone to see that night."

"I can see what attracts me. What an imagination!"

"Here's the half with my sense of humor. You disappeared Faith Nichols. It had to be fast, but loose ends take time. They kept you wondering. Hannah had a nickel-and-dime estate on paper. Sand saw to that. As far as California cares, Hannah is dead. She can come back, or stay dead. California gets the same out of it either way. That's that, then. The trouble is you had to get rid of Faith, and fast. A suddenly nervous sex worker is talking to me and to some Barnard graduate looking for a job. Where does she start cleaning out her conscience? She goes to the cops? Not impossible. Some of the people Hannah used in her kidnapping business were in Coombs's crowd, so they're up to their necks in how the man died. That drags you in.

"You have the Coombs crowd on your plate now. So you met Faith the night before you killed her and found out what she'd spilled. Once Faith was gone, there were the loose ends—me."

"And here we are, sharing a Joseph Phelps Insignia, and I'm trying to get you into bed to boot. I have better ways of throwing two hundred and fifty better-spent bucks out the window."

"You could shoot me, but it's not the style you inherited from Coombs."

"Don't go simple on me. I wouldn't shoot you?" The look she gave the tree outside the window showed all the intentions of a sincere thought.

"Let's begin with a name of someone you can trust completely, say an art lady named Bessel, someone with deep roots in the Coombs cult. First, of course, you had to get to me, which is when you noticed I'm hard to get to. You inquired, and found a detective on her way up. A friend of mine, Rene Forrest, was pleased to volunteer as the go-between. So you cooked up this caning routine. In time we're buddies, and here I am."

"It's the oddest thing," she said. "Bram Stoker just crossed my mind. I was always puzzled where Bram came up with that idea that the vampire had to be invited into the house rather than let himself in quietly for a pint of blood. You might enlighten me. Why, pray tell, don't I take my pint?"

"Wrong book you've been worried about. Consult your Old Testament. Why does Lucifer go to God and tell him to move over? He wants his half. Half of what? There's a void upon the earth. Half of a void? No. He's thinking ahead, working on an investment opportunity. God's about to populate the world. They'll go forth and multiply. Just think of all those souls. Will they all be good do-bees? Lucifer throws the dice. But it's a sure thing. He knows better. He'll get his share. He'll have an empire."

She took her G-string to the sofa and crossed her legs. That closed off the warmth of her loins. She put a hand on a cushion and braced the arm to keep from falling on her hand. "You're out of your mind." It was something to say while she kept an eye on me, not yet quite sure where all this was going. It might fall off a cliff, like "just kidding."

"Lucifer had his minions," I said. "Here's this dumb dropout domme, Elizabeth, in her little domme-shop at the English Department. Faith knew too much. She could disappear. She'd been invisible for years anyway. The perfect solution appears on a silver platter. Elizabeth is there for the suicide. No body. The mystery drifts forever, because you killed her after she got gas and groceries at the convenience store in Albion.

"My guess? When the two of you arrived at the gate to the beach house, Najda was waiting in your car. You moved Faith into your car. Najda went to the house, unloaded the groceries, and put a single line of footsteps to the shore."

"And makes you a witness to a possible murderer? I thought you were giving me more credit? Lucifer? Remember?"

"Let's leave Lucifer aside. That's not where you put a foot

wrong. Faith didn't know when to expect me. It's one of those loose ends like the latchkey in the murder mystery. It was nothing to think about. Faith hadn't said when I'd arrive and didn't care and, very possibly, hadn't mentioned the painting she was bringing with her. Najda barely had time to get the groceries out of the trunk, and I was hot on her heels. She had to think. Is it better that I see some figure hot-footing an escape from the house, or that I run into a friendly mermaid wandering into me from up the coast?

"Faith is dead, and if I don't step in, some tenants are wondering where the rent checks should go. The investigation of a suicide becomes interesting—the follow-the-money routine, such as who owns the house. From what Faith said, it would be hard to track that to Sand and Coombs, plus ownership that can't be tracked is pretty common these days, so I've heard. So if I pick up the slack and do the trustee thing, life goes on as before, and a suicide is the focus. And you know how that ends. I'm your girl."

"Aha. I was curious to see what you were going to do with those minions," she said.

"You needed me for the suicide. I was the closer. Clean things up. And the painting. Faith brought it with her to give to me. Najda hauled it out of Faith's car, put it against the front wheel, an eyesore of a thrift-store nothing. Wouldn't buy it for the frame. If she saw the signature at the bottom, what did that mean? And the eighteen hundred taped to the back? Najda never noticed."

Celia stayed cool, but the undisciplined expression meant she didn't know about the money, a loose end, and where was that taking me?

"Kill you or use you. I like your mind." She reached the cane and shook her head. "Twenty-nine ninety-five for this thing. How else would it have worked? How else would you have been played to get you here?"

"You didn't have to. I would have shown up anyway." I pointed at the bottle. "Let's have a toast to a preposterous cake."

"The latchkey?" she asked.

"To the whole preposterous scheme Walter Coombs dreamed up a lifetime ago."

No politician tolerates an indictment like I'd been dishing out with a quiet conscience. She ran a tongue over her lower lip and stuck it in a cheek. It poked a smile that had waited patiently for an excuse to laugh. She was still betting she would get that laugh. I hadn't turned over my last card.

"I have Coombs's ledger," I said, "and his war diary. The ledger records names and events of some pith and moment."

The cheek puffed out again.

"You're name's in it, your birthday, your mother's married name, and the name she used before she was married, the name you took your first steps with."

"Why would I care who writes my name in a ledger?"

"For one thing, it's not the name you've since used to dazzle the electorate. For another, there are two men in the ledger that Coombs associated intimately with your name. We'll take Leonard Cochran first. There's a dagger after his name, and a date in nineteen ninety-five. It means that Coombs knew he was dead, which is not what the situation was when Coombs dated the death, because as much as a month later Cochran was still being seen at his country club. That comes from eyewitnesses quoted in an article in the *Chronicle*. The article became news of interest after Cochran had gone on a vacation to Yellowstone with his daughter. Neither of them were seen again. Cochran had a business. He had partners. He had obligations. Naturally, people were looking for him. But he didn't have a daughter. Odd, then, that a waitress in a restaurant remembers a man telling her that the blond girl with him was his daughter, and she called him Dad. The waitress is sure that Cochran and his daughter were very happy. They were going on a cruise to South America. A month later it could not be verified that they got on any boat anywhere. Everyone was free to draw their own conclusions.

"Cochran first appears in the ledger with the conjunction of the Greek letters alpha and omega, the beginning and end. That was before he got the dagger. Coombs trusted you to see to it that Cochran and his daughter disappeared. You were the daughter. It was a long time ago. Nobody could positively identify you. But you know there's going to be evidence to find once people know where to look in that investigation. They know what they're not looking for this time."

She moved to another cushion. I didn't see a reason to move.

"Then there's a man named White," I said. "Same Greek letters, same dagger in the ledger. Now that we're getting to know each other, Ms. Taylor, for the sake of closure, how about telling me where Cochran and White are buried? Coombs skipped that part."

"I seem to be overexposed," she said. The voice was calm. Her eyes wandered through calculations, as if there might be an offer getting cooked up in there, nothing I could trust, and she knew it, and she was going on to the next thing after money that might interest me. She stared. It was the stare at what Ward Flowers must have stared at when he was told his rifle had been used in a murder.

"I suppose this ledger is in a safe place?" she said. She coughed in a fist, unwillingly it seemed. It was a dumb question but not necessarily a dumb way to ask a dumb question. Any answer would get her a clue.

"Why'd he do it?" I asked.

"I could tell you, and you wouldn't try to understand." She was suddenly tired of delivering a performance. "What the hell do you care about White? And by the way, what is it…this playing me along?"

I was feeling entitled now to be very calm about this. "You were the movie star with White, the brunette in the golf outfit with him at the Masters at Monterey. You were about to tour New Zealand and reappear at the West Side Tennis Club in Forest Hills in September. After Monterey you dropped off the map."

She got bigger, like a cat does it. A big stretch.

I didn't like the feel of what I was doing to her, nor what I was going to do to her. We were on the same page there. She could see she wouldn't like it. It happened slowly. Her fingers had wandered to her thigh and scratched, and kept scratching into the slot on the other side of the cushion. There was a lot of scratching where there didn't need to be any. Then it was fast. The phone was at her ear: "Get in here!"

The front door opened. The man who shut the door quietly behind himself was man enough to handle me. Celia's eyes were on me like a laser—this is your target. He walked deliberately, in case he had to take an inconvenient step to one side to scoop me off my feet. I might have had ideas of slipping around him. I had no such ideas. The idea I had was formed a long time ago. The windows at my back had been rolled open. Somebody with skills could launch themselves through the screen, land on their hands, tuck and roll, finish upright in a running position, and make a clean getaway. A great stunt in a movie.

I got a ring of keys in my left hand, and held the hand up to show him I meant business. That did all the convincing it was going to do. I turned to the window and got a step going in a run. There were much faster steps behind me, and then two arms closed around my waist. We crashed to the floor. The keys slid out of reach. The struggle to get them was just what I could manage with one arm. I pushed my left hand out. His left hand went farther. His right hand had a grip on my shirt: this far and no farther for me. He stretched out hard, inching a hand to the loop, and reeled the keys in. It was a bit too casual. He turned a smile at my face for a kiss to build a dream on. I had rotated my body counterclockwise. That freed my right hand. The first finger on that hand plunged into his right eye at somewhat of an angle. I felt the fingernail break as it hit against something hard.

The finger had gone in as far as it needed to go. He was no longer touching me. I jumped up and embraced Guon Yin in a bear hug. She wasn't in any way, shape, or form a gal you'd call light as a feather, but she and I took the short walk to a point where I dropped her—and not just dropped her. I let my weight fall with hers onto his hands. The hands were over his face. When I backed away from the crash, he was done. The motion in him was the dying momentum of things that an instant earlier had been moving casually in a body.

A second to catch my breath followed a second to notice that Celia had decided she ought to make another phone call. I got to her fast and hit her arm. "Put the phone away."

The impact on the arm could have sailed her hand off with the phone into the wall, but the impact drew a scream. I didn't punch her—not yet. I pointed at the other side of the coffee table, at how this might all end.

"Where's Edith?"

"Oh, God."

It was her first lie. She was doubled up behind her knees. Her eyes were wet, but the cheeks still dry. I punched her knee and questioned how many lies this approach would elicit. I pulled her up and kicked her legs out from under her. Her upper body plunked onto hard flooring. I knew I couldn't pick Guon Yin up off the floor. But I guessed I'd made a believer out of Celia. I got my arms around Guon Yin's head. I did one nice grunt…then the low shriek from the depths…and sobs. At the moment she was a believer. I let go of Guon Yin.

Slightly interrupting a sob, she got up on an elbow and looked at the quiet man next to her. This dead guy had meant something to her. "We should get help."

"His Hollywood days are over, Celia."

"Call an ambulance!"

"Even in the movies they expect them to breathe," I said. "Go ahead, run some tests yourself."

"He's dead!"

"He grabbed me. About what I would have looked like, is what I was thinking."

She turned on her side, and balled her knees up. "You stupid shit."

I went over to a sink next to the drinks table and washed my hands. I went to the front window and looked out. It had stayed the same out there during my first killing. The scene was as I saw it would be, and would stay as it was, if I ended up lucky. I put my phone flat on a palm and went into the directory.

Her body unrolled fast. "What are you doing?"

"Calling the police," I said. "You have the local number?"

She was up like a shot. Her hand went behind the cushion again. The next instant a ladies' automatic was in her hand. "Put the phone down!"

I dropped my arm. The gun went back and forth. It repeated that I put the phone down. I put the phone on the windowsill.

She looked at the mess on the floor. "You stupid shit." This time it could have meant him or me.

She drew her hand across her eyes. They went ahead and refilled themselves, and streams ran down both cheeks and dropped to the floor. I felt like I ought to go, just shut up and go. Then again, there was my side for the record. Then again, there was the gun in her hand when she said, "Get on the floor. On your stomach."

Chapter 29

MY RIGHT CHEEK WAS flat on the floor, but one eye had a narrow angle on the front door, and I caught sight of hair the tint of which was that special bleached blond you get around high noon at the ocean when the light collects from the rows of waves breaking on the shore. I'd seen that head of hair diving off a rock. I'd seen the tits, too. Drying off, her tits were hard young points gazing at the sky. They had no bounce in them, but they had a shimmer and an ulterior motive. They were a handy distraction—from whatever it had been I wasn't supposed to notice. Persistently afterwards, I'd linked her to Faith and the crazy mystery forever inhabiting that house.

She took three or four steps inside from where I'd first heard voices through an open door. I was dressed as I'd been the day we'd first met, when she'd said that I'd confused her, that she wanted a chance to get me right. This instant, she stopped and looked at me with the kind of satisfaction that comes a few times in a life. I was at her feet. With no attempt at expression, her eyes were menacing, and I recalled that remnant of weird danger in her presence at the beach, as if in a memory from an instant before a car crash.

Another woman, older and more interested to see what was what with two people on the floor, pushed past Najda and leaned her shoulder for support against a wall, and after a minute said,

"He looks dead. Shouldn't it be the other way around? Shouldn't she be dead?"

"It was an accident," Celia said.

That Celia would dismiss her with such an answer was the peculiarity that settled the pecking order of this bunch.

It was a death in a locked room, with a naked woman, a cane, and a woman prostrate on the floor, a sex/murder scene never before described, and not for its appearance as an event beyond description. It was beyond nonsense, a scene you couldn't understand regardless of any skill in assembling best guesses from a forensic examination.

An accident it wasn't. But what was it? This guy had crawled under a lump of wood, knocked it off its pedestal onto his head, and crawled away, and the head crawled with him?

The woman decided that was not what it was. "You shot him." She pushed her shoulder off the wall. As an unbelievable statement, this took high honors. "What on earth were the three of you playing at?"

She stepped over my arm and went to the body beyond my feet. The circumstances stared her in the face, circumstances that couldn't have happened.

"That fell on his head?" the woman asked. "God, he's a mess. This is some slick innovation in a caning." Dead people just didn't upset her.

"Why is she on the floor?" she asked.

Something heavy was put on the table. The gun was not in Celia's hand? I wouldn't get many chances to bolt for the door, wildly swinging at anyone in the way. So far the standing woman didn't know what the gun was for.

Celia covered that. "She's on the floor until I decide what to do with her. I'm getting dressed. Keep the gun on her. You see what happened to him. He didn't think he needed a gun."

Celia passed behind me out of my sight. From the other room a vicious thud to the wall was exhibit A. Celia was pissed as hell.

Najda said, "What happens to her?" The older woman didn't

answer, and didn't seem to think it was up to her to have a say in it just yet. Unless I challenged her.

A dash for the door would have been a royal performance. The comment from her that I was the one who should be dead was enough to cut off the thought that I had any chance of success. If I so much as shifted a hand, I'd get a foot on my neck. The gun would make it stick. Najda had killed Faith, or Faith was killed on her watch. There was that minute chance in the weight of a decision: I'd get up, start walking, dare anybody to kill me, and pray Najda complicated the older woman's predicament. That option would last until Celia came back.

Soft-soled shoes entered the room. Celia poured a glass and addressed the troubles. "We have to move him."

The older woman agreed. "Yes, we should make him more comfortable."

"He has to be moved, I meant to say."

"You have a wheelbarrow?"

"There's three of us."

"Roll him in a carpet?"

Celia put a stamp on the plan: "There's one in the bedroom."

The woman with the gun decided she was owed something. I couldn't fit an explanation, any more than the dead man. The look she gave Celia was the last of her tolerance. A second dead body on the floor wouldn't fill in the smallest hole in the puzzle.

She waved her gun. Her annoyance was at a simmer.

A cushion huffed as Celia fell into a back cushion. "She knows everything."

"You said we knew that before she came up here."

"We suspected that," Celia snapped. "Something tipped her off to a ledger Walter had been keeping."

"What ledger?"

"A ledger, all right? A diary, a daybook. You record your thoughts in it. You record whatever you feel like recording. Christ! Call it whatever. Am I clear?"

"I'm not intellectually paralyzed. I appreciate knowing how he became dead, okay?"

"Fine. There's a ledger somewhere. Your name's in it. My name's in it. Our connection to everyone we ever killed is in it. What, where, when, why, who, is in it. It's everything that's ever happened. Happy?"

I hadn't moved yet, but I was committed to blasting off before Celia got possession of the gun. Before that I might only take a bullet in the shoulder. The woman had the floor, not moving, as if in a farewell at the side of a grave. It came to her.

"She'll go to the cops with the ledger."

"That's what she led me to believe," Celia said. "I expected trouble, but maybe not. Maybe she couldn't figure out what happened to Faith. It didn't occur to me that she knew anything significant. She was merely where she shouldn't be. And she might be useful. I could use someone in her position. People open up to her. They trust her. There was no reason to decide one way or the other. I invited her here. You try to budge her butt out of the four walls of her business. I took it on the ass to get her here. This seemed to me the place for step two."

There was a shifting of position on the cushion. Celia was drinking and tinkering an explanation into an explanation-confession.

"It's my fault. I could have handled things with a gun. I didn't expect a confrontation, but I wanted someone outside in case. It became clear slowly, but then all of a sudden, that she marched to her own drummer. She wanted me to confess. I couldn't believe it. Why put up with her after that? I called him in. I shouldn't have. He didn't understand. She ran for the window. He tackled her."

"He would not…" When the groan subsided, she finished the sentence, "…tackle her!"

"You weren't here. He tackled her. You could ask her. He thought she was a threat to me. I thought so. I mean, why call him in otherwise? She thought he was a threat. They were both right. It escalated. He had his arms around her. They fell. He fell on her. She had keys ready to scratch his face. He had that covered. It looked like it was all she had to protect herself with.

The keys were knocked out of her hand when she hit the floor. He held her down while he stretched an arm to reach them. She stuck a finger in his eye."

"The scream," Najda said. "That was what we heard. We thought it was from up the hill. Someone had been hurt. We weren't sure where."

"She grabbed the bust and dropped it on him."

The older woman doubted the statement. "She picked up that?"

"That's what I said."

The woman went limp trying to make the sight of me launching a huge chunk of lumber work for her. The clothes identified a man without a recognizable facial feature. She looked as if at where a face had been. She pulled the top of her sweater over her mouth.

"You could see what she was doing," she said to Celia. "You should have shot her."

Celia spoke deliberately, and fed up. "Yes, knowing what I know now. It went too fast. I knew I had to get rid of her, but I never intended to shoot her here. When he came in, I assumed he could get her under control. If you can't see…forget it."

"The gun was in your hand at the time?"

"I'm telling you what I did at the time."

"He wouldn't have hurt her."

"Are we taking sides?" Celia asked. "You're freaking out. We all lost a friend. Have a drink with me and tell me how we get the journal."

"She didn't bring it with her?"

"Her car keys are over there. If it's in her car, it'll be the one good thing that's happened today."

Celia fetched my keys and walked them over to Najda. "Cross your fingers. It will save us a lot of trouble. It's the Mazda in the lot across from the gate."

Najda left. Celia shook her head. "It's a mess. We'll have to call Jonah and Seth. They can handle it."

"There's no other way?"

"I thought of that…before. There might have been. I'm open. You want to ask her where the ledger is?"

"She made copies. She'll say anything."

"Getting the whole bag of beans out of her, it'll be tricky to know for sure. I'll have to work with them. We've done it before. What she's going to go through, it works. Eventually. Always has. We'll keep her alive till we verify what she says."

They'd started in on me. A bit of this chatter should be plenty to get me to understand how to make it easy on myself.

"May have to poke an eye out to get there," Celia said. "You don't have to watch."

"I don't like it." The humane one.

"You want to ask her to join our group?" Celia said.

The older woman snarled at me, "You smashed his head." She dialed and put the phone to her ear. While she waited, she asked, "How did you get the journal?" The question didn't work. She fixed it. "He would have let you go." She instantly saw she had another bogus assertion to ignore. A voice said hello. She knew the voice. She gave the phone to Celia.

"Is Seth with you?" Celia said. "Tell him to stay there. We're coming up. Soon. We'll be leaving soon. Yeah, we have a problem. It's important. I want you and Seth to handle it. Not now. Tell you when we get there."

My phone was in my back pocket. It was turned off, so it wouldn't ring, but when Celia handed the phone off to the other woman, it was something to think about. Its outline was visible. Celia went into the other room. A short, barely seen move at my feet put her right shoe to my right side. My face hadn't moved. The sweat under my cheek was greasy. Terror fought with the impulse to jump up and get it over with. I felt a hand slip into a back pocket. I heard a pair of scissors in the process of getting the pocket cut open.

I heard a plop of water. My phone went into the pitcher.

"We'll need a second rug for her."

"We'll tie her up. I'll get the cords. We'll wait for Najda. Where is Najda? She should be back."

The older woman leaned her head to the window. "She's coming. No journal. Edith is with her."

———

FOOTSTEPS running across gravel sounded through the open window at the back. Victim's intuition—this wasn't a rescue. Edith Barlow ran into the room and saw two bodies. She was wiping her eyes.

"She killed Webster," Celia said, in case there was a question there.

Edith went to the body. I suppose she saw everything Najda had told her she'd see. I turned my face to watch her. She knelt at Webster's waist and tugged pointlessly at the fabric around his knees. Little by little she let go of a motion that might disturb him. She bent forward and crossed herself, and transferred the hand that had crossed her heart and forehead and pressed it flat on his chest, something he should take with him. She kissed him there, and said, "I'll bury him." The voice was cool and sure and full of preoccupations of her own that didn't need to concern any of us, but did.

"Where?" Celia asked.

Edith pushed up to her knees and curled her arms around her chest, and didn't move. "Above the turn at Lonnigan's Rock. We used to sit there in the evening."

"You and Sofia, then. Kylie, you help."

So the older woman was Kylie. She was no longer any image Ward Flowers had ever found fit to eroticize her with. Drugs and drink had dropped her face. Her hair was on its way to a dirty white. The flame of life was torched, a disguise that no collection of circulars advertising her wanted, dead or alive, would penetrate.

"He has family," Kylie said.

"They're in Georgia," Edith said. "They don't get together."

That answered that. I killed Webster.

"We'll take the van," Kylie said. "I'll drive. We'll put him in the back. That reminds me, the van is low on gas. We can fill it at the station at the freeway."

"We need to get her car out of here," Celia said.

"I have the keys," Najda said. "I can drive her car."

"What do we do with her?" Edith spoke to the group.

"We don't need a vote," Celia said. "For now, she has to be tied up."

"She has some handcuffs in her glove compartment," Najda said. "Just a minute."

Najda stood over me when she came back. She sat on my back. Her hand went around my right wrist and pulled, but the arm wouldn't move. The next thing of consequence took a bit of time, but it got done. My legs were clamped between two thighs. Celia had come up from behind. She camped on my knees. Kylie grabbed my wrist two-handed and twisted. My wrist was cuffed, and the other wrist was persuaded to allow itself to be cuffed to it.

"We'll put this pair on her ankles in the car," Najda said.

"Tie her to the car seat," Celia said.

"The seat belt should be enough," Edith said.

"Just don't get stopped. Where's Sofia?"

Edith said, "God, I've got to tell Sofia."

The carpet came out of an adjoining room. They slid it past my nose. It was a fine-weave carpet, big enough, and a lot to lift on its own. Najda and Kylie had rolled it up and dragged it, both of them coming into view butt first, gripping from the front. When Webster was rolled up there was an appreciation of what it would take to lift the bundle. They gamed the steps. The wheelbarrow plan was considered and discarded. The four of them bent the bundle around the corner and out the door. After the bend, as far as I could hear, it was just chatter.

They came back for me. Najda and Kylie had the detail. They each grabbed an upper arm at the shoulder and got me to my knees with little effort. I refused to get to my feet and said so, and said it so they knew they had to decide that the next ten minutes wouldn't be pretty. Najda went outside. I shouldn't get silly about this. She brought a rope back. Quick little thinker. They looped it through my arms and tied the knot at my back. Najda looked at me. I could decide what would happen if she did what she and Kylie chose to do.

They dragged me to the door and halfway onto the step.

Edith had a say at this point. "You drag her over the gravel, and there's going to be blood all over my car." I stood up and walked to the car.

I was tied to the passenger seat of Edith's car. Najda tested the cuffs on my ankles, and then glanced at me, eye to eye for a moment, without a trace of ever having met me. I was a dead woman. The come to judgment verdict was getting into shape. Celia transferred the gun to a carry bag. Why do this in my view? I was now a routine bore. Najda pressed the lock and shut the car door. The latch snapped. The door was locked.

––––––––

Najda was waiting in my Mazda two houses down from Celia's house. Kylie and Celia were in the van ahead of her. Najda stopped with them when they pulled off to gas up. Edith went straight ahead without a glance to the side, and I'll always remember the helpless frown on Celia's face, isolated in the passenger window of the van, aware when our little caravan had broken up that some final scheme of Coombs and Sand and all the rest of them was over and done now. I didn't know that for almost an hour. What was clear to me then was that whatever was ahead of her, Edith had not wanted to trail a van with Webster in the cargo hold.

Edith got up to the speed in a short stretch of open freeway in the right lane and stuck the car in tightly with the trucks and Class C motor homes, lurching, grinding, down-shifting in harmony with everything on six to eighteen wheels. There was no car to my right to flourish a distress signal with my eyes. The semi ahead of us was hauling a piano. A quarter-hour on we passed the cutoff to Napa. I was in a simple place, stretching an image of salvation over a desperate terror every which way. What I could do with a fender-bender. Her fat was in the fire, if only a trucker stopped and came to the window and said that he thought I looked a bit uncomfortable. I could believe in a fender-bender. That would be enough, and tomorrow would be believable.

We started up the rise to the top of the hill entering Petaluma. They'd finished widening the old two-lane strip to three lanes, and we passed quickly through the first burgeoning metropolis above Marin. I hated speed. Then up the grade and back to the grind-it-out freeway experience when the taillights came on. Edith hit the brakes, adjusted, rolled along till she needed a little shot of gas, but kept the foot ready for another go on the brakes. She must have picked up Najda's preferences for what they were going to do to me. Her hands hadn't moved. They'd gripped the wheel in exactly the same place where I'd first watched her pull from the curb and settle into the job of getting me to where it would happen.

A call arrived. It was Celia. "Where are you?"

"Petaluma."

"We're on the freeway. Pull off on Washington. There's a service station on the right at the corner. We'll meet there."

"I'm past Washington. I can go back."

"No. Keep going. Try Rohnert Park Expressway. Same thing. There's a station at the first corner."

Edith was working her phone one-handed, searching. We'd completely stopped over and over again on the up grade. On the other side, as we picked up speed, she said, "I'm leaving you off."

My mouth opened. As carefully as I possibly could, without looking at her, within one long slow breath, I thought as hard as I've ever thought. Shut up and think what not to say, I repeated twice silently. If this was some crap to keep me well behaved, I was ready to scream my insides out. I wasn't hunkering down to defeat in a silent plea. Every second until now had been nothing but a struggling phrase, reasoned, trial-and-error shots at calm, and ultimately begging. Not now.

The right lane off the expressway headed us to the restrooms at the side of a convenience mart. Edith swung the car right to give herself a space to curl up to the curb at the ladies' room. She pulled forward to the corner of the building, got out fast, and went along the sidewalk past the store entrance to the pumps along the cross street. She spoke to two men pumping gas. They shook their heads. She turned in place, taking into account everything to see in a full circle, and took off in a line.

Over at the corner, at the exit to the cross street, she bent at the waist and put her head close to a man on his haunches. A truck was getting air in its tires. The man stood, took off his hat, smoothed a hand through his hair, and put his hat back on, looking where Edith was pointing. He looked great looking at me. He untied a tarpaulin stretched across the back of a steel frame built onto the bed of the truck. A small door opened out. He bent inside and moved things from left to right, right to left. Then he climbed inside. He came out with a big pair of pliers. Edith opened the door. The man took a look, and kept looking.

He turned to her: "If you're in a hurry, leave her off. I'll take her as is."

"Get the bracelets off her. She'll take you as is."

"Just passing time," he said.

He bent my foot and said, "Keep it like that." The lever arms went together. A snap and the foot felt numb suddenly.

"You need this rope in one piece?" he asked.

"Please. As many pieces as it takes."

He cut the rope off in short lengths. He helped me out of the car. He cut my wrists free of each other.

"Bend your wrist like this," he said. *Snap*. "The other." *Snap*.

"I thought you were dead," I said to Edith.

She held her hand against discussion. "You're a good man, Lewis." She handed him a bill. "Can you give us a few minutes alone?"

"No charge for a good deed," he said. "I'll be in my truck."

Edith folded the bill together with five more hundreds. It was what I'd given her at the train station at Jack London Square. "This will get you home. Go with Lewis and keep going."

"I'm staying here," I said. "The little shit killed one of your mother's friends, a woman named Faith."

"It won't be good if you're here when they get here. Faith is in Montana. It was Celia's plan. Just so you know, the three of us were married in a church in Tahoe."

I thought a minute. She meant the three of them, she and Webster and Sofia. Nothing to say about it but "I'm sorry."

"I would have invited you. Webster didn't have a witness. Sofia didn't want one."

"Did you kill anyone?"

"Twice," she said. "Enthusiastically, the first time, a man in Tres Pinos, and reluctantly, a woman. They'll never know she's dead."

"You saved my life," I said.

"They're my family, Elizabeth."

"You can come with me."

"I have to bury my husband."

I'd said I was sorry. Once in one day was enough. She brushed my hand away. She opened the door and got in and shut it and watched traffic at the intersection, waiting for me to go.

Chapter 30

THE SUPERMARKET ACROSS the street from the service station was the large structure I'd been aware of but hadn't looked at. It was the anchor of a mall where I could plant myself unseen. I asked Lewis if he would do me a favor. Drive a few blocks till he was out of sight of where we had come from, then work his way back to the parking lot behind the mall. I gave him a phone number where he could reach me for the evening of his choice in San Francisco.

"I can't believe this," he said.

"I can't thank you enough. We'll see if we can make a believer out of you."

I entered a leisurewear outlet through the back entrance, and studied the service station from the front window. The space where Edith's car had been was empty. The pumps were deserted, mostly. Edith was gone.

I went to the corner AT&T store and bought a phone. I called for a car, and kept an eye out for ten minutes, watching what pulled off northbound traffic. While I waited I called Nora Kolenick. If I had news about Hamilton Van Eyck, she'd said I should call. An instinct must have told her to let the phone ring. She called back on my return to the City.

"What do you want?" she asked.

"Hamilton is dead," I said, "earlier today. They're driving him to where he'll be buried. I decided not to go. He was married to two women. He loved them, and they loved him. I don't know any more, except it was an accident, and I haven't the faintest idea how long it would take to tell the whole thing. Someone will have to do that. It looks like me. Another thing. They wished to be given their privacy, so there's that, too."

After a wait that I took to equal a thanks and a goodbye, she said she might call someday when she was in my area.

I called Dennis Meisters. A woman answered. She was his wife. She wanted to hear what I sounded like, and while she was at that, by way of news, Dennis was back from his trip in good health. Whatever we were investigating, he was happy doing it on money that came out of his own pocket. He was looking forward to a breakfast with me. I needed to talk to him sooner. If he was free, I'd like to meet him in an hour. I invited her, but she said she didn't understand detective work. She'd be all left feet, mess up the clues.

———

WE were in the same arrangement in the same chairs, same table, the same corner on the biscuit supply, the same breaking in a new server on how we liked to waste time around here, and how it was plenty worth her while. I'd never known remotely as well as I did at this moment, what it was worth to look a man in the eye who could toss off an explanation for a shot-up leg on the remark that he'd only been doing his job. Plenty of us wouldn't know what he was talking about.

California appreciation had found its way into his coffee. On a second cup, he let go with a compliment that we had a nice bay.

"Someday we'll get around to a real lunch in Sausalito," he said.

"Lunch on the patio at Luigi's with a San Francisco professional dominant," I said, "I'll see if you grab the check. I'll have to bring my best pitch."

"You might meet Effie," he said. "She wanted me to pass on some appreciation that these get-togethers we've been having are giving her insight on tall blondes. Just knowing they're out there keeps the others on their toes."

"I'm lucky I'm on my own toes," I said. I put a hand on his arm and held on longer than was comfortable for him. But he was a gentleman, and let me get something out of my system. Suddenly, exhaustion washed through my bones, and I fell back. My hand slipped off his arm, then off the table. I couldn't keep it in my lap. It hung loose at the end of my arm.

He leaned forward, his body bent over his elbows on the table. He could reach out and stop me falling off my chair.

"They're a law unto themselves," I said. "An hour and a half ago I was thinking you'd never know why I wasn't returning calls. It was close."

He was hearing and seeing. I was close to the edge.

"You prefer somewhere private?" he asked

"I'd lose it," I said. "If we stay here I can hold myself together."

"Are you in danger?"

"They don't know where I am, or I wouldn't be here."

"You called me. Can they track you?"

"I just bought a phone to call a car. I called you. My old phone is in a pitcher of water. I've made a lot of calls on it. It's a long list. Where would they start?"

His eyes were on mine, very much on mine.

"There's your wife's safety to consider. You should walk away, Dennis."

He did the tough smile. "From what? My wife wouldn't forgive me."

"I want a name. Who do you trust?"

"You trust me with what you know, and I'll call my wife. We'll think about it."

"I know who killed Trent Tubman in Tres Pinos."

"I can't call anybody about that. Not on a Sunday."

"And there's my City Supervisor, the one with a Ph.D. in economics from Berkeley. She took the opportunity to use her high office to persuade a woman to hold a gun on me. I have everything on them, everything they've done for fifty years. That includes nineteen murders, I's dotted, T's crossed, cold cases, including Clement. They were taking me somewhere where I'd tell them what they wanted me to tell them. I would have."

He got off his elbows and worked a thumb and finger on his chin. The stare was serious. "That's a lot of cold cases. You don't want to start something that doesn't have an end."

"I killed one of them."

"Anybody upset about it?"

"His wife let me go," I said. "She may be regretting it."

"Who would help her do this regretting?"

"My supervisor, Celia Taylor. She's the boss. She didn't have to get permission to kill me. She gave the job to two guys. Kylie Bessel and a sweetie by the name of Najda offered to help."

"Remind me?"

"Najda was the girl at the beach that day I was supposed to meet Faith. Faith was a suicide—supposedly. She's in Montana. Bessel was the name on the painting."

"You got a line on that?"

"The eighteen hundred dollars taped to the back is what convinced me Faith had been there. No one else knew what that amount meant."

"Why draw attention to Bessel?"

"Faith was stripping the Oakland house of Bessel leads on her way out. She grabs the painting, sticks the eighteen hundred in an envelope on the back—only one thing to carry. Faith gets groceries and gasses up on the way to the beach house. She meets Celia and Najda at the top of the drive to the beach house and gets in with Celia. Najda drives Faith's car to the beach house, unloads a painting with the groceries. Doesn't have time to notice an envelope. I arrived and pushed her into high gear. She did what she was supposed to do. She got a set of recent footprints from the house to the water."

We shared a blank look.

"It's even possible Faith was in the house?" he said.

"And she walked back to the car to meet up with Celia while I was at the beach? That would leave a set of prints going in the wrong direction."

"Your brain's frazzled, but it's working."

"I got my brains handed to me. Remember. The Friday I called Faith I offered to drop in on her that evening. She started to agree, but then suddenly decided she had to meet someone. We could meet the next day at the ocean. That made sense. The reason for meeting was Hannah. She'd stored some of Hannah's belongings in the attic at the beach house. She'd been turning over the idea of disappearing ever since Hannah had disappeared. What kept her in Oakland—who knows? Faith stepped into Hannah's shoes with Neville Drum. One client with his spare cash is a career, but with the body in the shed, she must have kept a bag packed.

"Anyway, as one day follows another, one day Sand kills himself, and the wheel of events is on a roll. A kid on a summer job with a little more spunk than the next kid calls Faith and then me, and I call Faith. That's one call too many for comfort. Faith sees the last warning she might ever get."

"You'd be her witness," he said.

"Sort of. Celia set it up to look like Faith disappeared from inside a locked room. I didn't know where the room was."

"Okay," he said. "They came to the house in two cars. Just to get this right, let's go over it carefully. Faith goes up to the market to get herself on security tape. Down the road she switches to the other car. Najda takes Faith's car to the house."

"And wearing gloves. That leaves Faith's prints on the groceries, as if she'd been setting up housekeeping—as Faith would have done."

"Why lock the gate behind her?" His eyes went over my head. "Wait a minute."

"I think that was it," I said. "They didn't know when I would arrive. Najda didn't want to be surprised. She'd hear me arrive and have enough time to get down to the beach. There'd be one set of shoe prints to the water. At that point they'd go in her bag."

"But Faith is alive?" he said.

"Edith says so. That's always their cover. No bodies."

Dennis was moving biscuits with a fork. He poked one. "Celia drove up the road. That's where she and Faith waited for Najda. All Faith had to do was keep her head down in back."

He'd been steadily prying chunks off a biscuit, segregating them with the prong of a fork, until a tuna melt arrived with a beer.

"A lot of space up there between houses," he said. "Swimmers must cut through private property occasionally. A half-naked nymph will attract attention. She's something to watch with binoculars. Nobody would call the law on her."

"I was thinking of a phrase," I said, 'recalled to life.'"

He nudged a basket of chips. "You want some?"

"It was on a note delivered to Jarvis Lorry on the London-to-Dover stage."

I picked up one potato chip and turned it in the light, and kept turning it thinking of Edith.

"She killed two people," I said out loud, but to myself, twisting the sound of it in my fingers. I was gripped with a feeling I would have to do something. I could see the first step and the last step. The first step was get going. It was all I had time for. I put my last hundred on the table and started walking toward the spot where my car wasn't. Dennis was behind me, but not close. Wherever I was going, I'd have to come back. I hit that point and turned, and asked, "Can I use your car?"

I was half frantic, the half that was trying to stay able to communicate.

He drove.

"Go to your place," I said quietly. "I'll need some money for gas."

"Where are you going?" he said.

"Phillipsville. She'll kill herself."

"Who?"

"Edith. She let me go. I didn't understand that. I didn't turn it down, either. That's what counted when I was shackled to a car seat."

"What's this to do with the London-to-Dover stage?"

"Salvation. Edith killed two people. The creep who owned the property in Tres Pinos, she killed him. They insisted she pull the trigger. She passed the test. But there was another killing. She probably didn't know about it at the time of the first one, but that's the cost of admission to the family. She was just a candidate at that point, but there was blood on her hands. They could use that to argue she's in for a penny. Two pennies? What's the difference? Nothing for some of them, really, merely kill someone they have no reason to kill. Somebody else has a reason. They may have explained the reason, but it wasn't Edith's reason, but she went along with the reason, she was joining the family. She was halfway in. One more step. It's the way it's done."

"Murder, Incorporated," he said. "They don't advertise. Edith doesn't know the password. How does she get to them?"

"The connection? Not sure."

"If you want to sic the cops on them, it'll come up. Every time you answer a question with you're not sure, it adds up."

"Why are you with me?" I said.

"It's still a long way to Phillipsville. I'm still interested."

"Sofia, Webster, Edith—they were married drifters. Webster would have heard of Bessel from Flowers. Webster might have met Bessel, or someone who knew Bessel. Maybe the contact was through Sofia. Webster or Sofia, one of them was in touch with somebody who could float the possibility of membership in a gang that got things done for people. This would be just a somebody, as far as they knew, they shared encounters with. One night this somebody is listening. Sofia is griping about a dirtbag she used to service in exchange for a shack he made available for some kids who thought they were in publishing. The dirtbag overlooked the rent for the fun Sofia provided him. But Sofia moved on to another life, and the dirtbag wanted real rent from the group in some form or other. He owns the property. It's his right."

"Before you disturb me with the graphic details," he said, "the guy who vanished in Tres Pinos, that was a professional hit. Whoever supplied the scaffolding on that job, they knew their way around, A to Z."

"Is it that hard to kill someone?" I said.

"Nobody bumps into expertise like that. This gang got a rumor going that Tubman was seen in an underground leather cafeteria. There are only hundreds. Investigations only go so far with characters who ask for their own troubles. Cops start thinking that maybe Tubman died with a smile on his face. It was a cold case from day one. That kind of expertise."

"They bumped into me. They were within a day or two of getting a rumor going for me."

He thought all the way past Healdsburg. "This isn't just a few gals getting Tubman to lay off hassling the Snap Judgment Press for rent."

"They're not in it for money."

"What box are you checking?"

"Social manure. It's a category. People who hurt people under the cover of hurting them for money. The gang worked out a condign way of killing them."

He smiled. "Hurting people under cover? Professional dominants?"

I let that go for a minute. "If I didn't need you, I'd open the door and get out."

He'd stepped in it. He tried to get his shoe out. "We'll talk about dumb cops one of these days. Look, if you can wrap up the two cop killings in two thousand ten, that would put you on higher ground than Celia Taylor. No cop can ignore that. We could have a tactical unit in Phillipsville when we get there."

"I just need you to get me there."

"And then what?"

I looked up Bud and Mary in Phillipsville, and called them.

"We're closing," Bud said.

"This is Elizabeth, the one you used to think was Hannah."

"New number you got. You married?"

"Just a new phone. I'm looking for the place where all those artists lived. It was on the mountain side of the highway. I'm on my way up 101. Where do I turn off?"

"Anderson Road. Used to be a sign, Coombs Clinic. Watch for the turnout on the left. Just after take a sharp right on Anderson. A minute on you come to the teardrop. Where Pearl Creek hits some rocks and goes underground. Dry now. Just a second, Mary's talking in my bad ear. Chained off, she says. Just another second. Go under the chain. You can walk from there."

"What about Lonnigan's Rock?"

"When you get to the clinic, they'll point you. Lonnigan's Rock? Not much of a rock. You know somethin' I don't?"

"I heard there's a great view up there."

"You can get yourself a better tourist agent. You lookin' for the lady that makes them cakes? Haven't seen her since Hannah left."

"She's at the clinic?" I said.

"Wait a minute. Mary says park on our street. Stop at the first turn. You'll see a private property sign. Don't worry about the sign. Whole field is doing nothing but bein' private. Ascension Trail passes your rock. It's beaten-down grass from where you park to where you turn up into the trees. You'll see, where the fence is broken."

"Is it far? Anything to keep a lookout for?"

"A dry creek in an open area. Twenty minutes, if you don't twist an ankle. Trail is tricky. It's not a national park."

"I can see the clinic from the trail?"

"Close along where you're goin', down the slope on your right, you'll see some of the buildings. I'd say stop by and say hello to me and Mary, but we'll be closed."

"I have a feeling I'll be dropping in again. Thanks for the directions."

———

THE light was fading when we found the break in the fence. The slope didn't look bad to me, but twenty minutes of it was Dennis's idea of nineteen minutes too much and then some. And for what? He would have expected Edith's car where we parked, but there were no cars. And he was right, as I discovered. There was no indication that anyone had been in the location of the rock any time recently. And Bud was right, it wasn't much of a rock. But you could see where the creek fell ten feet to a sparkling pool in season when there was rain, and you could see where two people would be happy alone together. Or three people.

Chapter 31

I SPENT A MONTH telling my story over and over while the investigation gathered up a team. My car had been found in a yard in Klamath Falls, Oregon. That made it an interstate case.

The butcher, the baker, the candlestick maker, I didn't know their names, or whether they had to hide for a while, or hide forever, or change names, or go on with the names they had in plain sight, but whatever that was, if their names were in the ledger, they were pinned to a thousand databanks and spread out as so much factual tissue. One thing the FBI has in its toolbox is the means to cross-index data. Five points of intersection identify just about anybody. A dozen points and you can stop the clock night or day and know what they're doing that instant. Starlight passed right through them.

Celia, Kylie, Najda, Edith, and Sofia were the names I knew. After a year they hadn't been located. They'd disappeared. The one thing they knew how to do.

It's been eleven years since a home-built aircraft, made from a manufacturer's kit, with registration number M485RB, dove nose first into the sand at Rincon Point. Dave Wheezer had come up from L.A. with a friend the day before. They'd stayed at Hobson Beach Park and were just starting on their way back on August 22 at 11:17 A.M. when Dave saw a plane pitch to the right over the Pacific Ocean and suddenly loop into a steep descent.

Dave was one of eighteen eyewitnesses. He had gotten out of his camper but hung back with no interest in a dead body. The couple who'd slammed to a stop in front of the camper both ran from the highway to the crash site. The wife stayed a long time at the crash. Dave and his friend and the husband talked at the car while the husband waited for his wife. The husband said his wife had seen the plane corkscrew on the way down. Dave didn't recall that, but the wife had a pilot's license, and she took a look inside the cabin. She'd returned to the car with a funny feeling about the crash. She thought the fuel tank selector valve handle was in an awkward location behind the pilot's shoulder. He would have had to turn ninety degrees to reach it to switch fuel tanks. If he'd done that, his right foot could have slammed the right rudder pedal, causing the craft to pitch right and stall. Anyway, if the pilot had failed to switch fuel tanks, out of fuel, the plane would have dropped like a stone.

Just before leaving L.A. the next day Dave called a woman in Zephyr Cove, Nevada, a retirement community along the eastern shore of Lake Tahoe. He'd missed her on the trip out. He wondered if he could stay the night on his return. The woman had been a colleague at the Department of Agriculture in Washington, D.C. He would reroute his vacation home via Highway 80, the way he'd come west. The woman agreed, and Dave decided to stay an extra day in the Tahoe area, one of those shapeless, incoherent decisions that derange the future. The next morning a brief item appeared on the front page of the *Tahoe Daily Press*. Andrew Simmons, a Tahoe local, had died in a plane crash at about noon on August 22 at Rincon Beach, California, on the first leg of a flight to Monterey.

When Dave returned to his home in Bethesda, he experienced the jolt of what vacations are all about. He felt rejuvenated by a new purpose. Maybe it was the woman. No matter. His mind had jumped a groove in the same way he had chosen botany as a career in college. It suddenly was what it was, exactly the subject he wanted to pursue, and he set out to learn what there was to learn about a seemingly irrelevant subject: light single-seat aircraft, specifically the WELD 4A, the type that had crashed at Rincon Point.

Three weeks later Dave found the obituary for Andrew Brunner Simmons in the *San Francisco Chronicle*. The short note seemed skimpy for a Berkeley law graduate, the managing partner of a law firm with branches in three states. Simmons had one surviving blood relative, a sister in Whitman, Nebraska. Dave thought she had a strong case for a lawsuit, and sent her a report of his findings, and the reason behind his interest in her brother's death. He sent a copy of "Design Deficiencies in Single-Seat Aircraft," jacketed in a white folder, to the Federal Aviation Administration in the Department of Transportation with a reference to his letter to the sister.

"SIMMONS turned up in the ledger," Dennis was saying.

We were on the patio in his backyard, ten feet apart, brown-bagging a picnic. I was sipping what I'd brought with me in a plastic glass I'd brought with me. Being careful. A virus had come in from China with a serious pedigree. An office worker in Wuhan had died of it. Or someone had died. Instinctually nervous people were being careful.

"The ledger put Simmons's mother on a camping trip in Myers Flat. Her son, Andrew, was born in a tent. After that it was shoe leather and note-taking, running down the mother's connections to more connections. They would have run the sister through the mill too, but she'd been solid in the community since her mother died. The paperboy could recall helping her install a new brass lock on her front door. She was putting it in upside down, and she'd figured that out herself. Her bunnies got loose once out of the back pens. Neighbors from all over had to round them up."

"The sister didn't pan out?" I said.

"They ran her dental records. Nothing. And it stood that way until one morning a fed, attached at the hip to fate, was looking at a name on a list. The name had popped out of a Department of Transportation article. The last name was Wheezer. It was the Wheezer report that made him walk around the office with a second cup of coffee that morning. Simmons's sister passed on a recommendation by Wheezer to pursue a lawsuit, a suit which she had a strong chance of winning. It brought the fed back to a second look at the sister's live-in housekeeper.

"It was too late. The housekeeper, Sharon Longley, had been to a reunion. Some old gals had put together an event in Eureka. When she returned to Nebraska she felt sick, the kind of over-all blahs that respond to bed rest and liquids and Miss Marple reruns. But on the fifth day she was admitted to the Red Hills Family Health Center. They would transport her to emergency care in Lincoln the next day. Overnight she died. Her physical profile left the fed with a cadaver in bad shape and no suspi-cions, certainly no reason to run down the Sharon Longleys of the world. But a body scan of the corpse showed old fractures in the right ulna and radius. That lined up with an item in the hospital record of someone else in the ledger, a former city supervisor in San Francisco, Celia Taylor. She'd taken a fall campaigning on the Sixteenth Avenue tiled steps."

"They found her," I said.

"Her dental records sealed the identification."

"It must have been a lonely life," I said.

"Whitman, Nebraska? Might have been better than prison. I wouldn't know."

I shrugged my shoulders. "Peculiar," I said. "She used that Nebraska area code. Seems like a mistake she wouldn't make."

"Probably thought that's what a good cop would think. Cops have hundreds of notes pinned up to corkboards. The threads point in hundreds of directions. It was Celia's trip to Eureka that got them to spread out a map of the city. They'd been onto Humboldt County, locating pot entrepreneurs for decades, so they had the area broken down into places where people on the run could set up a lean-to. Informants habitate in the weeds out there, but nothing came back on a description of Kylie Bessel. They were looking in the right place. She'd been beautiful in her day. Overnight, almost, she had perfected the art of appearing a withered loon.

"Flowers received a letter postmarked Redding. They didn't have to steam it open. The security video got an old hag in a wig slipping the letter in the outside drop box. She'd parked two blocks away. They got a fake license in the lot across from the Hertz agency. It was the same fake license they spotted in Eureka. The rest was paperwork."

"She killed the two officers on Valerio?"

"Once the feds enter the life of a quarter-wit in a prison in Alabama and lay it all out in simple sentences how he has one simple future, the miracle happens. They get a focus, and the focus does wonders for the memory. They get his life story for the record. He put an x at each robbery. The little x in Tickfaw, Louisiana, joined Flowers in possession of the rifle at the time it was used in San Francisco. The lies to your friend Rene nailed a guilty knowledge."

"Bessel didn't do it?" I said, wondering that all the hard logic was wrong.

"It was Flowers. When I came home my wife said as much. I was overthinking this thing, that an artist who could put big money in Bitcoin couldn't be so stupid as to keep a murder weapon and give it to a collector."

"Every good cop needs an Effie," I said.

"What I was thinking?"

"Najda?" I said.

"Small beer, an accessory to a disappearance, maybe a murder, chicken feed to what they're digging up in property records as far away as Cypress. All they'll have to do is stake out the beaches, look for black-haired beauties in polka-dot bikinis. They'll scoop her up. No hurry. She'll have that body when she's fifty."

"One guy did it all—Walter Coombs," I said, "a latter-day Rasputin."

"A nobody, unnoticed, no record even when he died—except the last entry in his own ledger. He saw a market in women's problems, and a demand for new identities. Real people and fake people. He created both."

We parted with a wave goodbye at ten feet. Effie had a right arm around her detective. I got to the corner of the cul-de-sac and hesitated. Right or left? They hadn't found Edith, and I was debating how smart I had to be to think she and Sofia were still together. They were married. It was the kind of marriage where the parties don't have to bother with a divorce. I had a hunch they'd be together, and for a second I saw them sunning on a couple rocks in a little stretch where the Amtrak line runs close to the ocean along Santa Claus Lane in Carpinteria. As a train approaches Edith lifts her arm…but I didn't see her wave at the engineer. She'd murdered a woman, and saved the life of a woman. It wasn't up to me to average that out. She had a conscience. I didn't want to think that over anymore.

I had another hunch. Sarah Feldman had another temporary job. I left her a message. I had an idea.

I turned left back to the City with a good reason to buy a bottle, and a good reason not to. I was still the trustee of an estate with eighteen hundred dollars and a painting I couldn't give away. And Hannah was still missing. Nobody had invented a way to find her. I had an idea about that, too.

———